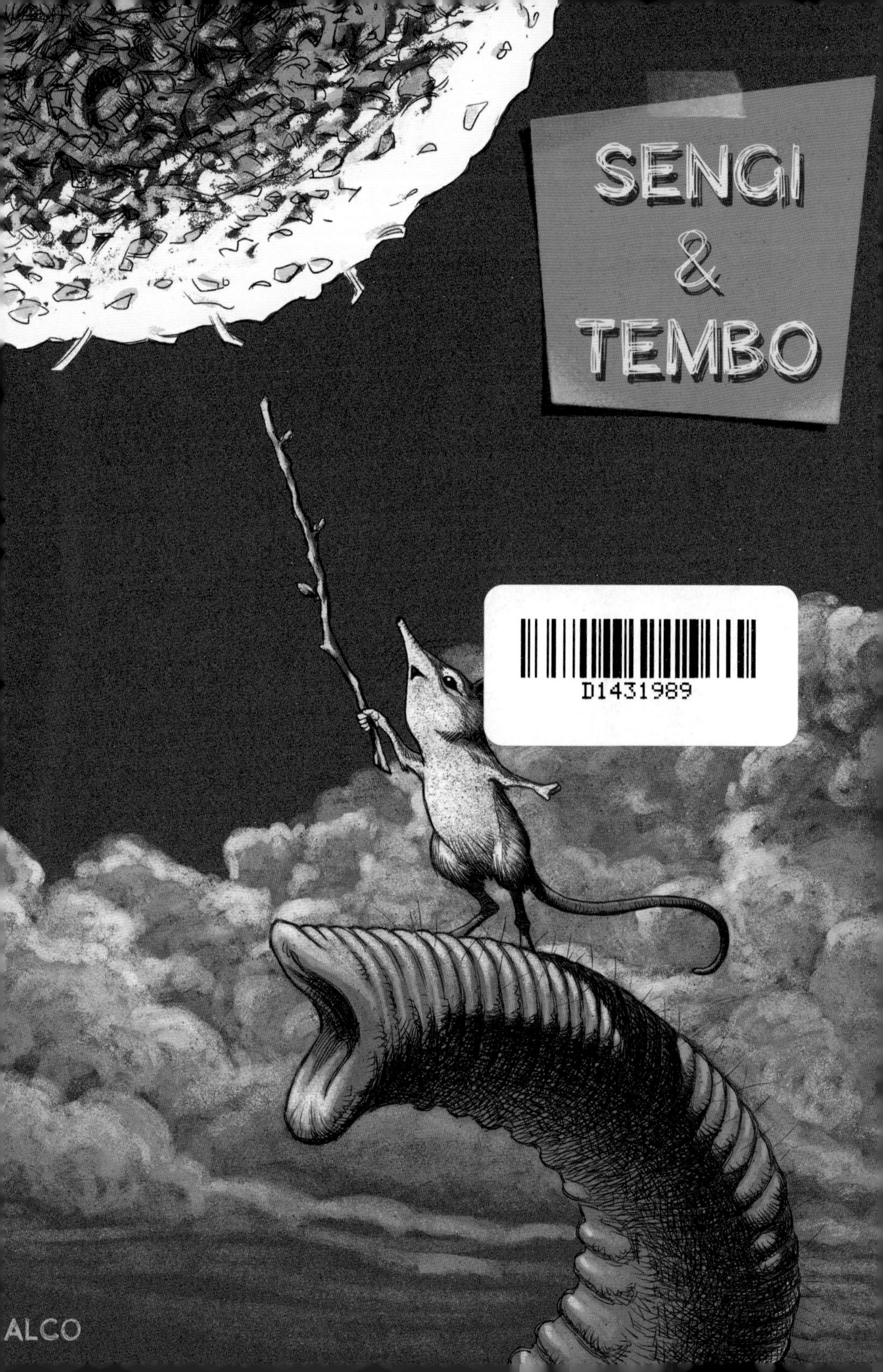
SENGI
&
TEMBO
ALCO

# SENGI AND TEMBO

**Writer/Artist**
**GIUSEPPE FALCO**

**Editor**
**ANDREA LORENZO MOLINARI**

**Scout Editor**
**WAYNE HALL**

**Scout Production**
**RICHARD RIVERA**

Brendan Deneen, *CEO*
James Pruett, *CCO*
Tennessee Edwards, *CSO*
James Haick III, *President*

Don Handfield, *CMO*
David Byrne, *Co-Publisher*
Charlie Stickney, *Co-Publisher*
Richard Rivera, *Associate Publ.*

Joel Rodriguez, *Head Of Design*

FB/TW/IG:
@Scoutcomics

LEARN MORE AT:
www.scoutcomics.com

SENGI AND TEMBO. TRADE PAPERBACK #1. 2021. Published by Scout Comics and Entertainment, Inc. All rights reserv contents copyright © 2021 by GIUSEPPE FALCO. All characters, events and institutions depicted herein are fictional. Any sim between any of the name, characters, persons, events, and/or institutions in this publication to actual names, characters, and per whether living or dead, events, and/or Institutions is unintended and purely coincidental. No portion of this book may be c or transmitted in any form without the express permission of creators or publisher, except for excerpts for journalistic and r purposes. For more information on Scout Comics and Entertainment, Inc., visit the website at www.scoutcomics.com. Printed in

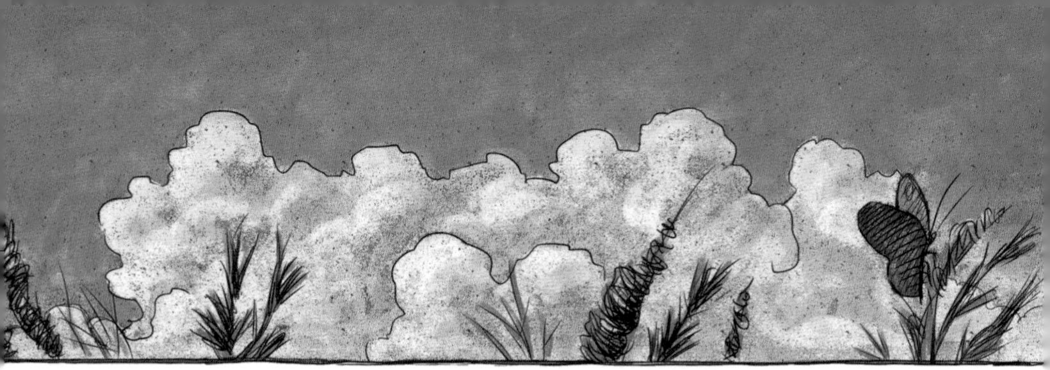

# SENGI AND TEMBO

FALCO

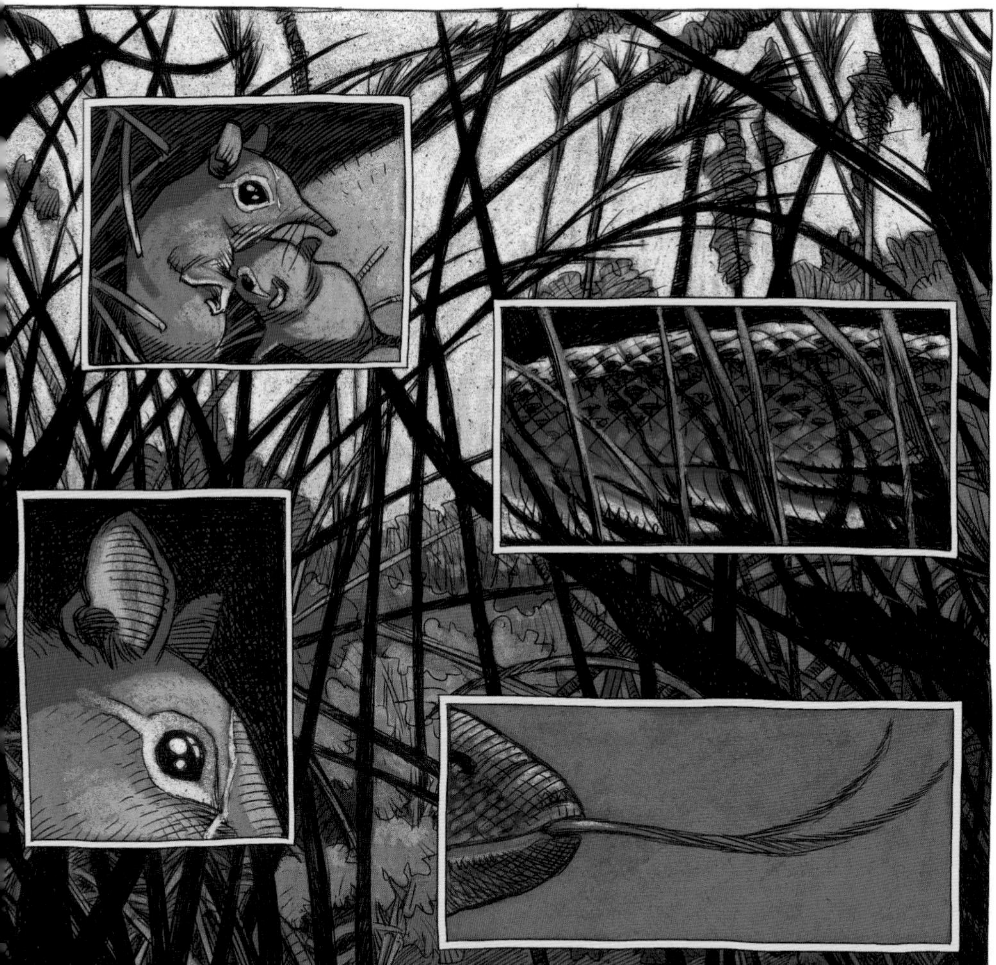

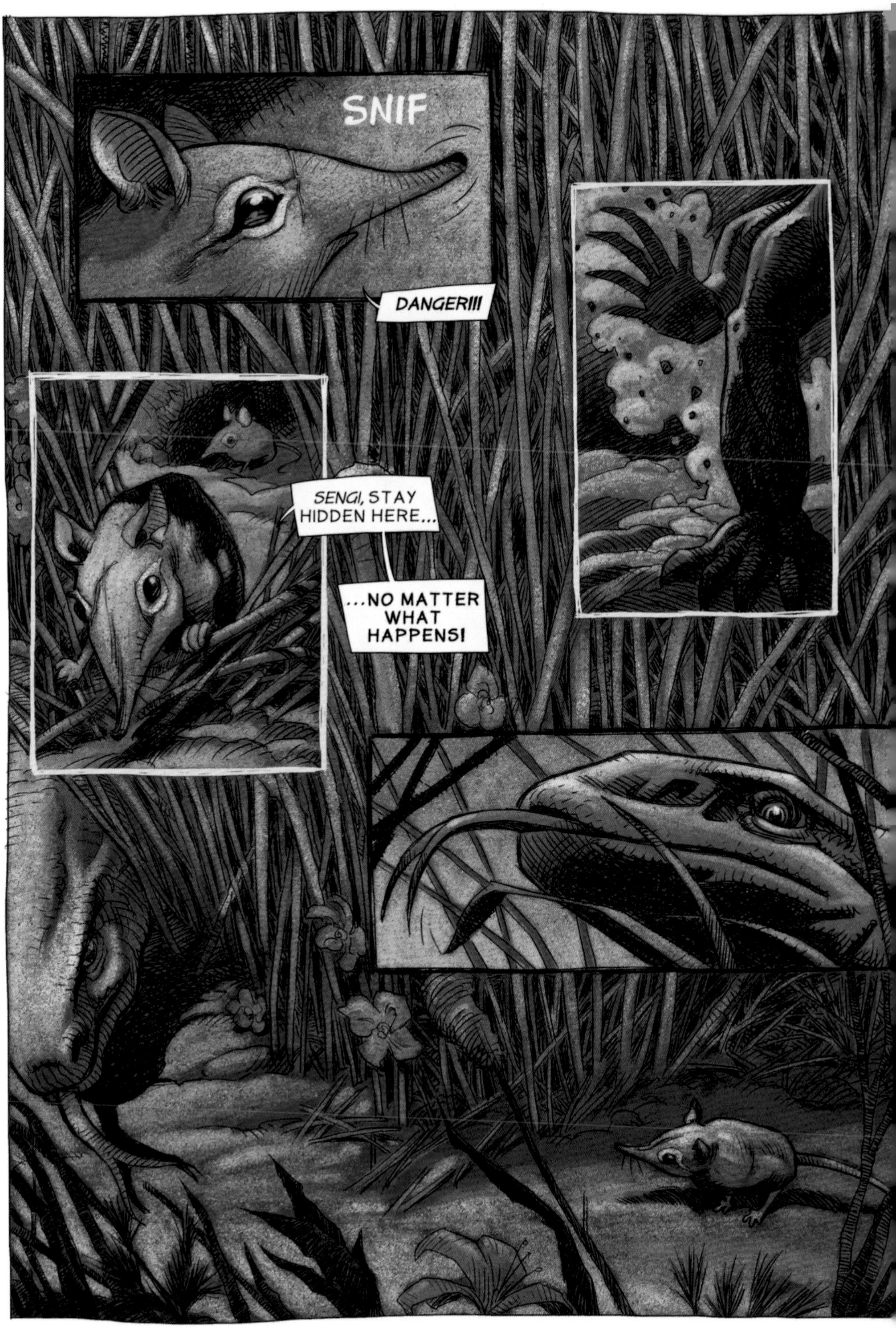
SNIF
DANGER!!!
SENGI, STAY HIDDEN HERE...
...NO MATTER WHAT HAPPENS!

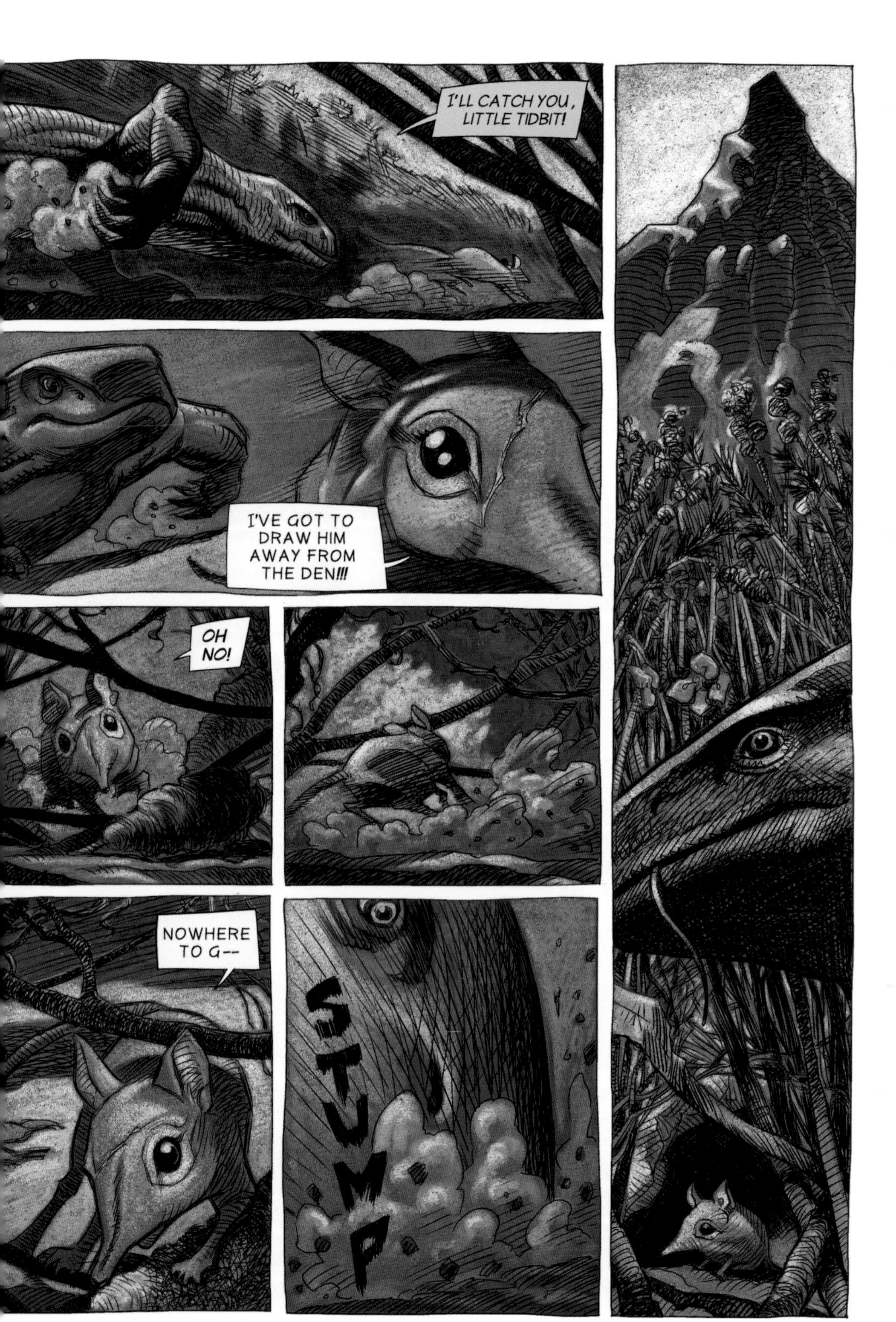
I'LL CATCH YOU, LITTLE TIDBIT!
I'VE GOT TO DRAW HIM AWAY FROM THE DEN!!!
OH NO!
NOWHERE TO G--
STUMP

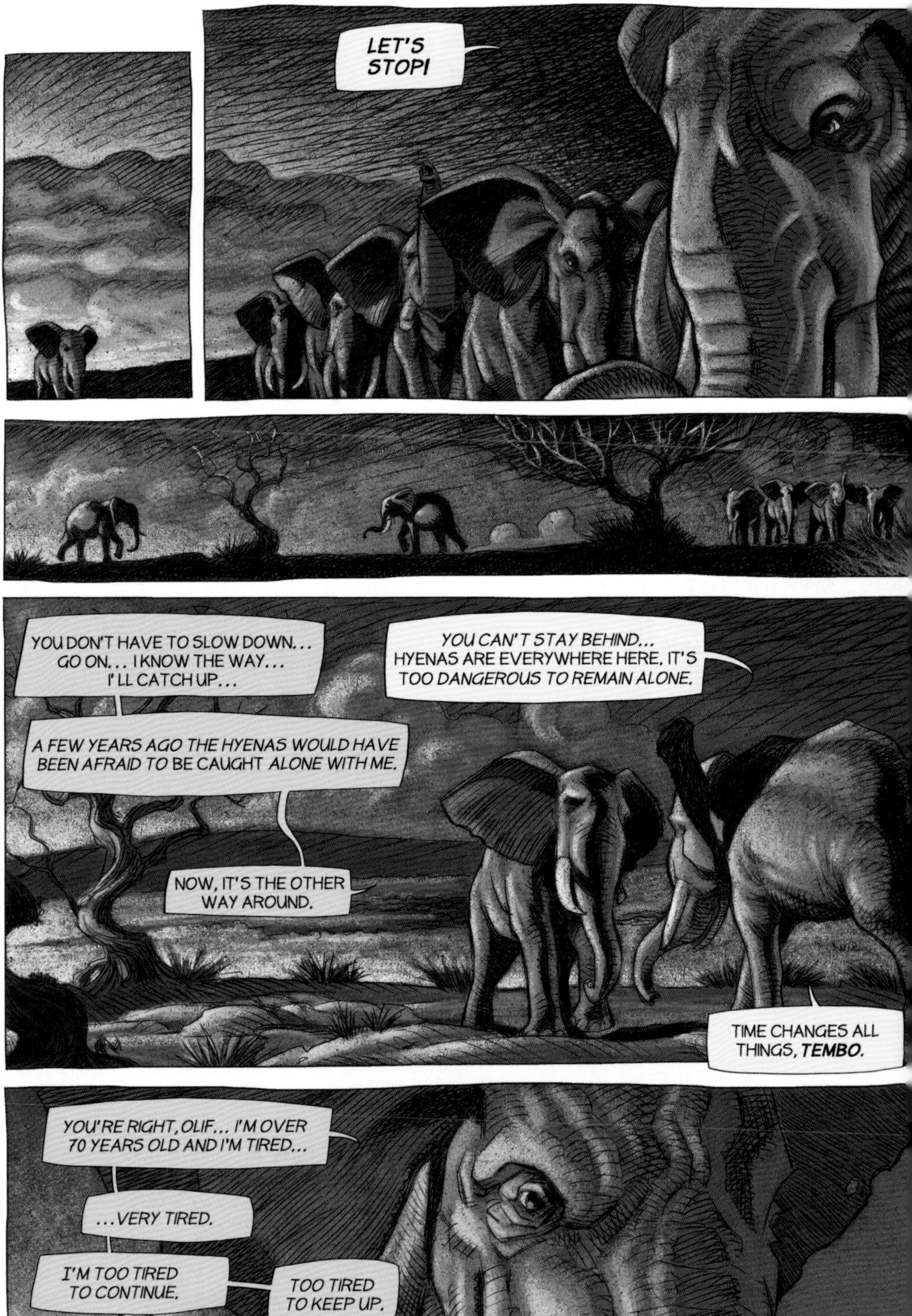

LET'S STOP!
YOU DON'T HAVE TO SLOW DOWN... GO ON... I KNOW THE WAY... I'LL CATCH UP...
A FEW YEARS AGO THE HYENAS WOULD HAVE BEEN AFRAID TO BE CAUGHT ALONE WITH ME.
NOW, IT'S THE OTHER WAY AROUND.
YOU CAN'T STAY BEHIND... HYENAS ARE EVERYWHERE HERE. IT'S TOO DANGEROUS TO REMAIN ALONE.
TIME CHANGES ALL THINGS, TEMBO.
YOU'RE RIGHT, OLIF... I'M OVER 70 YEARS OLD AND I'M TIRED...
...VERY TIRED.
I'M TOO TIRED TO CONTINUE.
TOO TIRED TO KEEP UP.

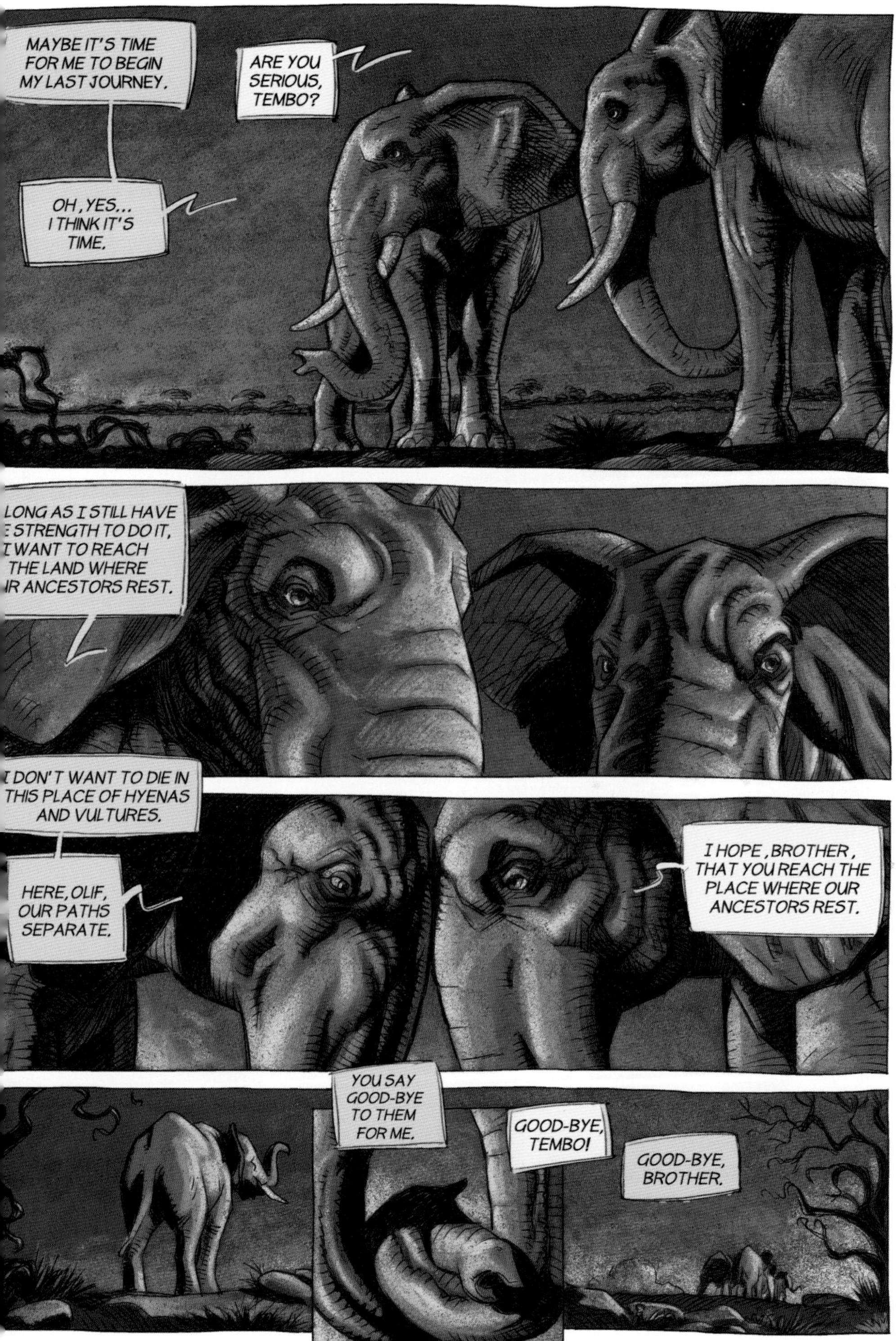
MAYBE IT'S TIME FOR ME TO BEGIN MY LAST JOURNEY.
ARE YOU SERIOUS, TEMBO?
OH, YES... I THINK IT'S TIME.
LONG AS I STILL HAVE STRENGTH TO DO IT, I WANT TO REACH THE LAND WHERE ANCESTORS REST.
I DON'T WANT TO DIE IN THIS PLACE OF HYENAS AND VULTURES.
HERE, OLIF, OUR PATHS SEPARATE.
I HOPE, BROTHER, THAT YOU REACH THE PLACE WHERE OUR ANCESTORS REST.
YOU SAY GOOD-BYE TO THEM FOR ME.
GOOD-BYE, TEMBO!
GOOD-BYE, BROTHER.

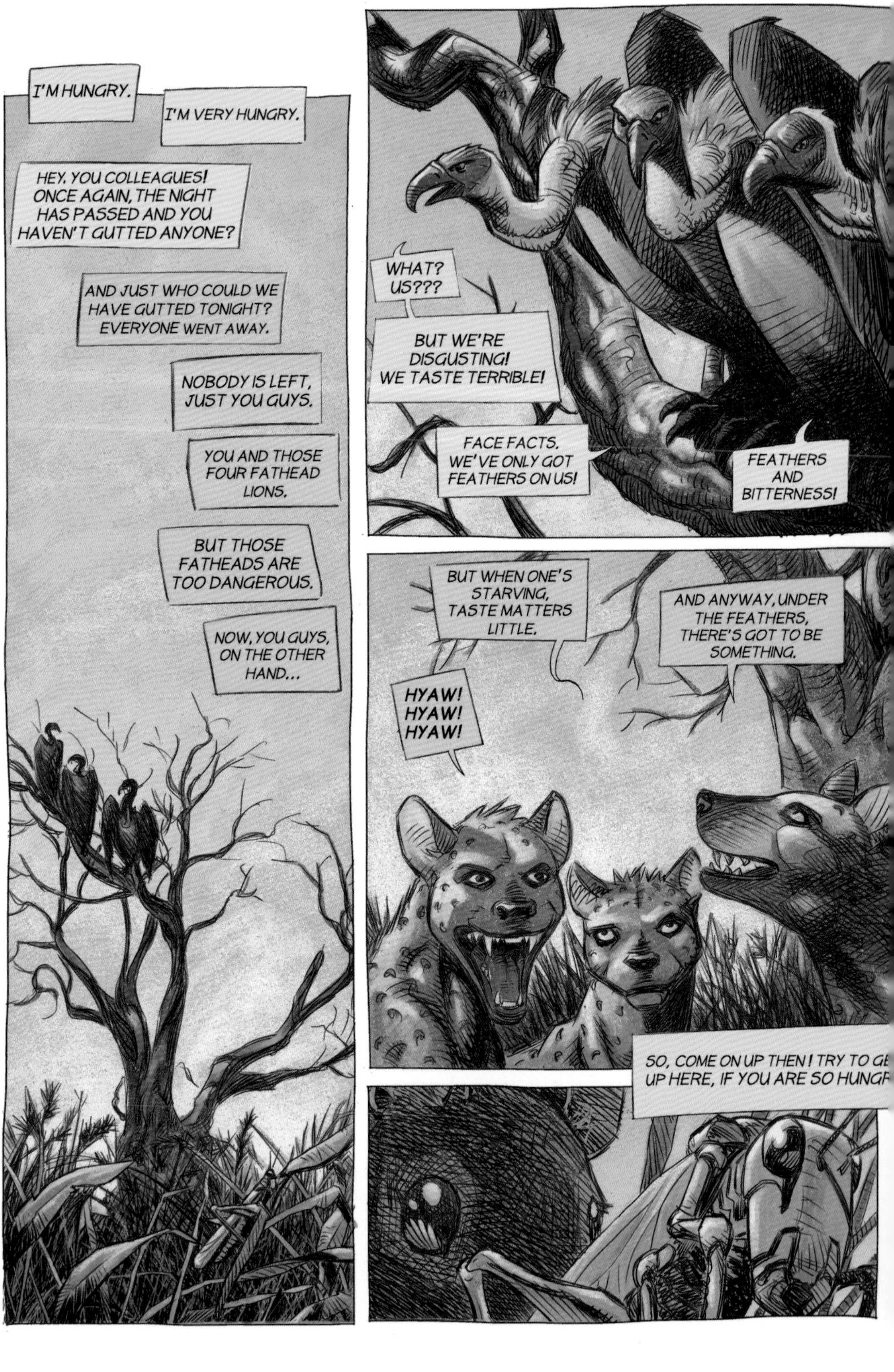
I'M HUNGRY.
I'M VERY HUNGRY.
HEY. YOU COLLEAGUES! ONCE AGAIN, THE NIGHT HAS PASSED AND YOU HAVEN'T GUTTED ANYONE?
AND JUST WHO COULD WE HAVE GUTTED TONIGHT? EVERYONE WENT AWAY.
NOBODY IS LEFT, JUST YOU GUYS.
YOU AND THOSE FOUR FATHEAD LIONS.
BUT THOSE FATHEADS ARE TOO DANGEROUS.
NOW, YOU GUYS, ON THE OTHER HAND...
WHAT? US???
BUT WE'RE DISGUSTING! WE TASTE TERRIBLE!
FACE FACTS. WE'VE ONLY GOT FEATHERS ON US!
FEATHERS AND BITTERNESS!
BUT WHEN ONE'S STARVING, TASTE MATTERS LITTLE.
AND ANYWAY, UNDER THE FEATHERS, THERE'S GOT TO BE SOMETHING.
HYAW! HYAW! HYAW!

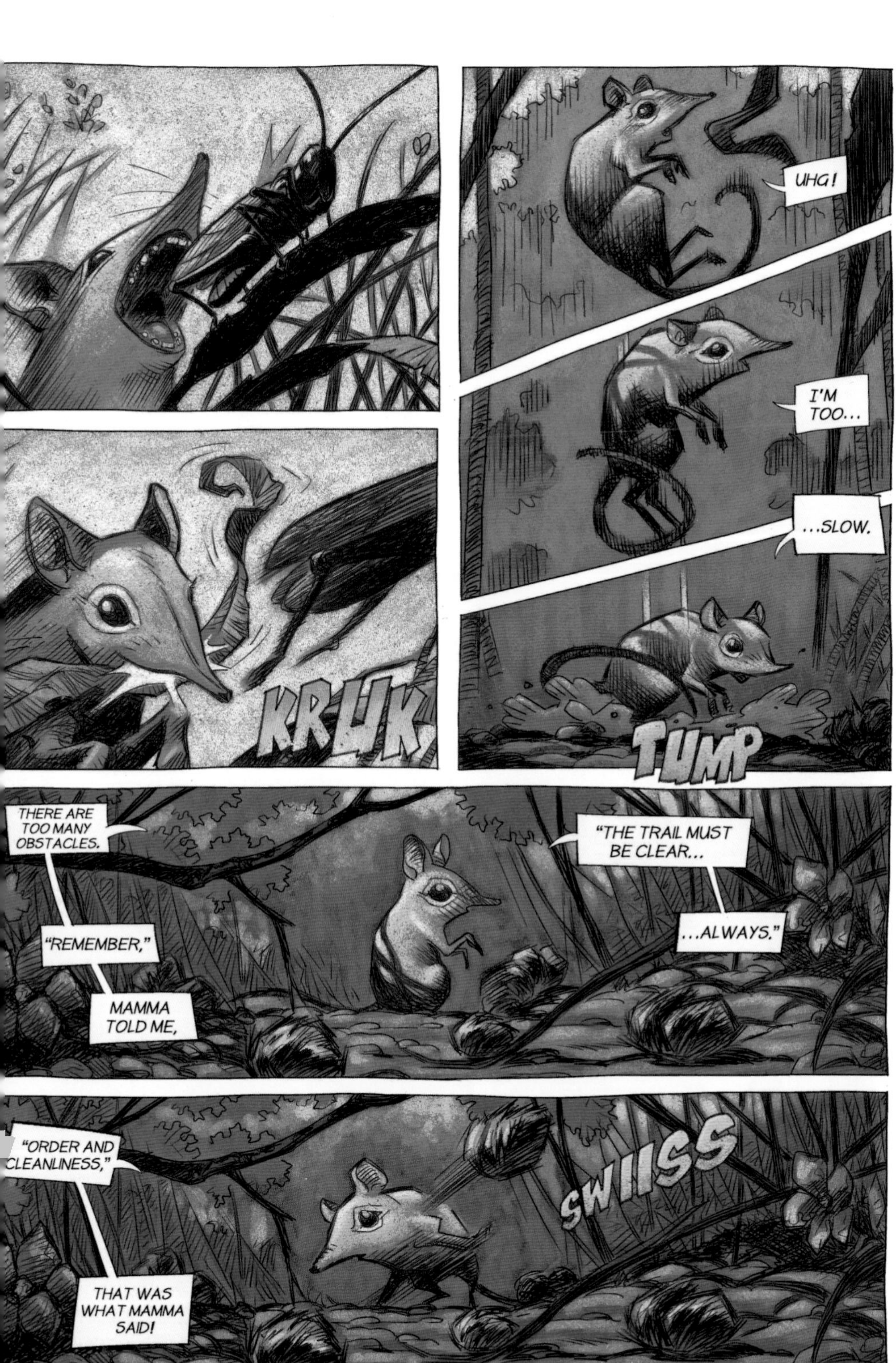
KRUK
UHG!
I'M TOO...
...SLOW.
TUMP
THERE ARE TOO MANY OBSTACLES.
"REMEMBER,"
MAMMA TOLD ME,
"THE TRAIL MUST BE CLEAR...
...ALWAYS."
"ORDER AND CLEANLINESS,"
THAT WAS WHAT MAMMA SAID!
SWIISS

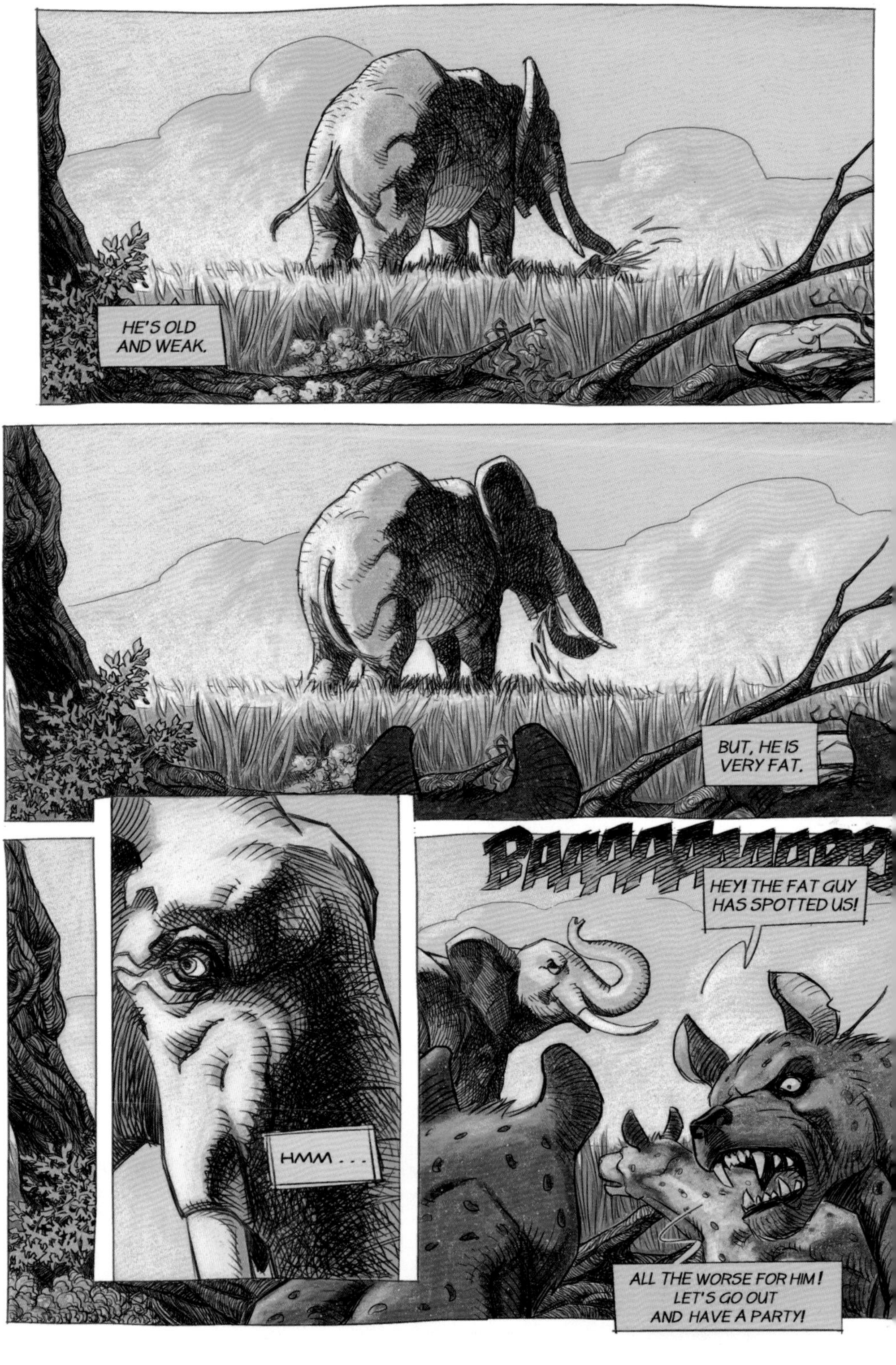
HE'S OLD AND WEAK.
BUT, HE IS VERY FAT.
HMM . . .
HEY! THE FAT GUY HAS SPOTTED US!
ALL THE WORSE FOR HIM! LET'S GO OUT AND HAVE A PARTY!

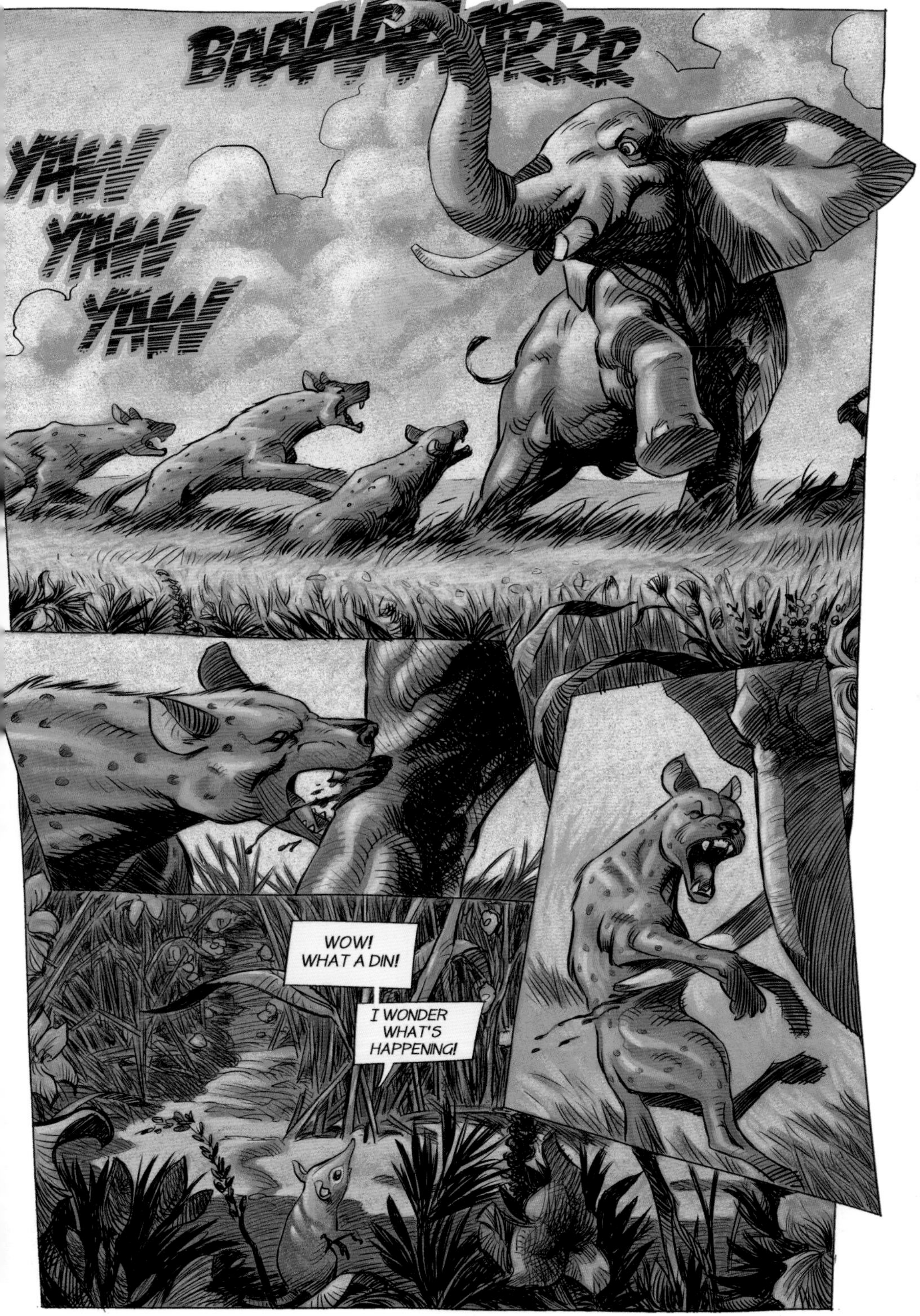
BAAAARRRR
YAW
YAW
YAW
WOW! WHAT A DIN!
I WONDER WHAT'S HAPPENING!

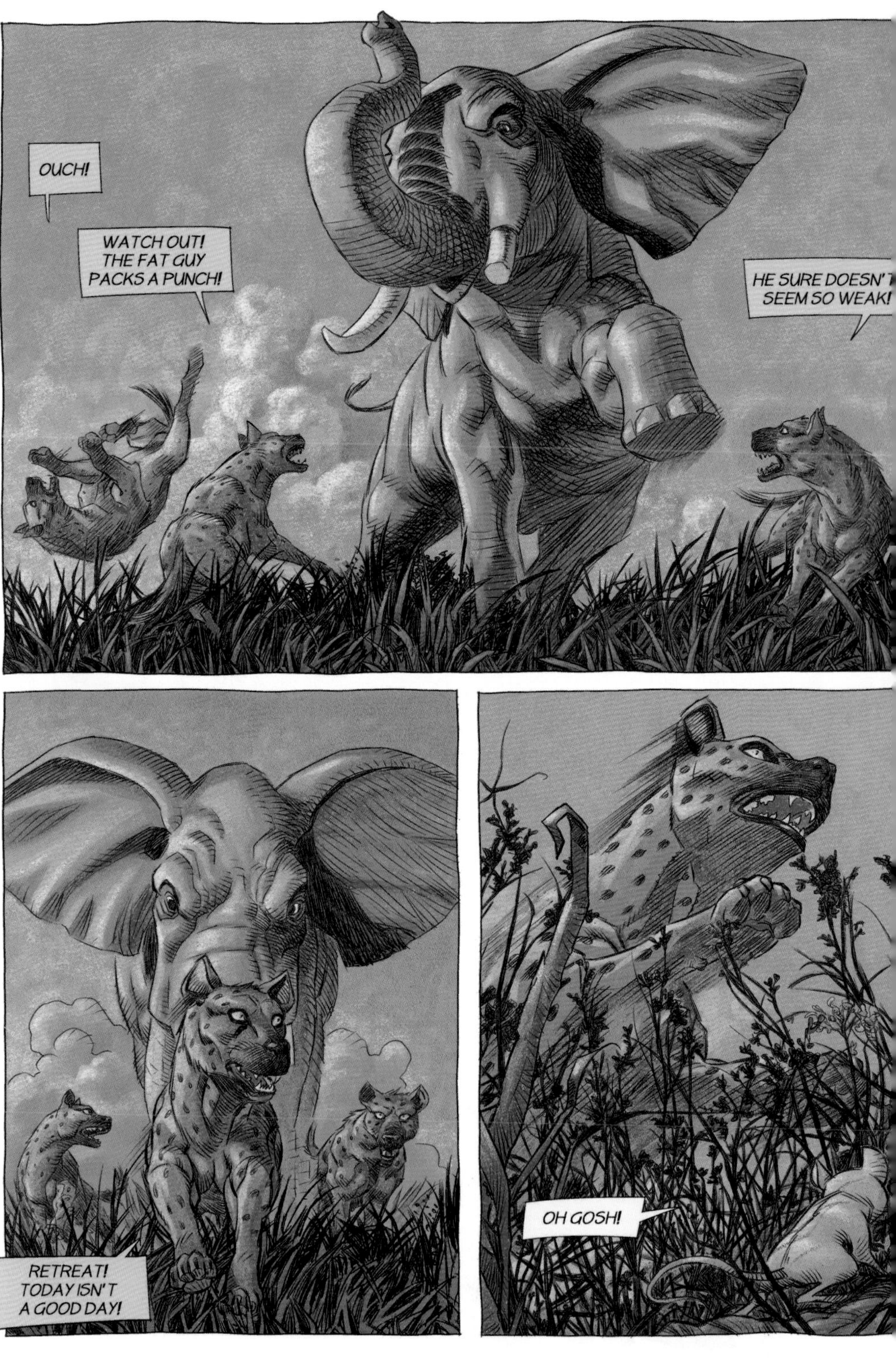
OUCH!
WATCH OUT! THE FAT GUY PACKS A PUNCH!
HE SURE DOESN'T SEEM SO WEAK!
RETREAT! TODAY ISN'T A GOOD DAY!
OH GOSH!

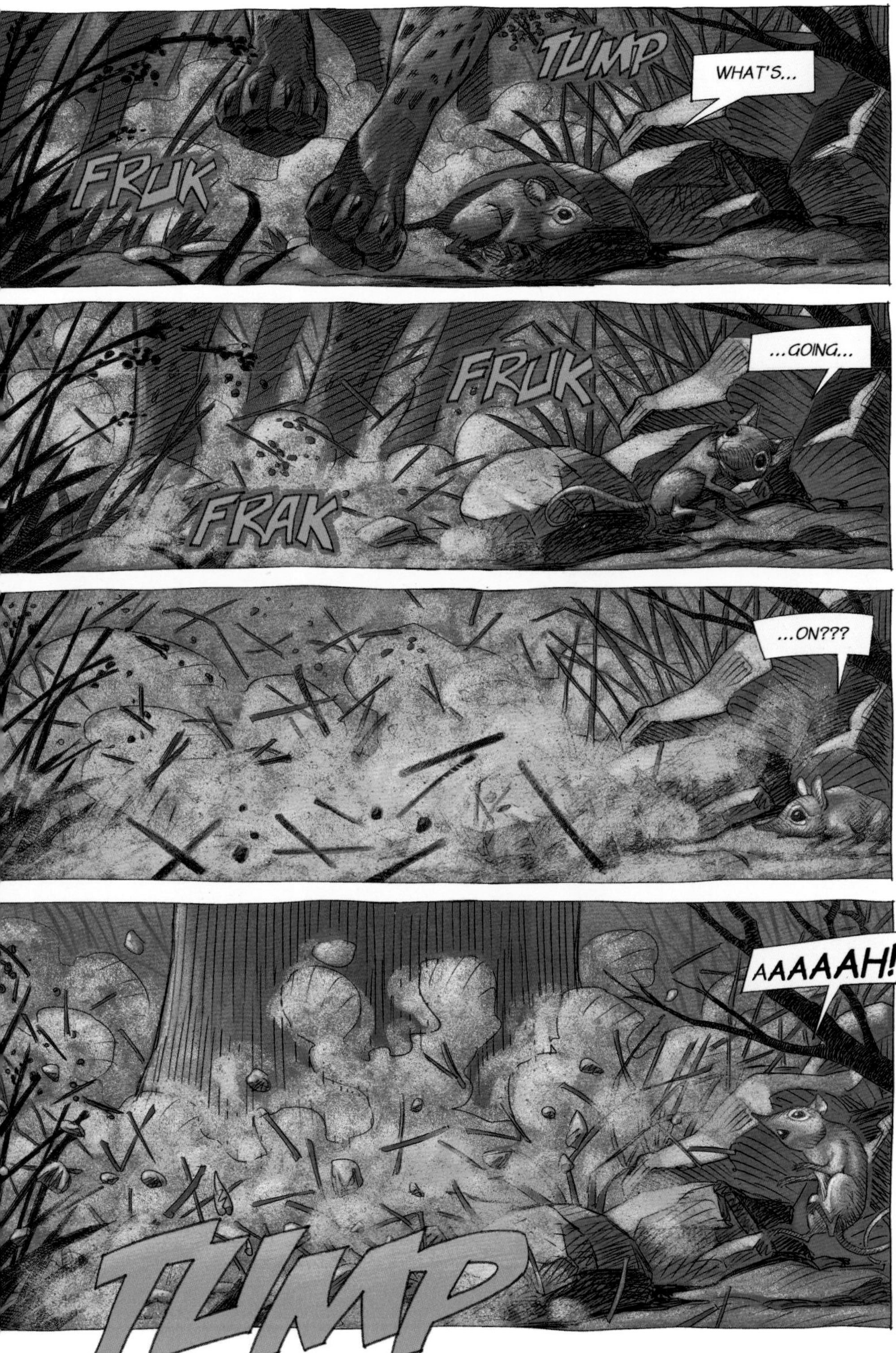
TUMP
WHAT'S...
FRUK
...GOING...
FRUK
FRAK
...ON???
AAAAAH!
TUMP

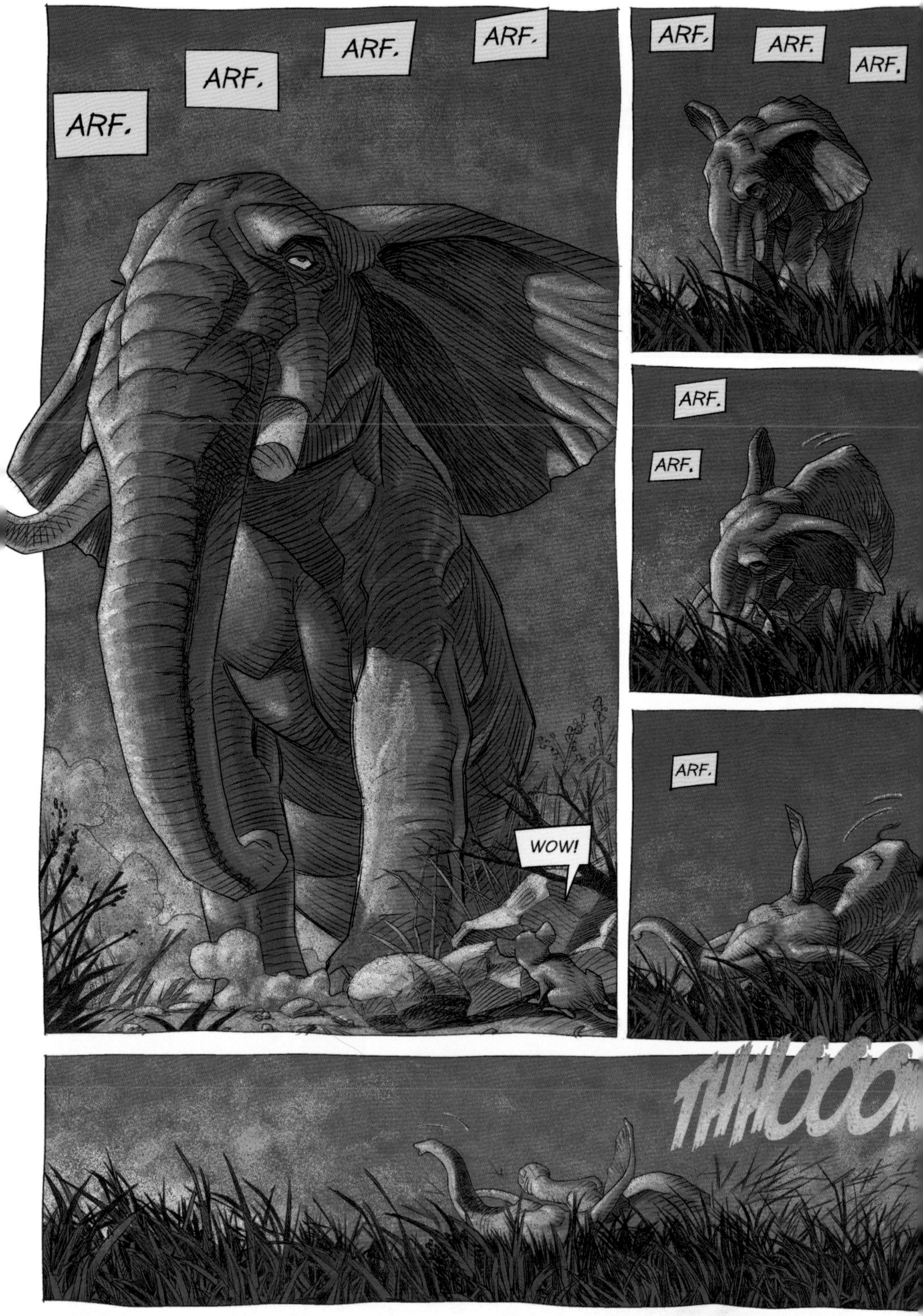

ARF.
ARF.
ARF.
ARF.
WOW!
ARF.
ARF.
ARF.
ARF.
ARF.
ARF.
THHOOOM

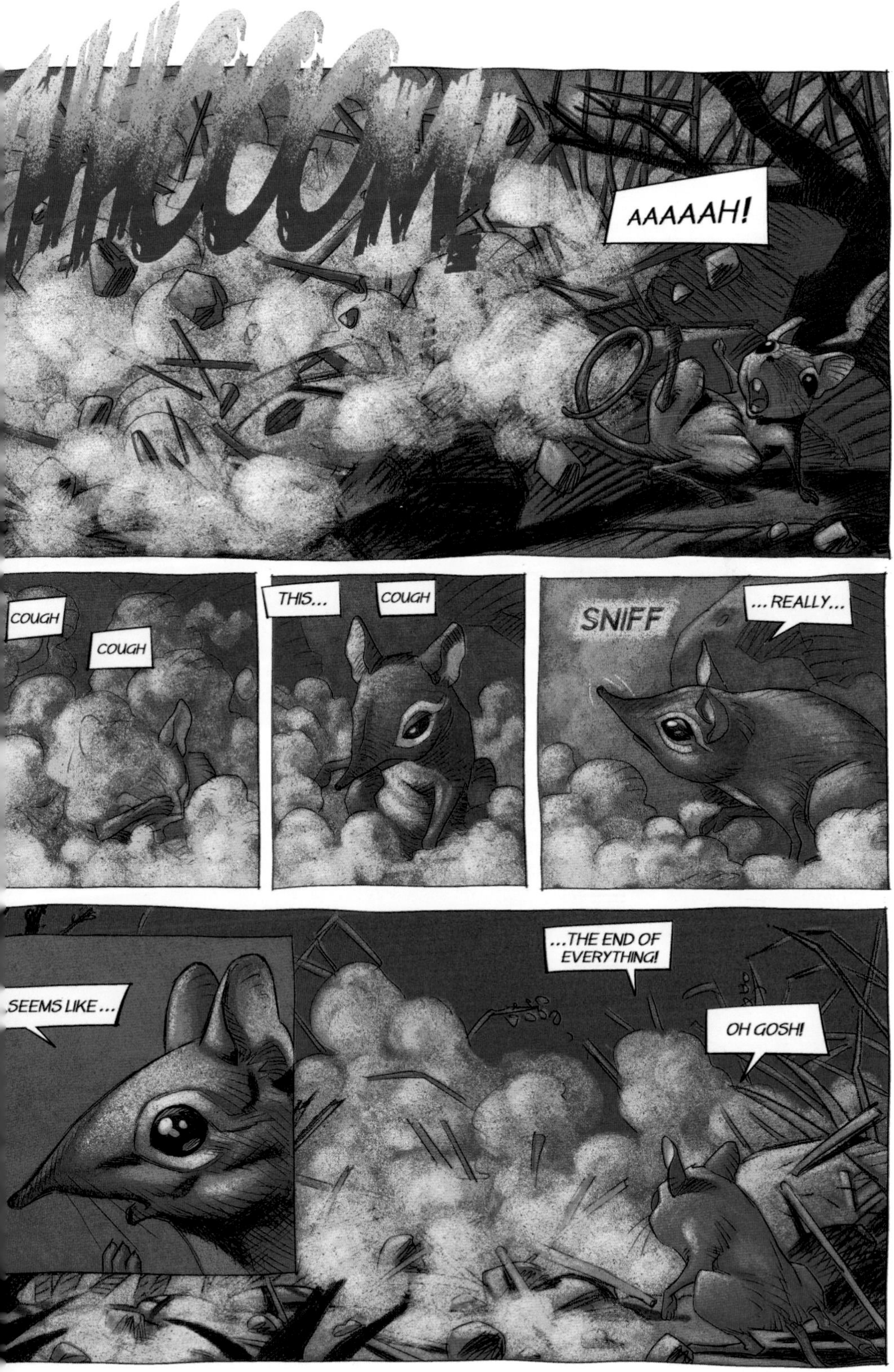
WHOOOM!
AAAAAH!
COUGH
COUGH
THIS...
COUGH
SNIFF
...REALLY...
SEEMS LIKE...
...THE END OF EVERYTHING!
OH GOSH!

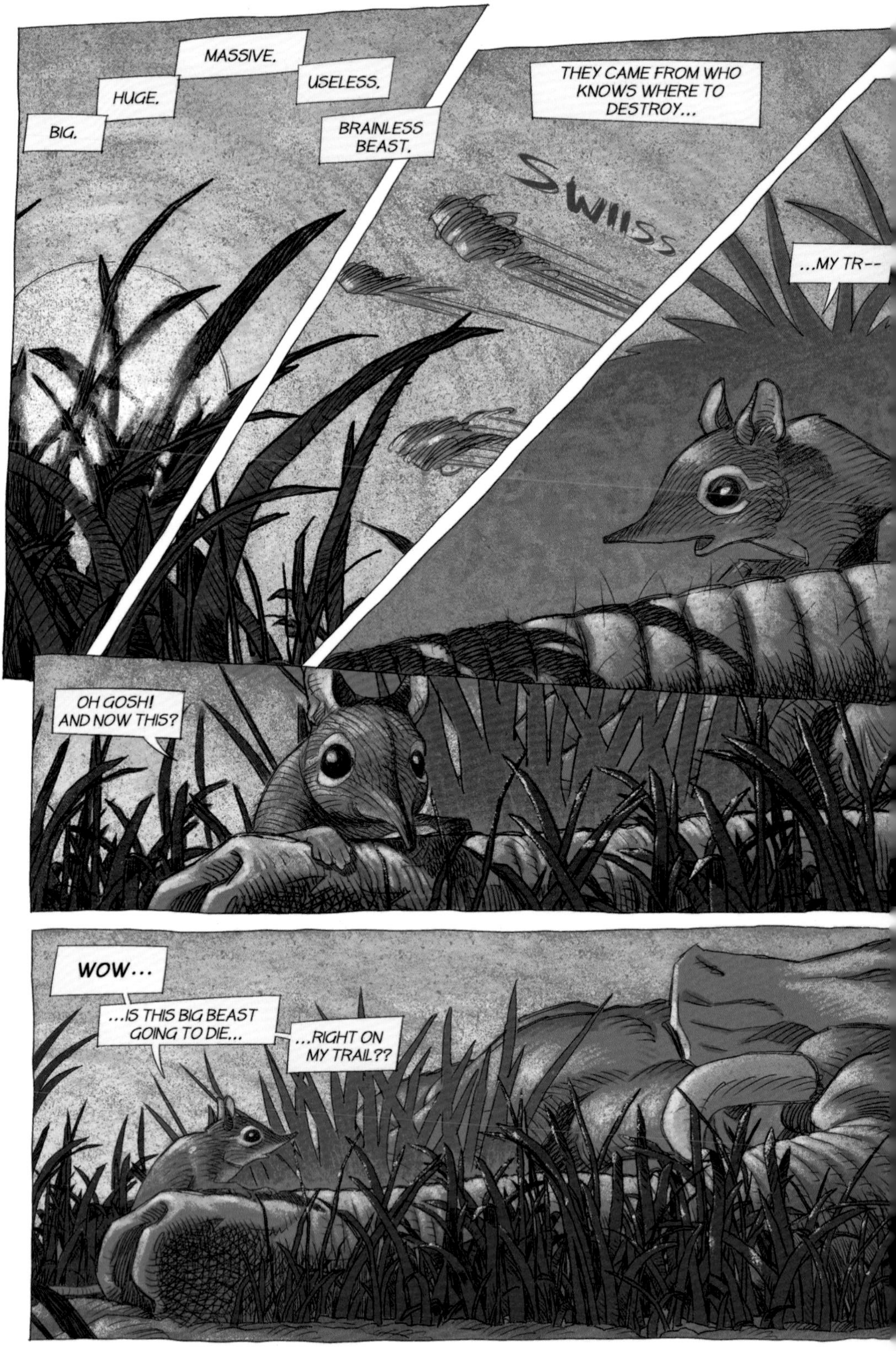
BIG.
HUGE.
MASSIVE.
USELESS.
BRAINLESS BEAST.
THEY CAME FROM WHO KNOWS WHERE TO DESTROY...
SWIISS
...MY TR--
OH GOSH! AND NOW THIS?
WOW...
...IS THIS BIG BEAST GOING TO DIE...
...RIGHT ON MY TRAIL??

HEY!

TUNF!

WELL, SINCE YOU'RE ALIVE...

...CAN YOU MOVE YOUR BIG NOSE OFF MY TRAIL?

. . .

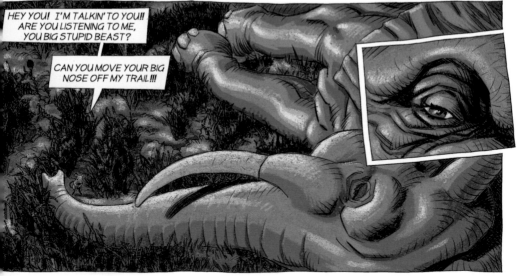

HEY YOU! I'M TALKIN' TO YOU!! ARE YOU LISTENING TO ME, YOU BIG STUPID BEAST?

CAN YOU MOVE YOUR BIG NOSE OFF MY TRAIL!!!

HEY! WHO ARE YOU??? WHY ARE YOU SHOUTING AT THIS HOUR OF NIGHT?
NIGHT??? WHAT NIGHT? IT'S MORNING ALREADY. HAS BEEN FOR QUITE A WHILE!
MMH... YOU'RE RIGHT
BUT I'M TOO TIRED... I'LL SLEEP HERE A LITTLE LONGER...
TUMP
FINE! YOU CAN SLEEP AS LONG AS YOU WANT! BUT MOVE YOUR BIG NOSE OFF MY TRAIL!
YOUR... WHAT??
TRAIL!!!
MY TRAIL! ARE YOU DEAF?
AND... WHERE WOULD THIS ... TRAIL BE?

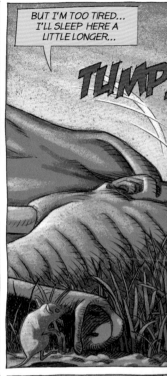

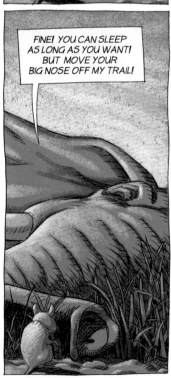

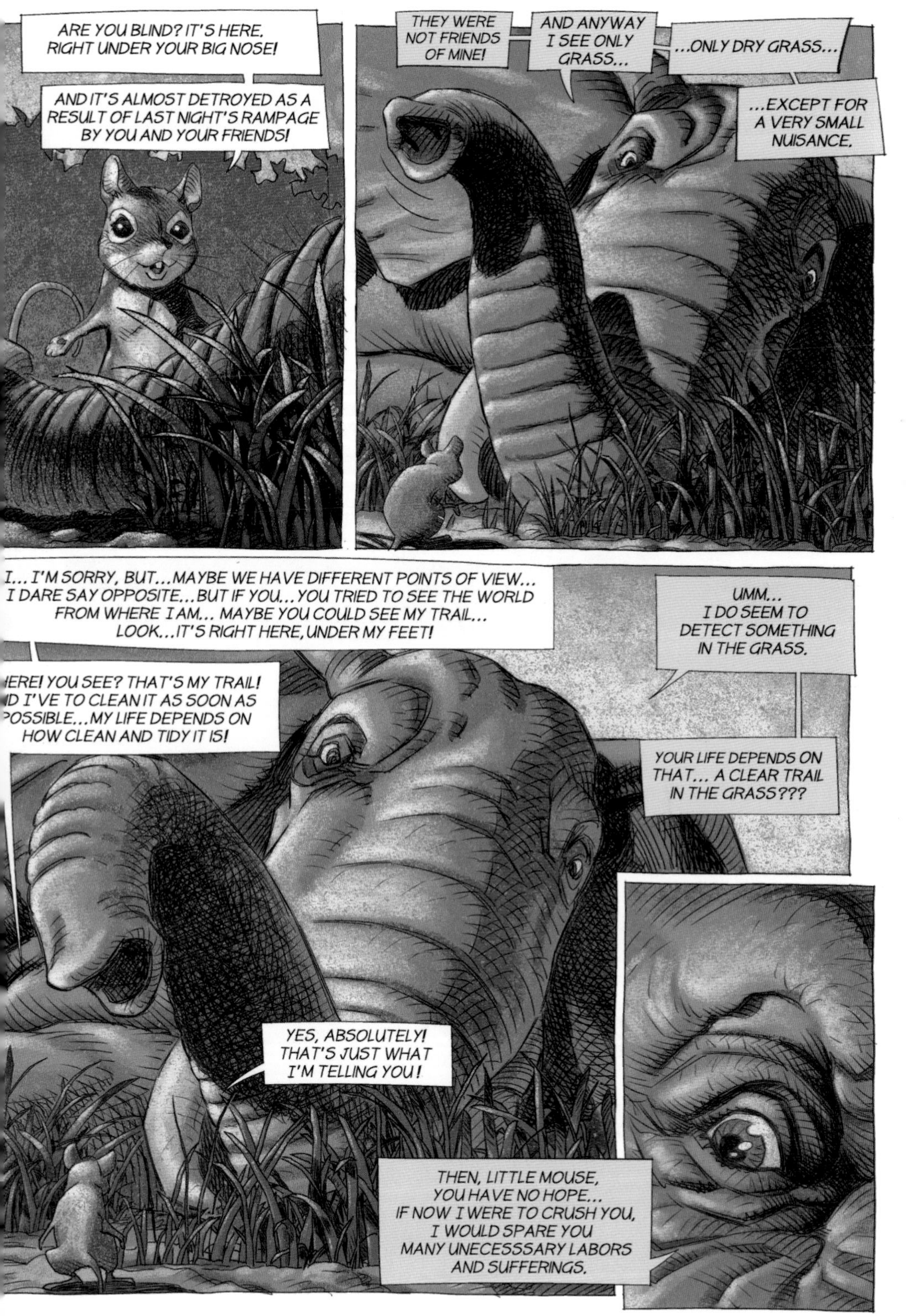
ARE YOU BLIND? IT'S HERE. RIGHT UNDER YOUR BIG NOSE!
AND IT'S ALMOST DETROYED AS A RESULT OF LAST NIGHT'S RAMPAGE BY YOU AND YOUR FRIENDS!
THEY WERE NOT FRIENDS OF MINE!
AND ANYWAY I SEE ONLY GRASS...
...ONLY DRY GRASS...
...EXCEPT FOR A VERY SMALL NUISANCE.
I... I'M SORRY, BUT... MAYBE WE HAVE DIFFERENT POINTS OF VIEW... I DARE SAY OPPOSITE... BUT IF YOU... YOU TRIED TO SEE THE WORLD FROM WHERE I AM... MAYBE YOU COULD SEE MY TRAIL... LOOK... IT'S RIGHT HERE, UNDER MY FEET!
UMM... I DO SEEM TO DETECT SOMETHING IN THE GRASS.
ERE! YOU SEE? THAT'S MY TRAIL! D I'VE TO CLEAN IT AS SOON AS OSSIBLE... MY LIFE DEPENDS ON HOW CLEAN AND TIDY IT IS!
YOUR LIFE DEPENDS ON THAT... A CLEAR TRAIL IN THE GRASS???
YES, ABSOLUTELY! THAT'S JUST WHAT I'M TELLING YOU!
THEN, LITTLE MOUSE, YOU HAVE NO HOPE... IF NOW I WERE TO CRUSH YOU, I WOULD SPARE YOU MANY UNECESSSARY LABORS AND SUFFERINGS.

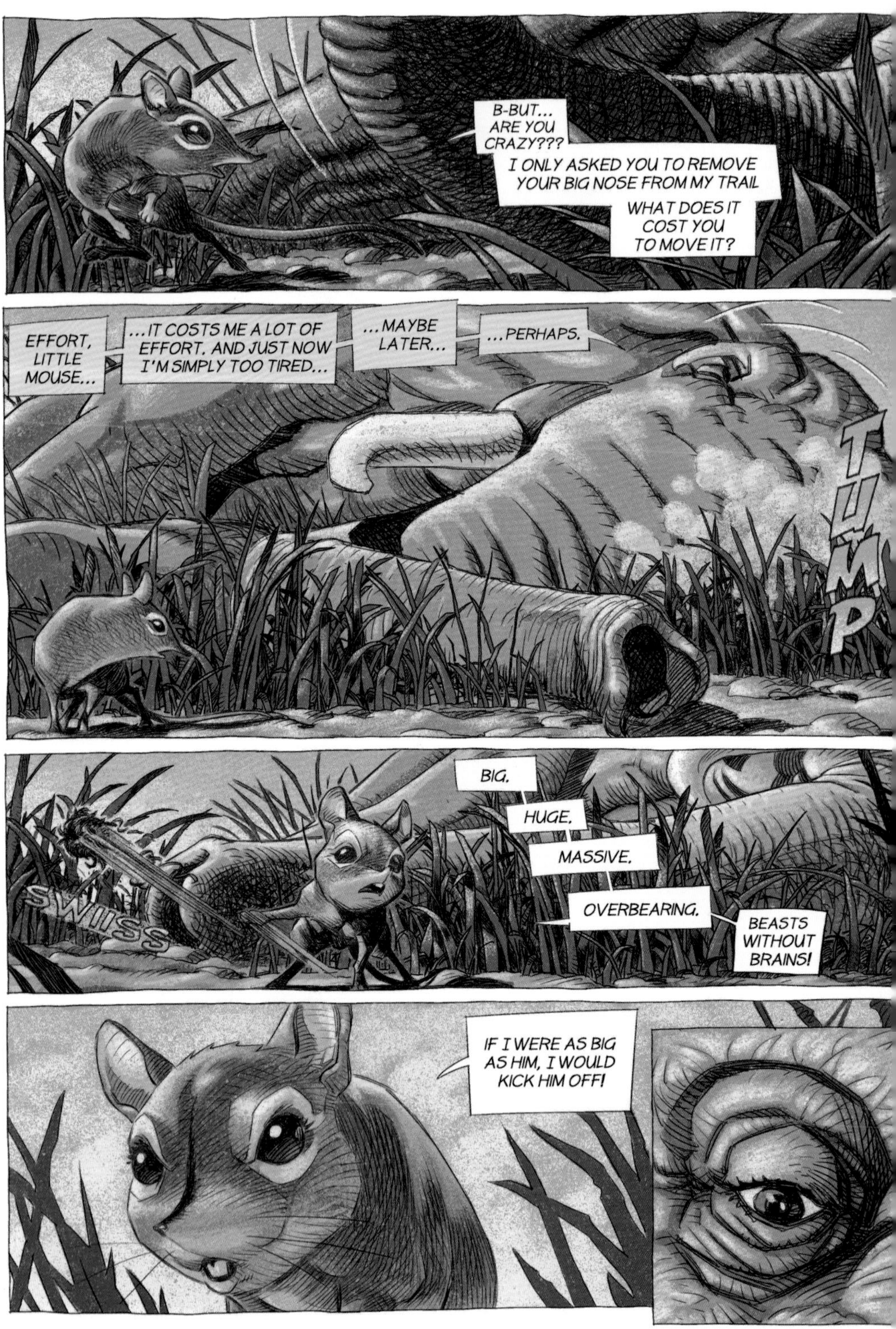

B-BUT... ARE YOU CRAZY???
I ONLY ASKED YOU TO REMOVE YOUR BIG NOSE FROM MY TRAIL
WHAT DOES IT COST YOU TO MOVE IT?
EFFORT, LITTLE MOUSE...
...IT COSTS ME A LOT OF EFFORT, AND JUST NOW I'M SIMPLY TOO TIRED...
...MAYBE LATER...
...PERHAPS.
TUMP
SWIISS
BIG.
HUGE.
MASSIVE.
OVERBEARING.
BEASTS WITHOUT BRAINS!
IF I WERE AS BIG AS HIM, I WOULD KICK HIM OFF!

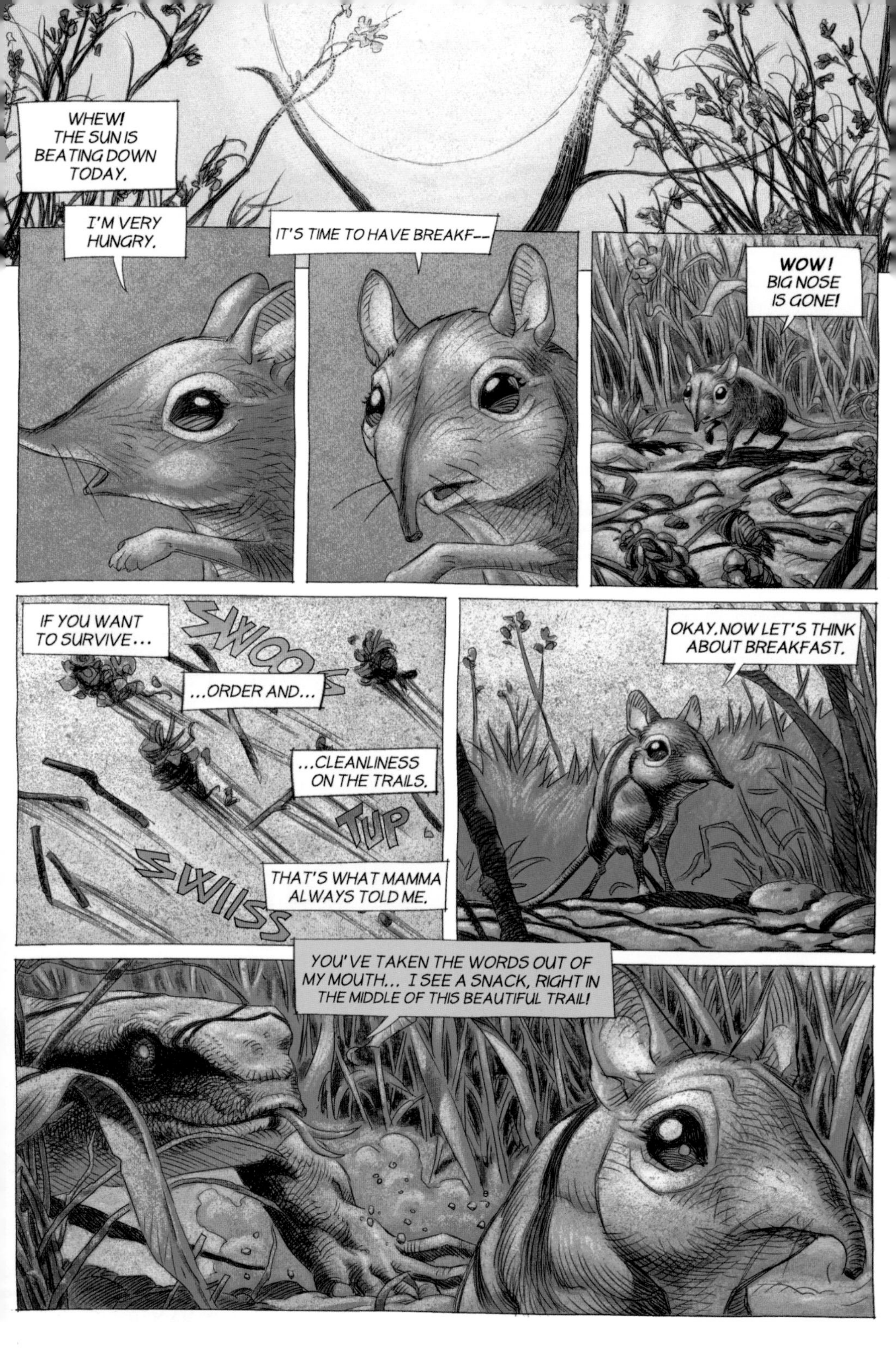
WHEW!
THE SUN IS
BEATING DOWN
TODAY.
I'M VERY
HUNGRY.
IT'S TIME TO HAVE BREAKF--
WOW!
BIG NOSE
IS GONE!
IF YOU WANT
TO SURVIVE...
SWOOSH
...ORDER AND...
...CLEANLINESS
ON THE TRAILS.
TUP
SWIISS
THAT'S WHAT MAMMA
ALWAYS TOLD ME.
OKAY. NOW LET'S THINK
ABOUT BREAKFAST.
YOU'VE TAKEN THE WORDS OUT OF
MY MOUTH... I SEE A SNACK, RIGHT IN
THE MIDDLE OF THIS BEAUTIFUL TRAIL!

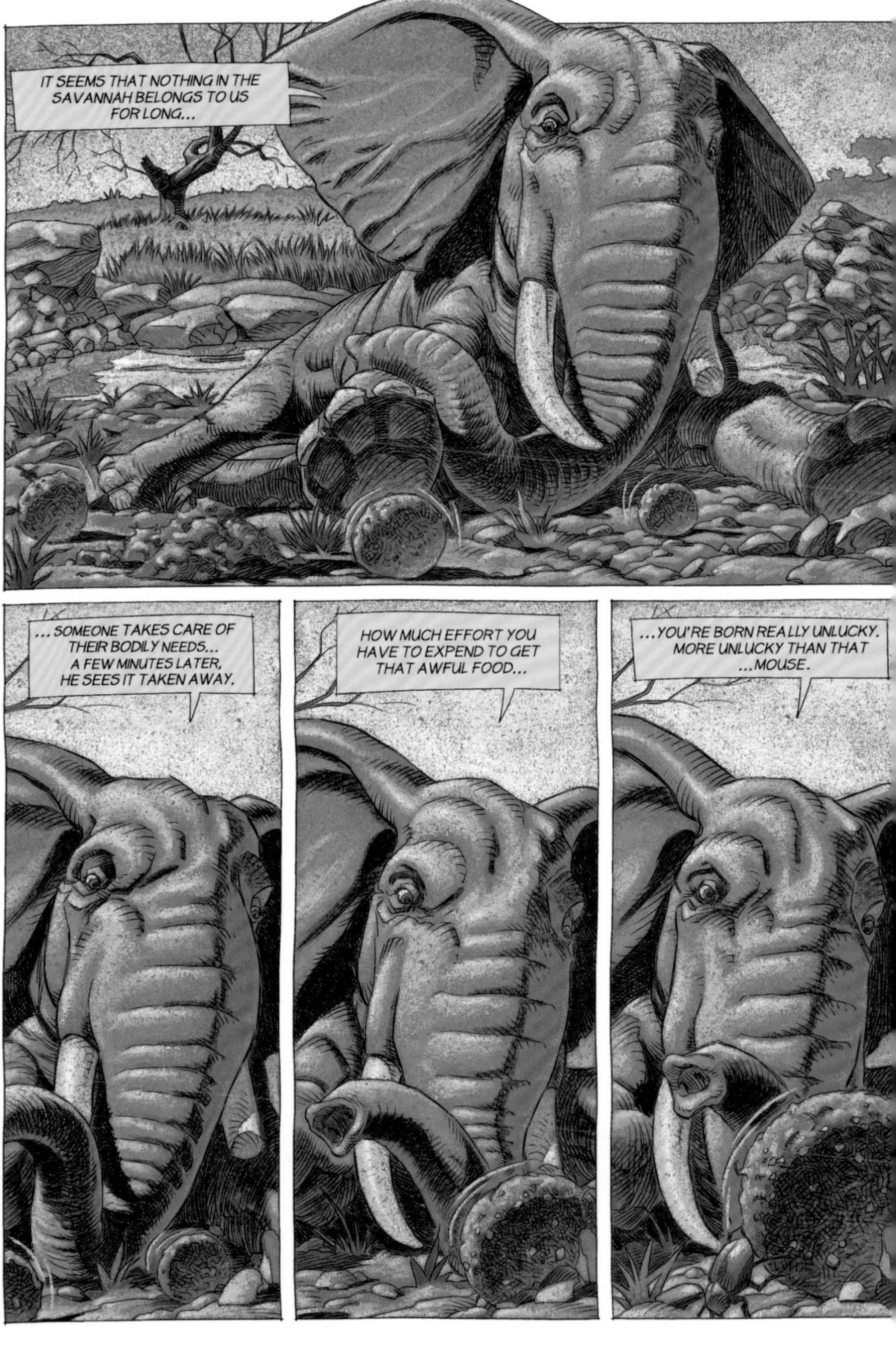
IT SEEMS THAT NOTHING IN THE SAVANNAH BELONGS TO US FOR LONG...
...SOMEONE TAKES CARE OF THEIR BODILY NEEDS... A FEW MINUTES LATER, HE SEES IT TAKEN AWAY.
HOW MUCH EFFORT YOU HAVE TO EXPEND TO GET THAT AWFUL FOOD...
...YOU'RE BORN REALLY UNLUCKY. MORE UNLUCKY THAN THAT ...MOUSE.

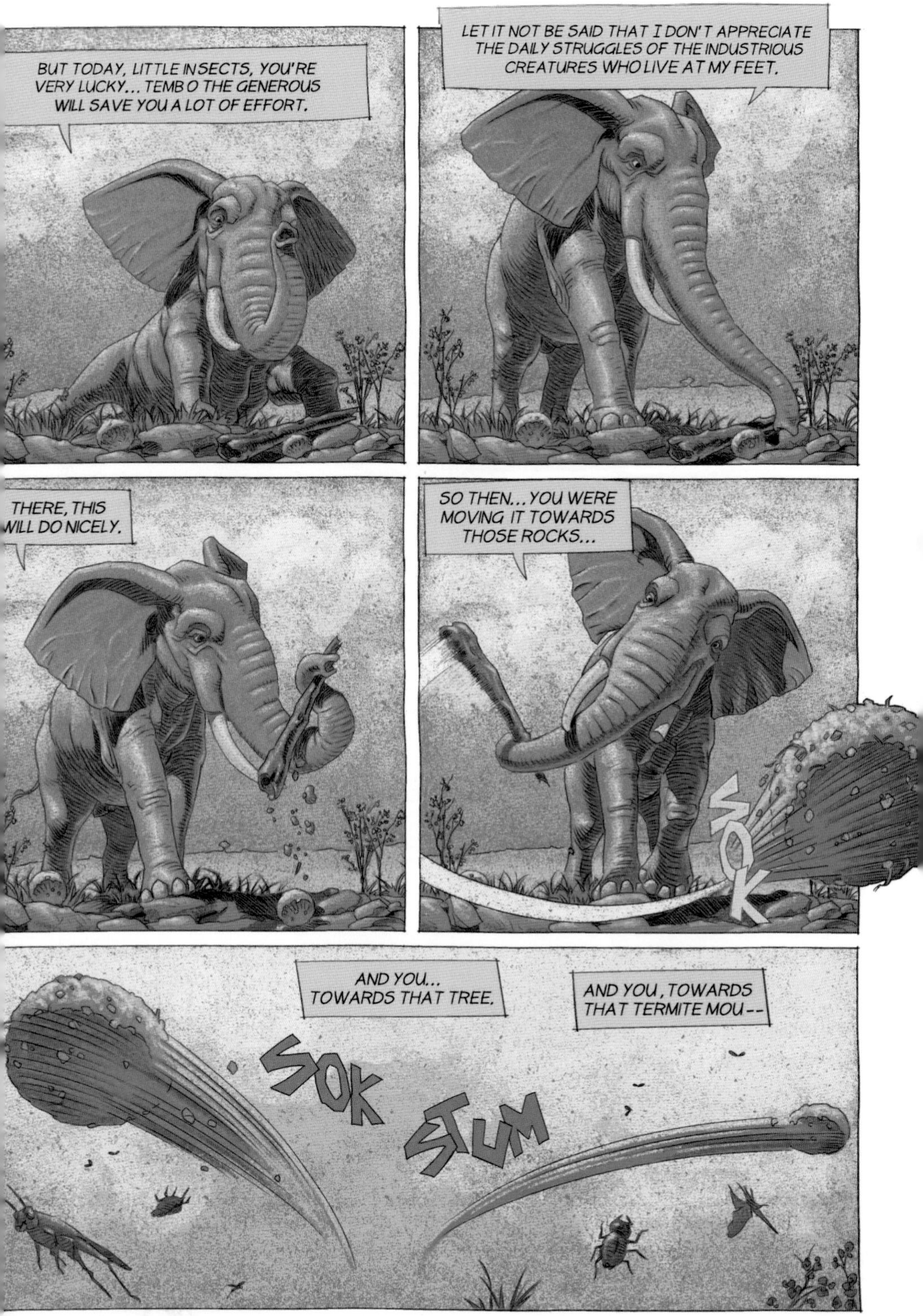
BUT TODAY, LITTLE INSECTS, YOU'RE VERY LUCKY... TEMBO THE GENEROUS WILL SAVE YOU A LOT OF EFFORT.
LET IT NOT BE SAID THAT I DON'T APPRECIATE THE DAILY STRUGGLES OF THE INDUSTRIOUS CREATURES WHO LIVE AT MY FEET.
THERE, THIS WILL DO NICELY.
SO THEN... YOU WERE MOVING IT TOWARDS THOSE ROCKS...
SOK
AND YOU... TOWARDS THAT TREE.
AND YOU, TOWARDS THAT TERMITE MOU--
SOK
STUM

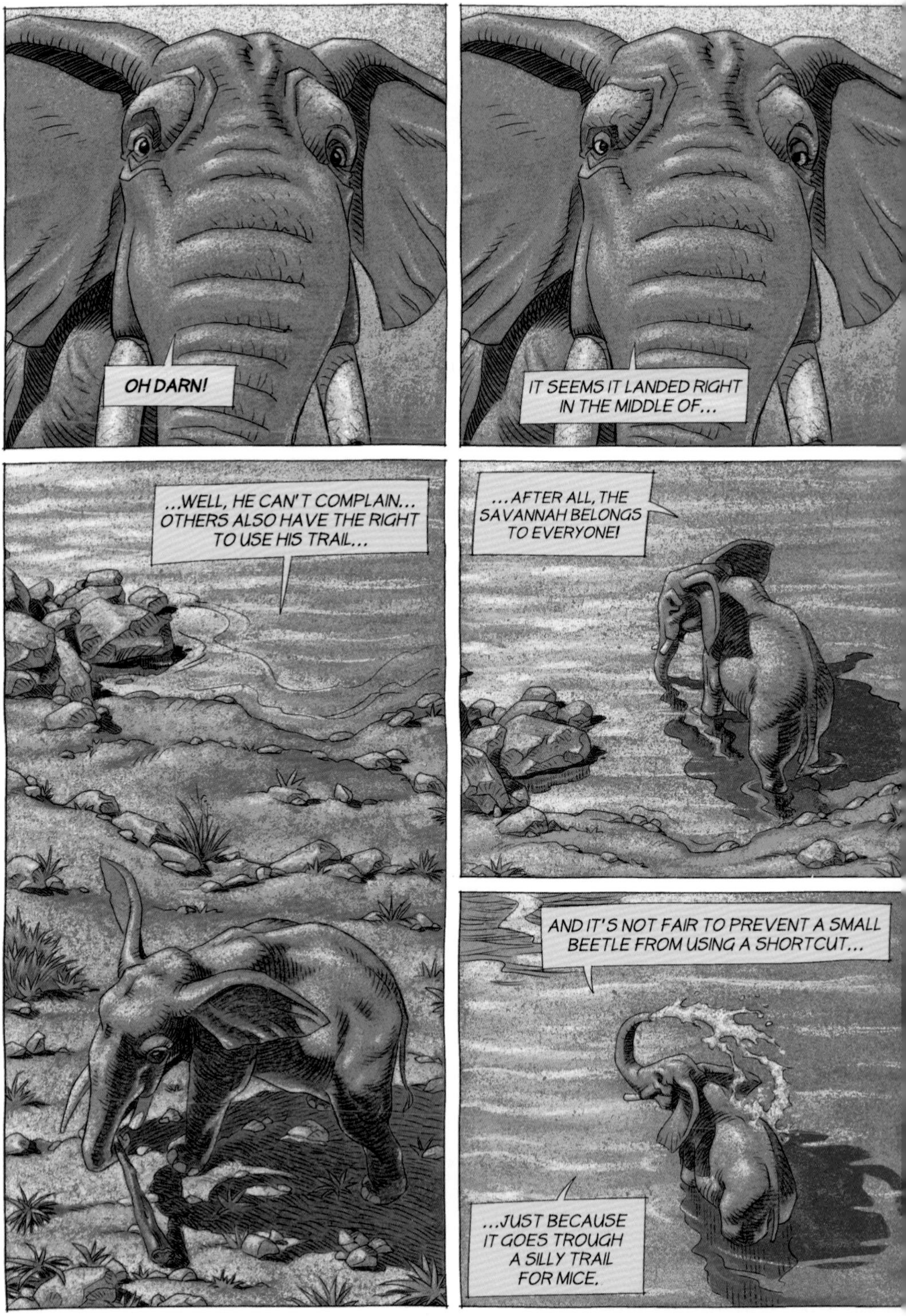
OH DARN!
IT SEEMS IT LANDED RIGHT IN THE MIDDLE OF...
...WELL, HE CAN'T COMPLAIN... OTHERS ALSO HAVE THE RIGHT TO USE HIS TRAIL...
...AFTER ALL, THE SAVANNAH BELONGS TO EVERYONE!
AND IT'S NOT FAIR TO PREVENT A SMALL BEETLE FROM USING A SHORTCUT...
...JUST BECAUSE IT GOES TROUGH A SILLY TRAIL FOR MICE.

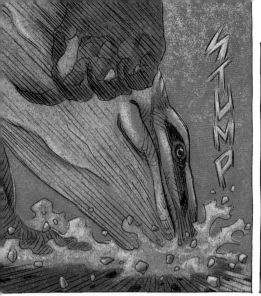

STUMP

STUPID! I'M REALLY STUPID!

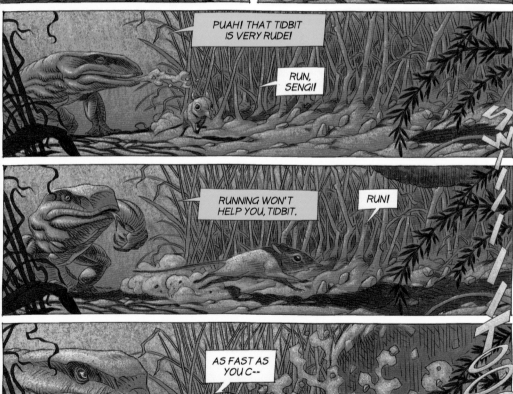

PUAH! THAT TIDBIT IS VERY RUDE!

RUN, SENGI!

SWIIIIIISH

RUNNING WON'T HELP YOU, TIDBIT.

RUN!

AS FAST AS YOU C--

YOUR SCENT WILL ALWAYS LEAD ME TO...

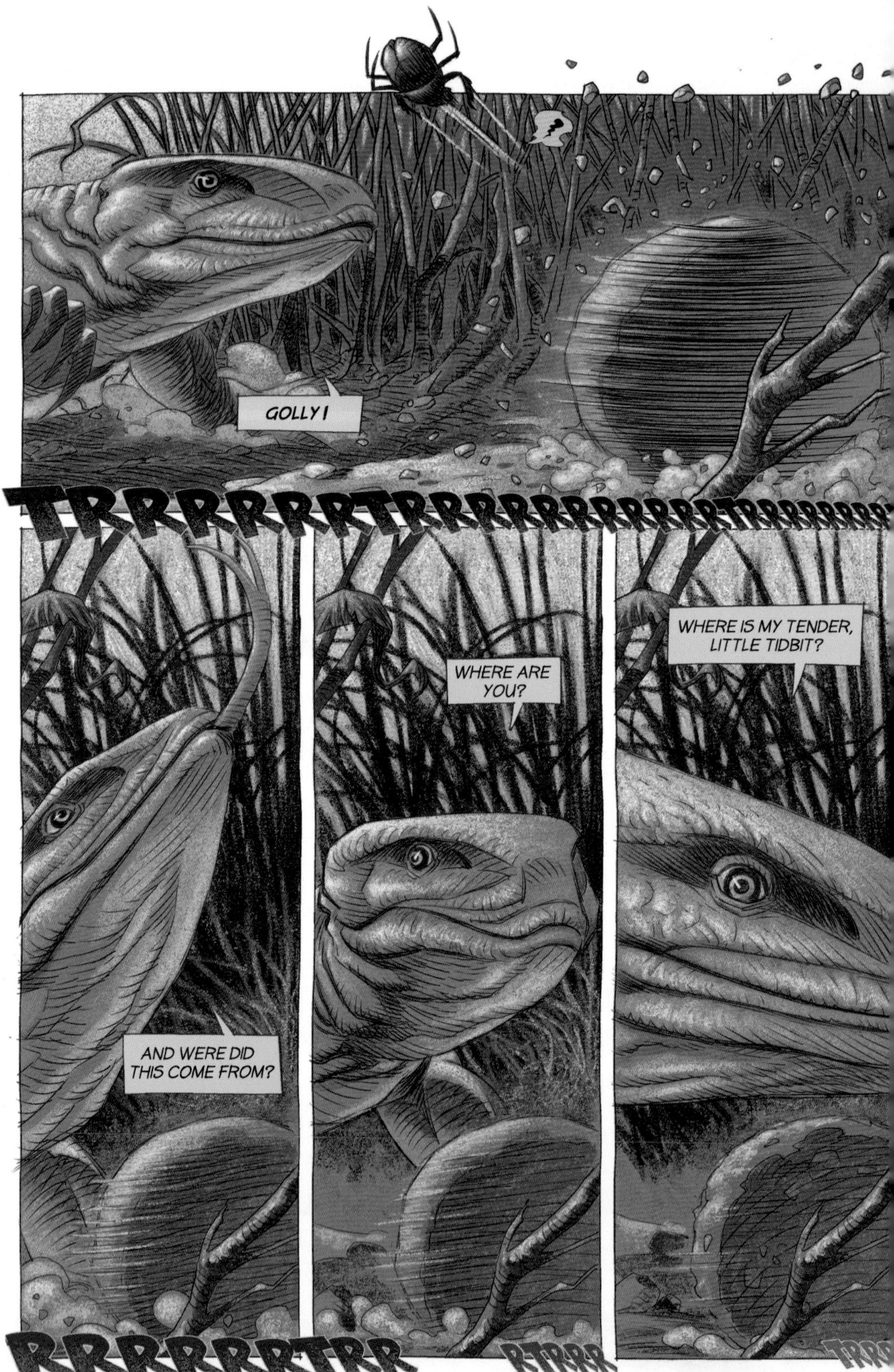
?
GOLLY!
TRRRRRRTRRRRRRRRRRRRRTRRRRRRR
AND WERE DID THIS COME FROM?
RRRRRRRTRR
WHERE ARE YOU?
RTRRR
WHERE IS MY TENDER, LITTLE TIDBIT?

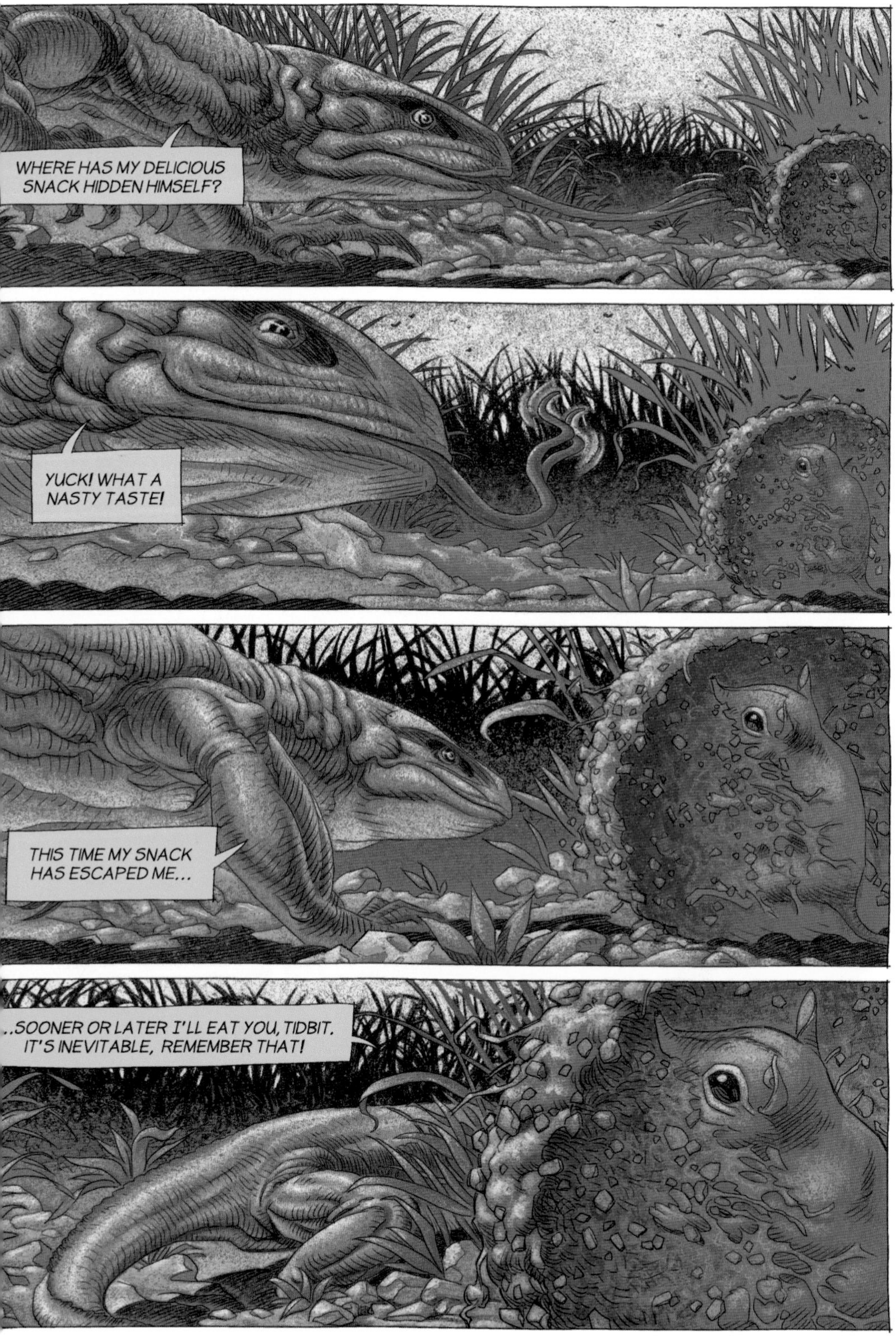
WHERE HAS MY DELICIOUS SNACK HIDDEN HIMSELF?
YUCK! WHAT A NASTY TASTE!
THIS TIME MY SNACK HAS ESCAPED ME...
...SOONER OR LATER I'LL EAT YOU, TIDBIT. IT'S INEVITABLE, REMEMBER THAT!

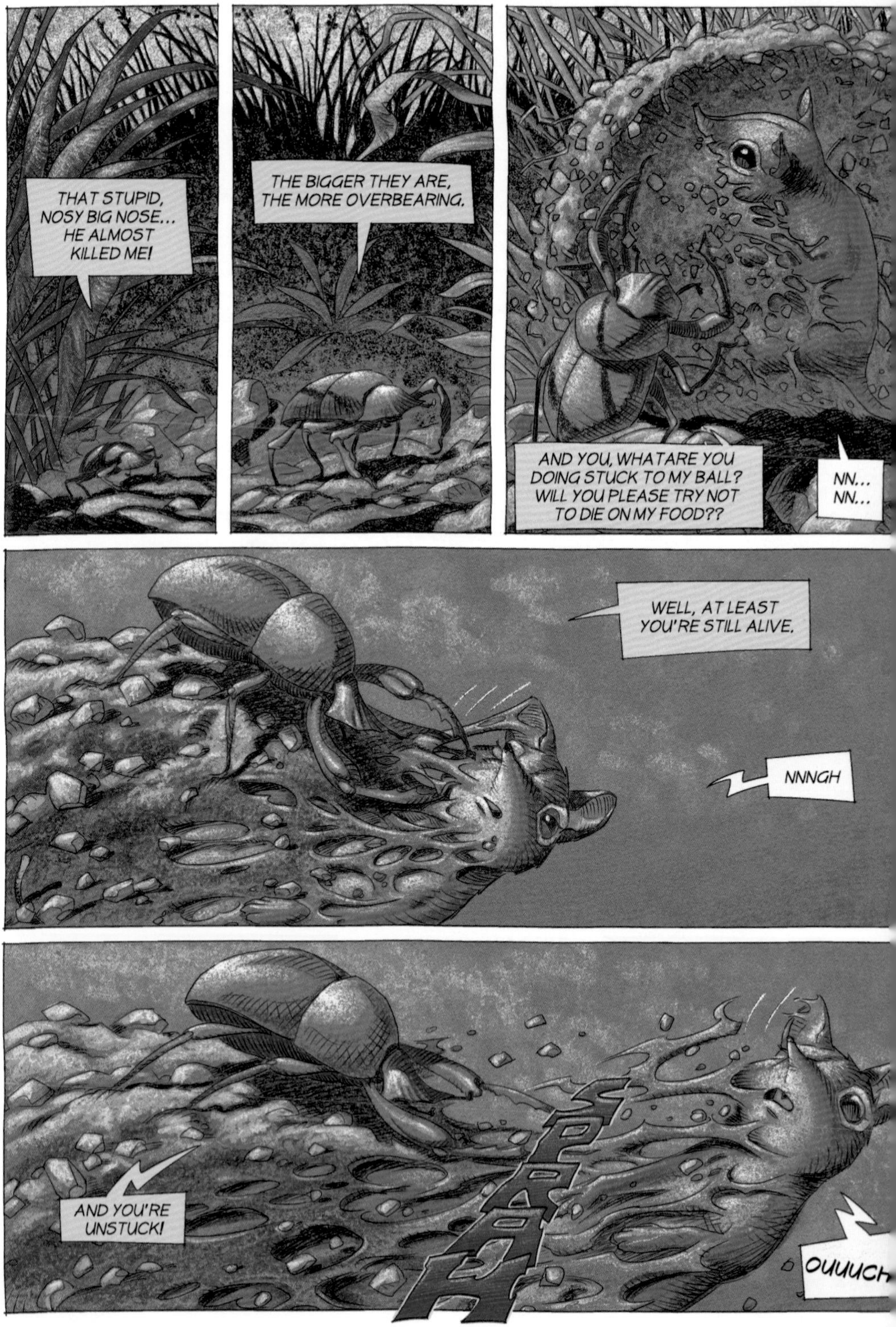
THAT STUPID, NOSY BIG NOSE... HE ALMOST KILLED ME!
THE BIGGER THEY ARE, THE MORE OVERBEARING.
AND YOU, WHATARE YOU DOING STUCK TO MY BALL? WILL YOU PLEASE TRY NOT TO DIE ON MY FOOD??
NN... NN...
WELL, AT LEAST YOU'RE STILL ALIVE.
NNNGH
SPLAAA
AND YOU'RE UNSTUCK!
OUUUCH

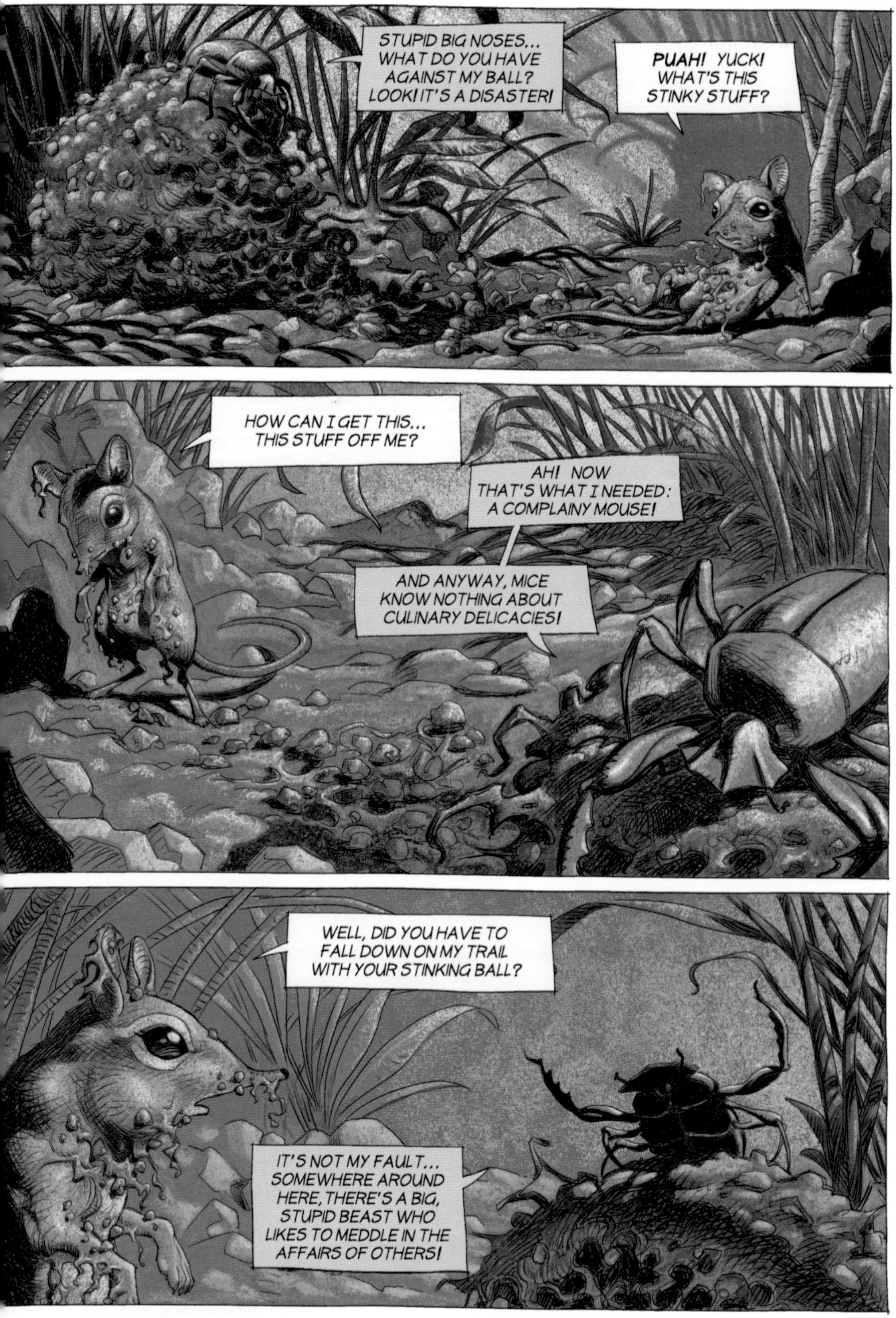
STUPID BIG NOSES... WHAT DO YOU HAVE AGAINST MY BALL? LOOK! IT'S A DISASTER!
PUAH! YUCK! WHAT'S THIS STINKY STUFF?
HOW CAN I GET THIS... THIS STUFF OFF ME?
AH! NOW THAT'S WHAT I NEEDED: A COMPLAINY MOUSE!
AND ANYWAY, MICE KNOW NOTHING ABOUT CULINARY DELICACIES!
WELL, DID YOU HAVE TO FALL DOWN ON MY TRAIL WITH YOUR STINKING BALL?
IT'S NOT MY FAULT... SOMEWHERE AROUND HERE, THERE'S A BIG, STUPID BEAST WHO LIKES TO MEDDLE IN THE AFFAIRS OF OTHERS!

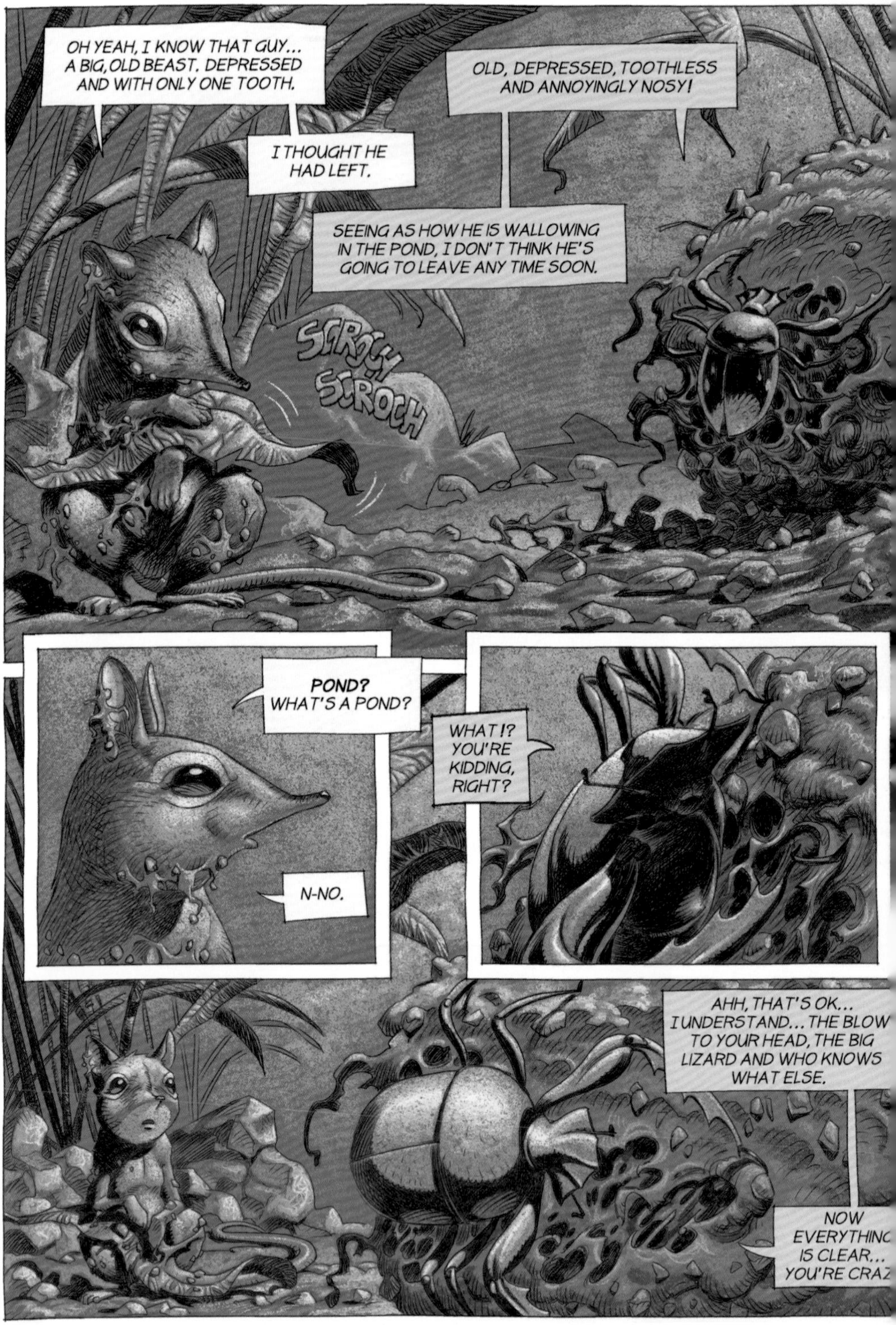
OH YEAH, I KNOW THAT GUY... A BIG, OLD BEAST. DEPRESSED AND WITH ONLY ONE TOOTH.
I THOUGHT HE HAD LEFT.
OLD, DEPRESSED, TOOTHLESS AND ANNOYINGLY NOSY!
SEEING AS HOW HE IS WALLOWING IN THE POND, I DON'T THINK HE'S GOING TO LEAVE ANY TIME SOON.
SCROCH SCROCH
POND? WHAT'S A POND?
WHAT!? YOU'RE KIDDING, RIGHT?
N-NO.
AHH, THAT'S OK... I UNDERSTAND... THE BLOW TO YOUR HEAD, THE BIG LIZARD AND WHO KNOWS WHAT ELSE.
NOW EVERYTHING IS CLEAR... YOU'RE CRAZ

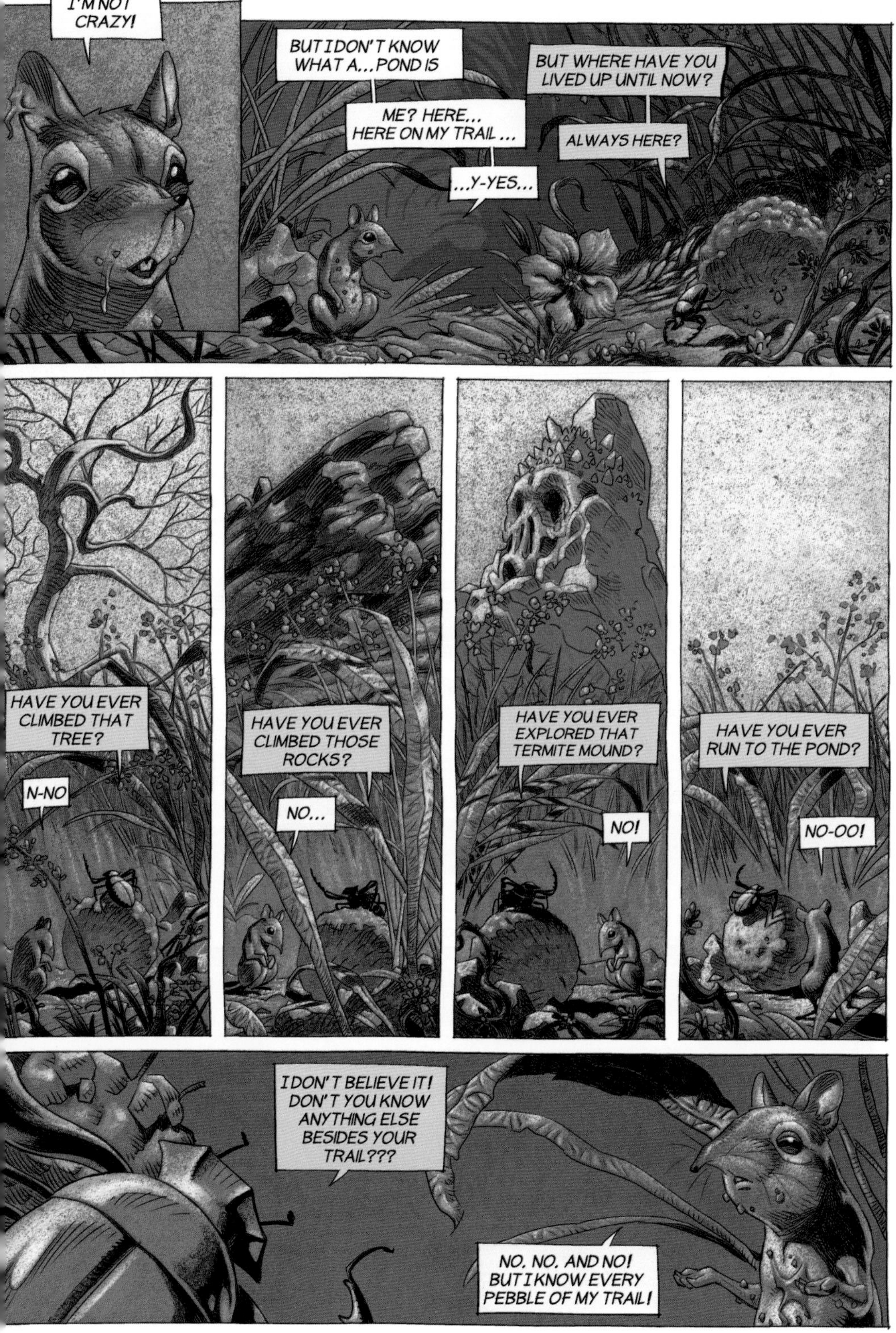
I'M NOT CRAZY!
BUT I DON'T KNOW WHAT A... POND IS
BUT WHERE HAVE YOU LIVED UP UNTIL NOW?
ME? HERE... HERE ON MY TRAIL ...
ALWAYS HERE?
...Y-YES...
HAVE YOU EVER CLIMBED THAT TREE?
N-NO
HAVE YOU EVER CLIMBED THOSE ROCKS?
NO...
HAVE YOU EVER EXPLORED THAT TERMITE MOUND?
NO!
HAVE YOU EVER RUN TO THE POND?
NO-OO!
I DON'T BELIEVE IT! DON'T YOU KNOW ANYTHING ELSE BESIDES YOUR TRAIL???
NO. NO. AND NO! BUT I KNOW EVERY PEBBLE OF MY TRAIL!

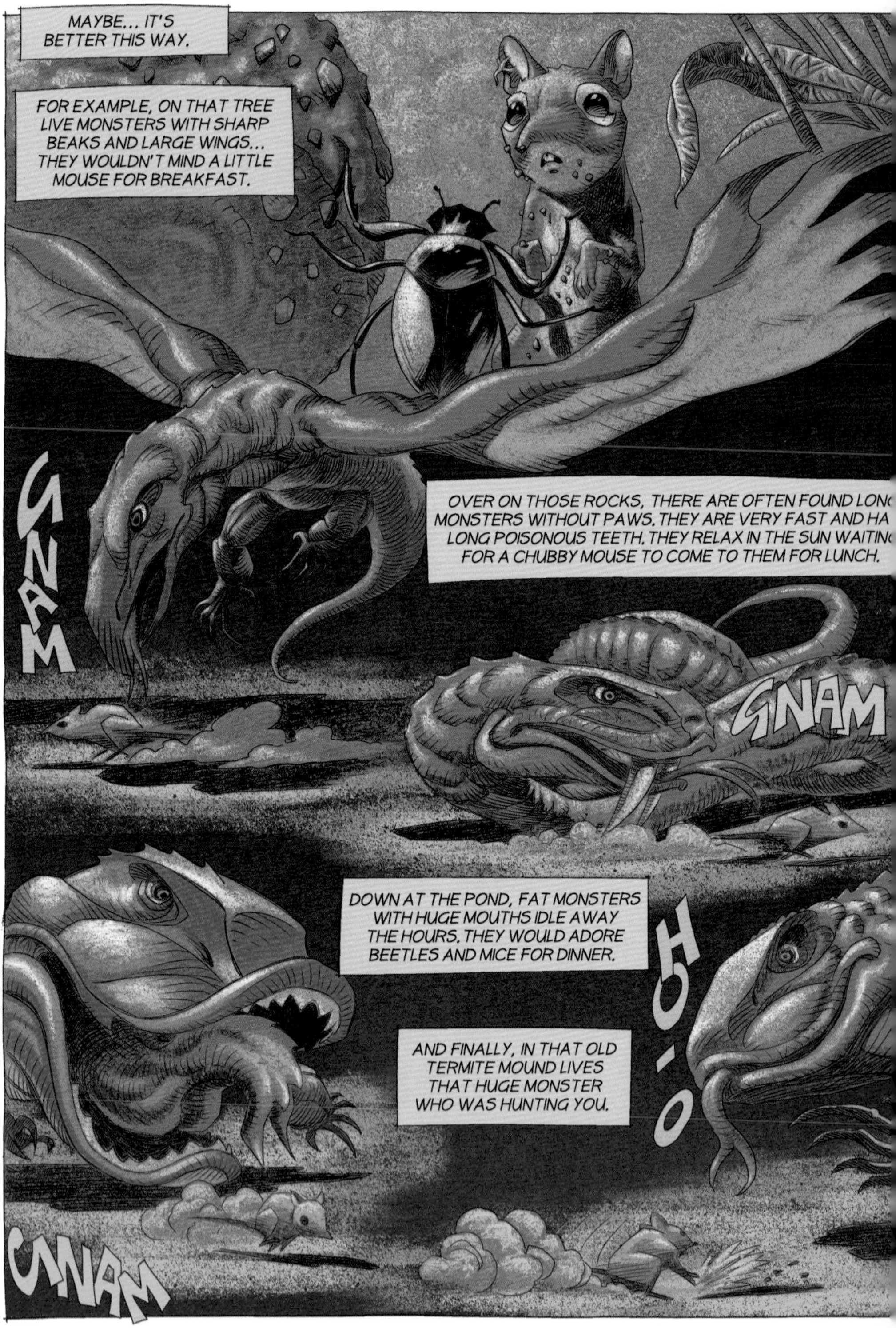
MAYBE... IT'S BETTER THIS WAY.
FOR EXAMPLE, ON THAT TREE LIVE MONSTERS WITH SHARP BEAKS AND LARGE WINGS... THEY WOULDN'T MIND A LITTLE MOUSE FOR BREAKFAST.
GNAM
OVER ON THOSE ROCKS, THERE ARE OFTEN FOUND LONG MONSTERS WITHOUT PAWS. THEY ARE VERY FAST AND HA LONG POISONOUS TEETH. THEY RELAX IN THE SUN WAITING FOR A CHUBBY MOUSE TO COME TO THEM FOR LUNCH.
GNAM
DOWN AT THE POND, FAT MONSTERS WITH HUGE MOUTHS IDLE AWAY THE HOURS. THEY WOULD ADORE BEETLES AND MICE FOR DINNER.
AND FINALLY, IN THAT OLD TERMITE MOUND LIVES THAT HUGE MONSTER WHO WAS HUNTING YOU.
GNAM

THAT UGLY MONSTER LIVES IN THERE???

YES, HE ARRIVED A FEW DAYS AGO.

THAT MONSTER ATE MY MOM... A FEW DAYS AGO.

I'M SORRY, BUDDY, BUT YOU CAN'T DO ANYTHING ABOUT IT... THAT'S LIFE.

I DON'T... I DON'T LIKE... THIS...LIFE.

EHM OK, I'M GOING, I'VE GOT TO PUSH THIS BALL UP THERE, BEFORE IT GETS DARK.

SEE YOU SOON BUDDY, IF SOMEONE DOESN'T EAT US.

S-SURE... S-SEE YOU SOON.

WHAT KIND OF WORLD IS OUT THERE???

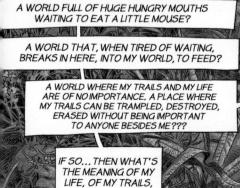

A WORLD FULL OF HUGE HUNGRY MOUTHS WAITING TO EAT A LITTLE MOUSE?

A WORLD THAT, WHEN TIRED OF WAITING, BREAKS IN HERE, INTO MY WORLD, TO FEED?

A WORLD WHERE MY TRAILS AND MY LIFE ARE OF NO IMPORTANCE, A PLACE WHERE MY TRAILS CAN BE TRAMPLED, DESTROYED, ERASED WITHOUT BEING IMPORTANT TO ANYONE BESIDES ME???

IF SO... THEN WHAT'S THE MEANING OF MY LIFE, OF MY TRAILS, OF MY RUNNING?

AM I JUST FOOD FOR ALL THOSE HORRIBLE MONSTERS???

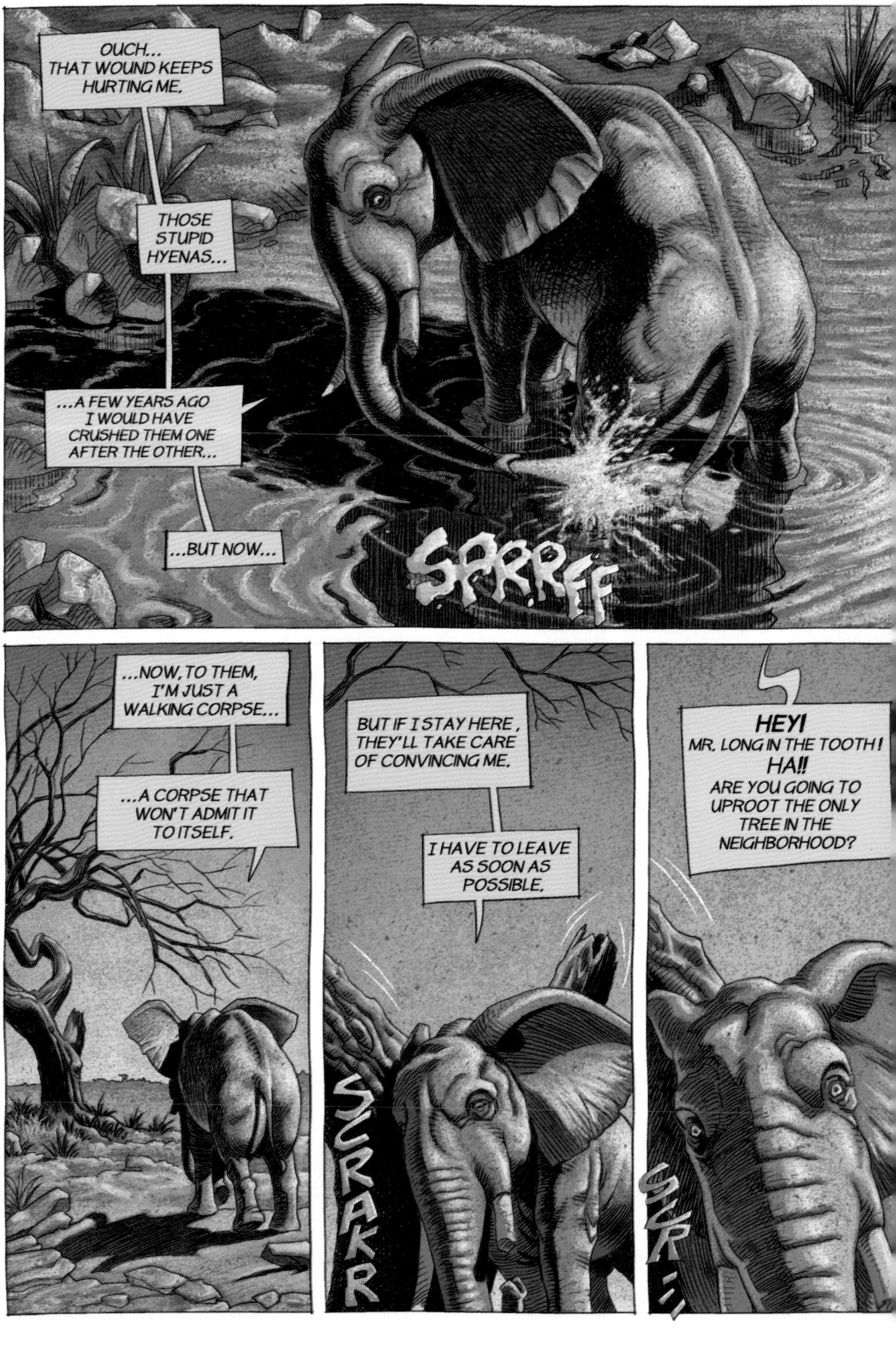
OUCH... THAT WOUND KEEPS HURTING ME.
THOSE STUPID HYENAS...
...A FEW YEARS AGO I WOULD HAVE CRUSHED THEM ONE AFTER THE OTHER...
...BUT NOW...
SPRRFF
...NOW, TO THEM, I'M JUST A WALKING CORPSE...
...A CORPSE THAT WON'T ADMIT IT TO ITSELF.
BUT IF I STAY HERE, THEY'LL TAKE CARE OF CONVINCING ME.
I HAVE TO LEAVE AS SOON AS POSSIBLE.
SCRAKR
HEY! MR. LONG IN THE TOOTH! HA!! ARE YOU GOING TO UPROOT THE ONLY TREE IN THE NEIGHBORHOOD?
SCR...

I WAS JUST SCRATCHING MY BACK!

BUT IF YOU CALL ME, MR. LONG IN THE TOOTH, AGAIN...

HO! AND NOW YOU'RE SENSITIVE?

YOU'RE THE VICTIM?

PERHAPS, RATHER THE FOOL?

EHM...AND HOW'S YOUR WOUND DOING?

IT HURTS, RIGHT?

MUCH?

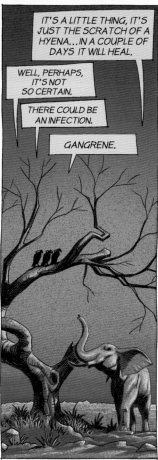

IT'S A LITTLE THING, IT'S JUST THE SCRATCH OF A HYENA...IN A COUPLE OF DAYS IT WILL HEAL.

WELL, PERHAPS, IT'S NOT SO CERTAIN.

THERE COULD BE AN INFECTION.

GANGRENE.

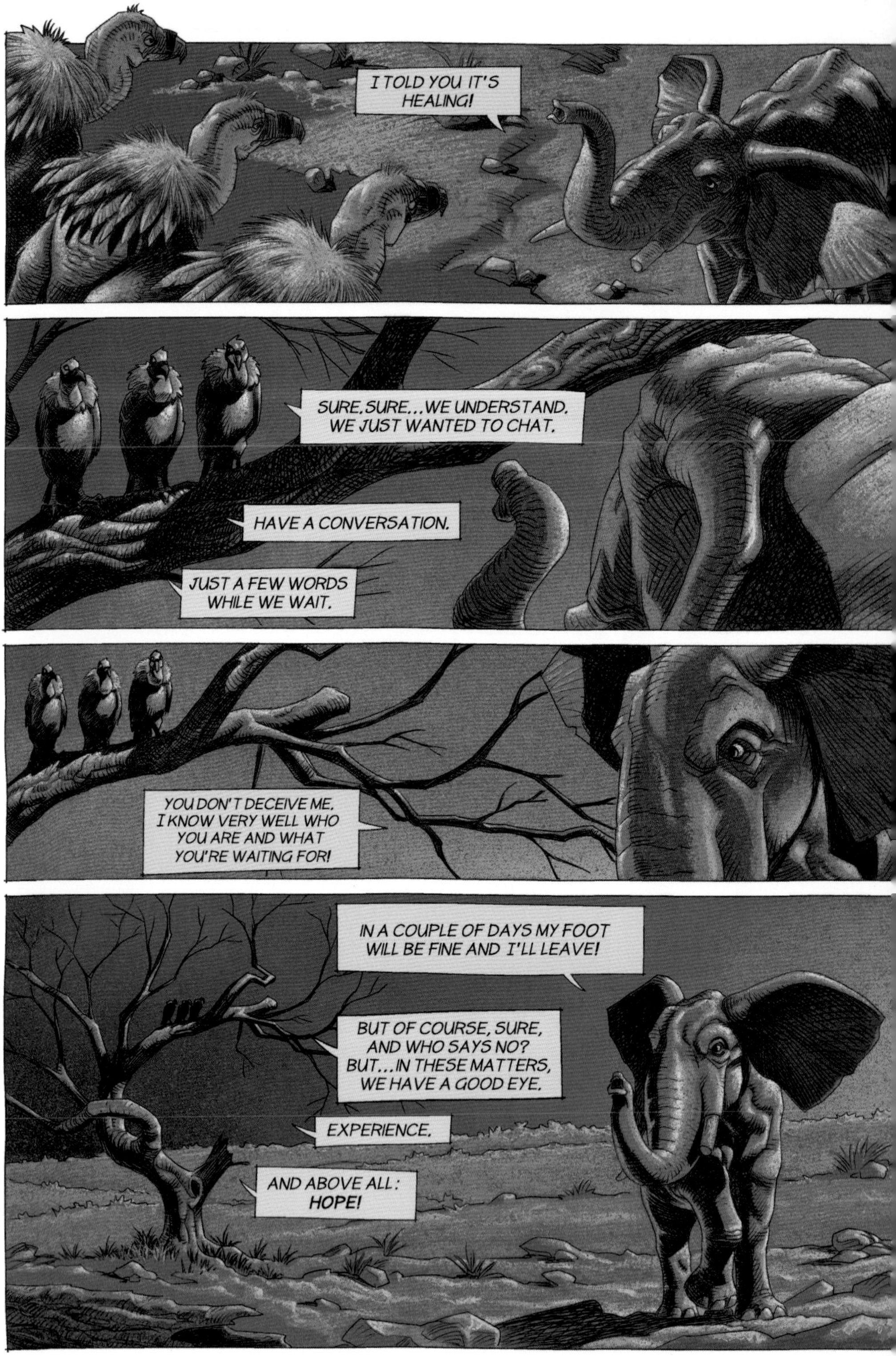
I TOLD YOU IT'S HEALING!
SURE, SURE...WE UNDERSTAND. WE JUST WANTED TO CHAT.
HAVE A CONVERSATION.
JUST A FEW WORDS WHILE WE WAIT.
YOU DON'T DECEIVE ME. I KNOW VERY WELL WHO YOU ARE AND WHAT YOU'RE WAITING FOR!
IN A COUPLE OF DAYS MY FOOT WILL BE FINE AND I'LL LEAVE!
BUT OF COURSE, SURE, AND WHO SAYS NO? BUT...IN THESE MATTERS, WE HAVE A GOOD EYE.
EXPERIENCE.
AND ABOVE ALL: HOPE!

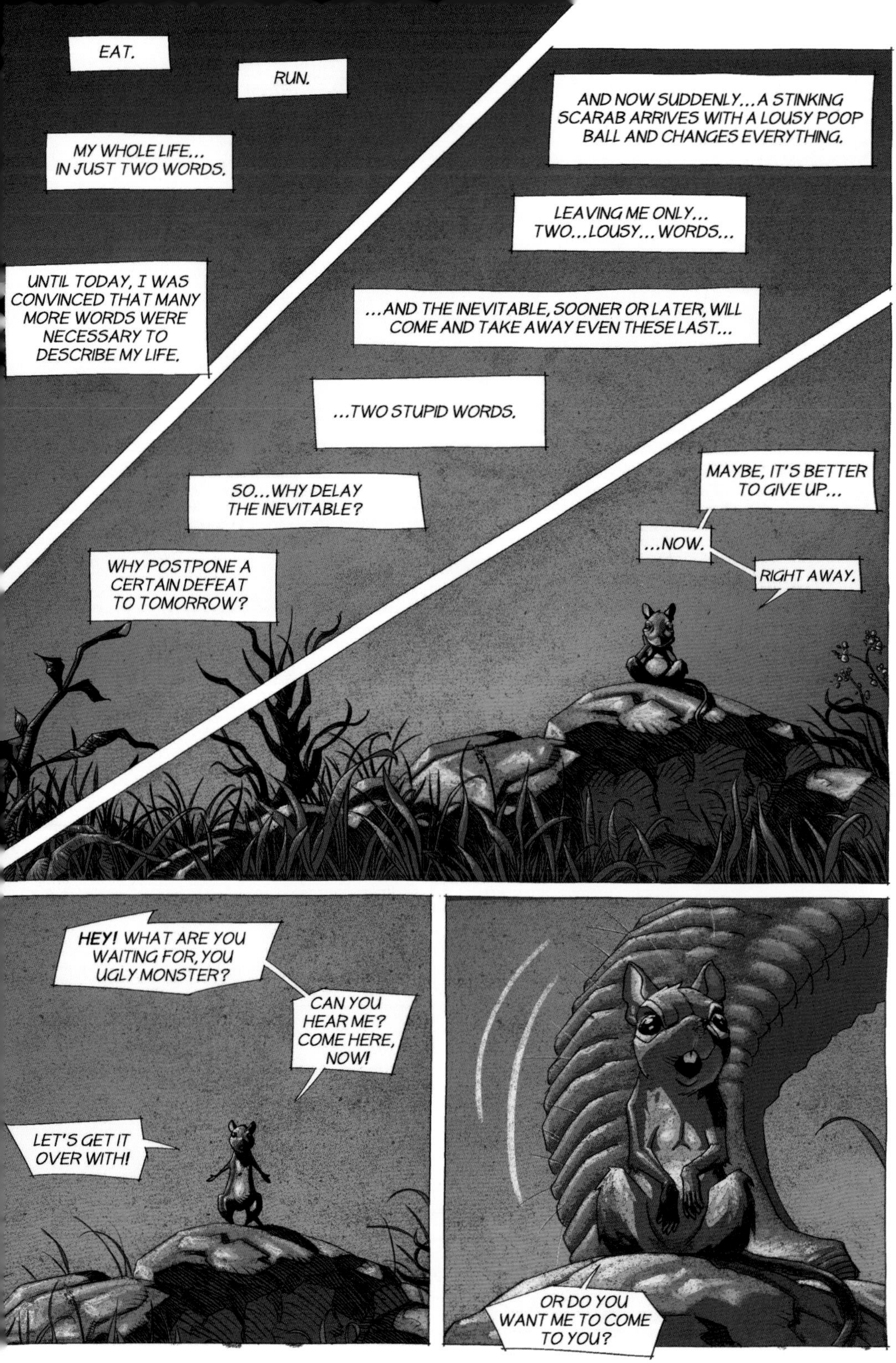
EAT.
RUN.
MY WHOLE LIFE... IN JUST TWO WORDS.
UNTIL TODAY, I WAS CONVINCED THAT MANY MORE WORDS WERE NECESSARY TO DESCRIBE MY LIFE.
AND NOW SUDDENLY... A STINKING SCARAB ARRIVES WITH A LOUSY POOP BALL AND CHANGES EVERYTHING.
LEAVING ME ONLY... TWO... LOUSY... WORDS...
...AND THE INEVITABLE, SOONER OR LATER, WILL COME AND TAKE AWAY EVEN THESE LAST...
...TWO STUPID WORDS.
SO... WHY DELAY THE INEVITABLE?
WHY POSTPONE A CERTAIN DEFEAT TO TOMORROW?
MAYBE, IT'S BETTER TO GIVE UP...
...NOW.
RIGHT AWAY.
HEY! WHAT ARE YOU WAITING FOR, YOU UGLY MONSTER?
CAN YOU HEAR ME? COME HERE, NOW!
LET'S GET IT OVER WITH!
OR DO YOU WANT ME TO COME TO YOU?

I'M HERE...

...SO WHAT DO YOU HAVE AGAINST ME?

AAAAAH!

OHH! IT'S ONLY YOU.

NOTHING...

...I'VE NOTHING AGAINST YOU.

WELL, YES!

IT WAS YOU!

IT'S ALL YOUR FAULT!

IT'S MY FAULT? WHAT IS?

THE WORLD!

THE WORLD THAT'S OUT THERE!

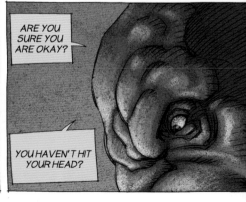

ARE YOU SURE YOU ARE OKAY?

YOU HAVEN'T HIT YOUR HEAD?

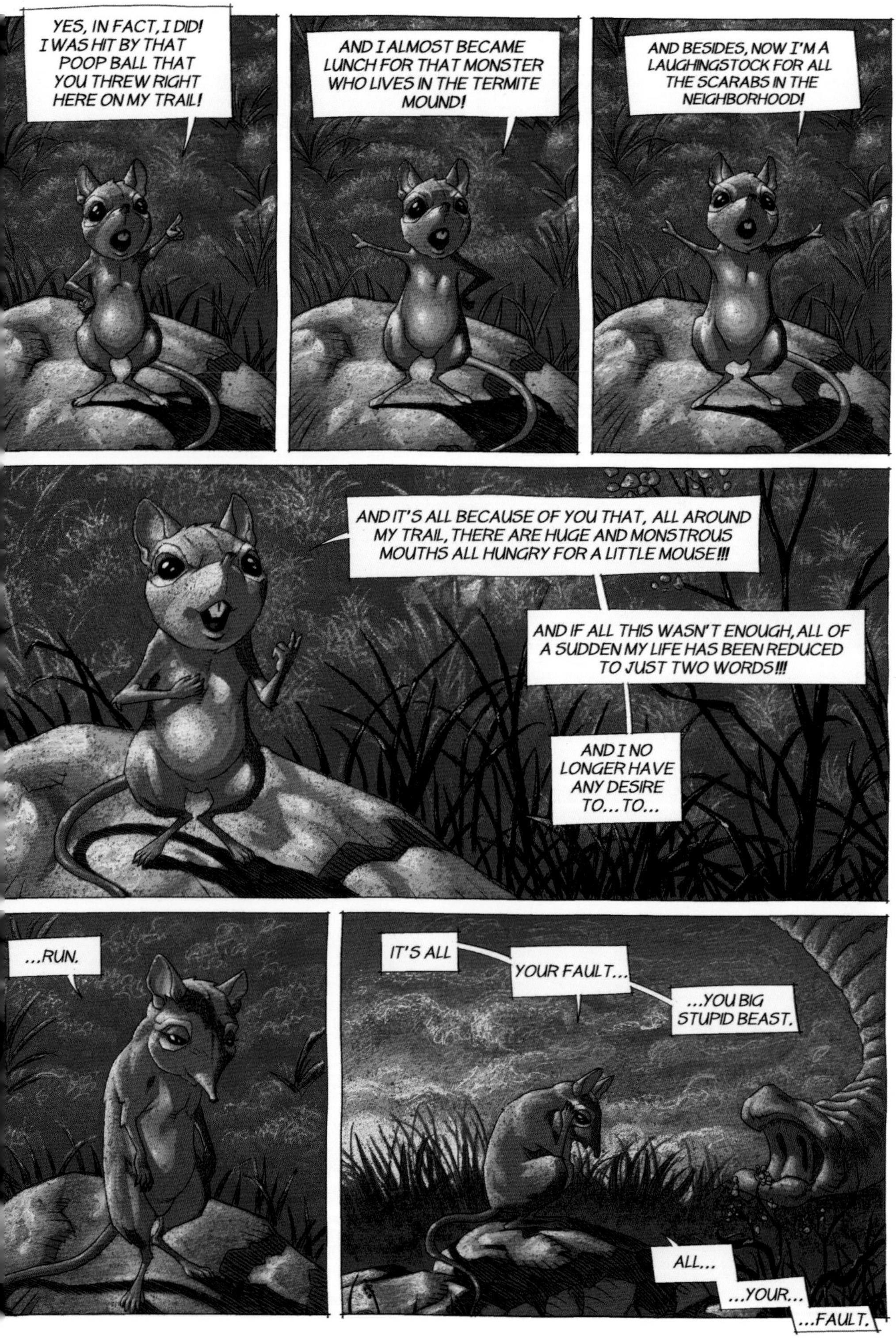
YES, IN FACT, I DID! I WAS HIT BY THAT POOP BALL THAT YOU THREW RIGHT HERE ON MY TRAIL!
AND I ALMOST BECAME LUNCH FOR THAT MONSTER WHO LIVES IN THE TERMITE MOUND!
AND BESIDES, NOW I'M A LAUGHINGSTOCK FOR ALL THE SCARABS IN THE NEIGHBORHOOD!
AND IT'S ALL BECAUSE OF YOU THAT, ALL AROUND MY TRAIL, THERE ARE HUGE AND MONSTROUS MOUTHS ALL HUNGRY FOR A LITTLE MOUSE!!!
AND IF ALL THIS WASN'T ENOUGH, ALL OF A SUDDEN MY LIFE HAS BEEN REDUCED TO JUST TWO WORDS!!!
AND I NO LONGER HAVE ANY DESIRE TO... TO...
...RUN.
IT'S ALL
YOUR FAULT...
...YOU BIG STUPID BEAST.
ALL...
...YOUR...
...FAULT.

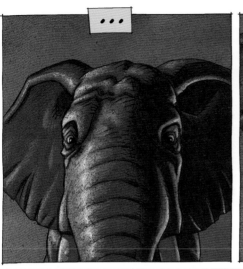

OF COURSE!
SURE!
NOW IT'S ALL
MY FAULT!

BECAUSE WHEN SOMEONE IS AS BIG AS ME,
POOP BALLS ARE NOTHING MORE THAN...

...THAN POOP BALLS!

AND AS FOR US GIANTS, WE DON'T IMAGINE THAT
THROWING THEM COULD UPSET THE RIDICULOUS
LIVES OF YOU PEOPLE WHO IGNORE ALL THAT IS
OUTSIDE YOUR MISERABLE, INSIGNIFICANT WORLDS!
YOU ONLY SEEK TO CONTINUE TO CRADLE
YOURSELF IN YOUR DULL COMFORT!

CO-COMFORT???

AND...AND I'M
THE ONE WHO
HIT HIS HEAD?

LOOK AT ME!!
LOOK AT ME AND
TELL ME WHAT
YOU SEE!

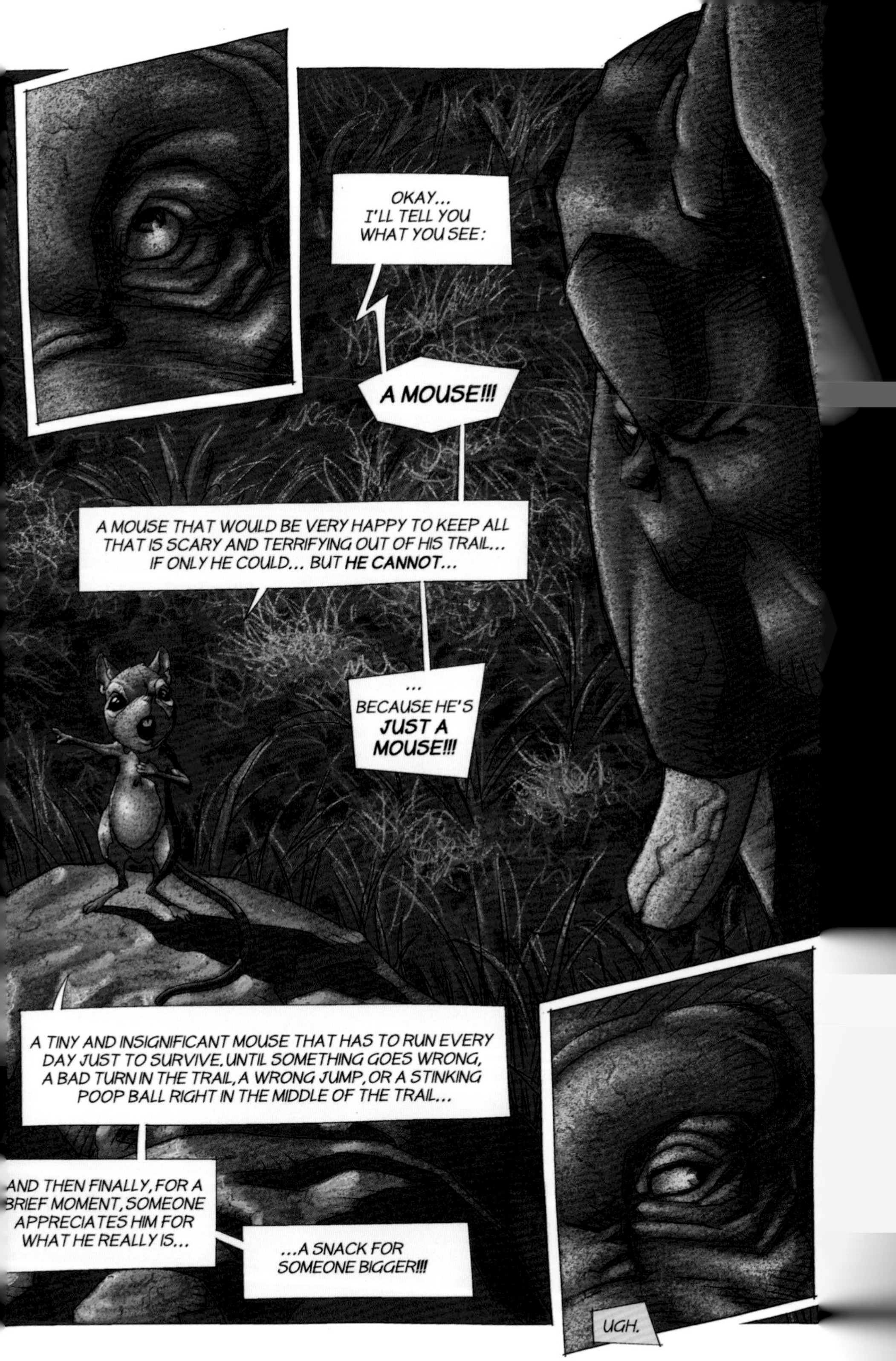
OKAY... I'LL TELL YOU WHAT YOU SEE:
A MOUSE!!!
A MOUSE THAT WOULD BE VERY HAPPY TO KEEP ALL THAT IS SCARY AND TERRIFYING OUT OF HIS TRAIL... IF ONLY HE COULD... BUT HE CANNOT...
... BECAUSE HE'S JUST A MOUSE!!!
A TINY AND INSIGNIFICANT MOUSE THAT HAS TO RUN EVERY DAY JUST TO SURVIVE, UNTIL SOMETHING GOES WRONG, A BAD TURN IN THE TRAIL, A WRONG JUMP, OR A STINKING POOP BALL RIGHT IN THE MIDDLE OF THE TRAIL...
AND THEN FINALLY, FOR A BRIEF MOMENT, SOMEONE APPRECIATES HIM FOR WHAT HE REALLY IS...
...A SNACK FOR SOMEONE BIGGER!!!
UGH.

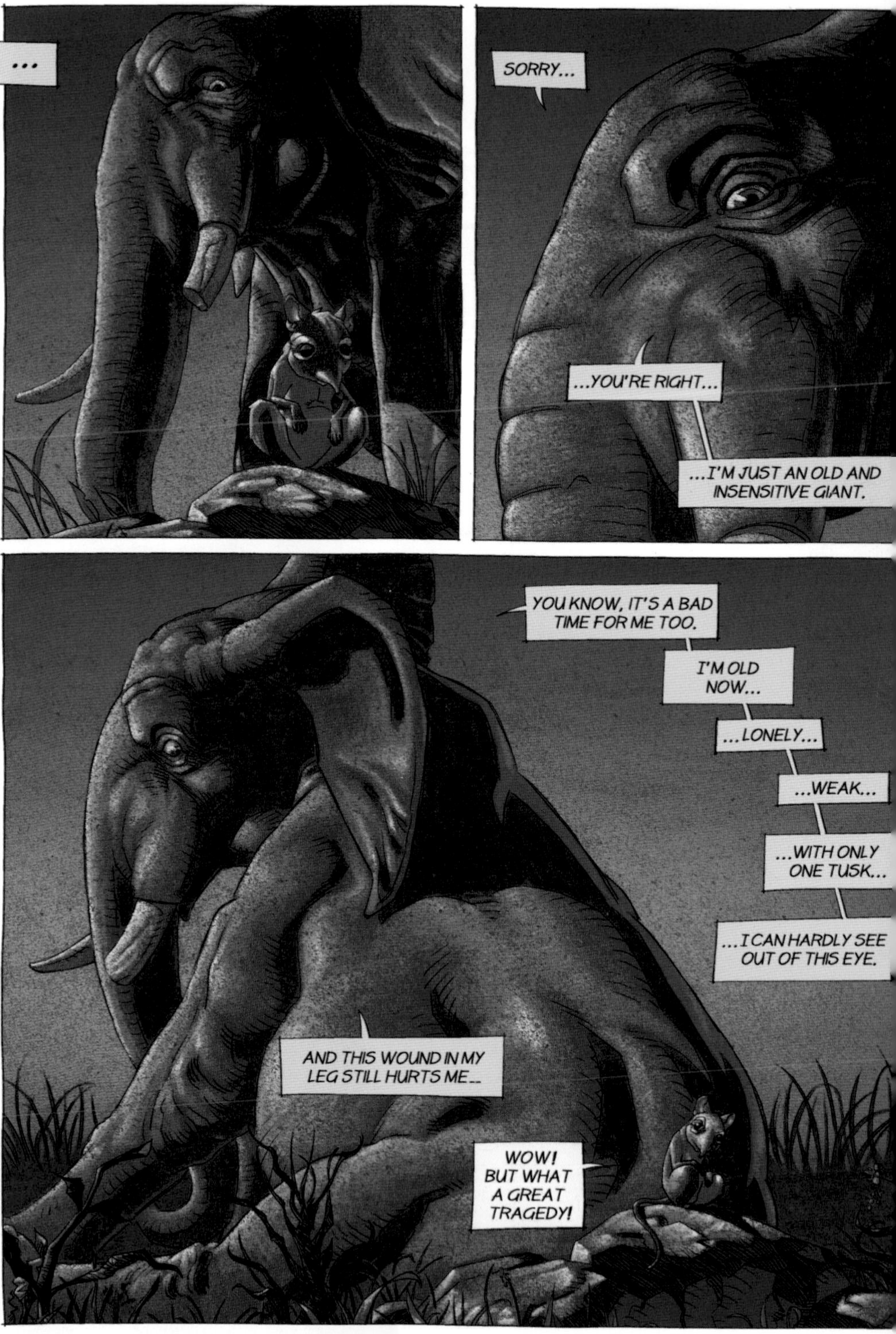
...
SORRY...
...YOU'RE RIGHT...
...I'M JUST AN OLD AND INSENSITIVE GIANT.
YOU KNOW, IT'S A BAD TIME FOR ME TOO.
I'M OLD NOW...
...LONELY...
...WEAK...
...WITH ONLY ONE TUSK...
...I CAN HARDLY SEE OUT OF THIS EYE.
AND THIS WOUND IN MY LEG STILL HURTS ME...
WOW! BUT WHAT A GREAT TRAGEDY!

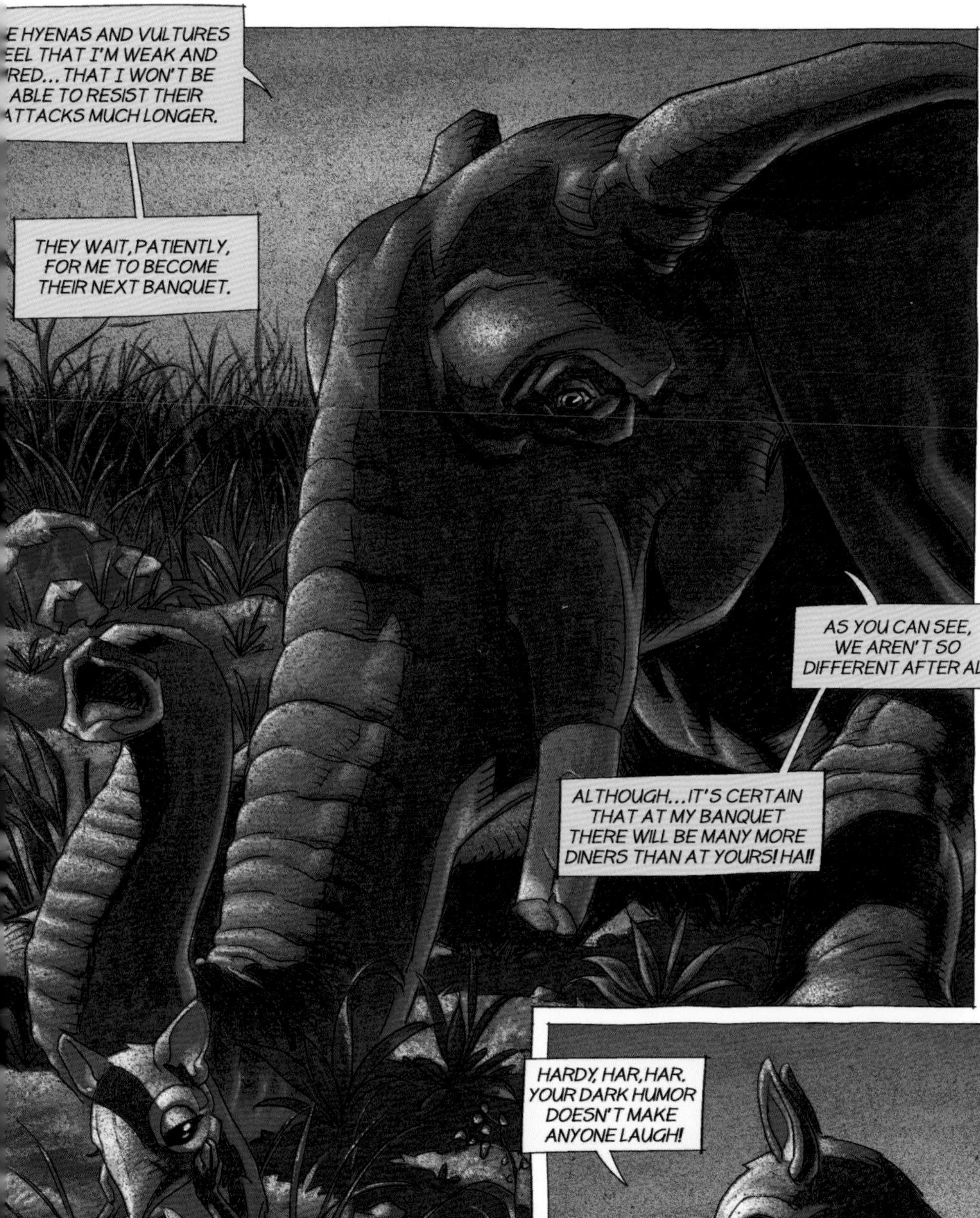
E HYENAS AND VULTURES EEL THAT I'M WEAK AND RED... THAT I WON'T BE ABLE TO RESIST THEIR ATTACKS MUCH LONGER.
THEY WAIT, PATIENTLY, FOR ME TO BECOME THEIR NEXT BANQUET.
AS YOU CAN SEE, WE AREN'T SO DIFFERENT AFTER ALL.
ALTHOUGH... IT'S CERTAIN THAT AT MY BANQUET THERE WILL BE MANY MORE DINERS THAN AT YOURS! HA!!

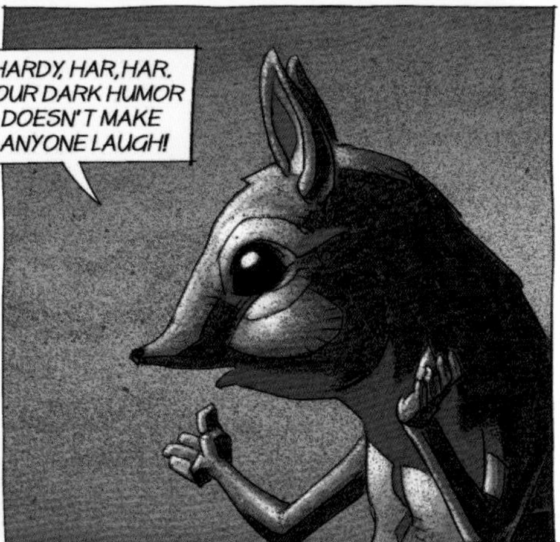
HARDY, HAR, HAR. YOUR DARK HUMOR DOESN'T MAKE ANYONE LAUGH!

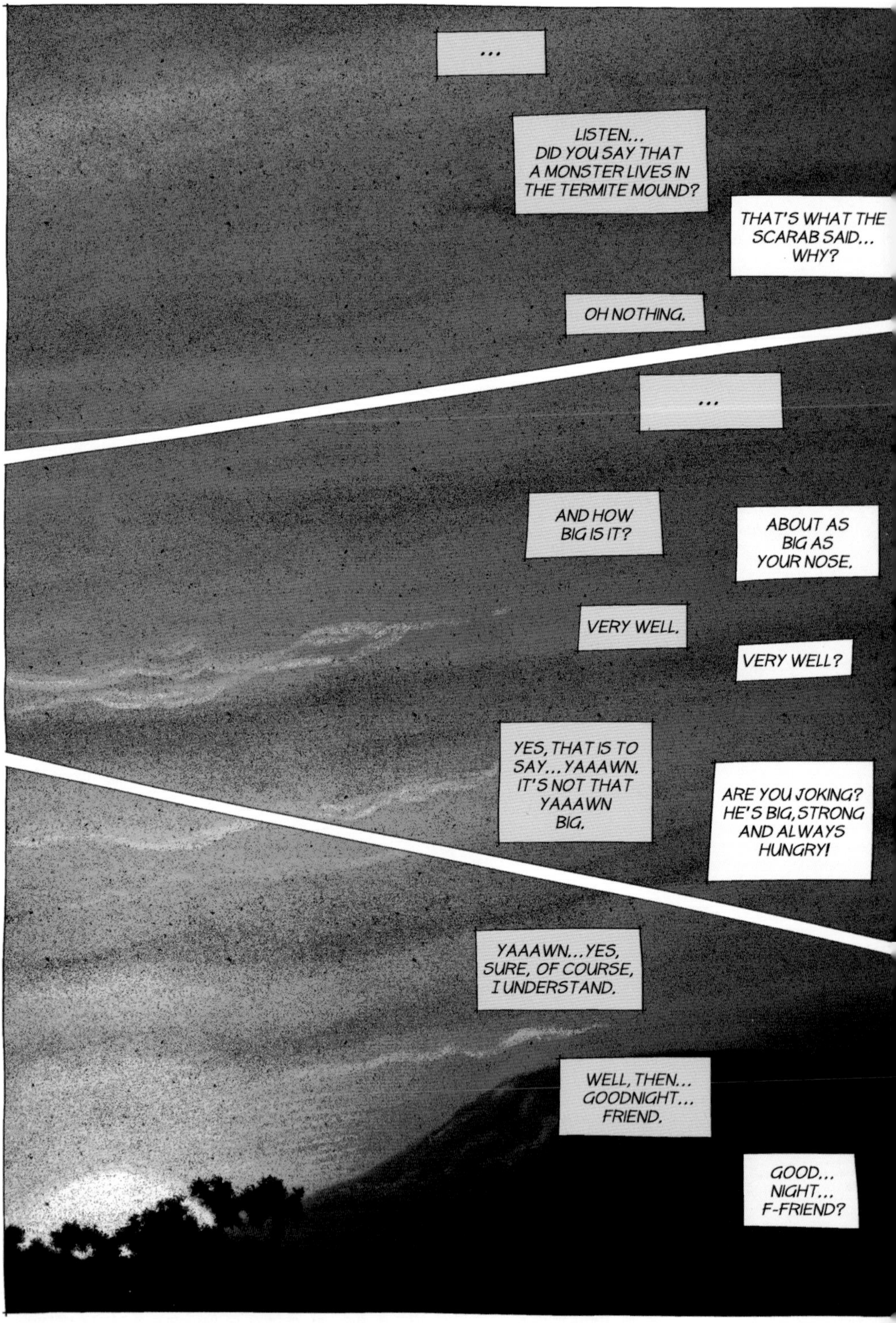
...
LISTEN... DID YOU SAY THAT A MONSTER LIVES IN THE TERMITE MOUND?
THAT'S WHAT THE SCARAB SAID... WHY?
OH NOTHING.
...
AND HOW BIG IS IT?
ABOUT AS BIG AS YOUR NOSE.
VERY WELL.
VERY WELL?
YES, THAT IS TO SAY... YAAAWN. IT'S NOT THAT YAAAWN BIG.
ARE YOU JOKING? HE'S BIG, STRONG AND ALWAYS HUNGRY!
YAAAWN... YES, SURE, OF COURSE, I UNDERSTAND.
WELL, THEN... GOODNIGHT... FRIEND.
GOOD... NIGHT... F-FRIEND?

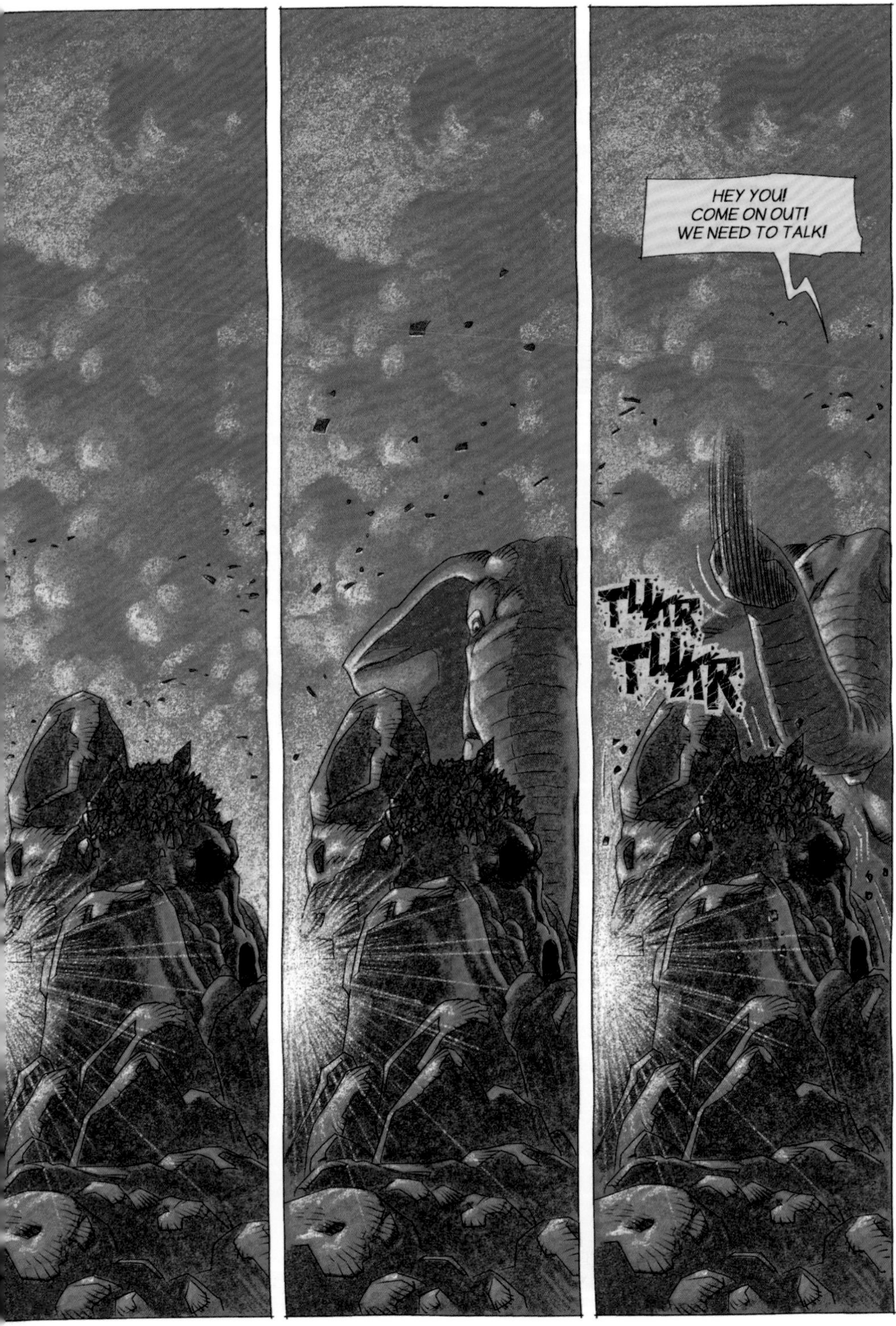
HEY YOU!
COME ON OUT!
WE NEED TO TALK!
THWR THWR

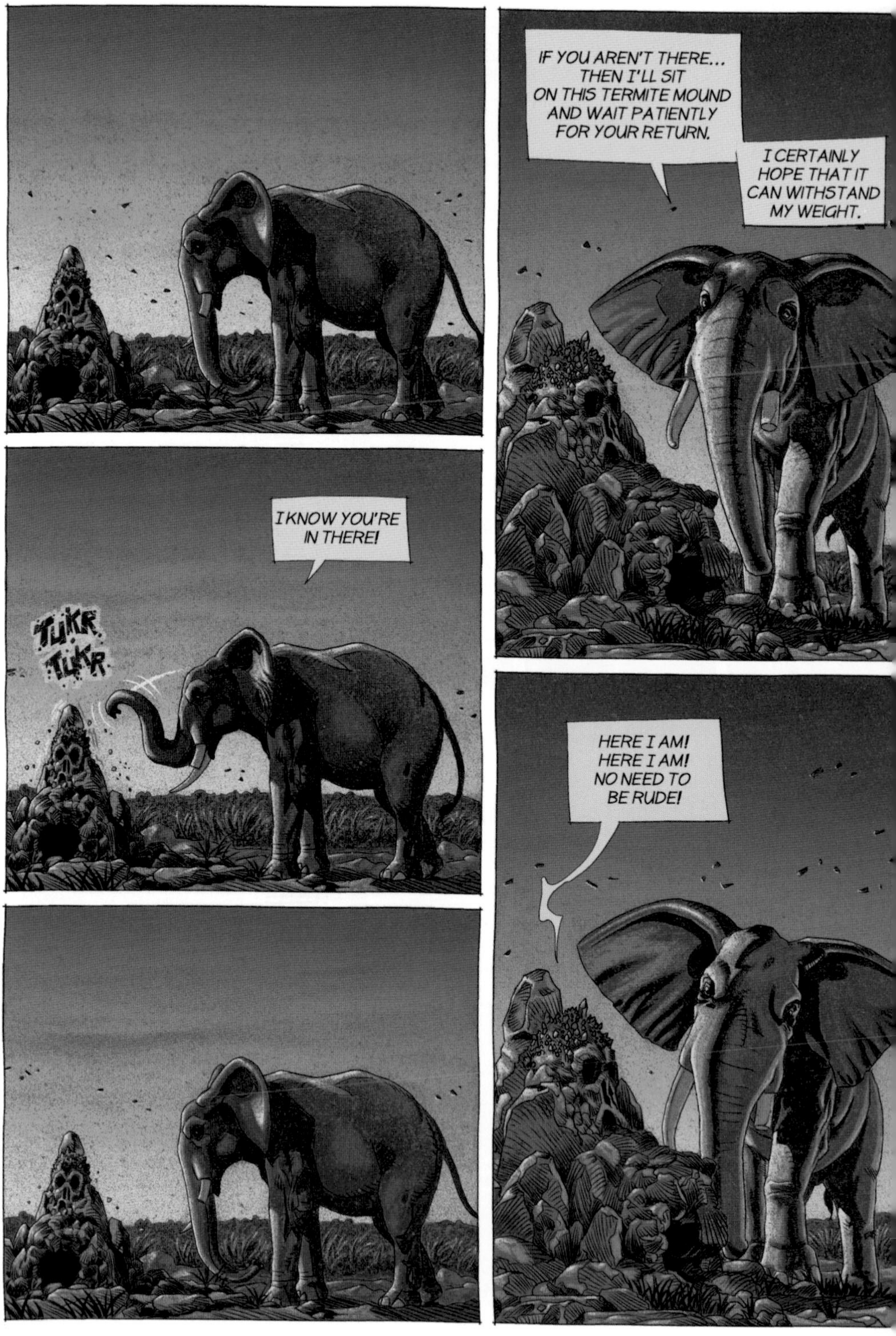
I KNOW YOU'RE IN THERE!
TUKR TUKR
IF YOU AREN'T THERE... THEN I'LL SIT ON THIS TERMITE MOUND AND WAIT PATIENTLY FOR YOUR RETURN.
I CERTAINLY HOPE THAT IT CAN WITHSTAND MY WEIGHT.
HERE I AM! HERE I AM! NO NEED TO BE RUDE!

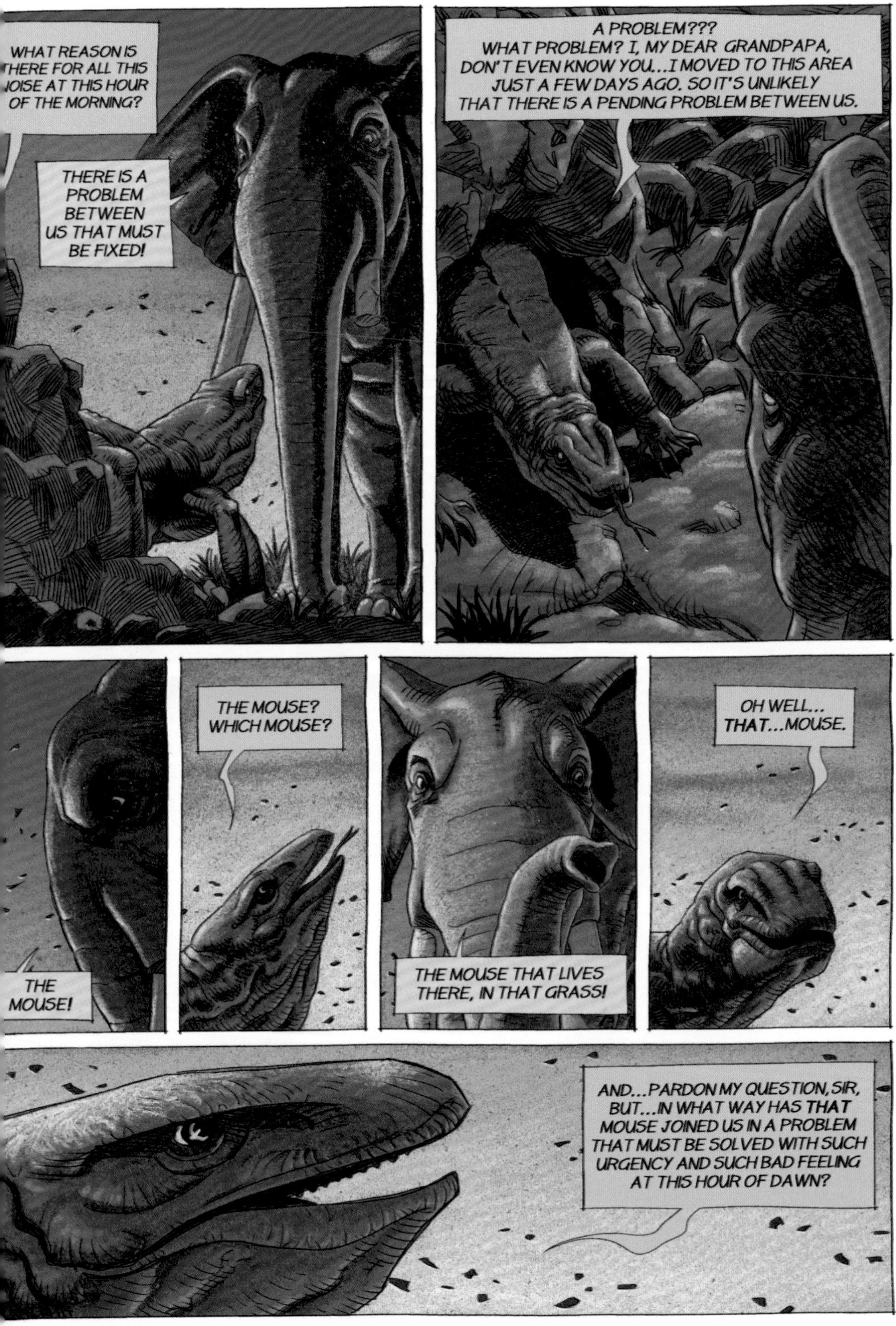
WHAT REASON IS THERE FOR ALL THIS NOISE AT THIS HOUR OF THE MORNING?
THERE IS A PROBLEM BETWEEN US THAT MUST BE FIXED!
A PROBLEM??? WHAT PROBLEM? I, MY DEAR GRANDPAPA, DON'T EVEN KNOW YOU...I MOVED TO THIS AREA JUST A FEW DAYS AGO. SO IT'S UNLIKELY THAT THERE IS A PENDING PROBLEM BETWEEN US.
THE MOUSE!
THE MOUSE? WHICH MOUSE?
THE MOUSE THAT LIVES THERE, IN THAT GRASS!
OH WELL... THAT...MOUSE.
AND...PARDON MY QUESTION, SIR, BUT...IN WHAT WAY HAS THAT MOUSE JOINED US IN A PROBLEM THAT MUST BE SOLVED WITH SUCH URGENCY AND SUCH BAD FEELING AT THIS HOUR OF DAWN?

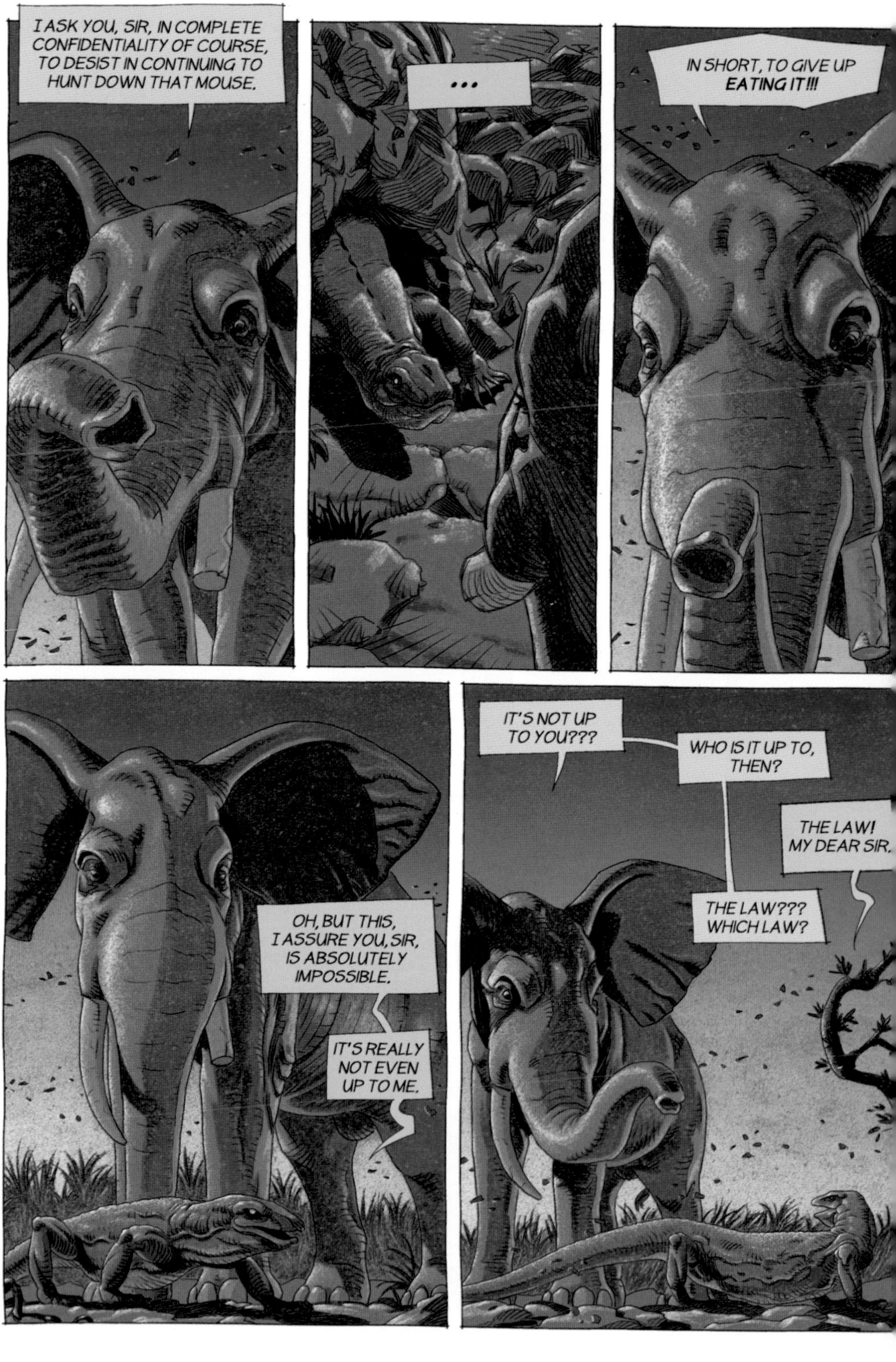
I ASK YOU, SIR, IN COMPLETE CONFIDENTIALITY OF COURSE, TO DESIST IN CONTINUING TO HUNT DOWN THAT MOUSE.
...
IN SHORT, TO GIVE UP **EATING IT!!!**
OH, BUT THIS, I ASSURE YOU, SIR, IS ABSOLUTELY IMPOSSIBLE.
IT'S REALLY NOT EVEN UP TO ME.
IT'S NOT UP TO YOU???
WHO IS IT UP TO, THEN?
THE LAW! MY DEAR SIR.
THE LAW??? WHICH LAW?

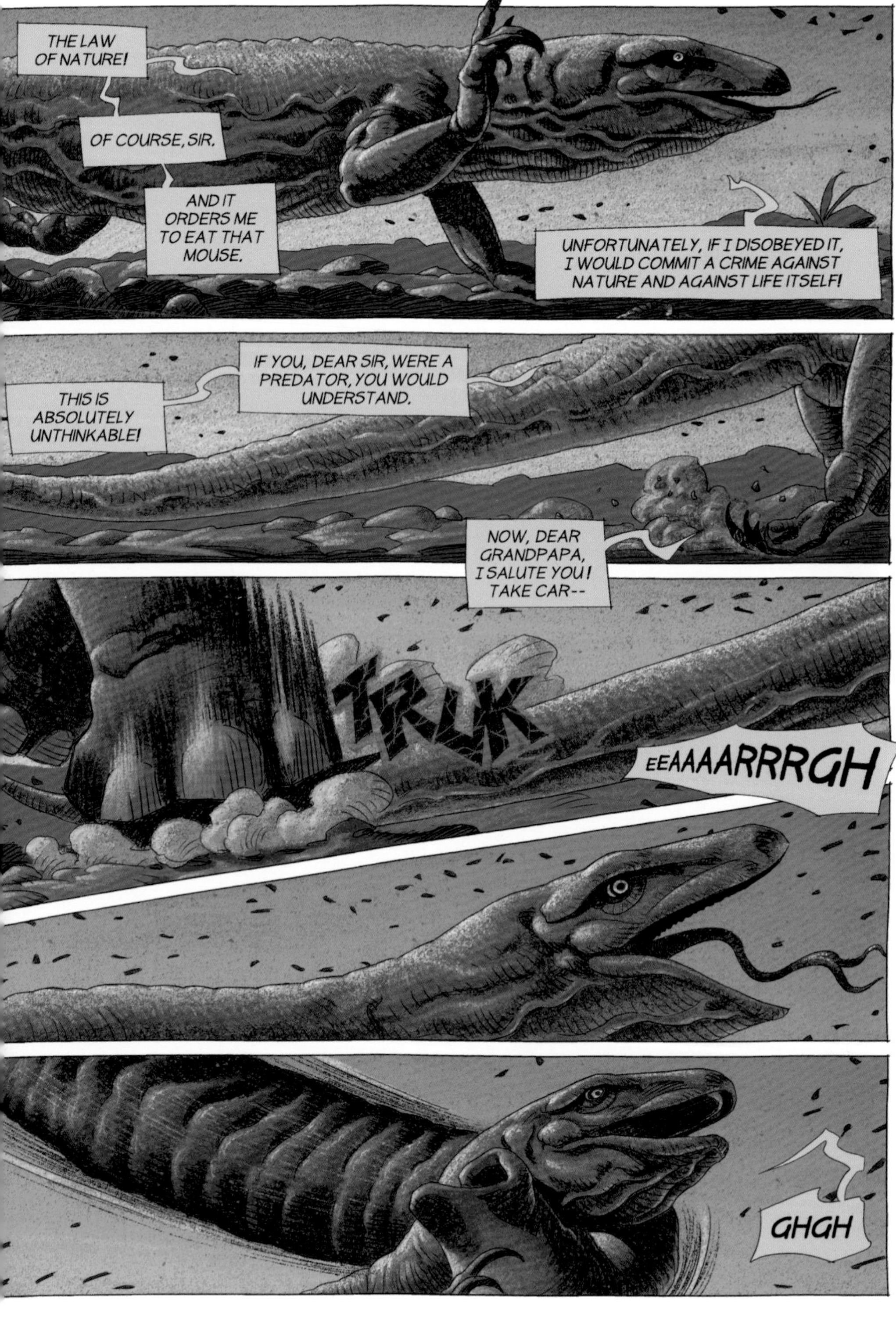
THE LAW OF NATURE!
OF COURSE, SIR.
AND IT ORDERS ME TO EAT THAT MOUSE.
UNFORTUNATELY, IF I DISOBEYED IT, I WOULD COMMIT A CRIME AGAINST NATURE AND AGAINST LIFE ITSELF!
THIS IS ABSOLUTELY UNTHINKABLE!
IF YOU, DEAR SIR, WERE A PREDATOR, YOU WOULD UNDERSTAND.
NOW, DEAR GRANDPAPA, I SALUTE YOU! TAKE CAR--
TRUK
EEAAAARRRGH
GHGH

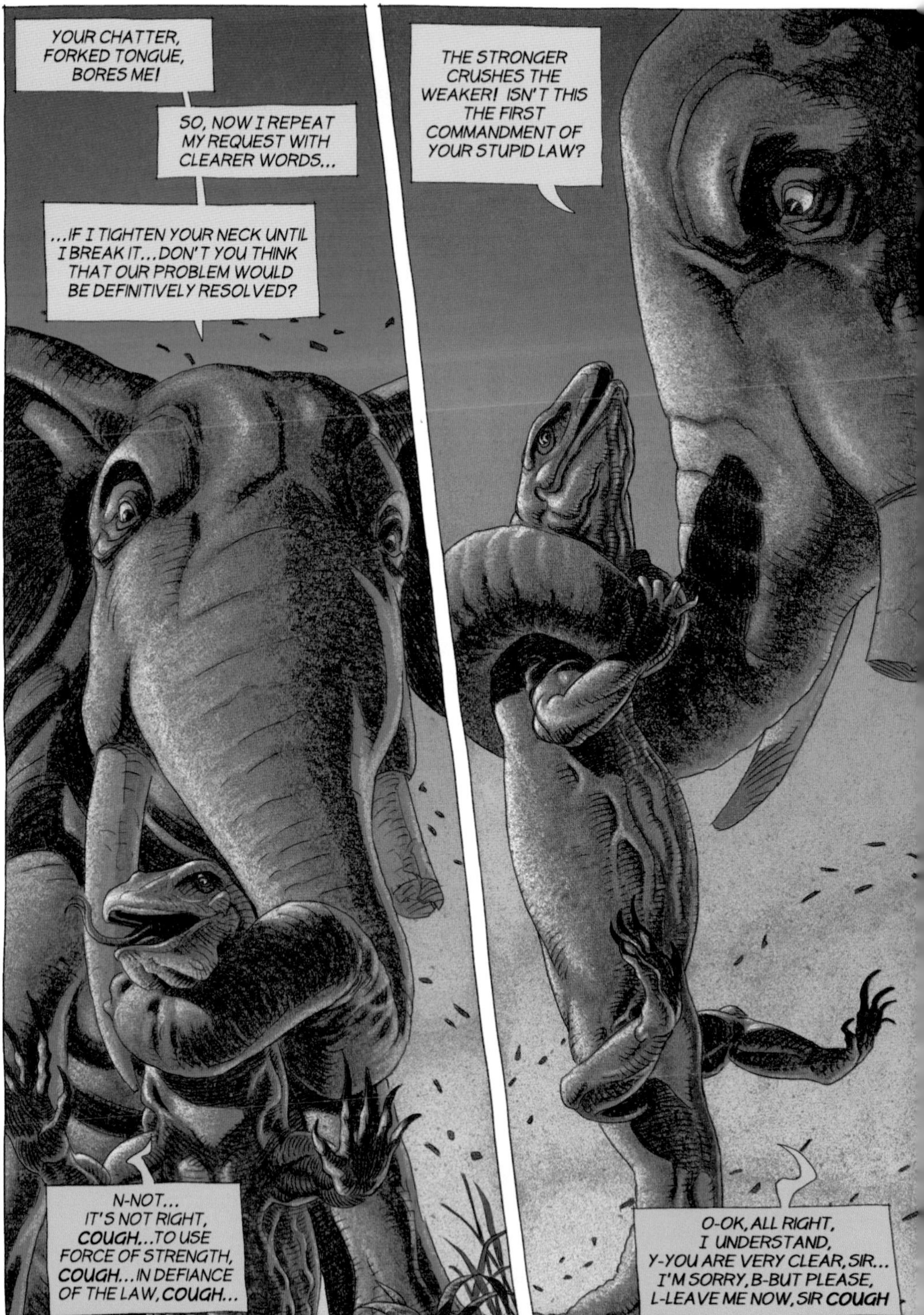
YOUR CHATTER, FORKED TONGUE, BORES ME!
SO, NOW I REPEAT MY REQUEST WITH CLEARER WORDS...
...IF I TIGHTEN YOUR NECK UNTIL I BREAK IT...DON'T YOU THINK THAT OUR PROBLEM WOULD BE DEFINITIVELY RESOLVED?
N-NOT... IT'S NOT RIGHT, COUGH...TO USE FORCE OF STRENGTH, COUGH...IN DEFIANCE OF THE LAW, COUGH...
THE STRONGER CRUSHES THE WEAKER! ISN'T THIS THE FIRST COMMANDMENT OF YOUR STUPID LAW?
O-OK, ALL RIGHT, I UNDERSTAND, Y-YOU ARE VERY CLEAR, SIR... I'M SORRY, B-BUT PLEASE, L-LEAVE ME NOW, SIR COUGH

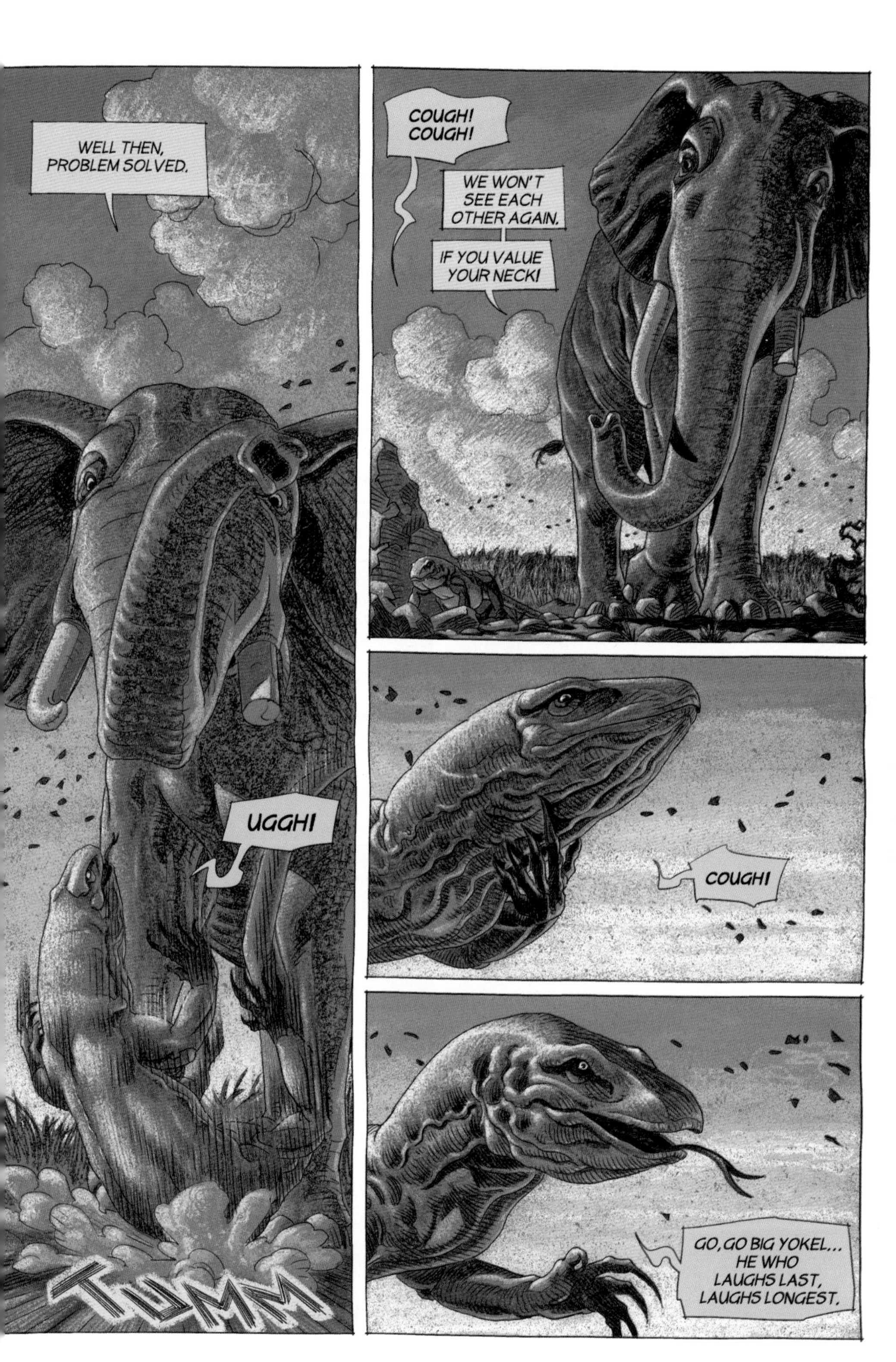
WELL THEN, PROBLEM SOLVED.
UGGH!
TUMM
COUGH! COUGH!
WE WON'T SEE EACH OTHER AGAIN.
IF YOU VALUE YOUR NECK!
COUGH!
GO, GO BIG YOKEL... HE WHO LAUGHS LAST, LAUGHS LONGEST.

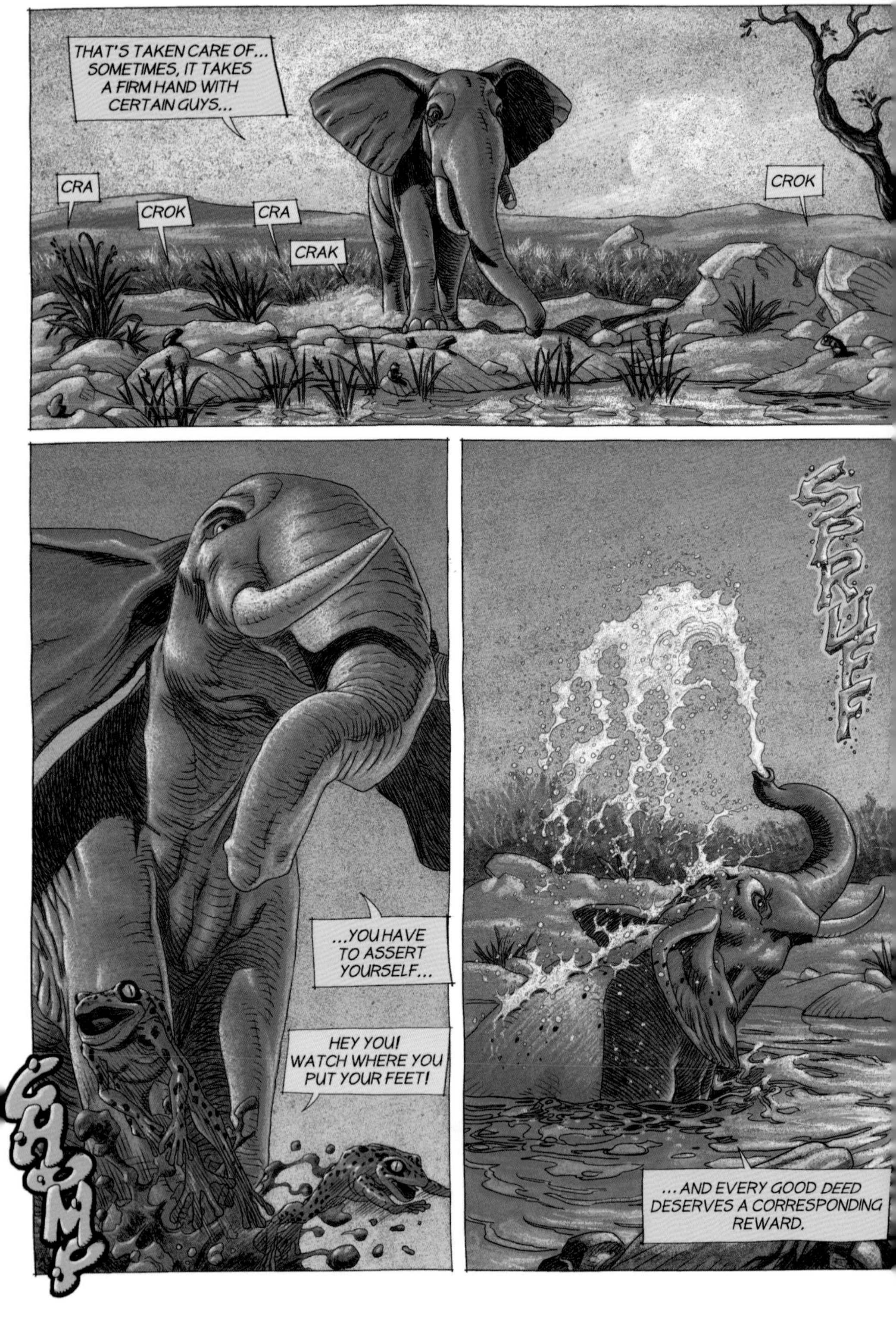
THAT'S TAKEN CARE OF... SOMETIMES, IT TAKES A FIRM HAND WITH CERTAIN GUYS...
CRA
CROK
CRA
CRAK
CROK
...YOU HAVE TO ASSERT YOURSELF...
HEY YOU! WATCH WHERE YOU PUT YOUR FEET!
CHOMP
SPRUFF
...AND EVERY GOOD DEED DESERVES A CORRESPONDING REWARD.

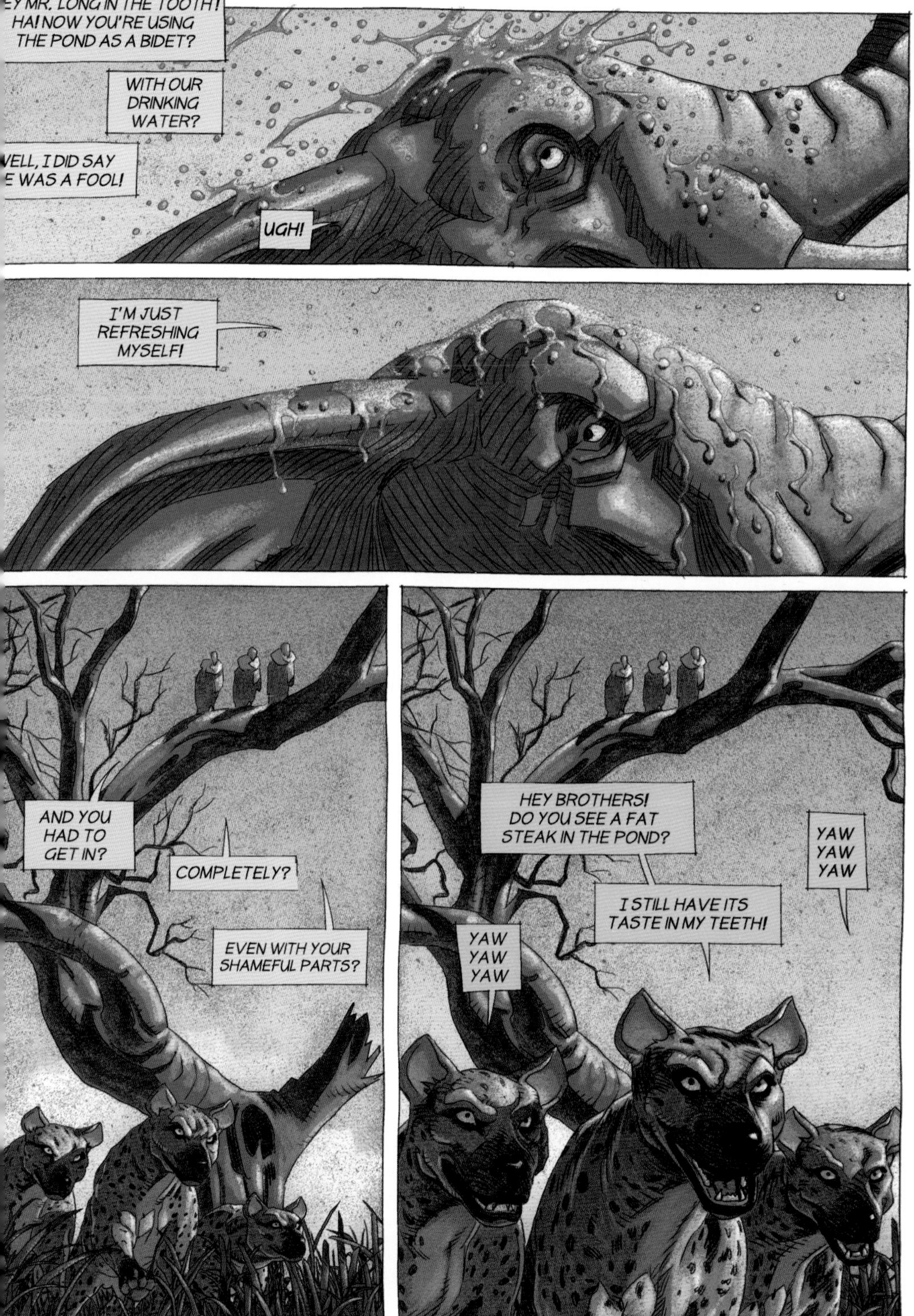
EY MR. LONG IN THE TOOTH! HA! NOW YOU'RE USING THE POND AS A BIDET?
WITH OUR DRINKING WATER?
VELL, I DID SAY E WAS A FOOL!
UGH!
I'M JUST REFRESHING MYSELF!
AND YOU HAD TO GET IN?
COMPLETELY?
EVEN WITH YOUR SHAMEFUL PARTS?
HEY BROTHERS! DO YOU SEE A FAT STEAK IN THE POND?
I STILL HAVE ITS TASTE IN MY TEETH!
YAW YAW YAW
YAW YAW YAW

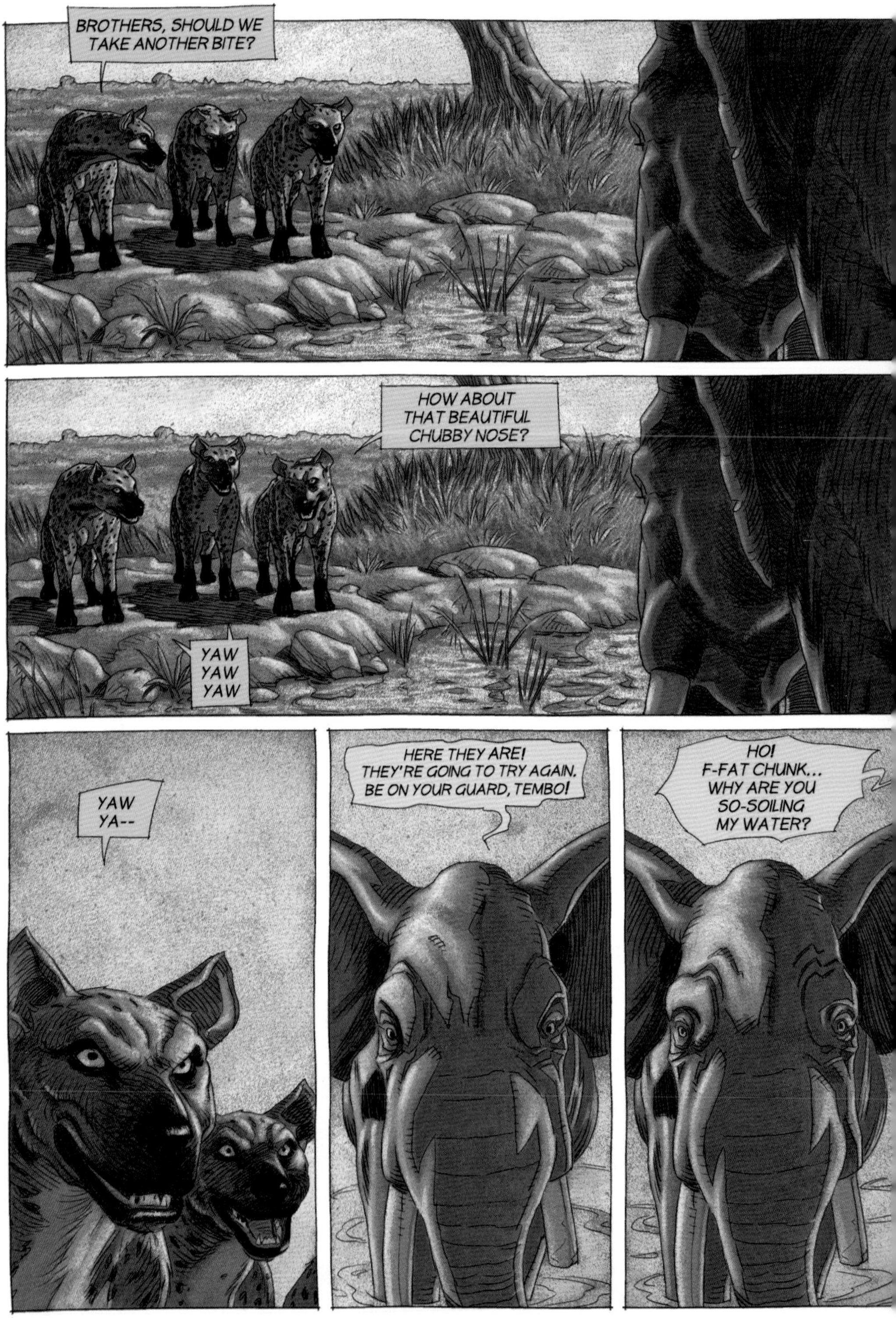
BROTHERS, SHOULD WE TAKE ANOTHER BITE?
HOW ABOUT THAT BEAUTIFUL CHUBBY NOSE?
YAW YAW YAW
YAW YA--
HERE THEY ARE! THEY'RE GOING TO TRY AGAIN. BE ON YOUR GUARD, TEMBO!
HO! F-FAT CHUNK... WHY ARE YOU SO-SOILING MY WATER?

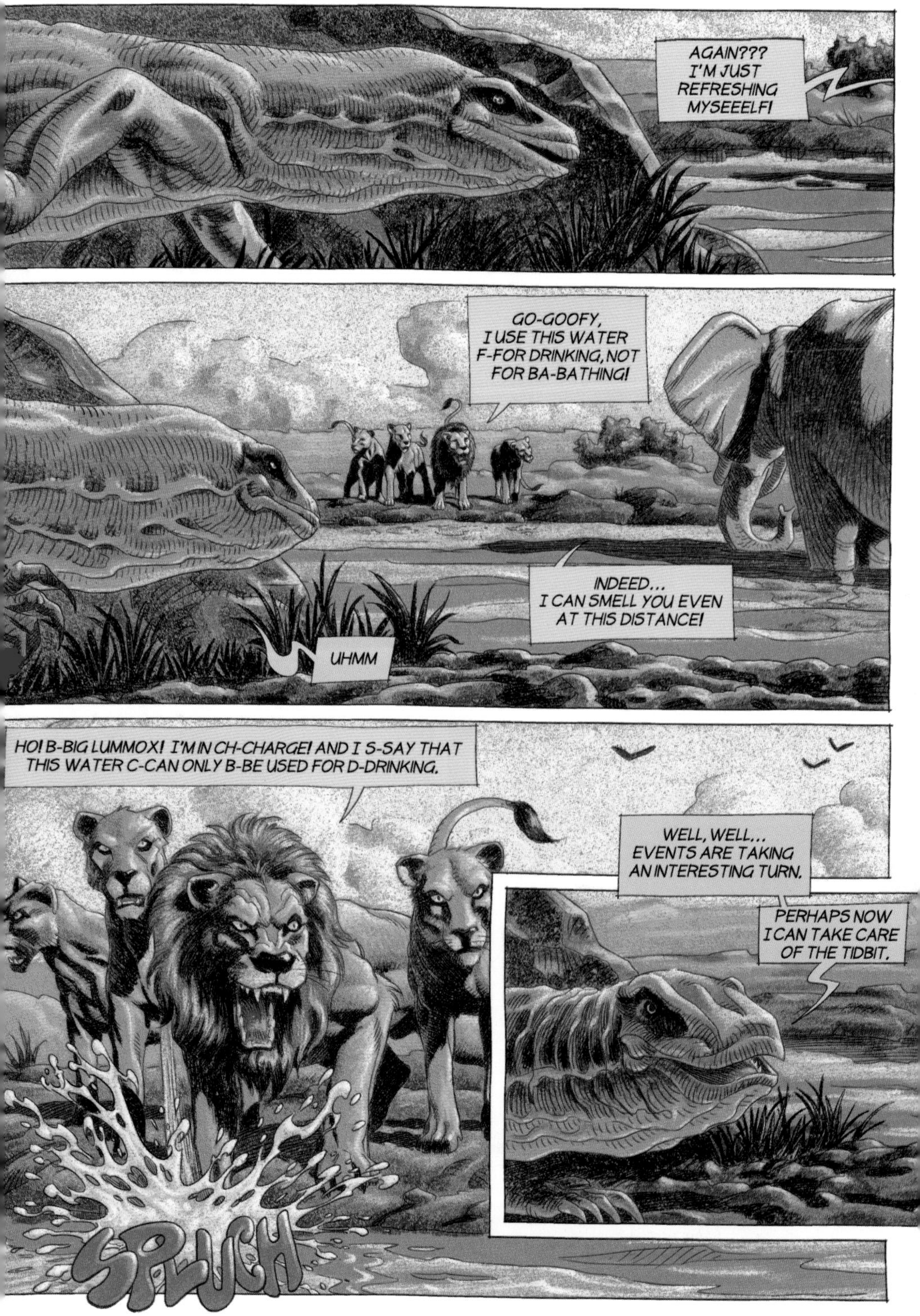
AGAIN??? I'M JUST REFRESHING MYSEEELF!
GO-GOOFY, I USE THIS WATER F-FOR DRINKING, NOT FOR BA-BATHING!
INDEED... I CAN SMELL YOU EVEN AT THIS DISTANCE!
UHMM
HO! B-BIG LUMMOX! I'M IN CH-CHARGE! AND I S-SAY THAT THIS WATER C-CAN ONLY B-BE USED FOR D-DRINKING.
WELL, WELL... EVENTS ARE TAKING AN INTERESTING TURN.
PERHAPS NOW I CAN TAKE CARE OF THE TIDBIT.
SPLUCH

TO BE...

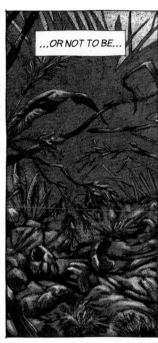

...OR NOT TO BE...

...THIS IS THE QUESTION.

TO LIVE OR SIMPLY SURVIVE?

HAVING TO CONTINUE TO ENDURE THE DAILY WORRIES...

...TO SUFFER, RESIGNED, THE CLAWS OF BAD LUCK...

TRIK

...OR TURN... AND FIGHT?

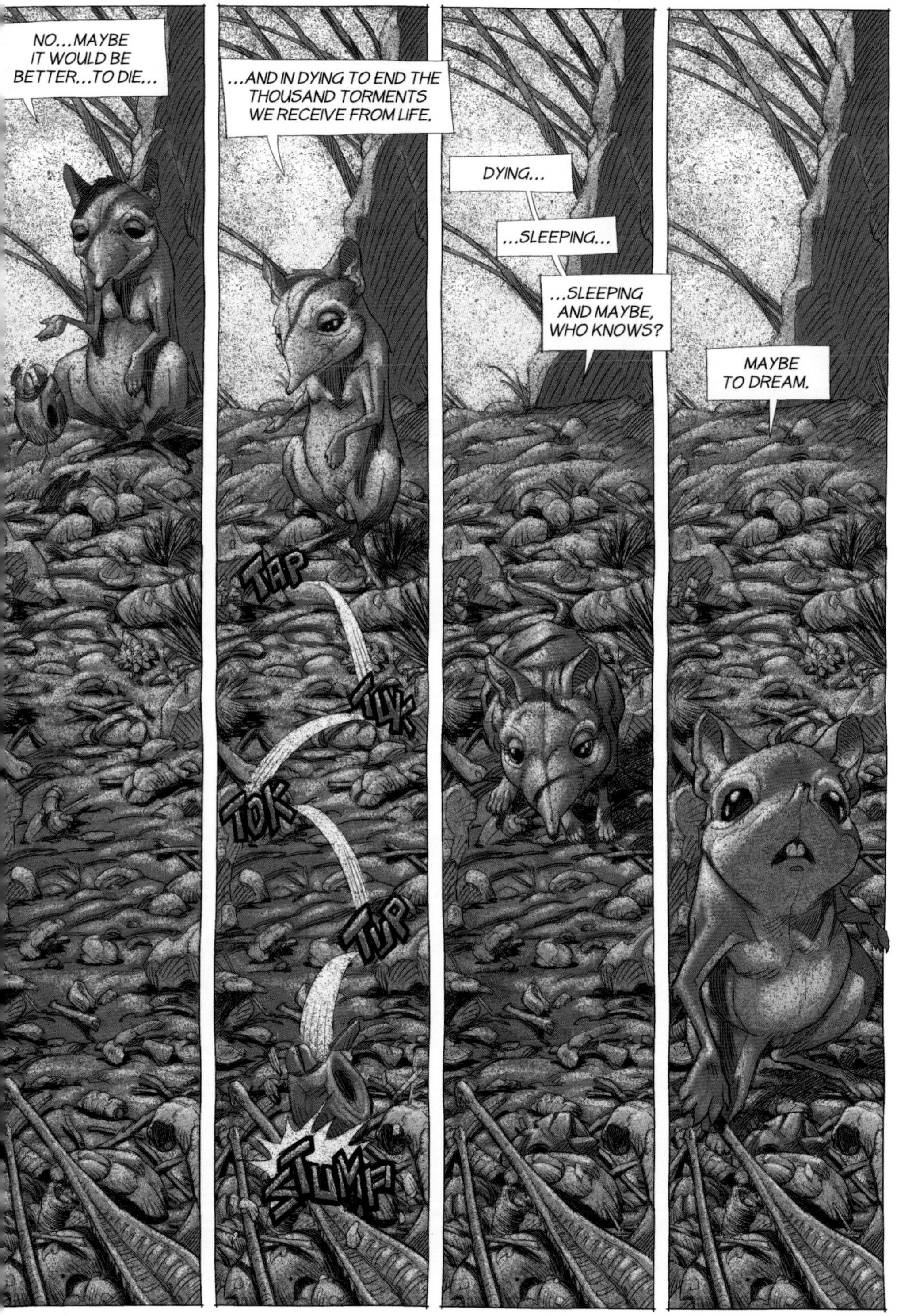

NO...MAYBE IT WOULD BE BETTER...TO DIE...
...AND IN DYING TO END THE THOUSAND TORMENTS WE RECEIVE FROM LIFE.
TAP
TUK
TOK
TUP
STUMP
DYING...
...SLEEPING...
...SLEEPING AND MAYBE, WHO KNOWS?
MAYBE TO DREAM.

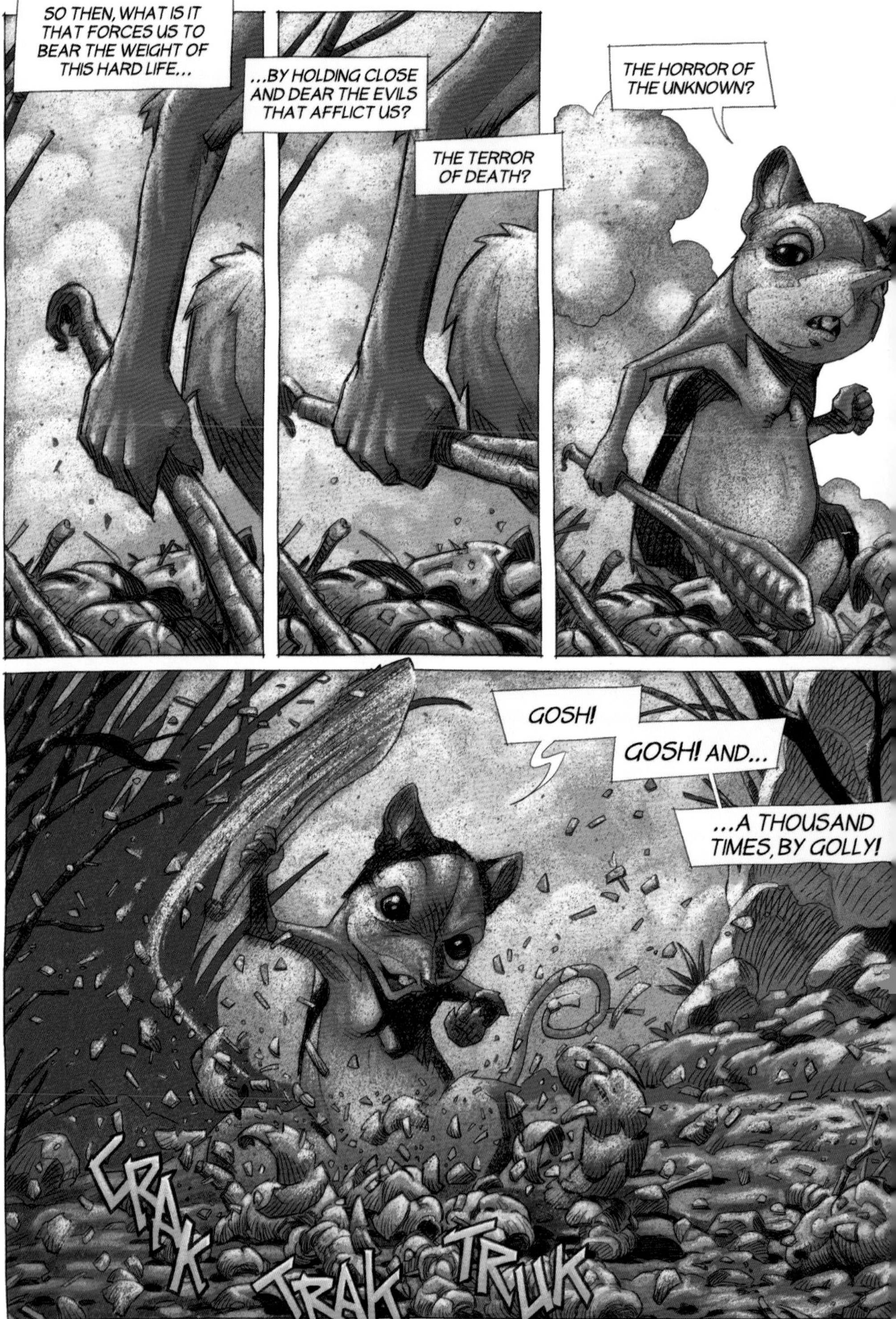
SO THEN, WHAT IS IT THAT FORCES US TO BEAR THE WEIGHT OF THIS HARD LIFE...
...BY HOLDING CLOSE AND DEAR THE EVILS THAT AFFLICT US?
THE TERROR OF DEATH?
THE HORROR OF THE UNKNOWN?
GOSH!
GOSH! AND...
...A THOUSAND TIMES, BY GOLLY!
CRAK
TRAK
TRUK

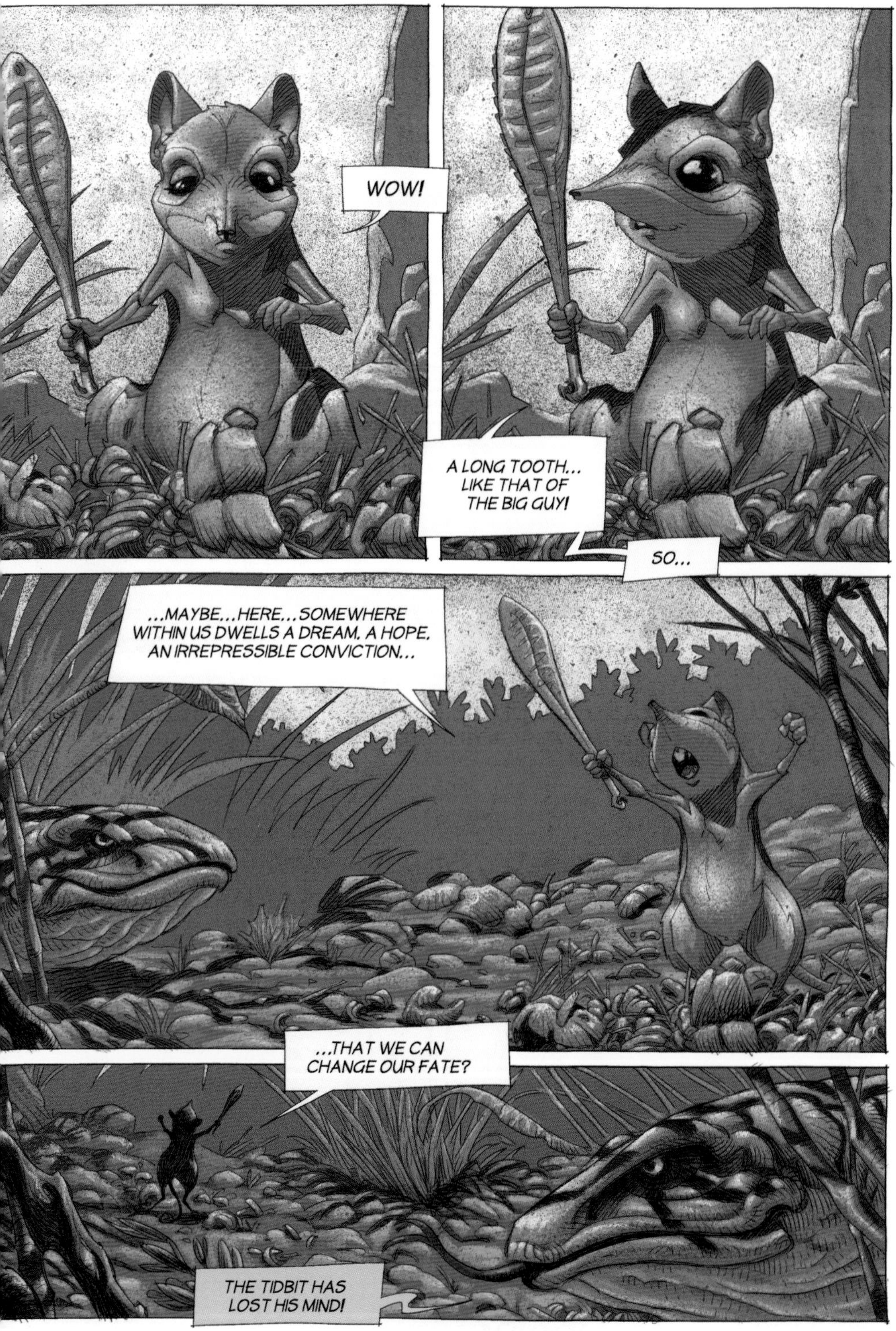
WOW!
A LONG TOOTH... LIKE THAT OF THE BIG GUY!
SO...
...MAYBE...HERE...SOMEWHERE WITHIN US DWELLS A DREAM, A HOPE, AN IRREPRESSIBLE CONVICTION...
...THAT WE CAN CHANGE OUR FATE?
THE TIDBIT HAS LOST HIS MIND!

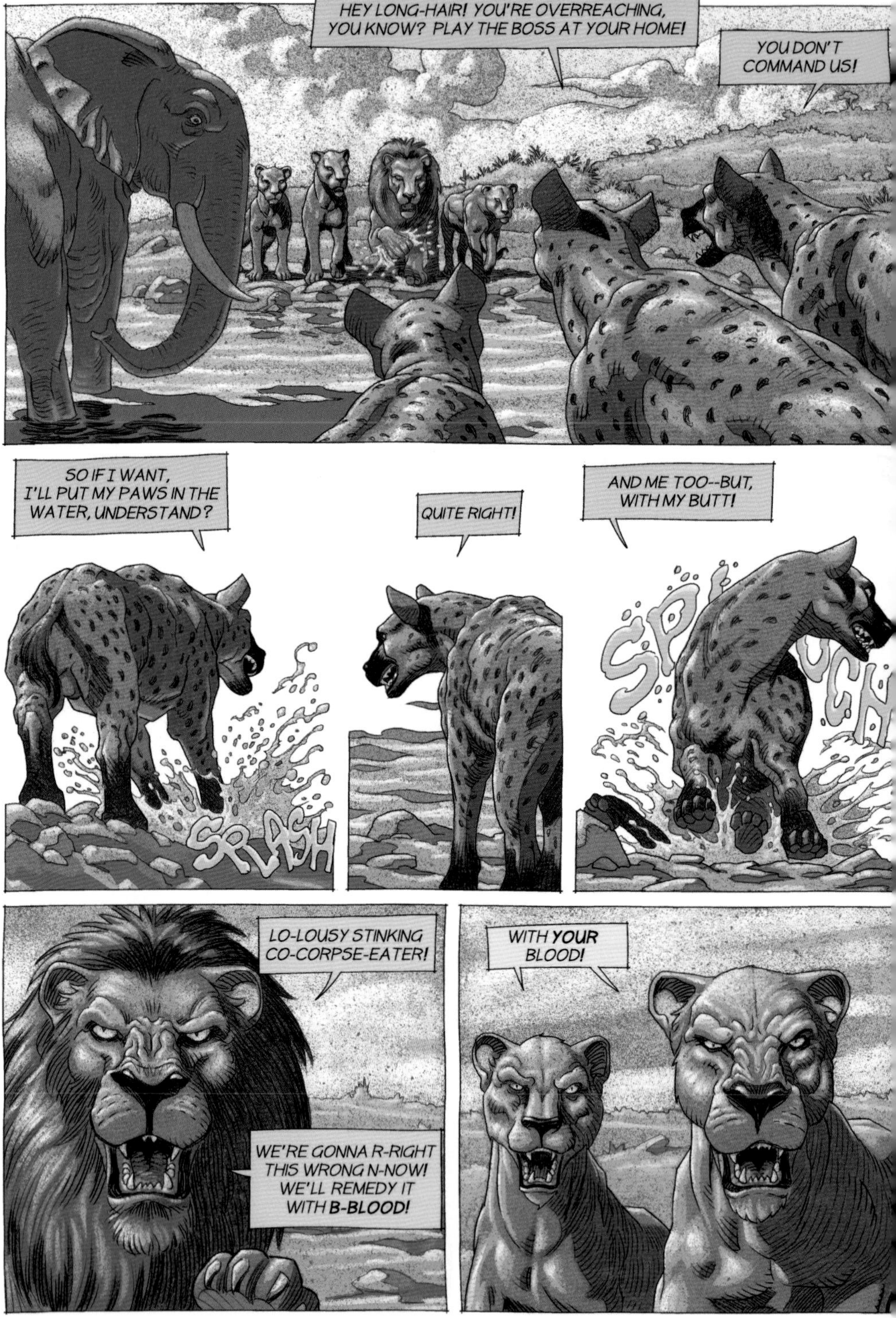
HEY LONG-HAIR! YOU'RE OVERREACHING, YOU KNOW? PLAY THE BOSS AT YOUR HOME!
YOU DON'T COMMAND US!
SO IF I WANT, I'LL PUT MY PAWS IN THE WATER, UNDERSTAND?
SPLASH
QUITE RIGHT!
AND ME TOO--BUT, WITH MY BUTT!
LO-LOUSY STINKING CO-CORPSE-EATER!
WE'RE GONNA R-RIGHT THIS WRONG N-NOW! WE'LL REMEDY IT WITH **B-BLOOD!**
WITH **YOUR** BLOOD!

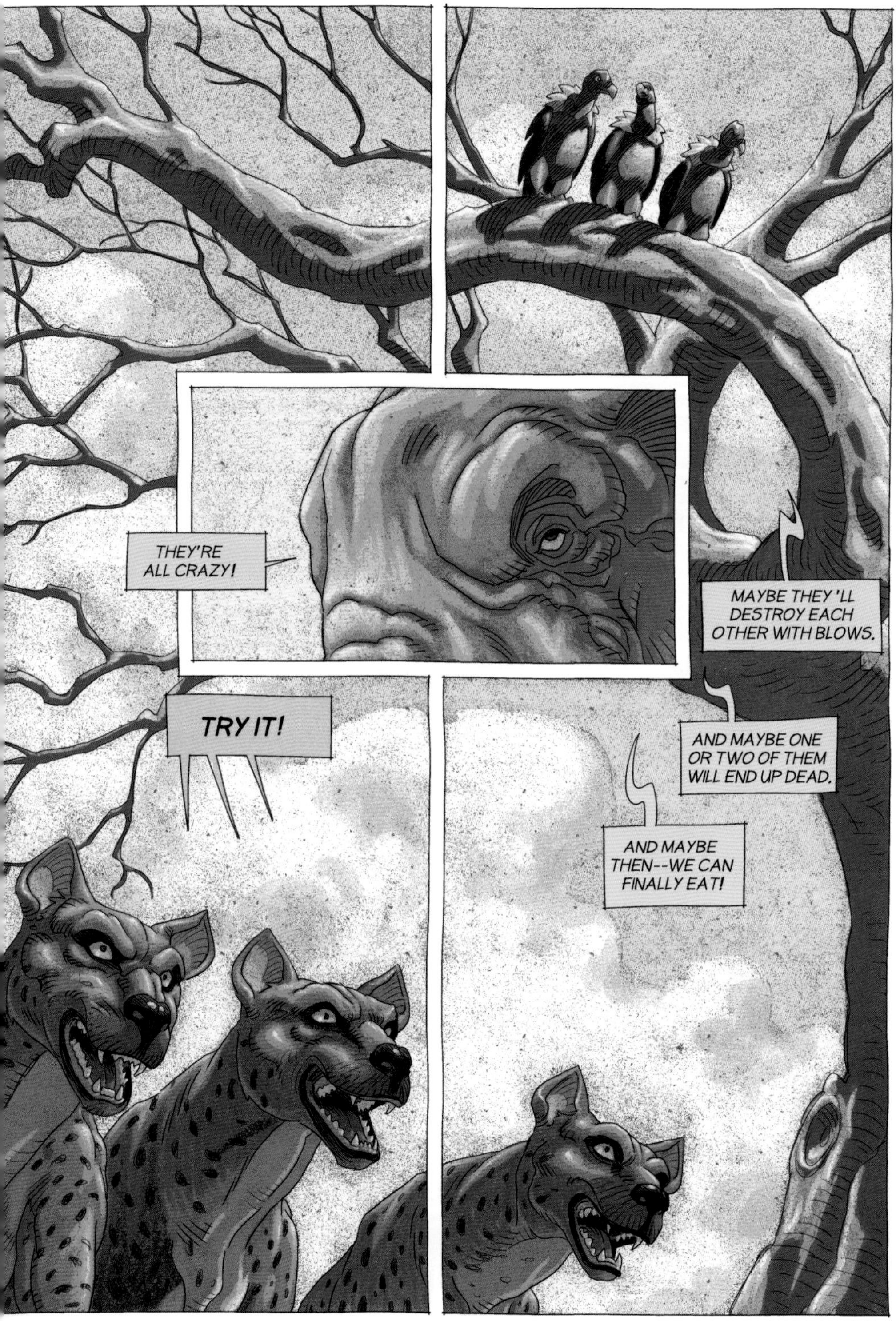
THEY'RE ALL CRAZY!
MAYBE THEY'LL DESTROY EACH OTHER WITH BLOWS.
TRY IT!
AND MAYBE ONE OR TWO OF THEM WILL END UP DEAD.
AND MAYBE THEN--WE CAN FINALLY EAT!

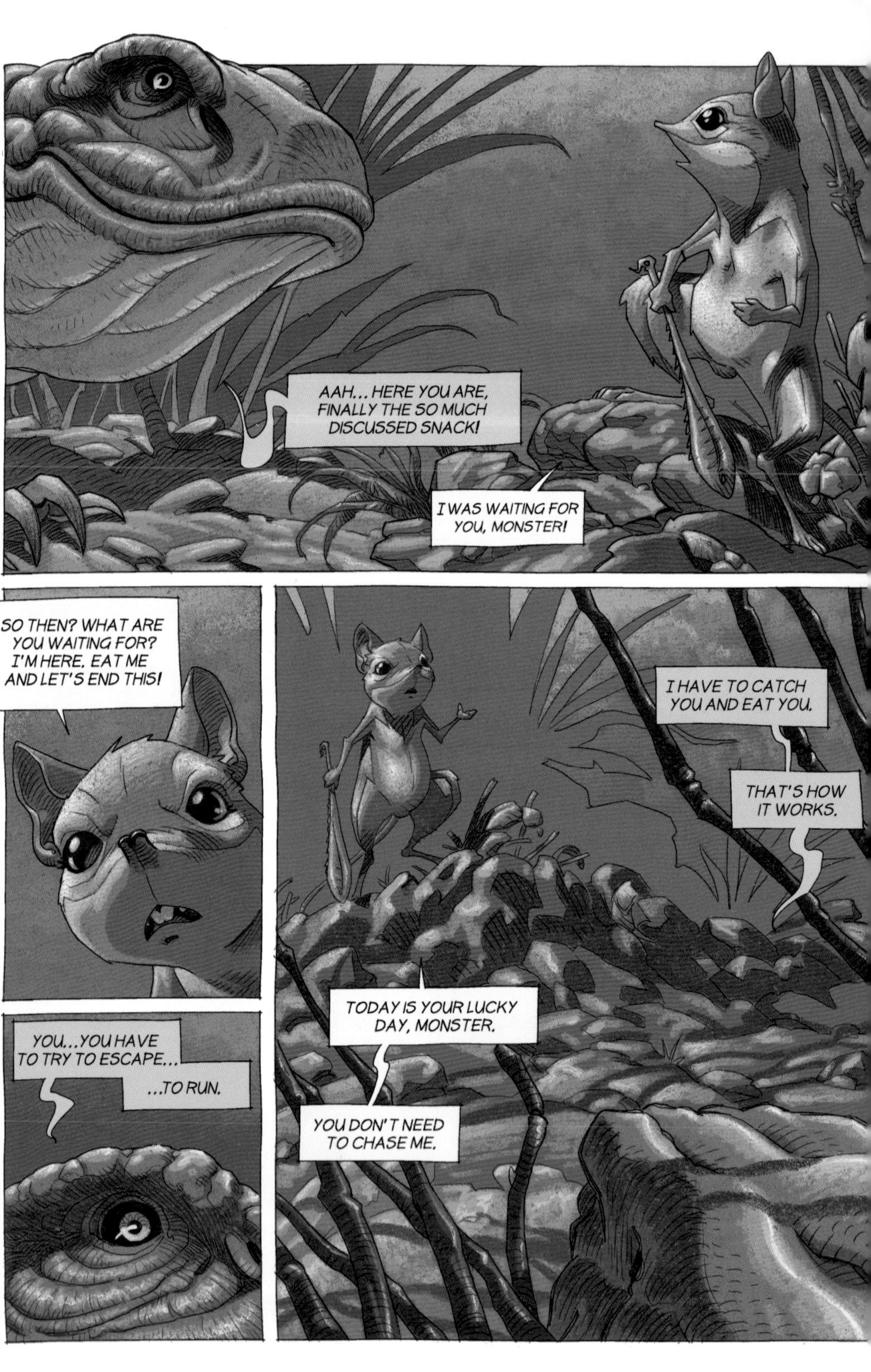
AAH... HERE YOU ARE, FINALLY THE SO MUCH DISCUSSED SNACK!
I WAS WAITING FOR YOU, MONSTER!
SO THEN? WHAT ARE YOU WAITING FOR? I'M HERE. EAT ME AND LET'S END THIS!
YOU...YOU HAVE TO TRY TO ESCAPE...
...TO RUN.
I HAVE TO CATCH YOU AND EAT YOU.
THAT'S HOW IT WORKS.
TODAY IS YOUR LUCKY DAY, MONSTER.
YOU DON'T NEED TO CHASE ME.

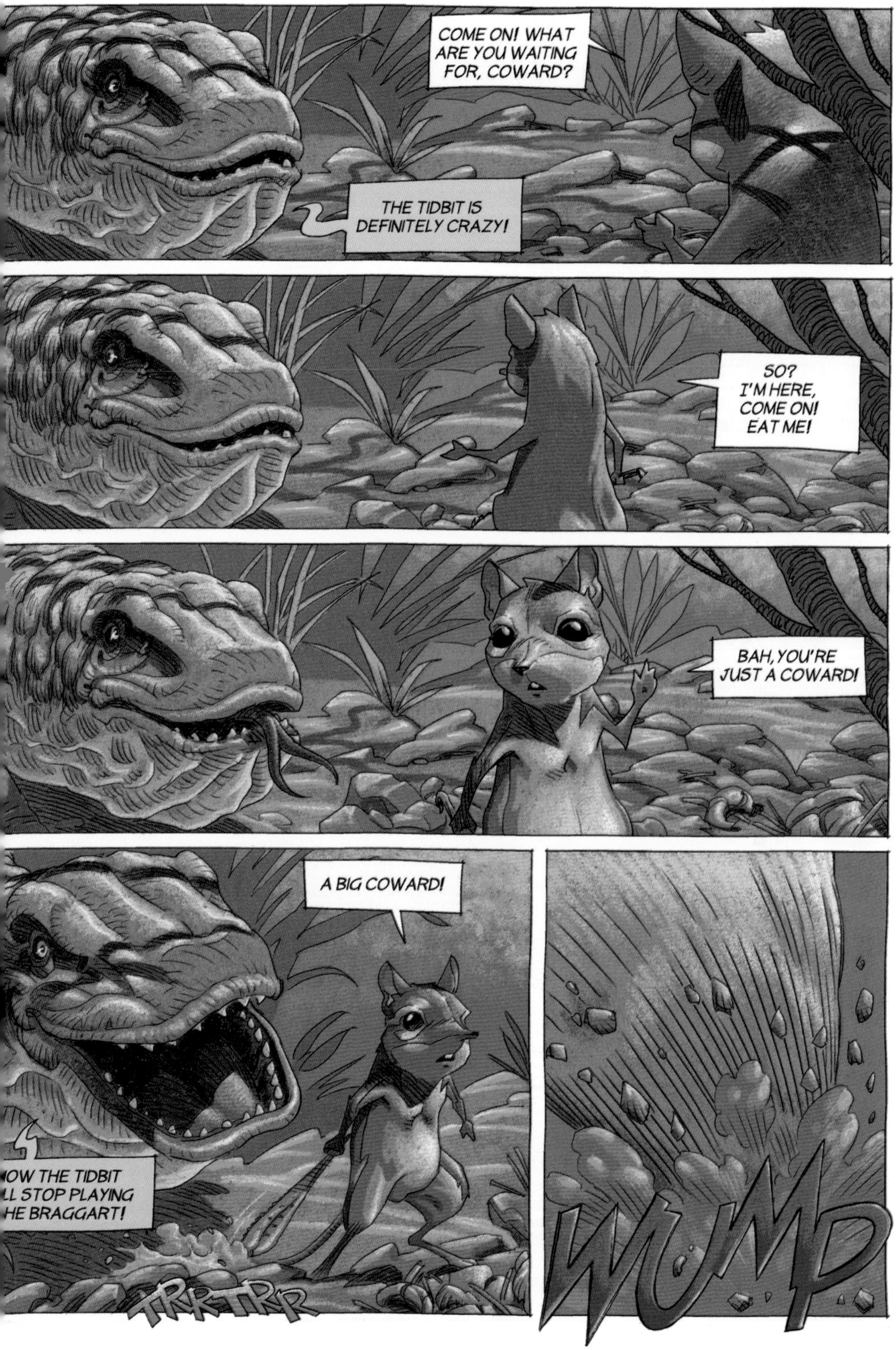
COME ON! WHAT ARE YOU WAITING FOR, COWARD?
THE TIDBIT IS DEFINITELY CRAZY!
SO? I'M HERE, COME ON! EAT ME!
BAH, YOU'RE JUST A COWARD!
A BIG COWARD!
OW THE TIDBIT LL STOP PLAYING HE BRAGGART!
TRRTRR
WUMP

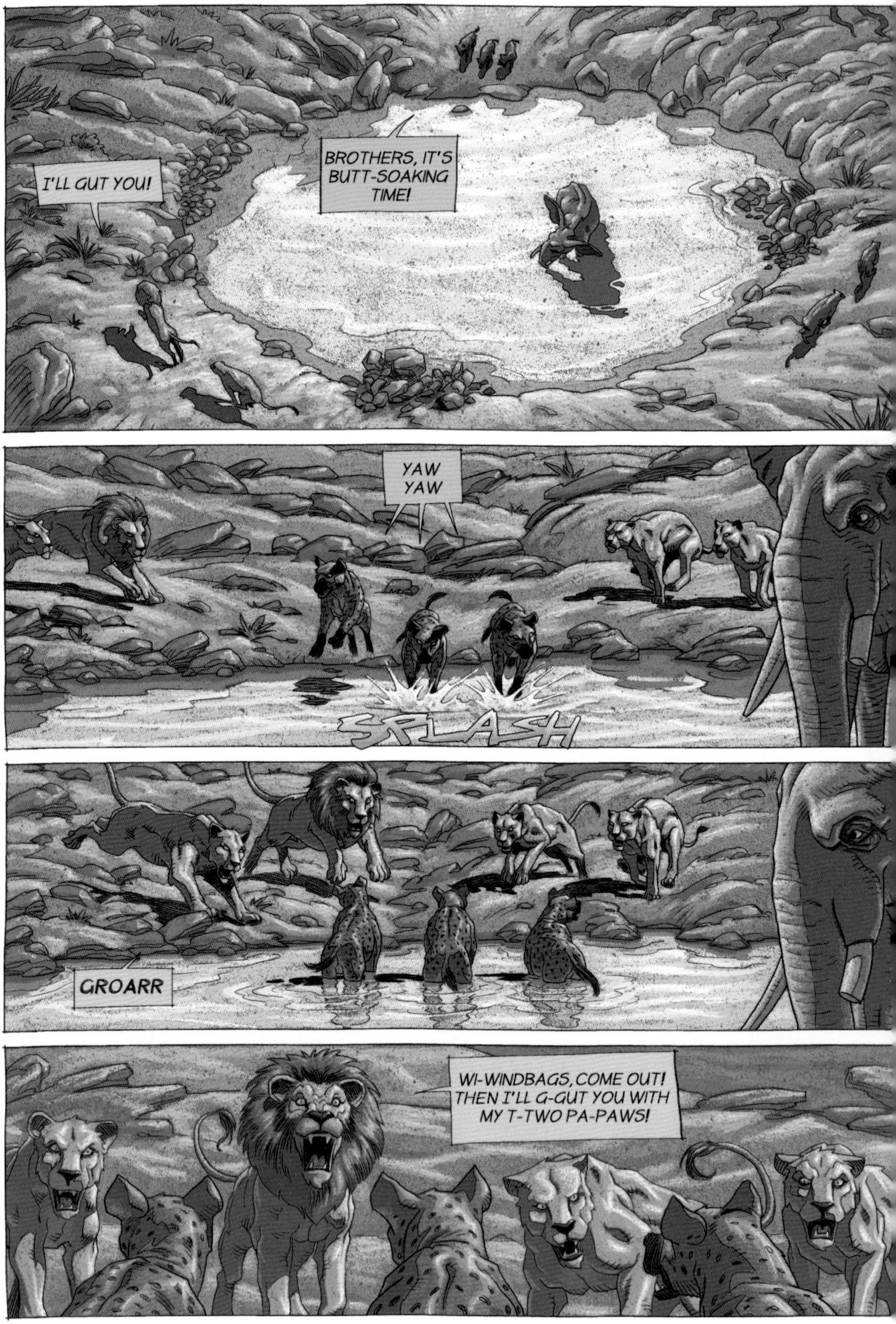
I'LL GUT YOU!
BROTHERS, IT'S BUTT-SOAKING TIME!
YAW YAW
SPLASH
GROARR
WI-WINDBAGS, COME OUT! THEN I'LL G-GUT YOU WITH MY T-TWO PA-PAWS!

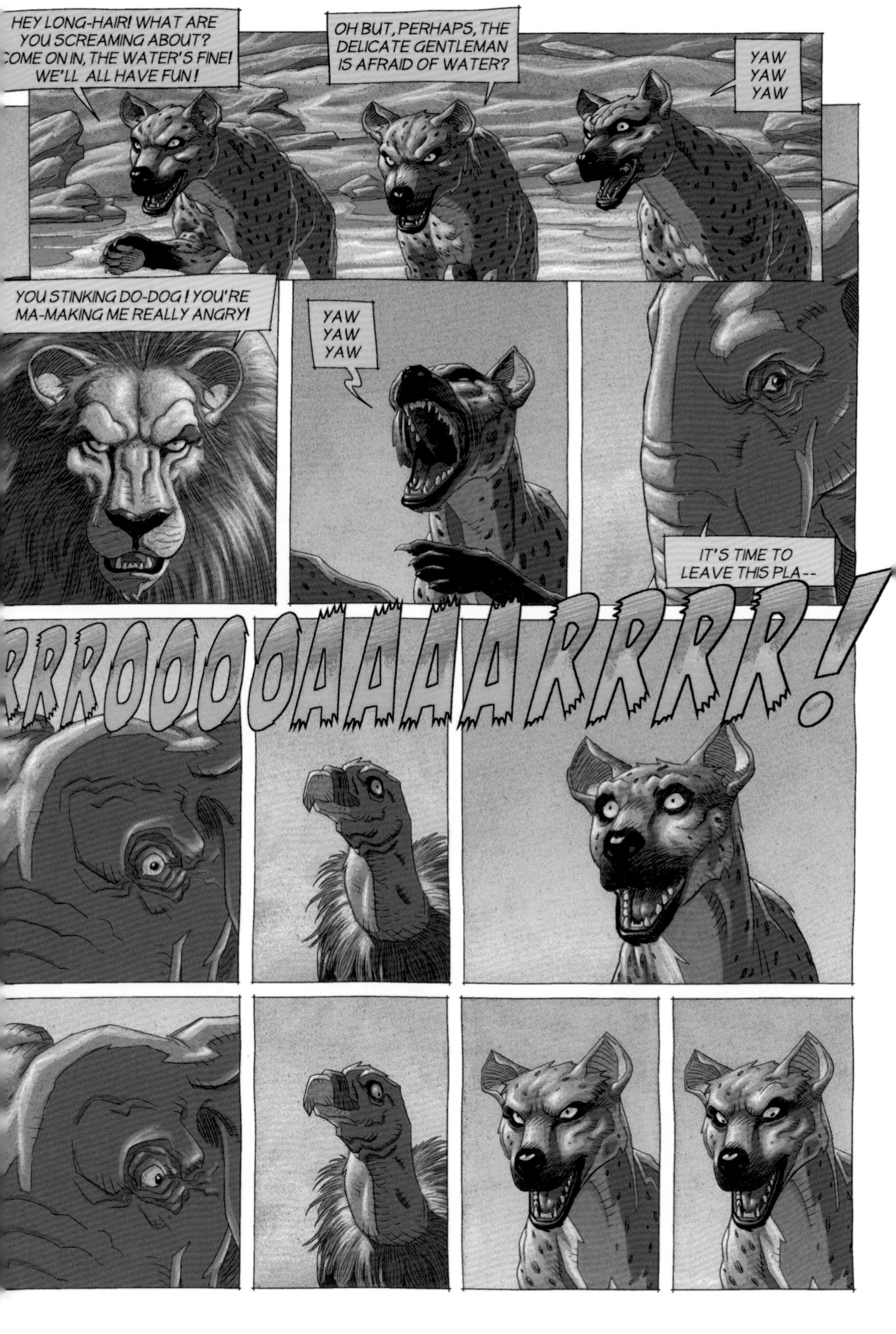
HEY LONG-HAIR! WHAT ARE YOU SCREAMING ABOUT? COME ON IN, THE WATER'S FINE! WE'LL ALL HAVE FUN!
OH BUT, PERHAPS, THE DELICATE GENTLEMAN IS AFRAID OF WATER?
YAW YAW YAW
YOU STINKING DO-DOG! YOU'RE MA-MAKING ME REALLY ANGRY!
YAW YAW YAW
IT'S TIME TO LEAVE THIS PLA--
RRROOOOAAAAARRRRR!

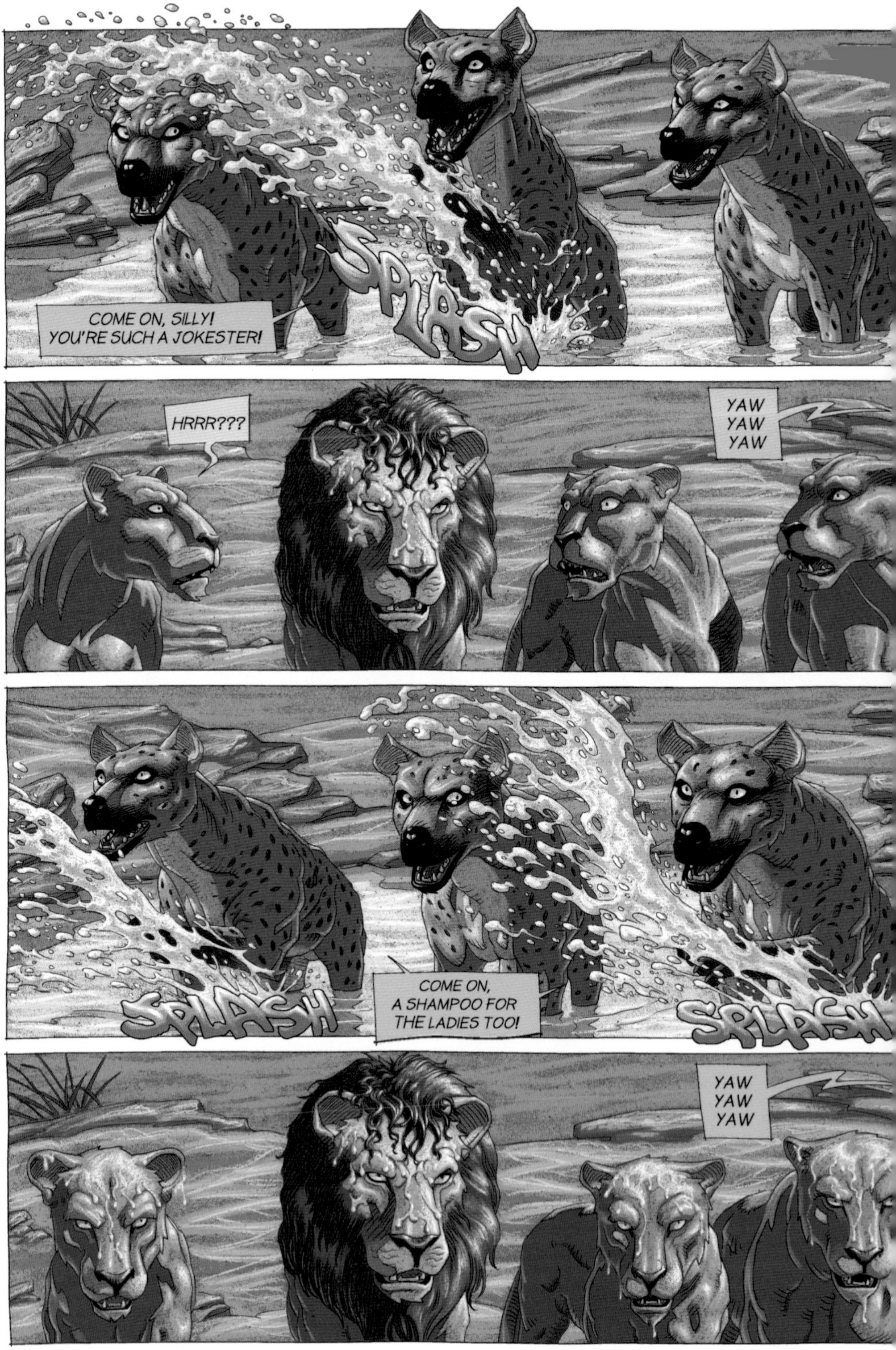
COME ON, SILLY! YOU'RE SUCH A JOKESTER!
SPLASH
HRRR???
YAW YAW YAW
SPLASH
COME ON, A SHAMPOO FOR THE LADIES TOO!
SPLASH
YAW YAW YAW

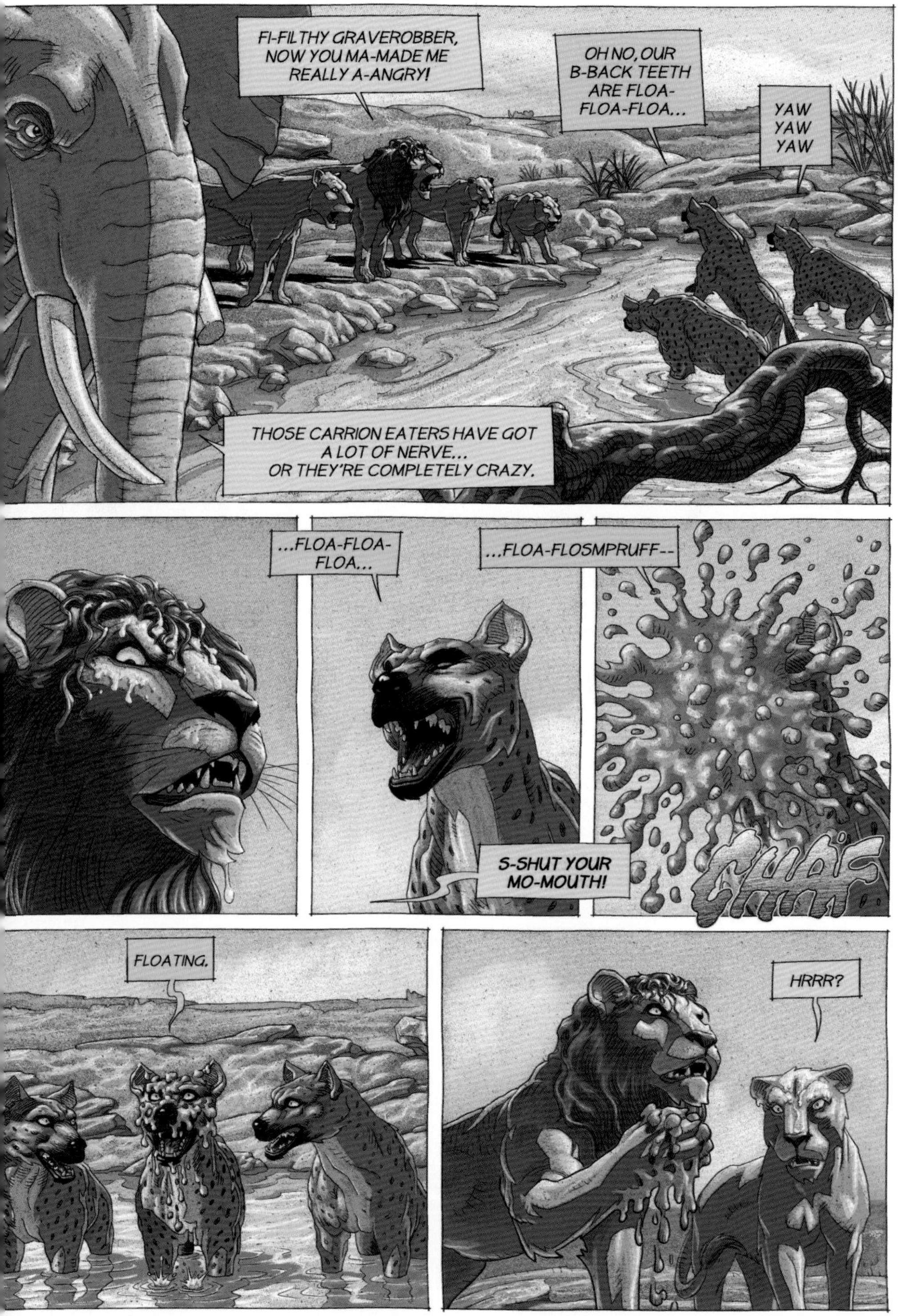
FI-FILTHY GRAVEROBBER, NOW YOU MA-MADE ME REALLY A-ANGRY!
OH NO, OUR B-BACK TEETH ARE FLOA-FLOA-FLOA-FLOA...
YAW YAW YAW
THOSE CARRION EATERS HAVE GOT A LOT OF NERVE... OR THEY'RE COMPLETELY CRAZY.
...FLOA-FLOA-FLOA...
...FLOA-FLOSMPRUFF--
S-SHUT YOUR MO-MOUTH!
FLOATING.
HRRR?

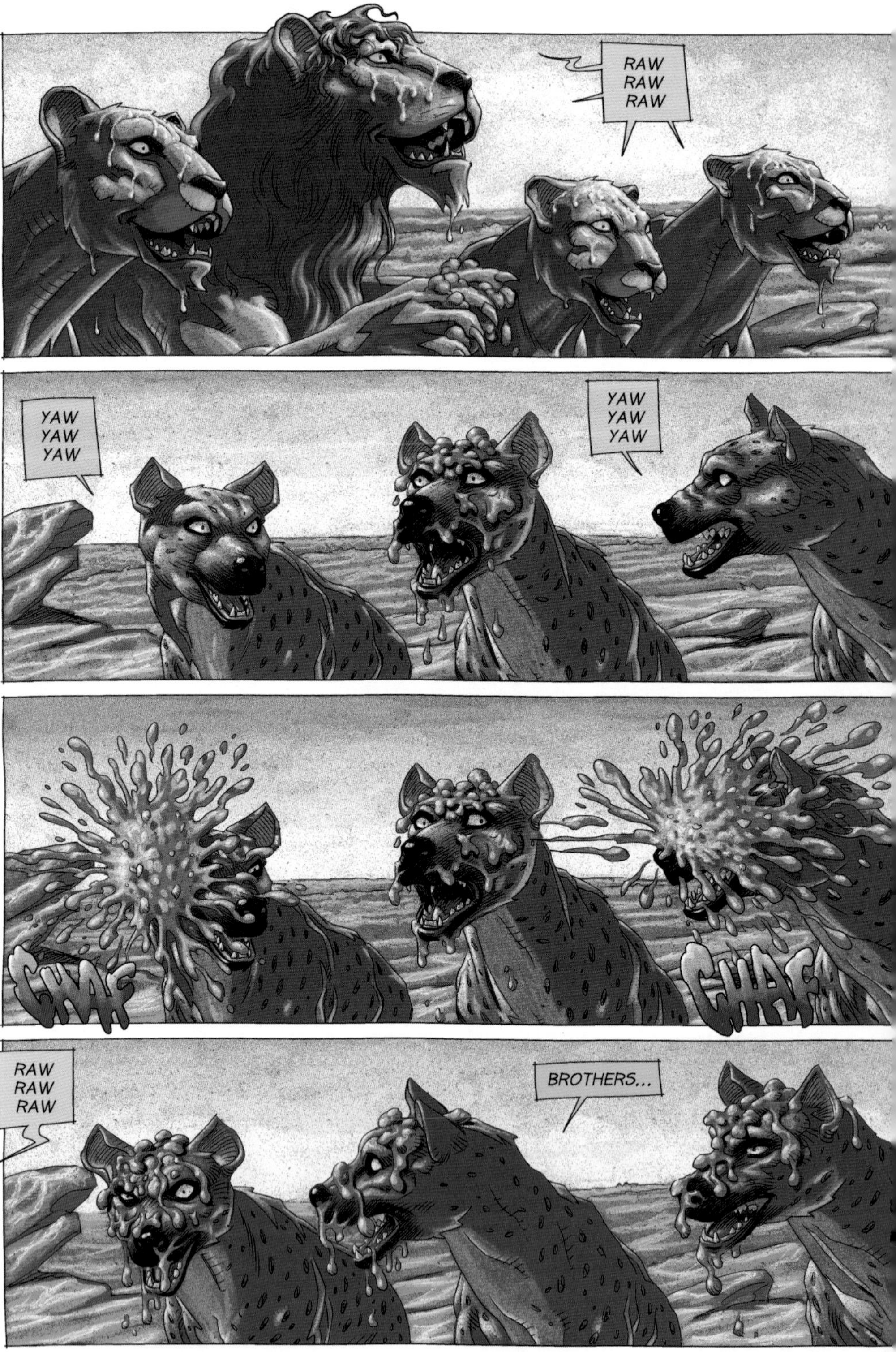
RAW RAW RAW
YAW YAW YAW
YAW YAW YAW
CHAF
CHAF
RAW RAW RAW
BROTHERS...

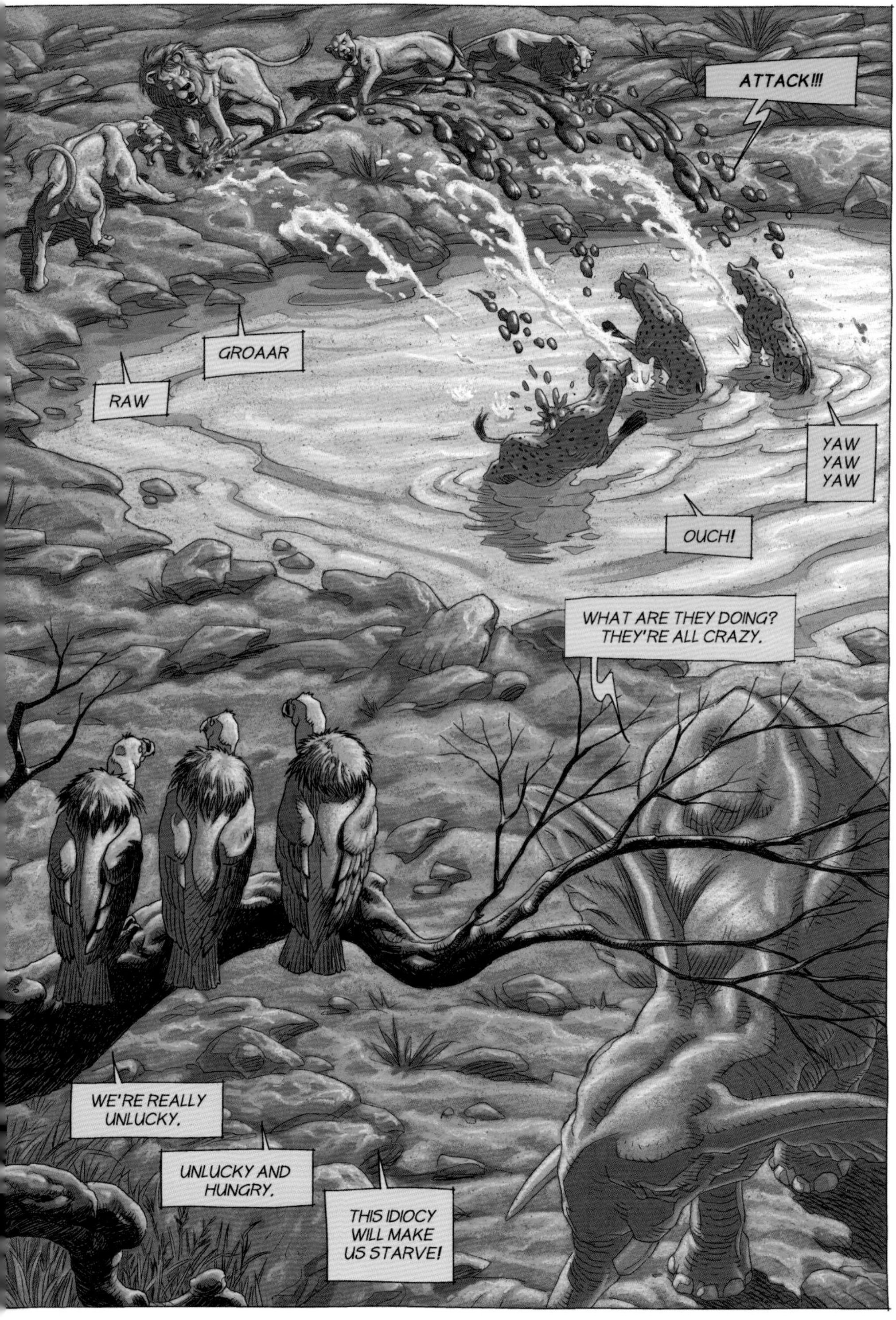
ATTACK!!!
GROOAR
RAW
YAW YAW YAW
OUCH!
WHAT ARE THEY DOING? THEY'RE ALL CRAZY.
WE'RE REALLY UNLUCKY.
UNLUCKY AND HUNGRY.
THIS IDIOCY WILL MAKE US STARVE!

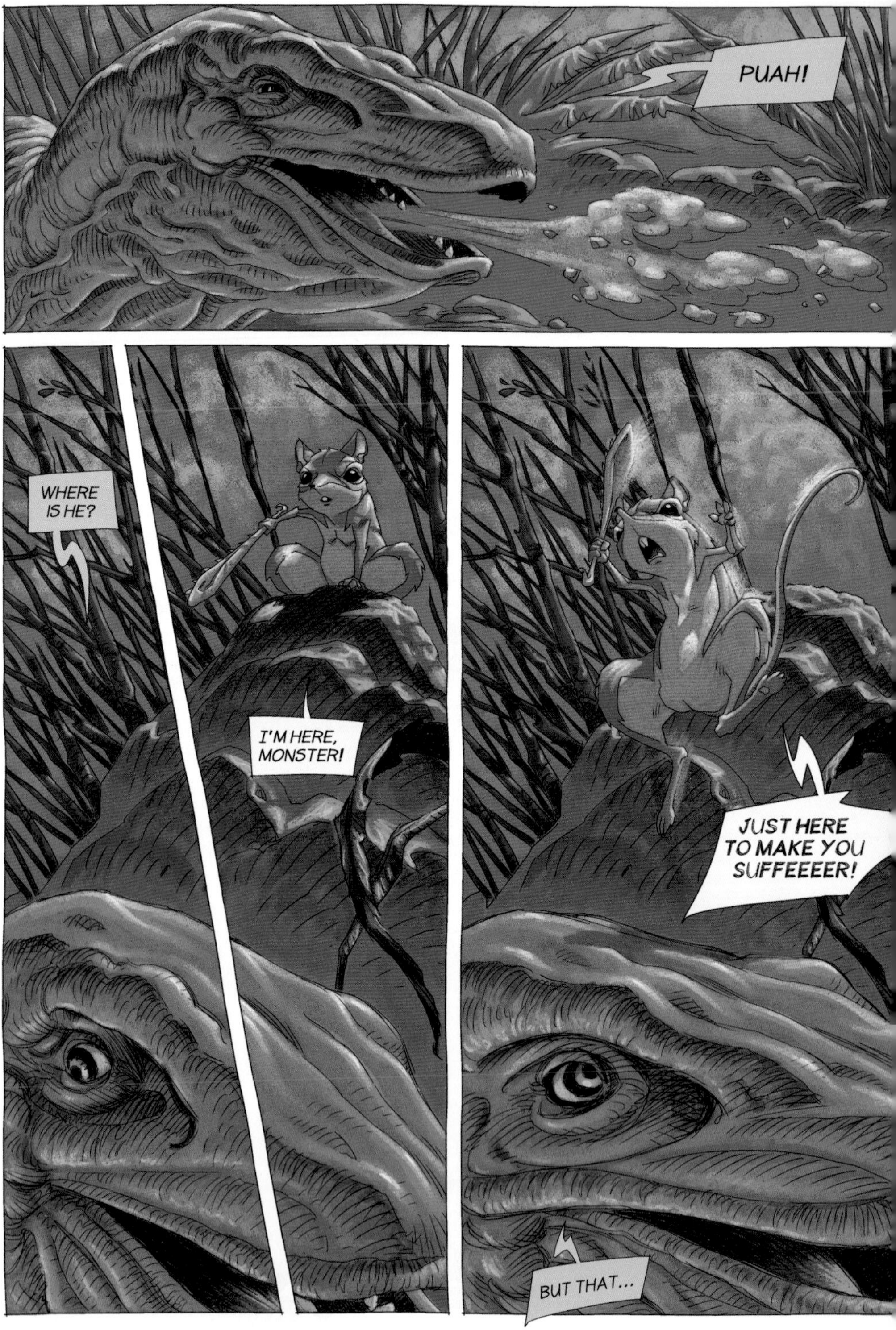
PUAH!
WHERE IS HE?
I'M HERE, MONSTER!
JUST HERE TO MAKE YOU SUFFEEEER!
BUT THAT...

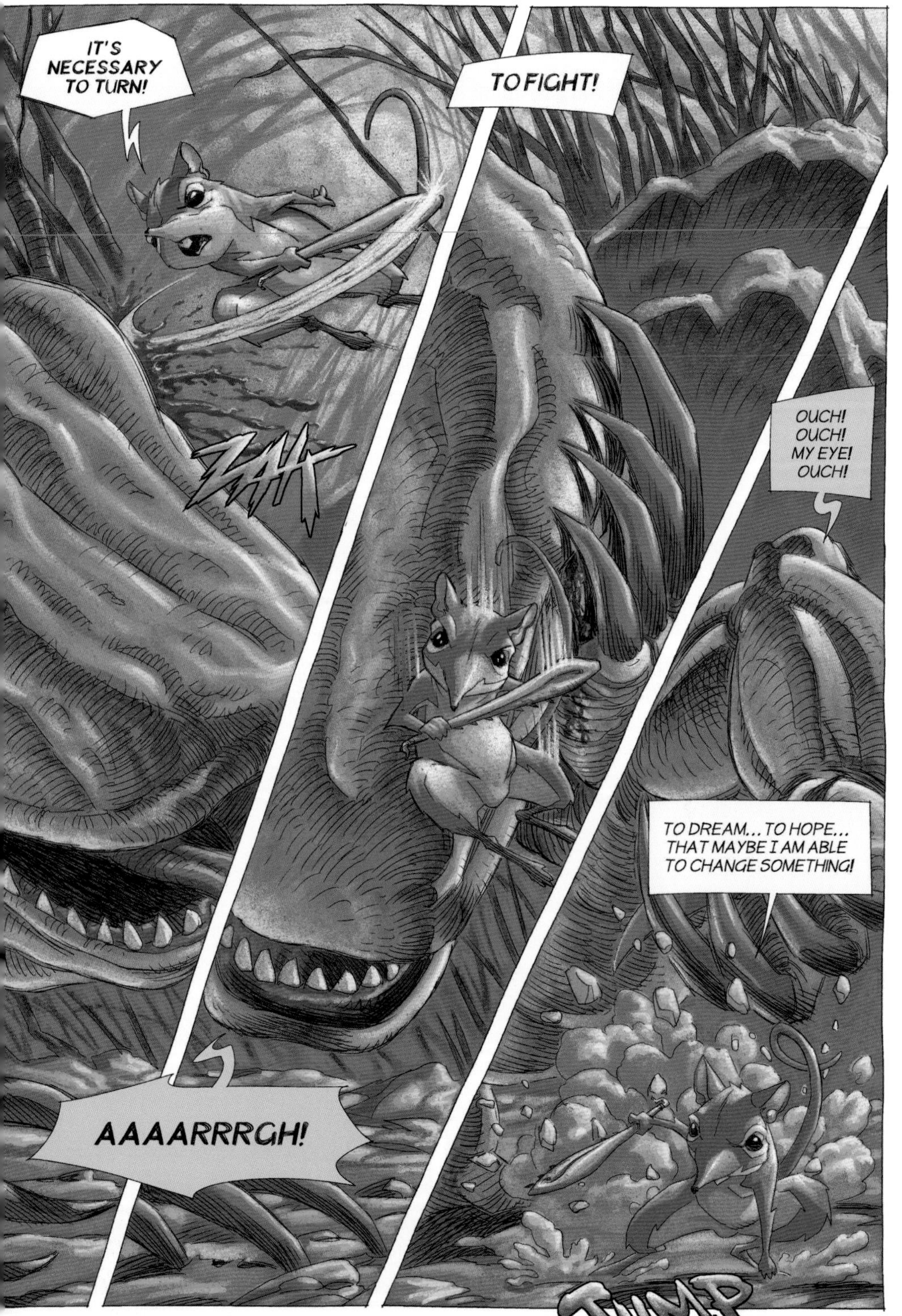
IT'S NECESSARY TO TURN!
ZAAK
TO FIGHT!
AAAARRRGH!
OUCH! OUCH! MY EYE! OUCH!
TO DREAM... TO HOPE... THAT MAYBE I AM ABLE TO CHANGE SOMETHING!
TUMP

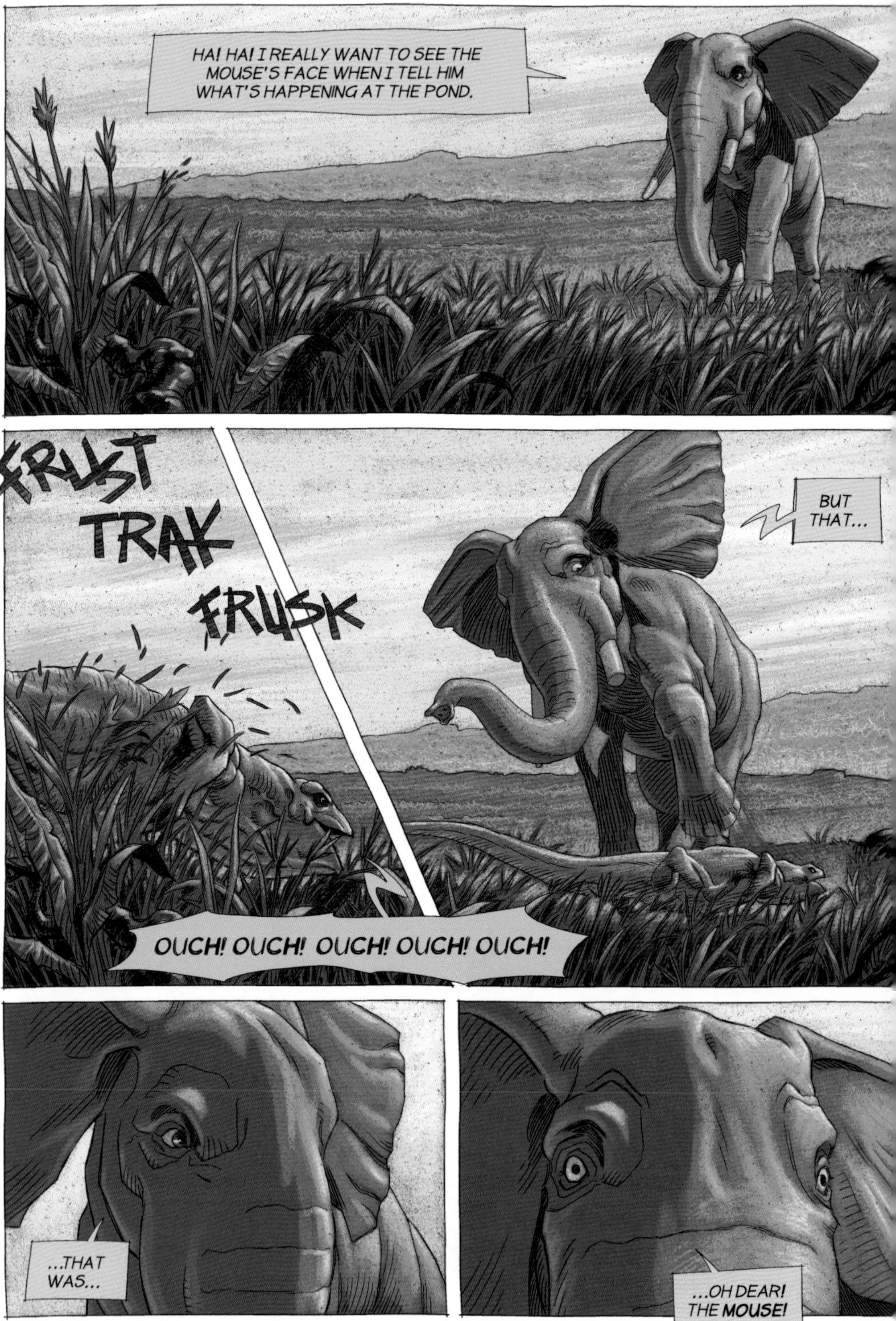
HA! HA! I REALLY WANT TO SEE THE MOUSE'S FACE WHEN I TELL HIM WHAT'S HAPPENING AT THE POND.
FRUST
TRAK
FRUSK
BUT THAT...
OUCH! OUCH! OUCH! OUCH! OUCH!
...THAT WAS...
...OH DEAR! THE MOUSE!

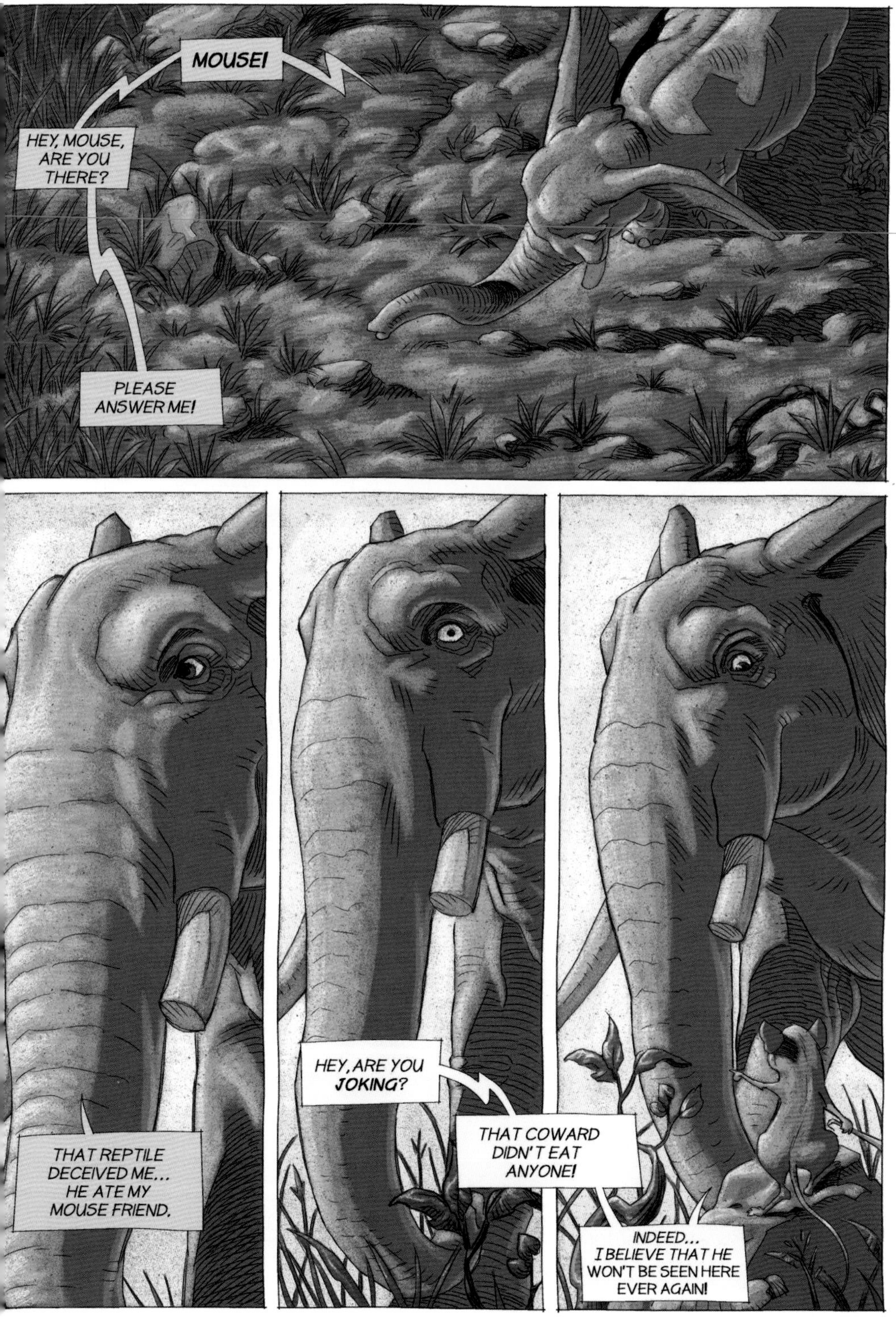
MOUSE!
HEY, MOUSE, ARE YOU THERE?
PLEASE ANSWER ME!
THAT REPTILE DECEIVED ME... HE ATE MY MOUSE FRIEND.
HEY, ARE YOU JOKING?
THAT COWARD DIDN'T EAT ANYONE!
INDEED... I BELIEVE THAT HE WON'T BE SEEN HERE EVER AGAIN!

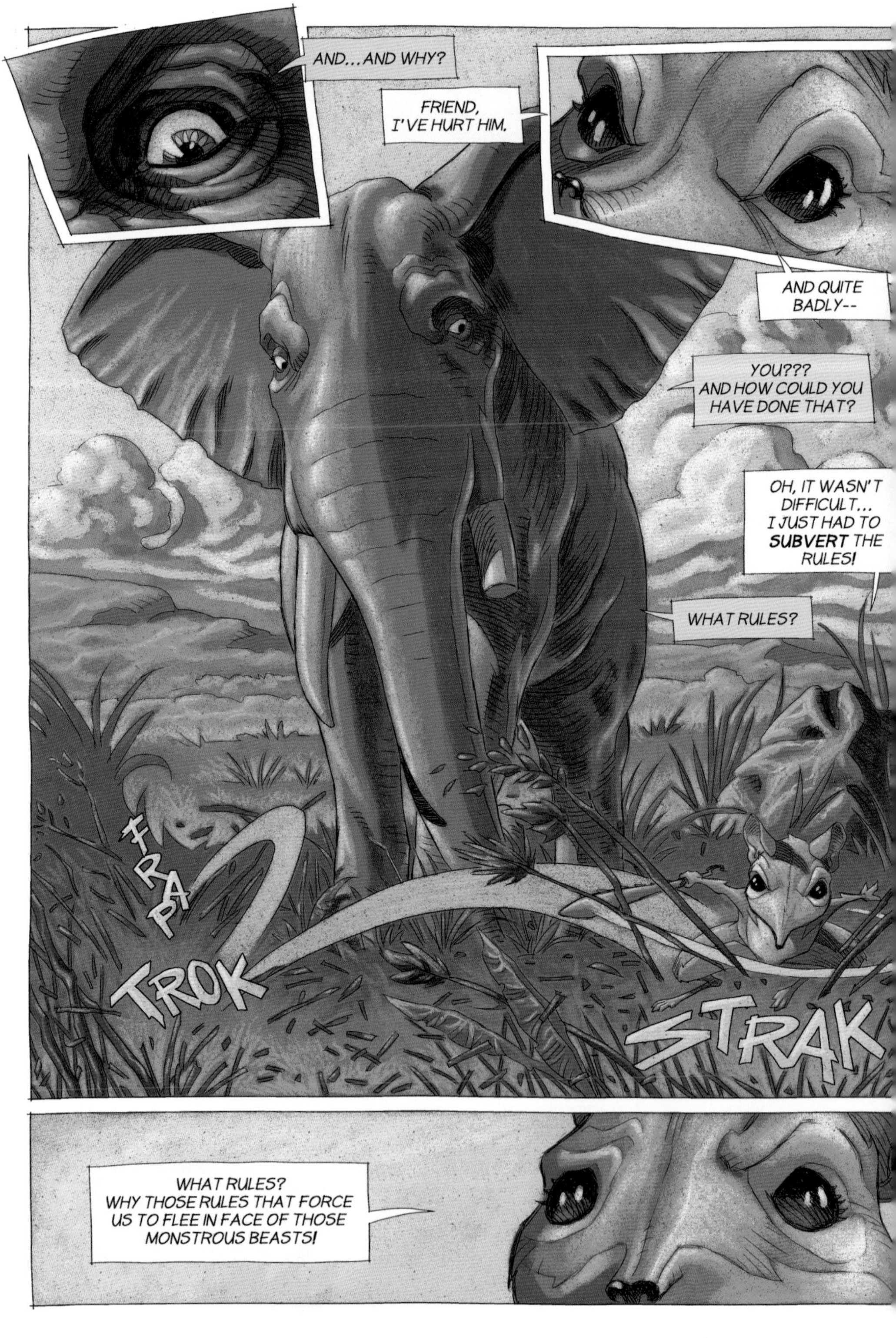
AND... AND WHY?
FRIEND, I'VE HURT HIM.
AND QUITE BADLY--
YOU??? AND HOW COULD YOU HAVE DONE THAT?
OH, IT WASN'T DIFFICULT... I JUST HAD TO **SUBVERT** THE RULES!
WHAT RULES?
FRAP
TROK
STRAK
WHAT RULES? WHY THOSE RULES THAT FORCE US TO FLEE IN FACE OF THOSE MONSTROUS BEASTS!

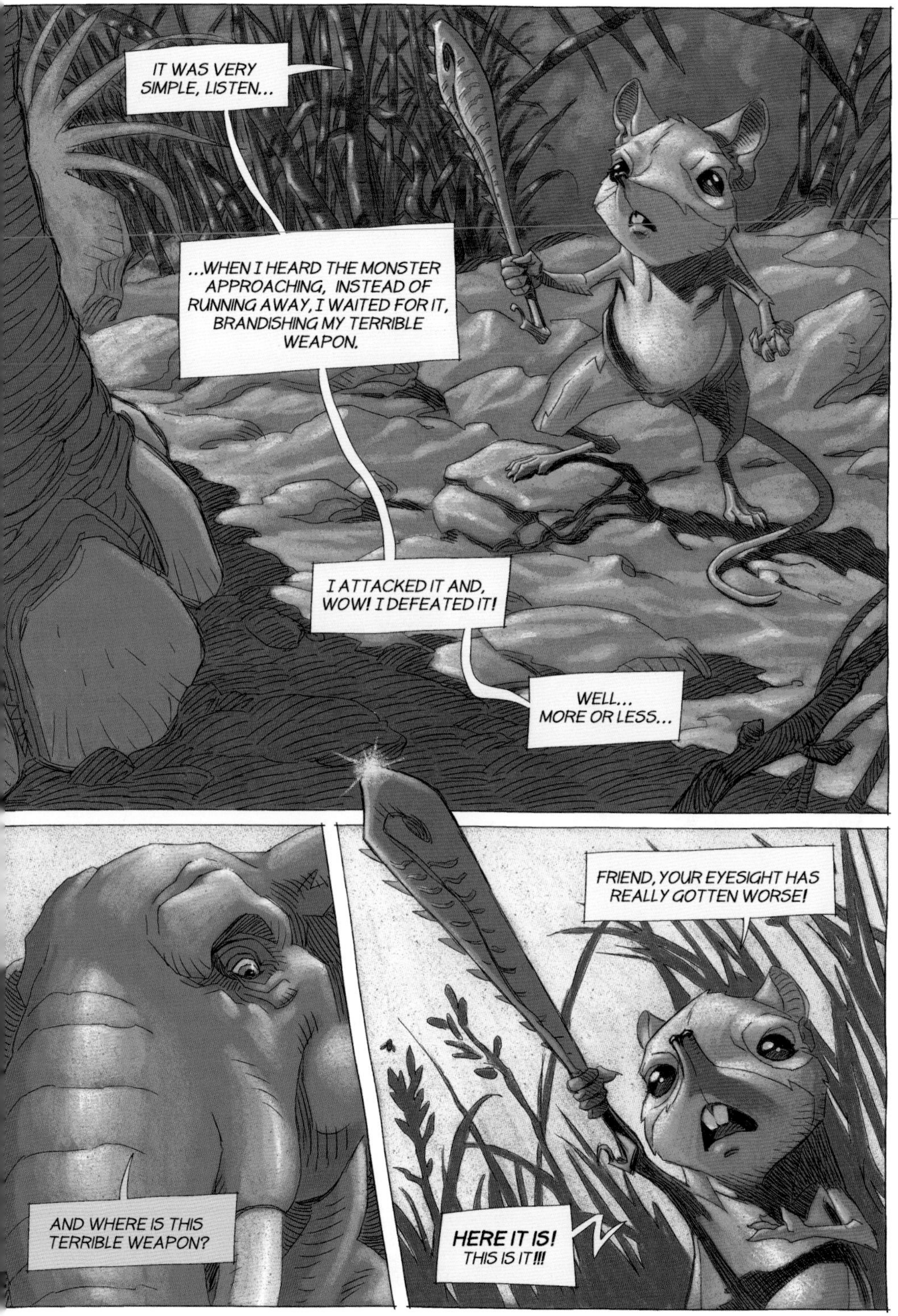
IT WAS VERY SIMPLE, LISTEN...
...WHEN I HEARD THE MONSTER APPROACHING, INSTEAD OF RUNNING AWAY, I WAITED FOR IT, BRANDISHING MY TERRIBLE WEAPON.
I ATTACKED IT AND, WOW! I DEFEATED IT!
WELL... MORE OR LESS...
AND WHERE IS THIS TERRIBLE WEAPON?
FRIEND, YOUR EYESIGHT HAS REALLY GOTTEN WORSE!
HERE IT IS! THIS IS IT!!!

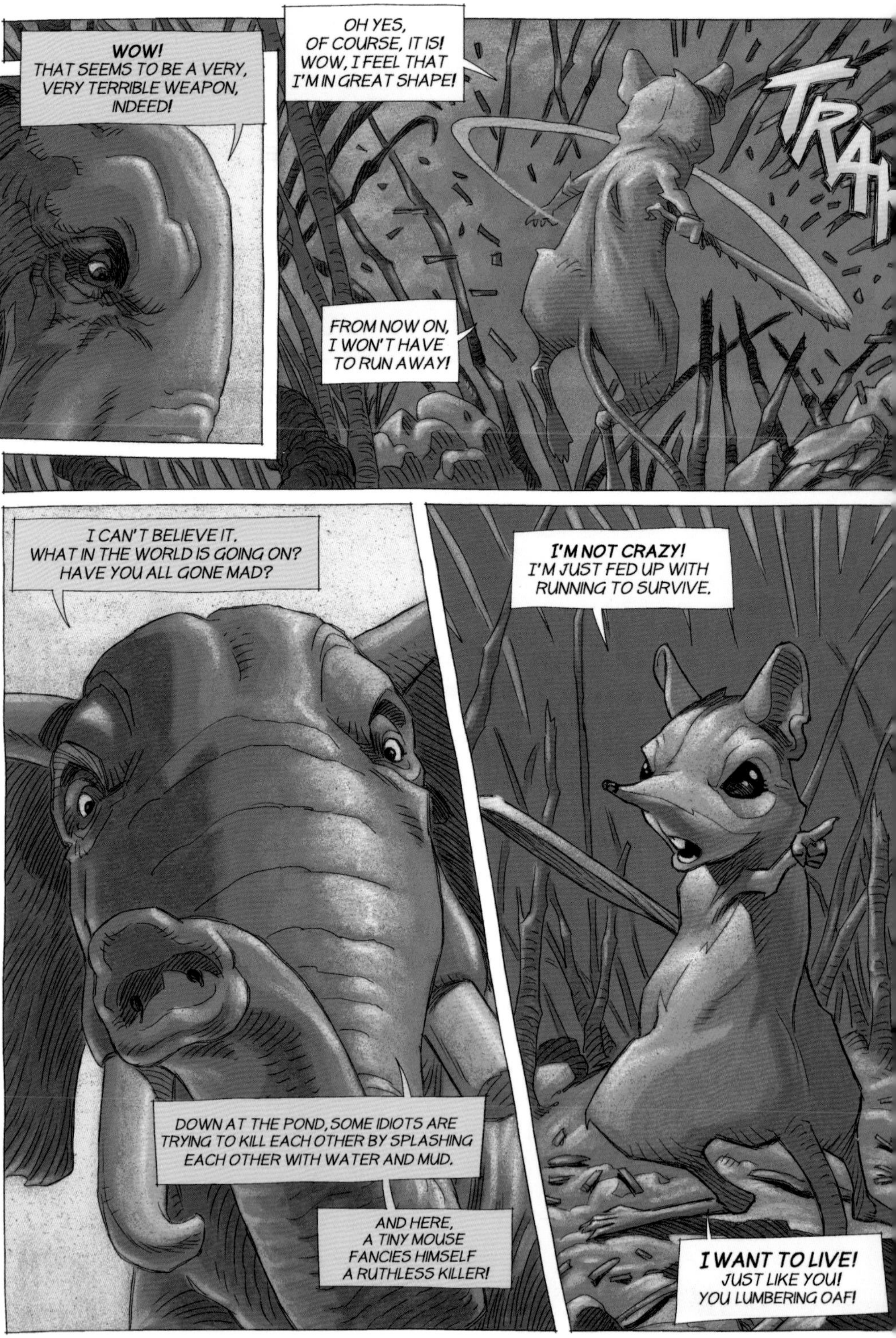
WOW!
THAT SEEMS TO BE A VERY, VERY TERRIBLE WEAPON, INDEED!
OH YES, OF COURSE, IT IS! WOW, I FEEL THAT I'M IN GREAT SHAPE!
TRAH
FROM NOW ON, I WON'T HAVE TO RUN AWAY!
I CAN'T BELIEVE IT. WHAT IN THE WORLD IS GOING ON? HAVE YOU ALL GONE MAD?
I'M NOT CRAZY!
I'M JUST FED UP WITH RUNNING TO SURVIVE.
DOWN AT THE POND, SOME IDIOTS ARE TRYING TO KILL EACH OTHER BY SPLASHING EACH OTHER WITH WATER AND MUD.
AND HERE, A TINY MOUSE FANCIES HIMSELF A RUTHLESS KILLER!
I WANT TO LIVE!
JUST LIKE YOU! YOU LUMBERING OAF!

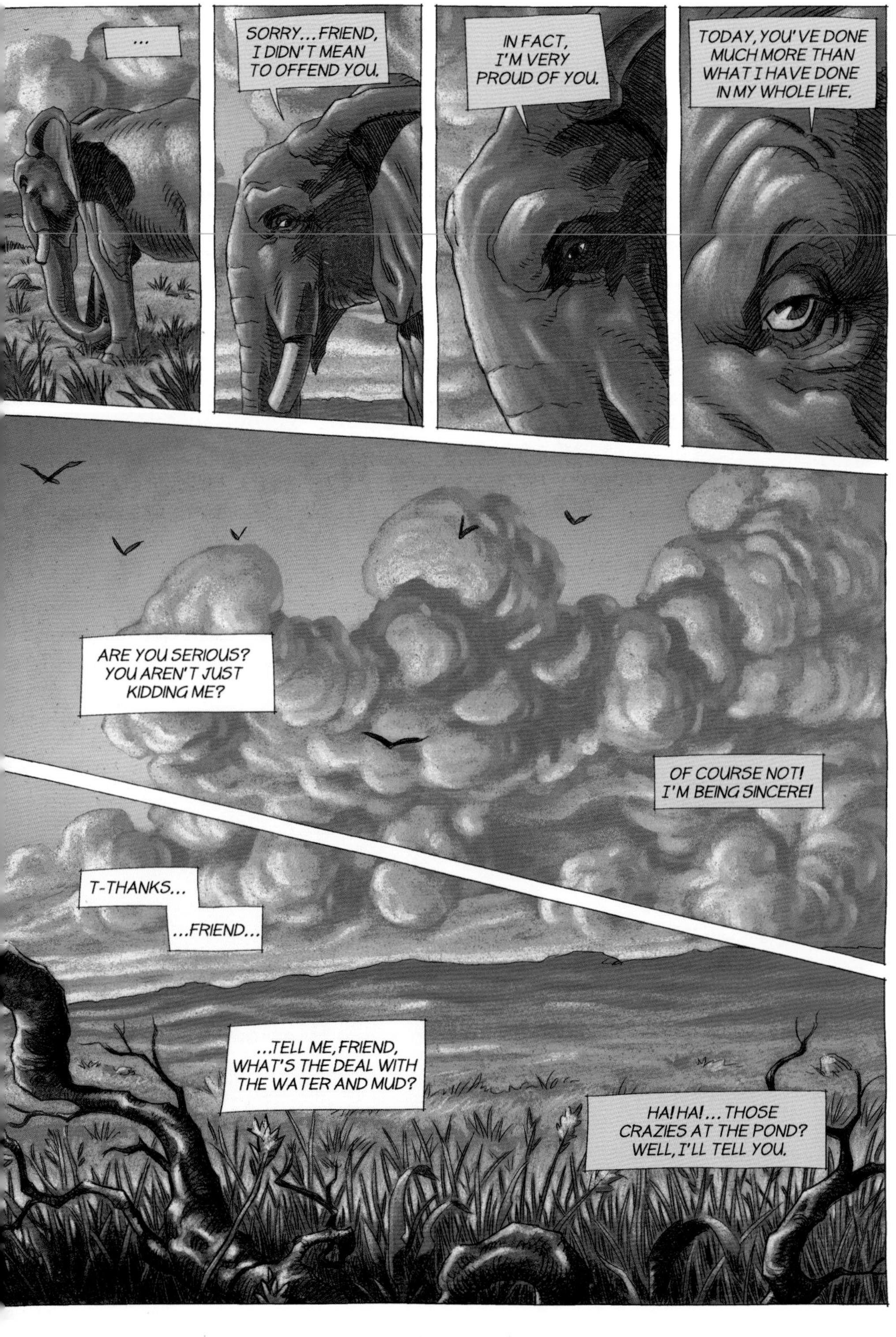
...
SORRY... FRIEND, I DIDN'T MEAN TO OFFEND YOU.
IN FACT, I'M VERY PROUD OF YOU.
TODAY, YOU'VE DONE MUCH MORE THAN WHAT I HAVE DONE IN MY WHOLE LIFE.
ARE YOU SERIOUS? YOU AREN'T JUST KIDDING ME?
OF COURSE NOT! I'M BEING SINCERE!
T-THANKS...
...FRIEND...
...TELL ME, FRIEND, WHAT'S THE DEAL WITH THE WATER AND MUD?
HA! HA! ... THOSE CRAZIES AT THE POND? WELL, I'LL TELL YOU.

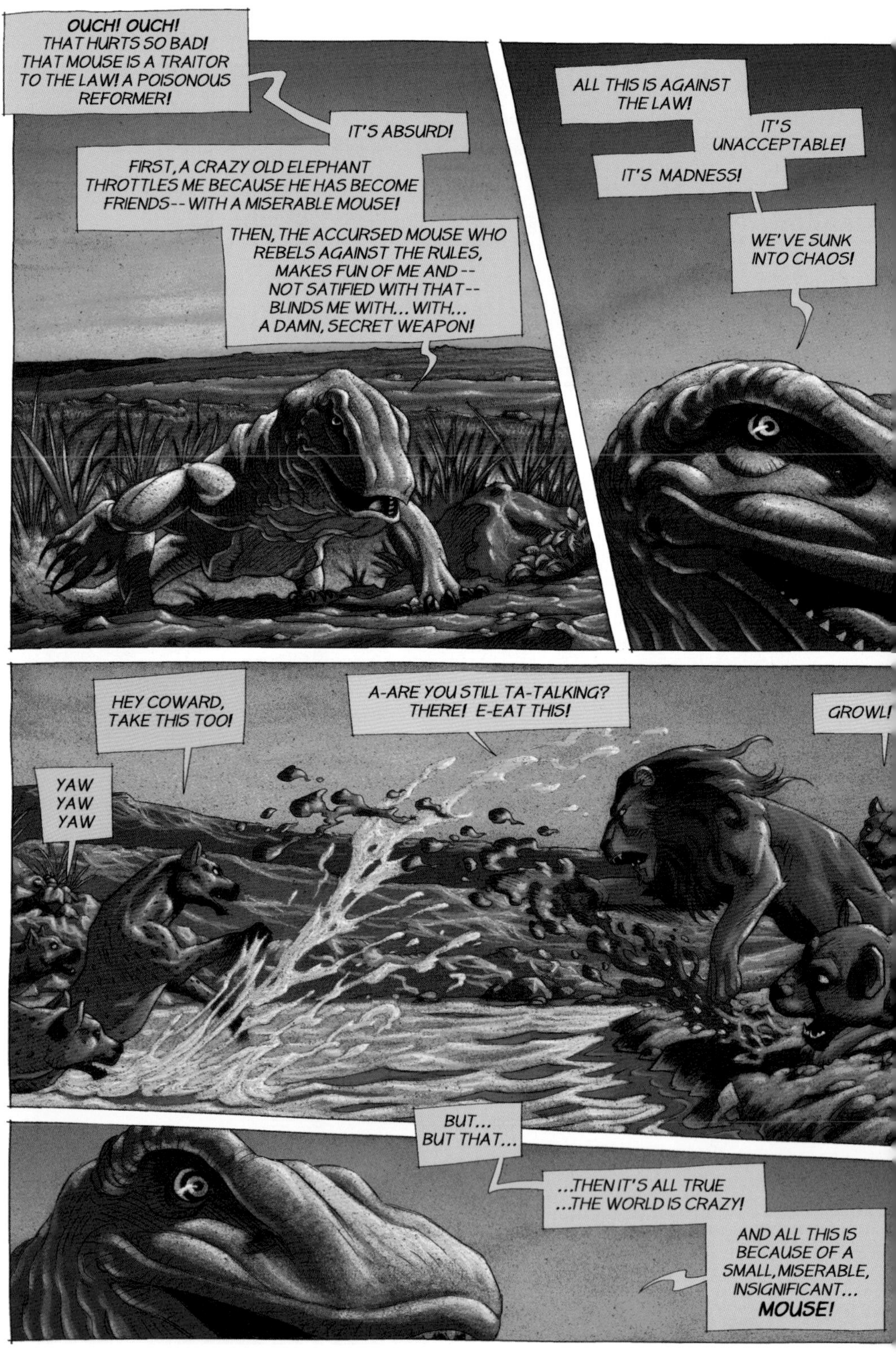
OUCH! OUCH! THAT HURTS SO BAD! THAT MOUSE IS A TRAITOR TO THE LAW! A POISONOUS REFORMER!
IT'S ABSURD!
FIRST, A CRAZY OLD ELEPHANT THROTTLES ME BECAUSE HE HAS BECOME FRIENDS-- WITH A MISERABLE MOUSE!
THEN, THE ACCURSED MOUSE WHO REBELS AGAINST THE RULES, MAKES FUN OF ME AND -- NOT SATIFIED WITH THAT-- BLINDS ME WITH... WITH... A DAMN, SECRET WEAPON!
ALL THIS IS AGAINST THE LAW!
IT'S UNACCEPTABLE!
IT'S MADNESS!
WE'VE SUNK INTO CHAOS!
HEY COWARD, TAKE THIS TOO!
YAW YAW YAW
A-ARE YOU STILL TA-TALKING? THERE! E-EAT THIS!
GROWL!
BUT... BUT THAT...
...THEN IT'S ALL TRUE ...THE WORLD IS CRAZY!
AND ALL THIS IS BECAUSE OF A SMALL, MISERABLE, INSIGNIFICANT... MOUSE!

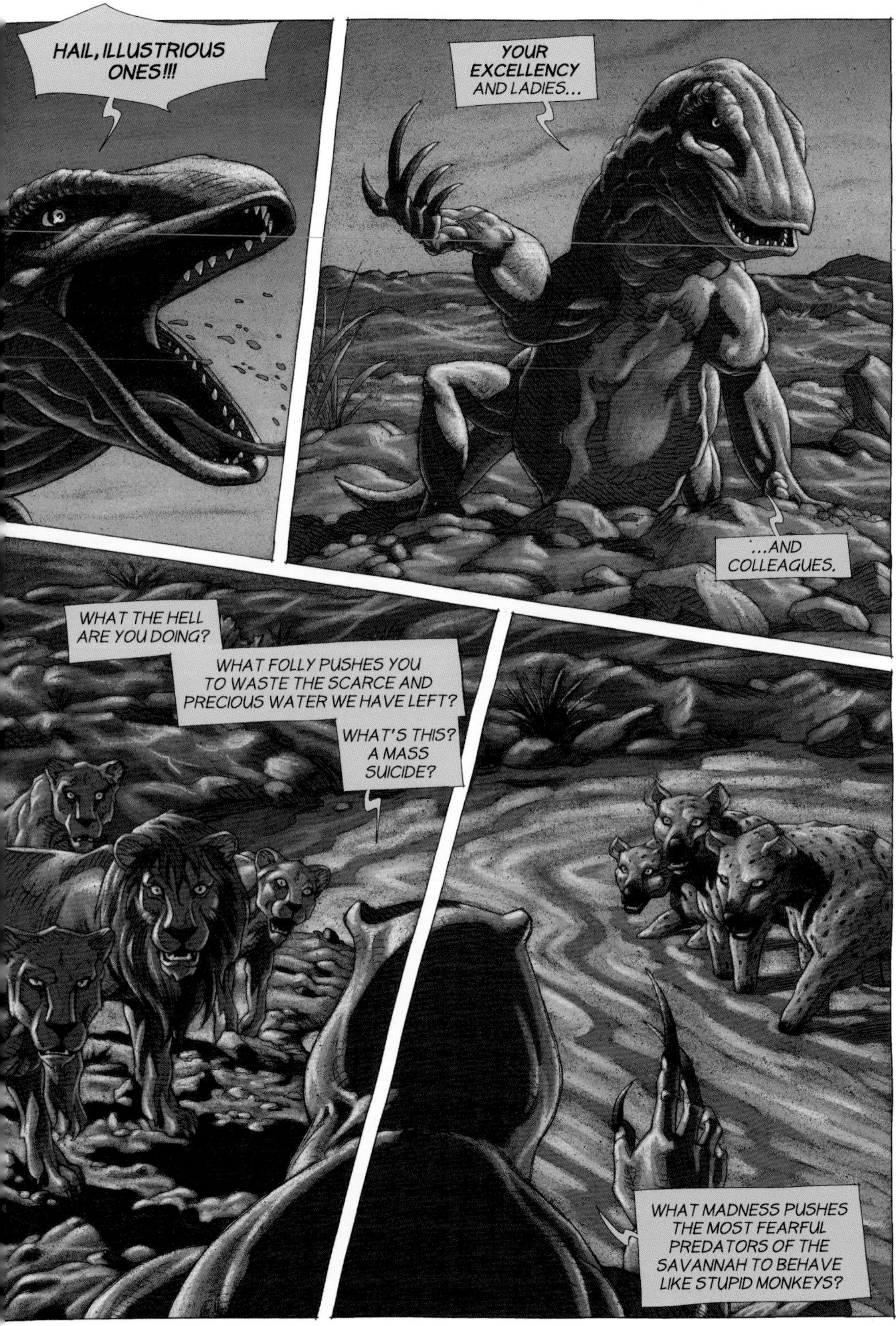
HAIL, ILLUSTRIOUS ONES!!!
YOUR EXCELLENCY AND LADIES...
...AND COLLEAGUES.
WHAT THE HELL ARE YOU DOING?
WHAT FOLLY PUSHES YOU TO WASTE THE SCARCE AND PRECIOUS WATER WE HAVE LEFT?
WHAT'S THIS? A MASS SUICIDE?
WHAT MADNESS PUSHES THE MOST FEARFUL PREDATORS OF THE SAVANNAH TO BEHAVE LIKE STUPID MONKEYS?

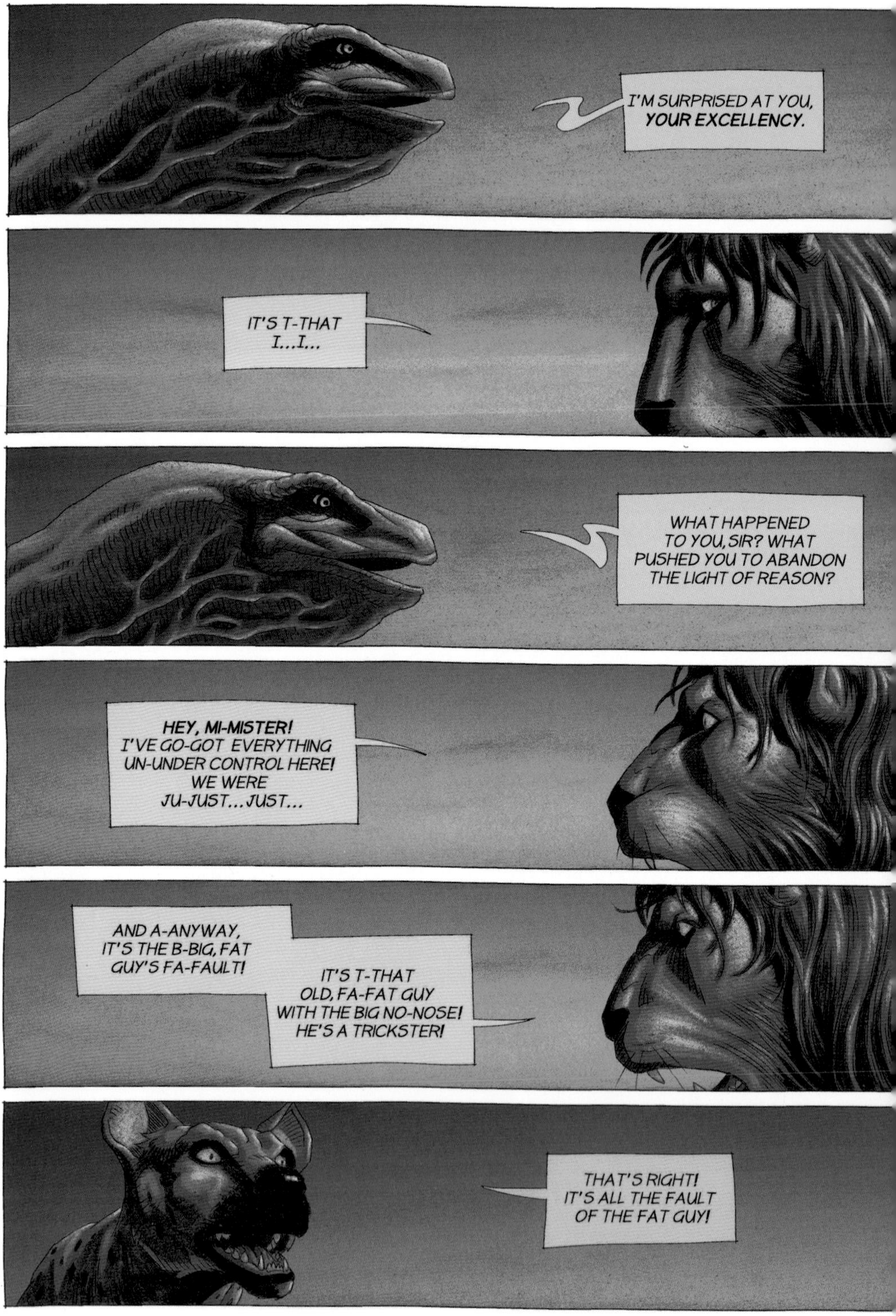
I'M SURPRISED AT YOU, YOUR EXCELLENCY.
IT'S T-THAT I...I...
WHAT HAPPENED TO YOU, SIR? WHAT PUSHED YOU TO ABANDON THE LIGHT OF REASON?
HEY, MI-MISTER! I'VE GO-GOT EVERYTHING UN-UNDER CONTROL HERE! WE WERE JU-JUST... JUST...
AND A-ANYWAY, IT'S THE B-BIG, FAT GUY'S FA-FAULT!
IT'S T-THAT OLD, FA-FAT GUY WITH THE BIG NO-NOSE! HE'S A TRICKSTER!
THAT'S RIGHT! IT'S ALL THE FAULT OF THE FAT GUY!

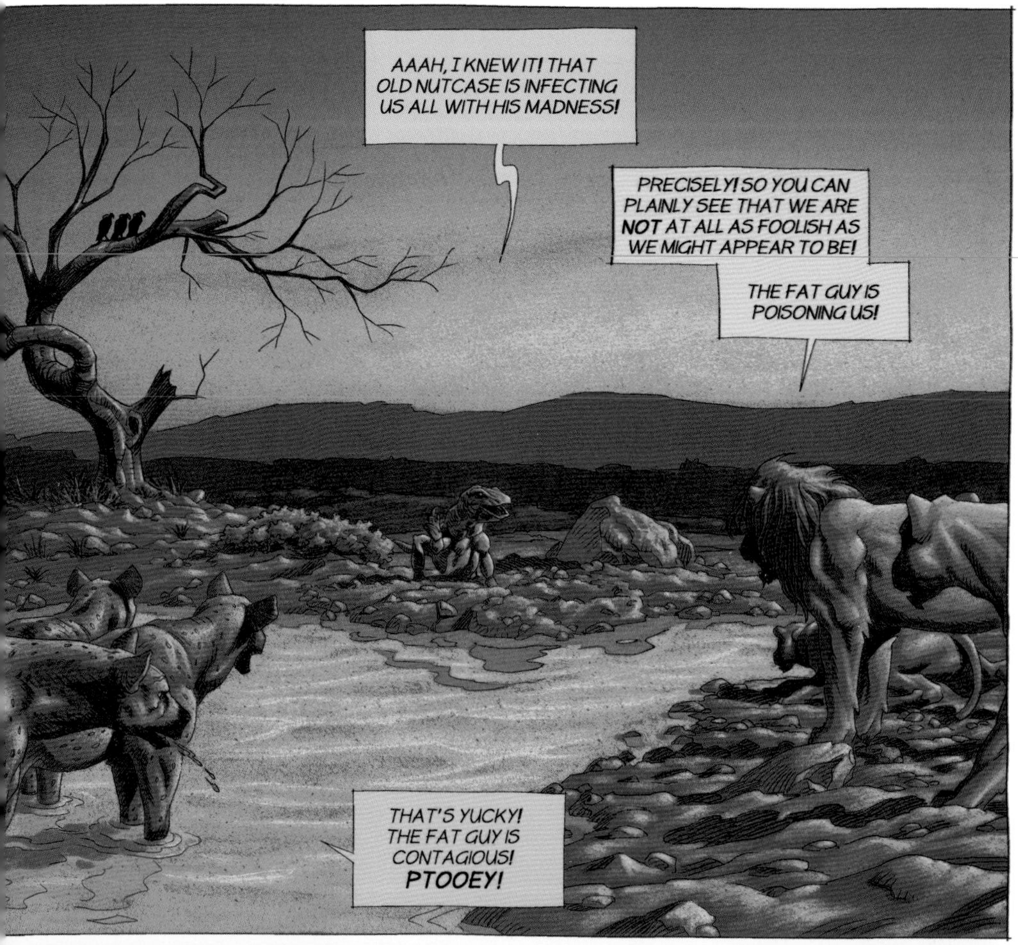
AAAH, I KNEW IT! THAT OLD NUTCASE IS INFECTING US ALL WITH HIS MADNESS!
PRECISELY! SO YOU CAN PLAINLY SEE THAT WE ARE **NOT** AT ALL AS FOOLISH AS WE MIGHT APPEAR TO BE!
THE FAT GUY IS POISONING US!
THAT'S YUCKY! THE FAT GUY IS CONTAGIOUS! **PTOOEY!**

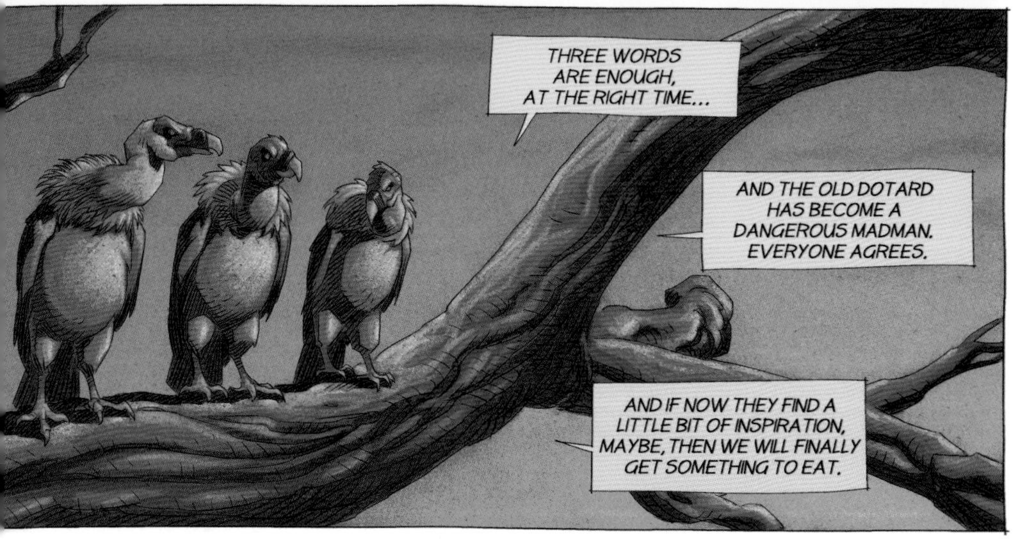
THREE WORDS ARE ENOUGH, AT THE RIGHT TIME...
AND THE OLD DOTARD HAS BECOME A DANGEROUS MADMAN. EVERYONE AGREES.
AND IF NOW THEY FIND A LITTLE BIT OF INSPIRATION, MAYBE, THEN WE WILL FINALLY GET SOMETHING TO EAT.

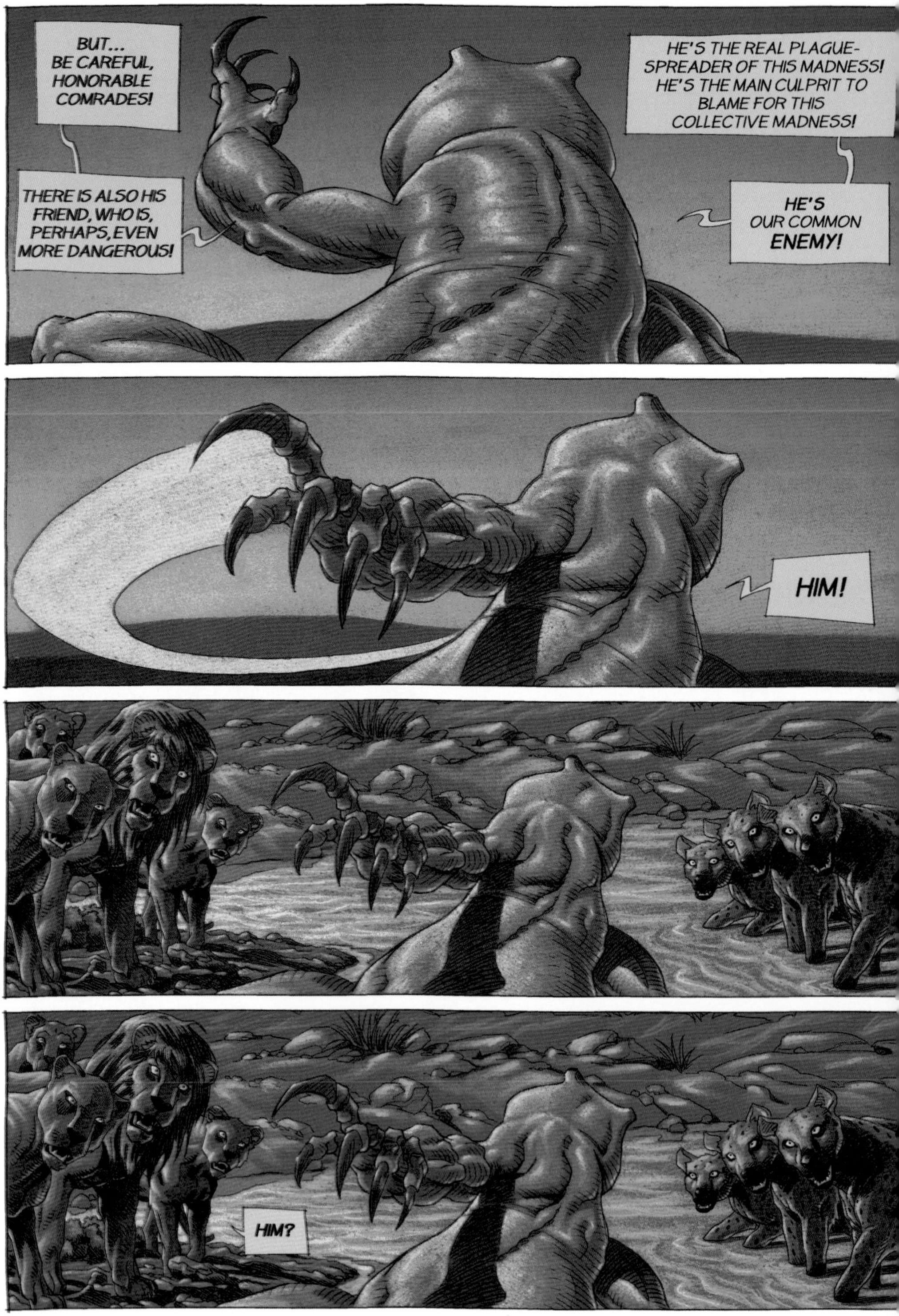
BUT... BE CAREFUL, HONORABLE COMRADES!
THERE IS ALSO HIS FRIEND, WHO IS, PERHAPS, EVEN MORE DANGEROUS!
HE'S THE REAL PLAGUE-SPREADER OF THIS MADNESS! HE'S THE MAIN CULPRIT TO BLAME FOR THIS COLLECTIVE MADNESS!
HE'S OUR COMMON ENEMY!
HIM!
HIM?

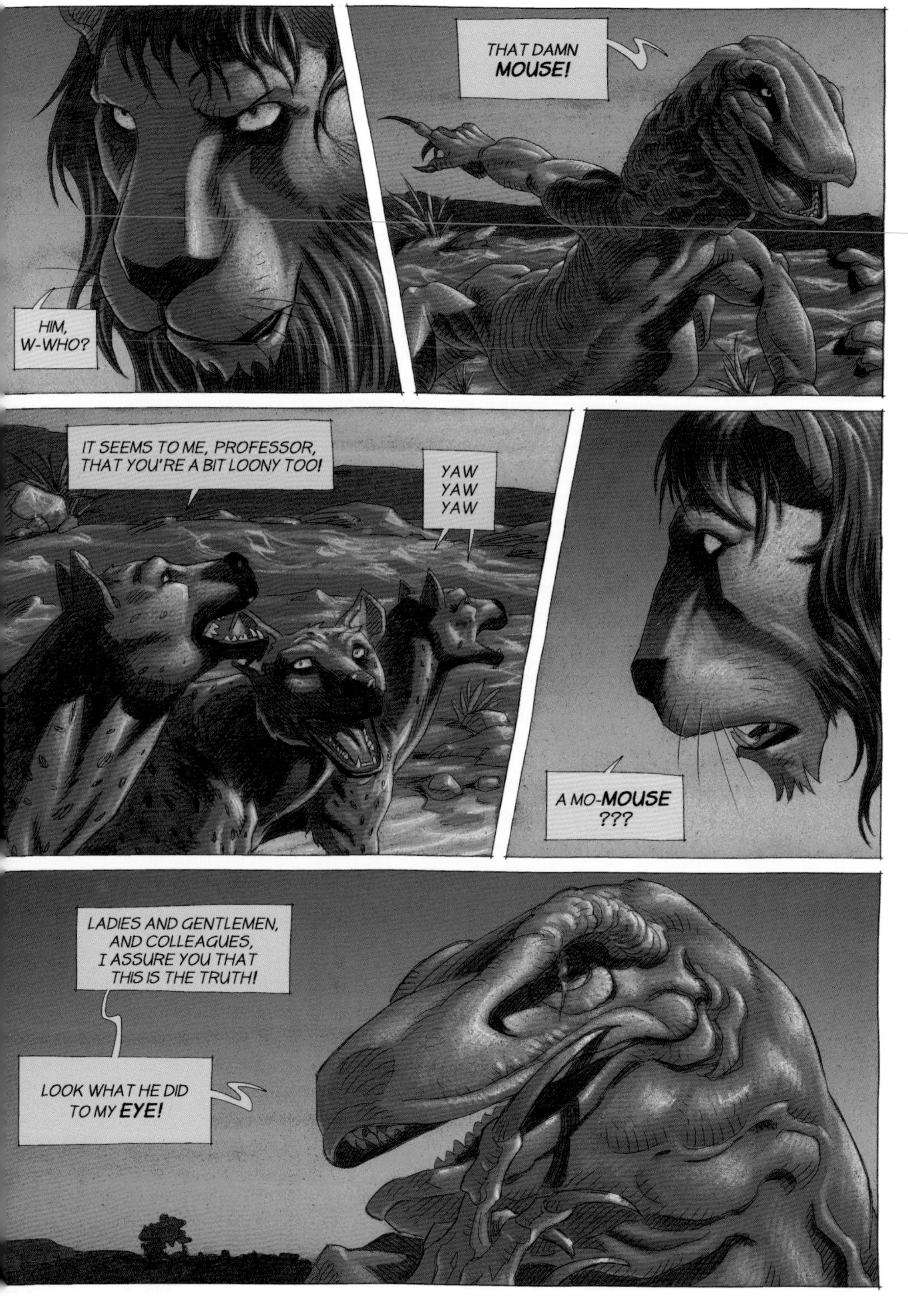
HIM, W-WHO?
THAT DAMN MOUSE!
IT SEEMS TO ME, PROFESSOR, THAT YOU'RE A BIT LOONY TOO!
YAW YAW YAW
A MO-MOUSE ???
LADIES AND GENTLEMEN, AND COLLEAGUES, I ASSURE YOU THAT THIS IS THE TRUTH!
LOOK WHAT HE DID TO MY EYE!

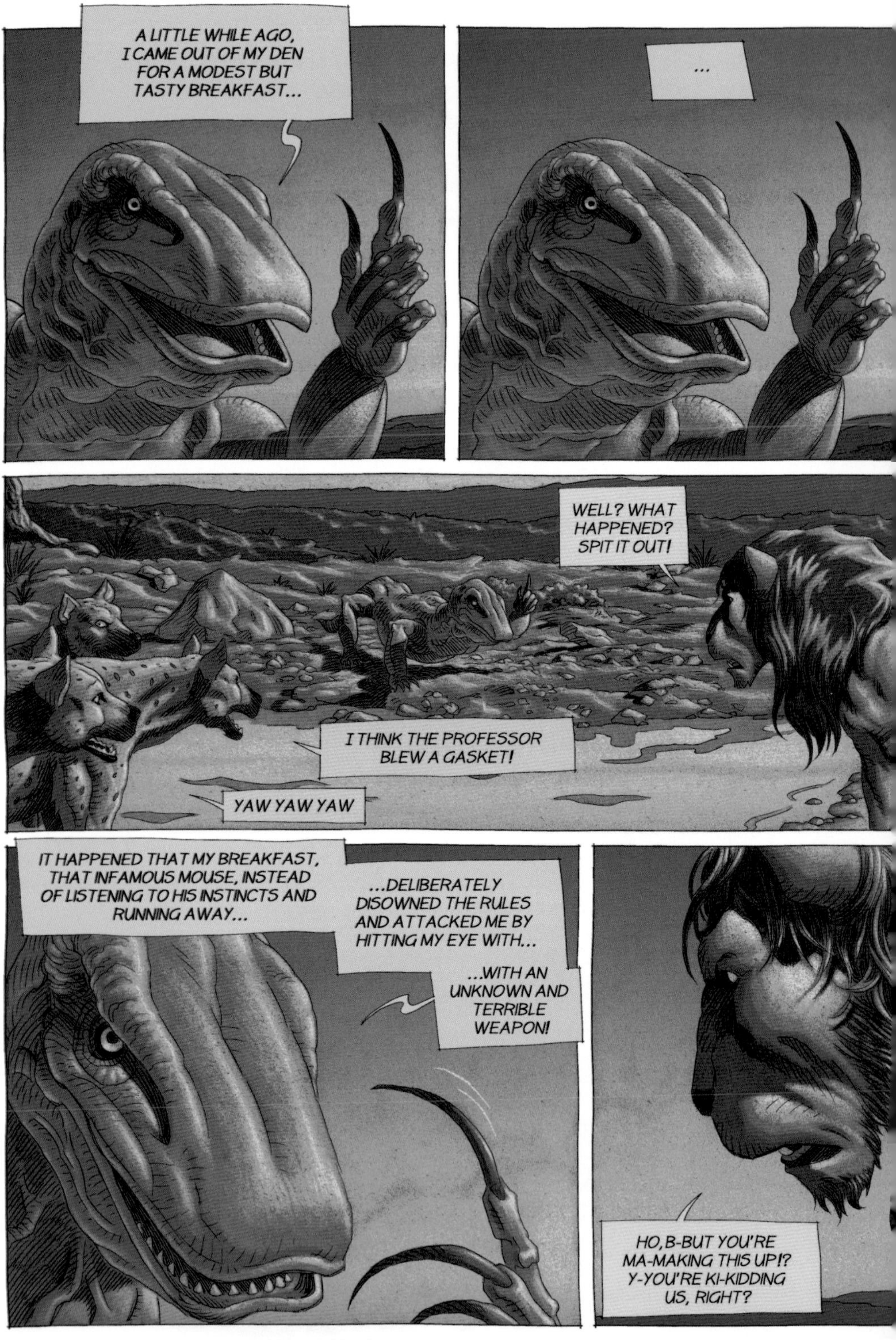
A LITTLE WHILE AGO, I CAME OUT OF MY DEN FOR A MODEST BUT TASTY BREAKFAST...
...
WELL? WHAT HAPPENED? SPIT IT OUT!
I THINK THE PROFESSOR BLEW A GASKET!
YAW YAW YAW
IT HAPPENED THAT MY BREAKFAST, THAT INFAMOUS MOUSE, INSTEAD OF LISTENING TO HIS INSTINCTS AND RUNNING AWAY...
...DELIBERATELY DISOWNED THE RULES AND ATTACKED ME BY HITTING MY EYE WITH...
...WITH AN UNKNOWN AND TERRIBLE WEAPON!
HO, B-BUT YOU'RE MA-MAKING THIS UP!? Y-YOU'RE KI-KIDDING US, RIGHT?

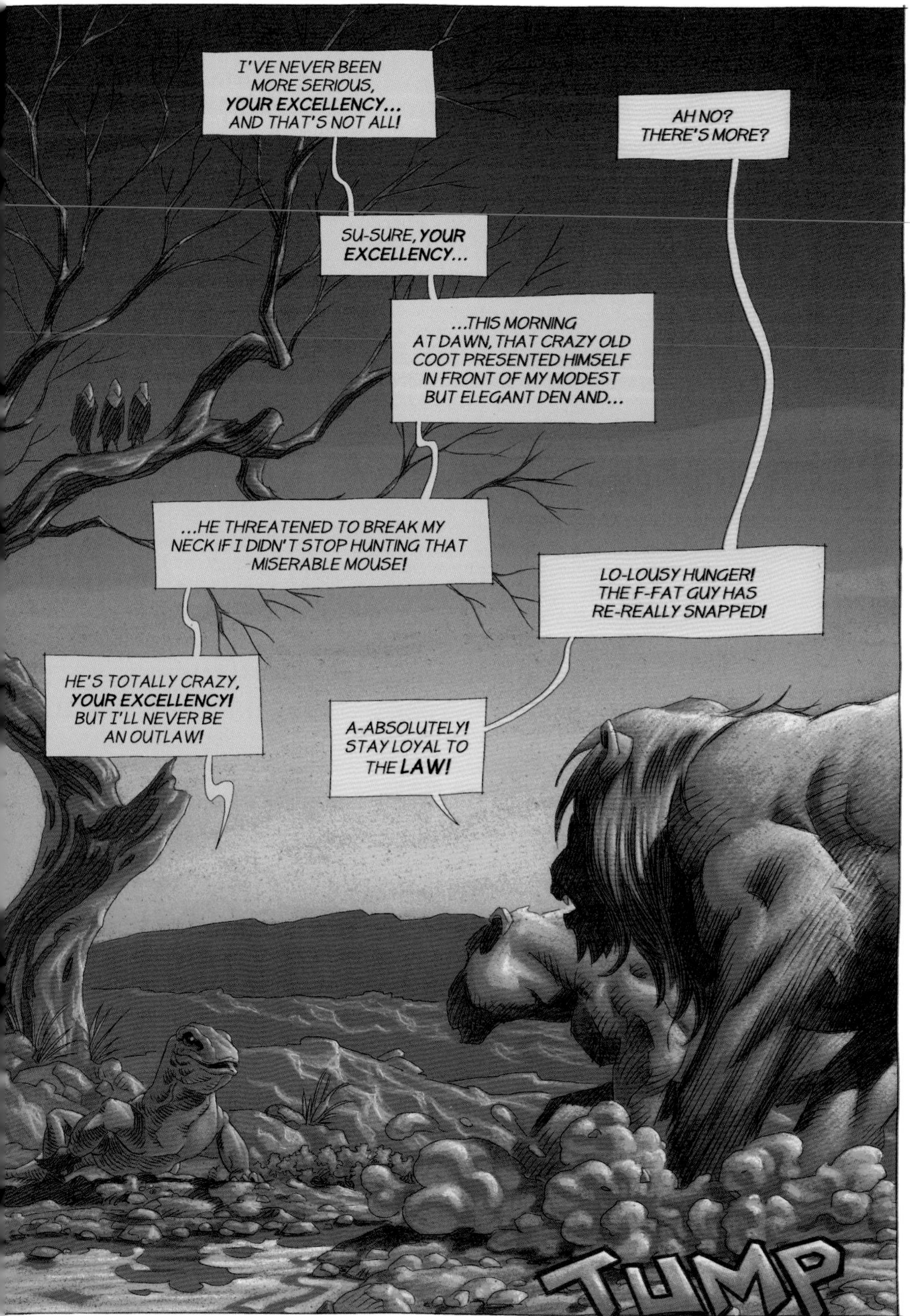
I'VE NEVER BEEN MORE SERIOUS, YOUR EXCELLENCY... AND THAT'S NOT ALL!
AH NO? THERE'S MORE?
SU-SURE, YOUR EXCELLENCY...
...THIS MORNING AT DAWN, THAT CRAZY OLD COOT PRESENTED HIMSELF IN FRONT OF MY MODEST BUT ELEGANT DEN AND...
...HE THREATENED TO BREAK MY NECK IF I DIDN'T STOP HUNTING THAT MISERABLE MOUSE!
LO-LOUSY HUNGER! THE F-FAT GUY HAS RE-REALLY SNAPPED!
HE'S TOTALLY CRAZY, YOUR EXCELLENCY! BUT I'LL NEVER BE AN OUTLAW!
A-ABSOLUTELY! STAY LOYAL TO THE LAW!
TUMP

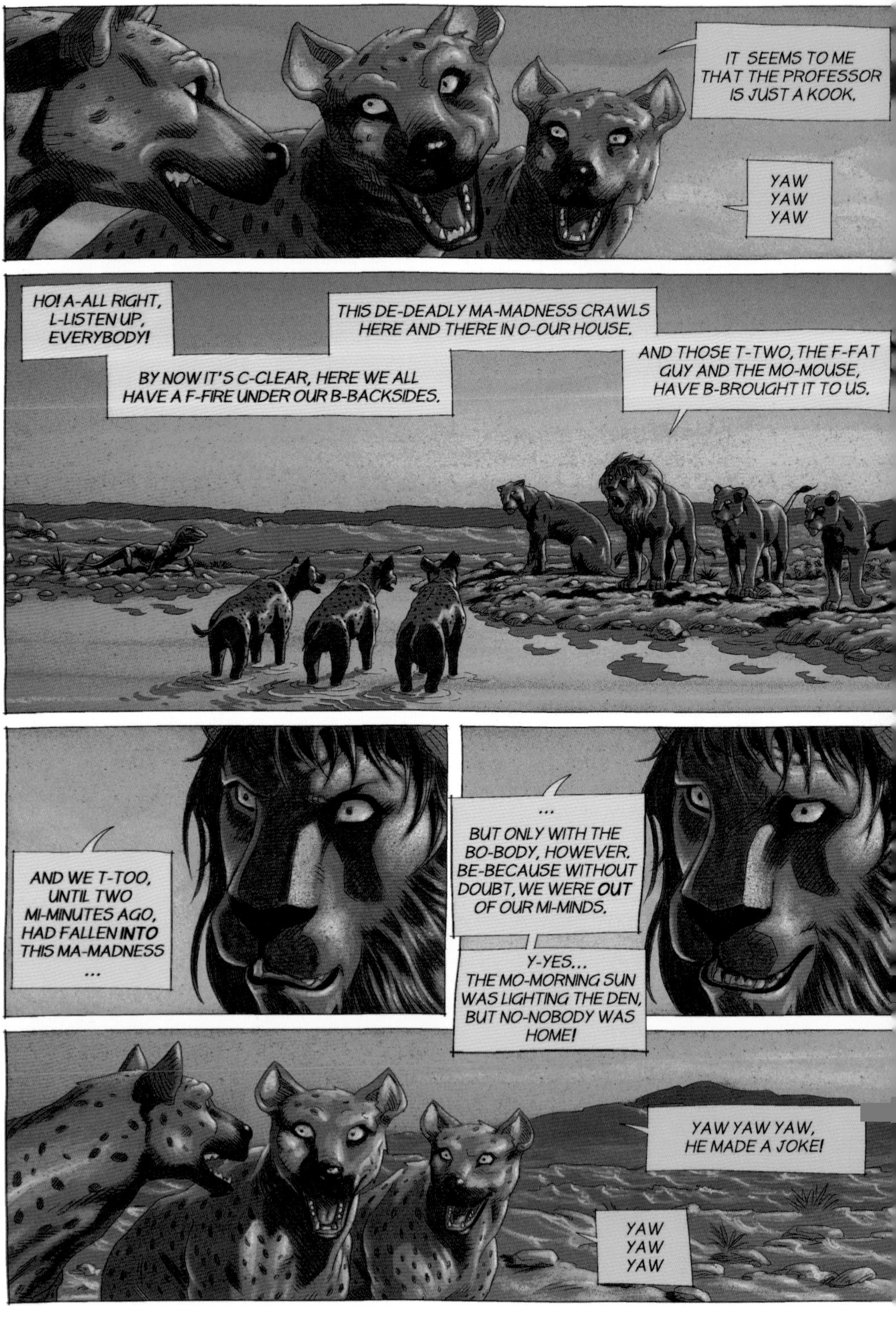
IT SEEMS TO ME THAT THE PROFESSOR IS JUST A KOOK.
YAW YAW YAW
HO! A-ALL RIGHT, L-LISTEN UP, EVERYBODY!
BY NOW IT'S C-CLEAR, HERE WE ALL HAVE A F-FIRE UNDER OUR B-BACKSIDES.
THIS DE-DEADLY MA-MADNESS CRAWLS HERE AND THERE IN O-OUR HOUSE.
AND THOSE T-TWO, THE F-FAT GUY AND THE MO-MOUSE, HAVE B-BROUGHT IT TO US.
AND WE T-TOO, UNTIL TWO MI-MINUTES AGO, HAD FALLEN **INTO** THIS MA-MADNESS ...
... BUT ONLY WITH THE BO-BODY, HOWEVER. BE-BECAUSE WITHOUT DOUBT, WE WERE **OUT** OF OUR MI-MINDS.
Y-YES... THE MO-MORNING SUN WAS LIGHTING THE DEN, BUT NO-NOBODY WAS HOME!
YAW YAW YAW, HE MADE A JOKE!
YAW YAW YAW

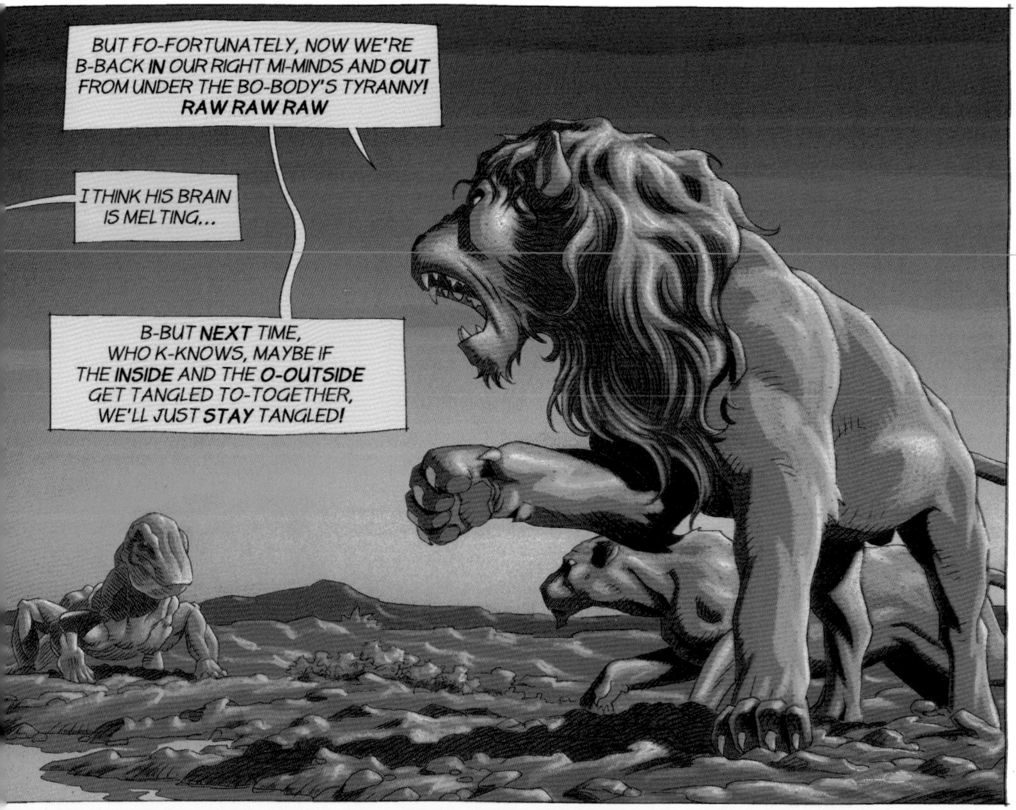
BUT FO-FORTUNATELY, NOW WE'RE B-BACK IN OUR RIGHT MI-MINDS AND OUT FROM UNDER THE BO-BODY'S TYRANNY! RAW RAW RAW
I THINK HIS BRAIN IS MELTING...
B-BUT NEXT TIME, WHO K-KNOWS, MAYBE IF THE INSIDE AND THE O-OUTSIDE GET TANGLED TO-TOGETHER, WE'LL JUST STAY TANGLED!

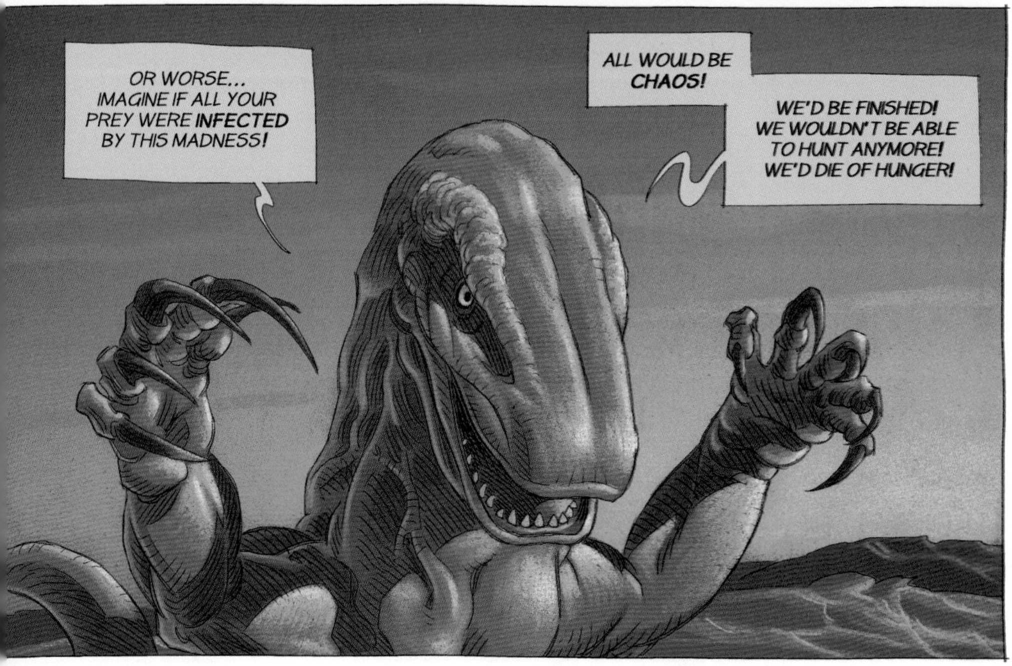
OR WORSE... IMAGINE IF ALL YOUR PREY WERE INFECTED BY THIS MADNESS!
ALL WOULD BE CHAOS!
WE'D BE FINISHED! WE WOULDN'T BE ABLE TO HUNT ANYMORE! WE'D DIE OF HUNGER!

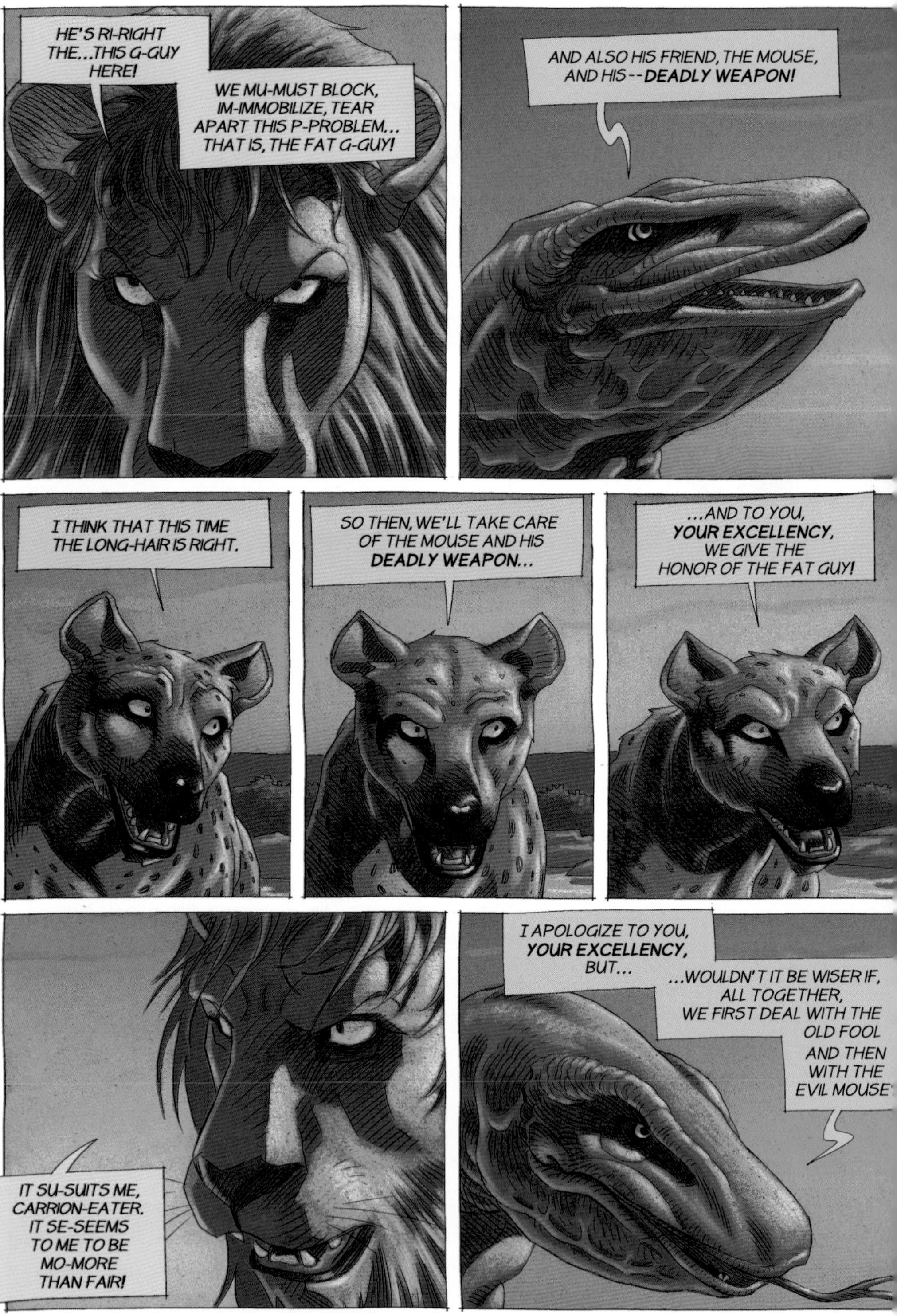
HE'S RI-RIGHT THE...THIS G-GUY HERE!
WE MU-MUST BLOCK, IM-IMMOBILIZE, TEAR APART THIS P-PROBLEM... THAT IS, THE FAT G-GUY!
AND ALSO HIS FRIEND, THE MOUSE, AND HIS--DEADLY WEAPON!
I THINK THAT THIS TIME THE LONG-HAIR IS RIGHT.
SO THEN, WE'LL TAKE CARE OF THE MOUSE AND HIS DEADLY WEAPON...
...AND TO YOU, YOUR EXCELLENCY, WE GIVE THE HONOR OF THE FAT GUY!
IT SU-SUITS ME, CARRION-EATER. IT SE-SEEMS TO ME TO BE MO-MORE THAN FAIR!
I APOLOGIZE TO YOU, YOUR EXCELLENCY, BUT...
...WOULDN'T IT BE WISER IF, ALL TOGETHER, WE FIRST DEAL WITH THE OLD FOOL AND THEN WITH THE EVIL MOUSE?

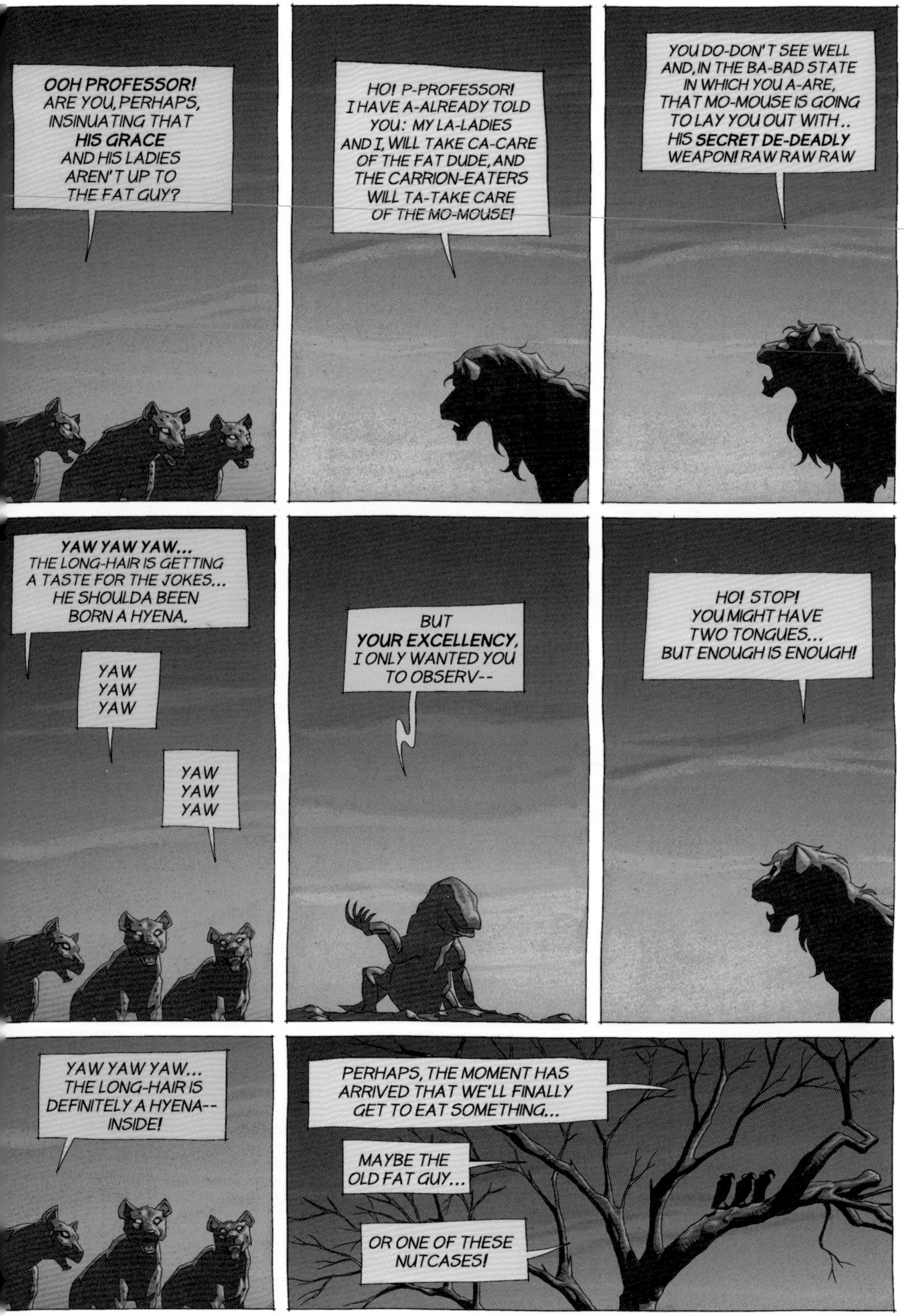
OOH PROFESSOR! ARE YOU, PERHAPS, INSINUATING THAT HIS GRACE AND HIS LADIES AREN'T UP TO THE FAT GUY?
HO! P-PROFESSOR! I HAVE A-ALREADY TOLD YOU: MY LA-LADIES AND I, WILL TAKE CA-CARE OF THE FAT DUDE, AND THE CARRION-EATERS WILL TA-TAKE CARE OF THE MO-MOUSE!
YOU DO-DON'T SEE WELL AND, IN THE BA-BAD STATE IN WHICH YOU A-ARE, THAT MO-MOUSE IS GOING TO LAY YOU OUT WITH.. HIS SECRET DE-DEADLY WEAPON! RAW RAW RAW
YAW YAW YAW... THE LONG-HAIR IS GETTING A TASTE FOR THE JOKES... HE SHOULDA BEEN BORN A HYENA.
YAW YAW YAW
YAW YAW YAW
BUT YOUR EXCELLENCY, I ONLY WANTED YOU TO OBSERV--
HO! STOP! YOU MIGHT HAVE TWO TONGUES... BUT ENOUGH IS ENOUGH!
YAW YAW YAW... THE LONG-HAIR IS DEFINITELY A HYENA-- INSIDE!
PERHAPS, THE MOMENT HAS ARRIVED THAT WE'LL FINALLY GET TO EAT SOMETHING...
MAYBE THE OLD FAT GUY...
OR ONE OF THESE NUTCASES!

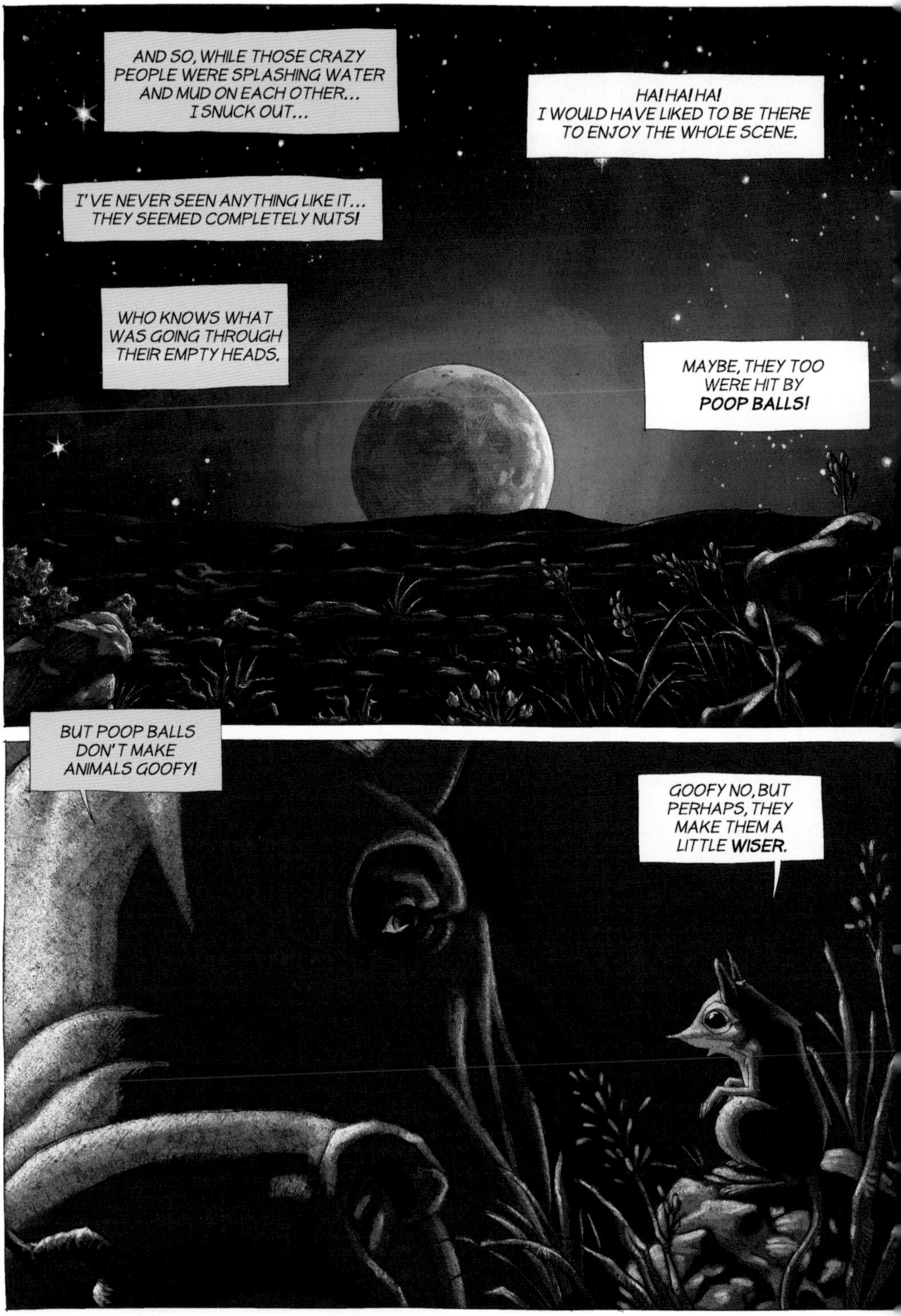
AND SO, WHILE THOSE CRAZY PEOPLE WERE SPLASHING WATER AND MUD ON EACH OTHER... I SNUCK OUT...
HA! HA! HA! I WOULD HAVE LIKED TO BE THERE TO ENJOY THE WHOLE SCENE.
I'VE NEVER SEEN ANYTHING LIKE IT... THEY SEEMED COMPLETELY NUTS!
WHO KNOWS WHAT WAS GOING THROUGH THEIR EMPTY HEADS.
MAYBE, THEY TOO WERE HIT BY **POOP BALLS!**
BUT POOP BALLS DON'T MAKE ANIMALS GOOFY!
GOOFY NO, BUT PERHAPS, THEY MAKE THEM A LITTLE **WISER.**

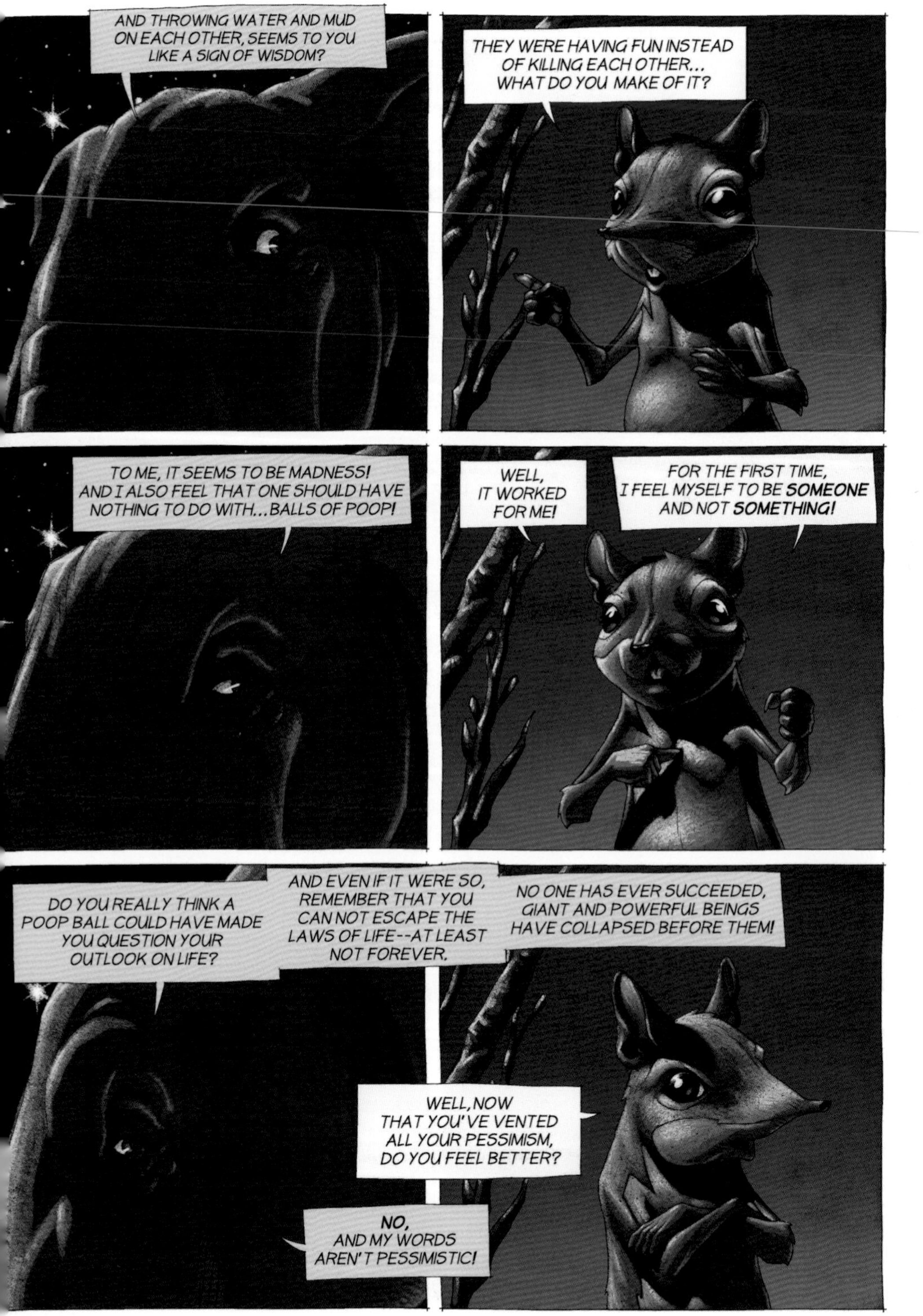
AND THROWING WATER AND MUD ON EACH OTHER, SEEMS TO YOU LIKE A SIGN OF WISDOM?
THEY WERE HAVING FUN INSTEAD OF KILLING EACH OTHER... WHAT DO YOU MAKE OF IT?
TO ME, IT SEEMS TO BE MADNESS! AND I ALSO FEEL THAT ONE SHOULD HAVE NOTHING TO DO WITH...BALLS OF POOP!
WELL, IT WORKED FOR ME!
FOR THE FIRST TIME, I FEEL MYSELF TO BE **SOMEONE** AND NOT **SOMETHING!**
DO YOU REALLY THINK A POOP BALL COULD HAVE MADE YOU QUESTION YOUR OUTLOOK ON LIFE?
AND EVEN IF IT WERE SO, REMEMBER THAT YOU CAN NOT ESCAPE THE LAWS OF LIFE--AT LEAST NOT FOREVER.
NO ONE HAS EVER SUCCEEDED, GIANT AND POWERFUL BEINGS HAVE COLLAPSED BEFORE THEM!
WELL, NOW THAT YOU'VE VENTED ALL YOUR PESSIMISM, DO YOU FEEL BETTER?
**NO,** AND MY WORDS AREN'T PESSIMISTIC!

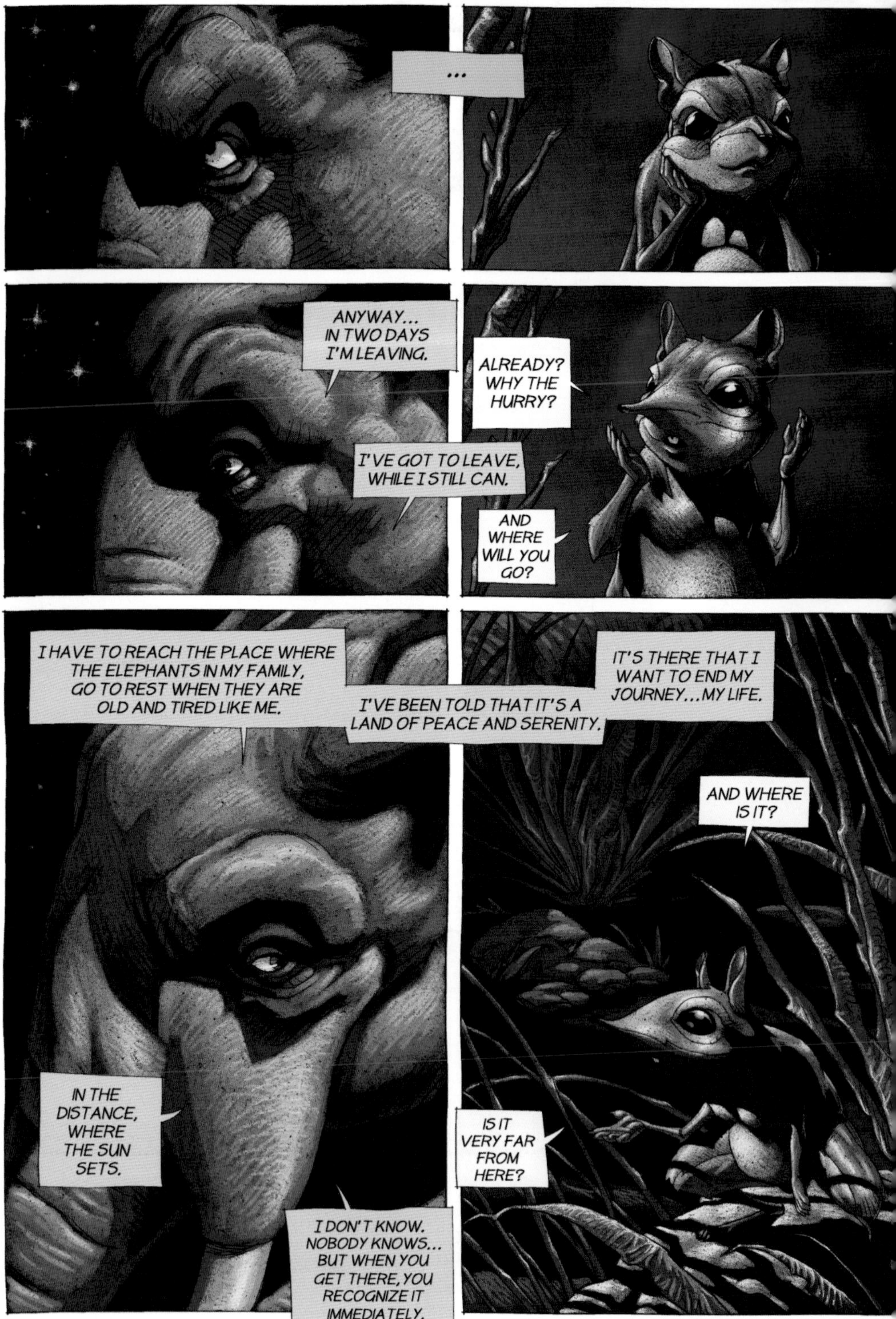
...
ANYWAY... IN TWO DAYS I'M LEAVING.
ALREADY? WHY THE HURRY?
I'VE GOT TO LEAVE, WHILE I STILL CAN.
AND WHERE WILL YOU GO?
I HAVE TO REACH THE PLACE WHERE THE ELEPHANTS IN MY FAMILY, GO TO REST WHEN THEY ARE OLD AND TIRED LIKE ME.
I'VE BEEN TOLD THAT IT'S A LAND OF PEACE AND SERENITY.
IT'S THERE THAT I WANT TO END MY JOURNEY... MY LIFE.
AND WHERE IS IT?
IN THE DISTANCE, WHERE THE SUN SETS.
IS IT VERY FAR FROM HERE?
I DON'T KNOW. NOBODY KNOWS... BUT WHEN YOU GET THERE, YOU RECOGNIZE IT IMMEDIATELY.

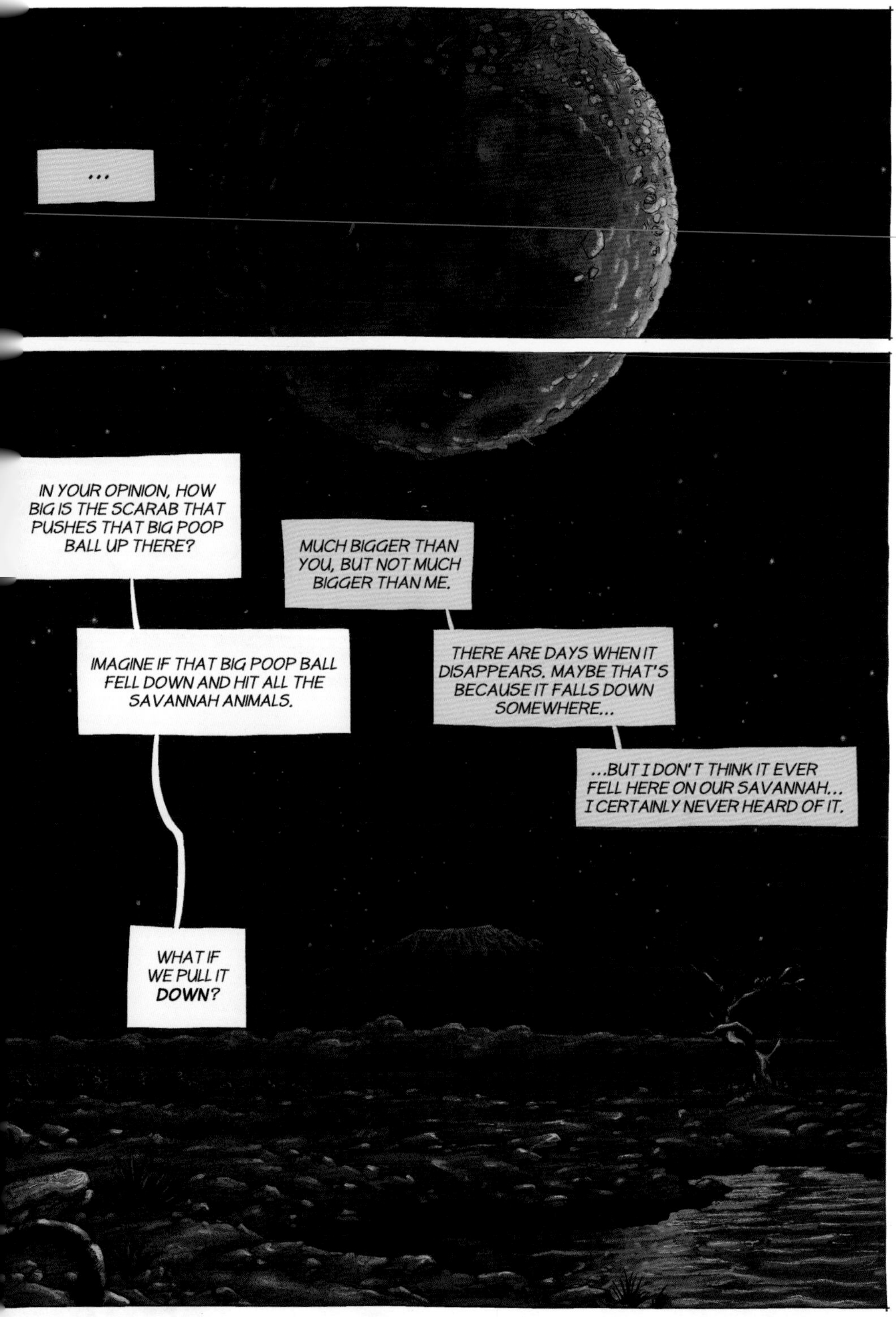
...
IN YOUR OPINION, HOW BIG IS THE SCARAB THAT PUSHES THAT BIG POOP BALL UP THERE?
IMAGINE IF THAT BIG POOP BALL FELL DOWN AND HIT ALL THE SAVANNAH ANIMALS.
MUCH BIGGER THAN YOU, BUT NOT MUCH BIGGER THAN ME.
THERE ARE DAYS WHEN IT DISAPPEARS. MAYBE THAT'S BECAUSE IT FALLS DOWN SOMEWHERE...
...BUT I DON'T THINK IT EVER FELL HERE ON OUR SAVANNAH... I CERTAINLY NEVER HEARD OF IT.
WHAT IF WE PULL IT DOWN?

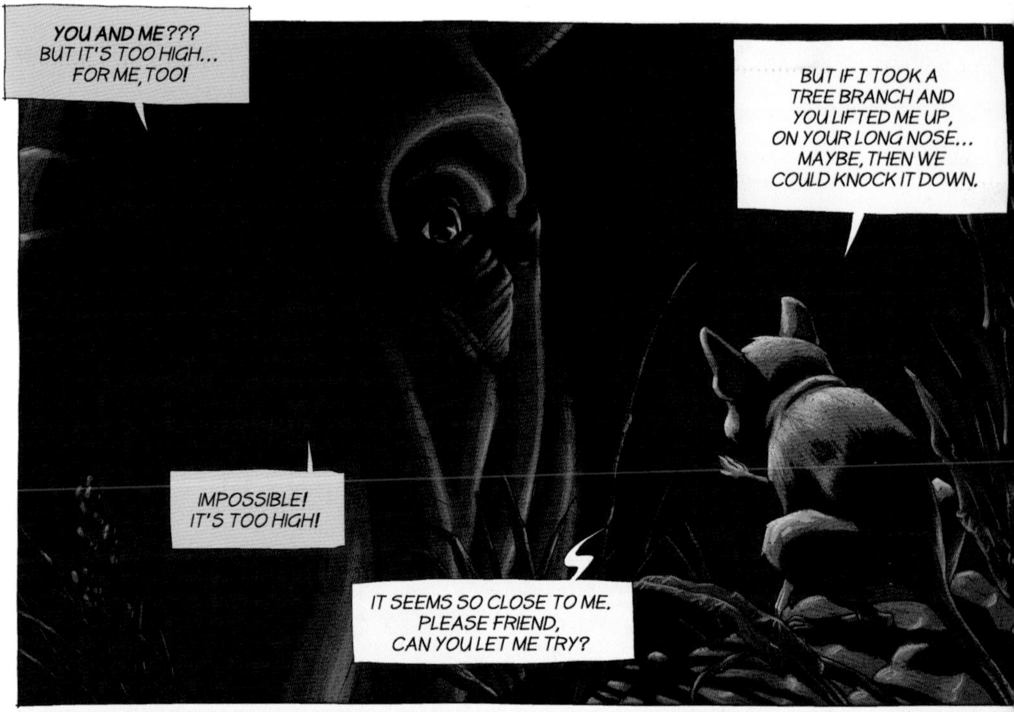
YOU AND ME???
BUT IT'S TOO HIGH...
FOR ME, TOO!
BUT IF I TOOK A TREE BRANCH AND YOU LIFTED ME UP, ON YOUR LONG NOSE... MAYBE, THEN WE COULD KNOCK IT DOWN.
IMPOSSIBLE! IT'S TOO HIGH!
IT SEEMS SO CLOSE TO ME. PLEASE FRIEND, CAN YOU LET ME TRY?

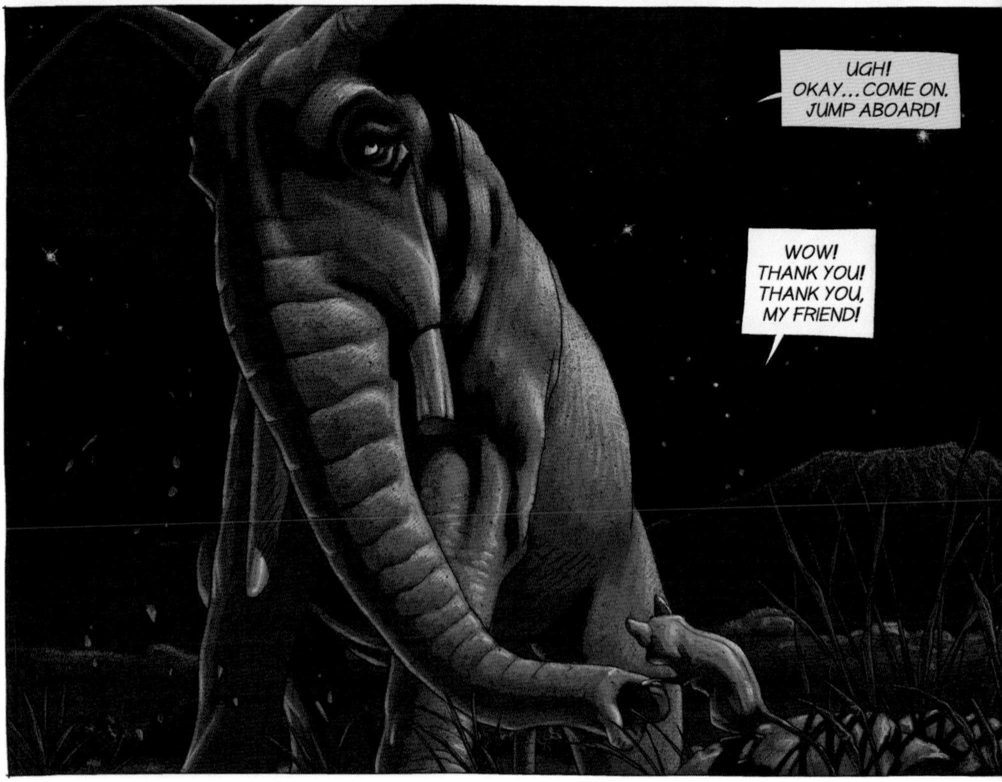
UGH! OKAY... COME ON. JUMP ABOARD!
WOW! THANK YOU! THANK YOU, MY FRIEND!

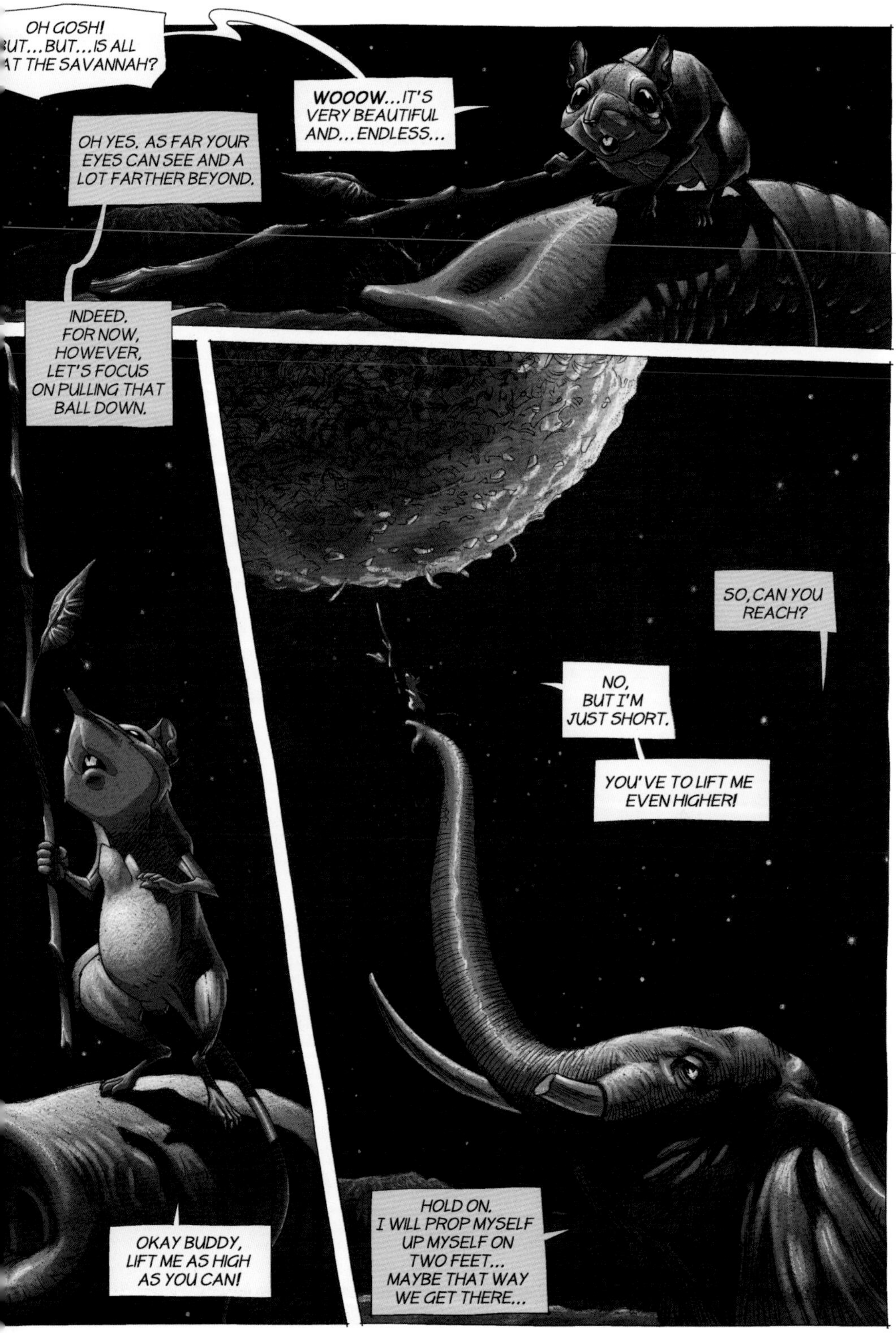
OH GOSH! BUT... BUT... IS ALL AT THE SAVANNAH?
WOOOW... IT'S VERY BEAUTIFUL AND... ENDLESS...
OH YES. AS FAR YOUR EYES CAN SEE AND A LOT FARTHER BEYOND.
INDEED. FOR NOW, HOWEVER, LET'S FOCUS ON PULLING THAT BALL DOWN.
SO, CAN YOU REACH?
NO, BUT I'M JUST SHORT.
YOU'VE TO LIFT ME EVEN HIGHER!
OKAY BUDDY, LIFT ME AS HIGH AS YOU CAN!
HOLD ON. I WILL PROP MYSELF UP MYSELF ON TWO FEET... MAYBE THAT WAY WE GET THERE...

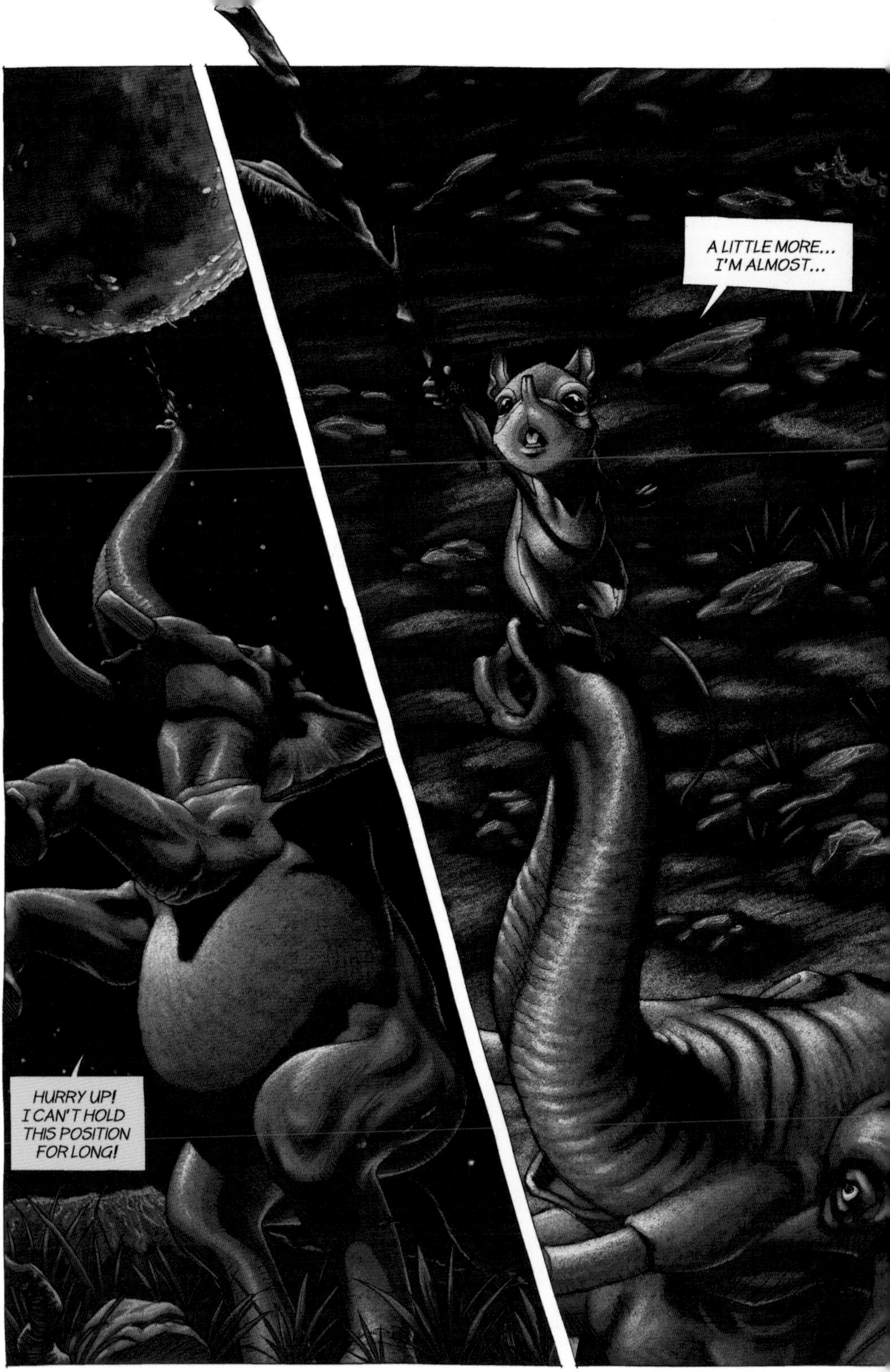
HURRY UP! I CAN'T HOLD THIS POSITION FOR LONG!
A LITTLE MORE... I'M ALMOST...

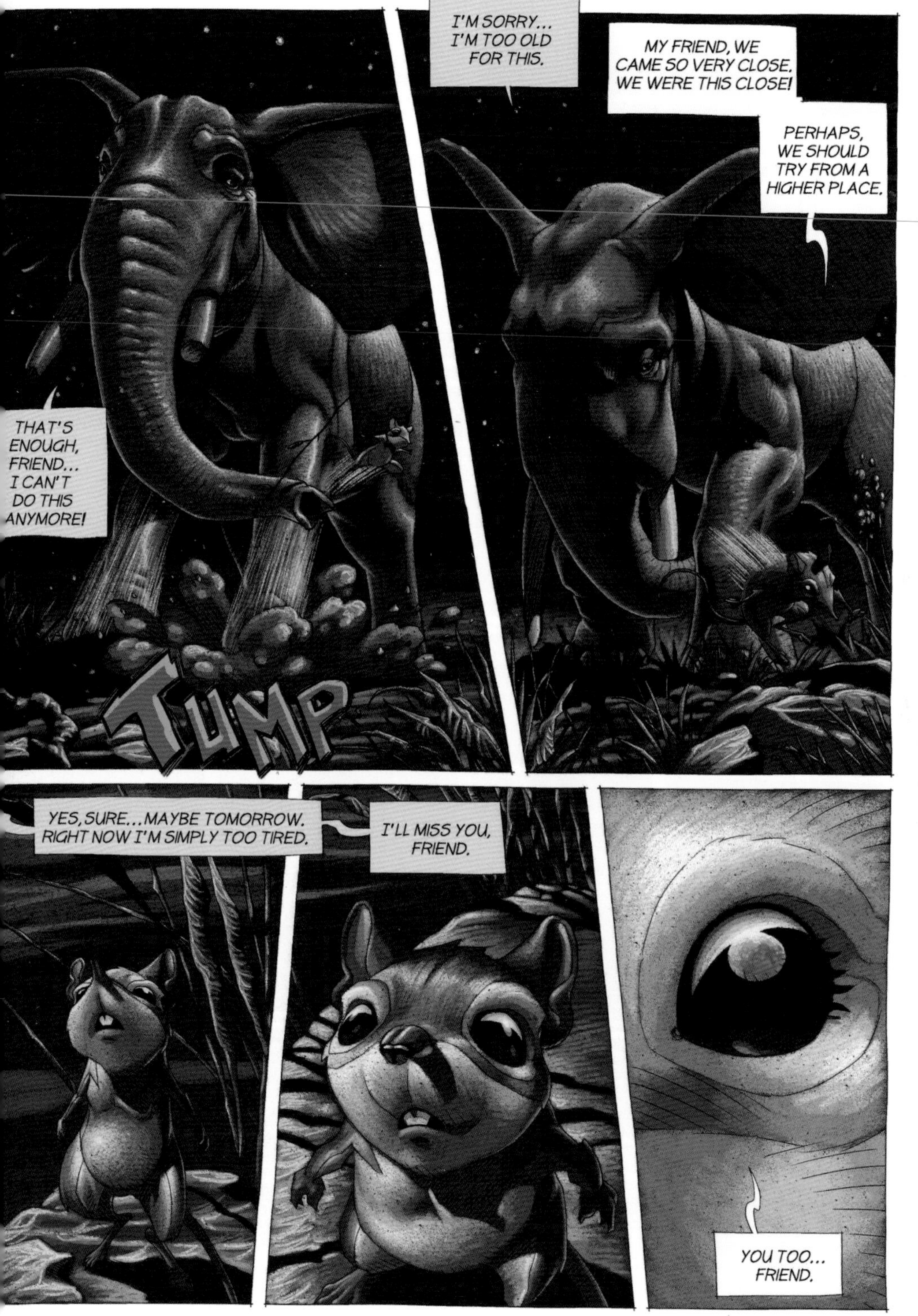
I'M SORRY... I'M TOO OLD FOR THIS.
MY FRIEND, WE CAME SO VERY CLOSE. WE WERE THIS CLOSE!
THAT'S ENOUGH, FRIEND... I CAN'T DO THIS ANYMORE!
TUMP
PERHAPS, WE SHOULD TRY FROM A HIGHER PLACE.
YES, SURE... MAYBE TOMORROW. RIGHT NOW I'M SIMPLY TOO TIRED.
I'LL MISS YOU, FRIEND.
YOU TOO... FRIEND.

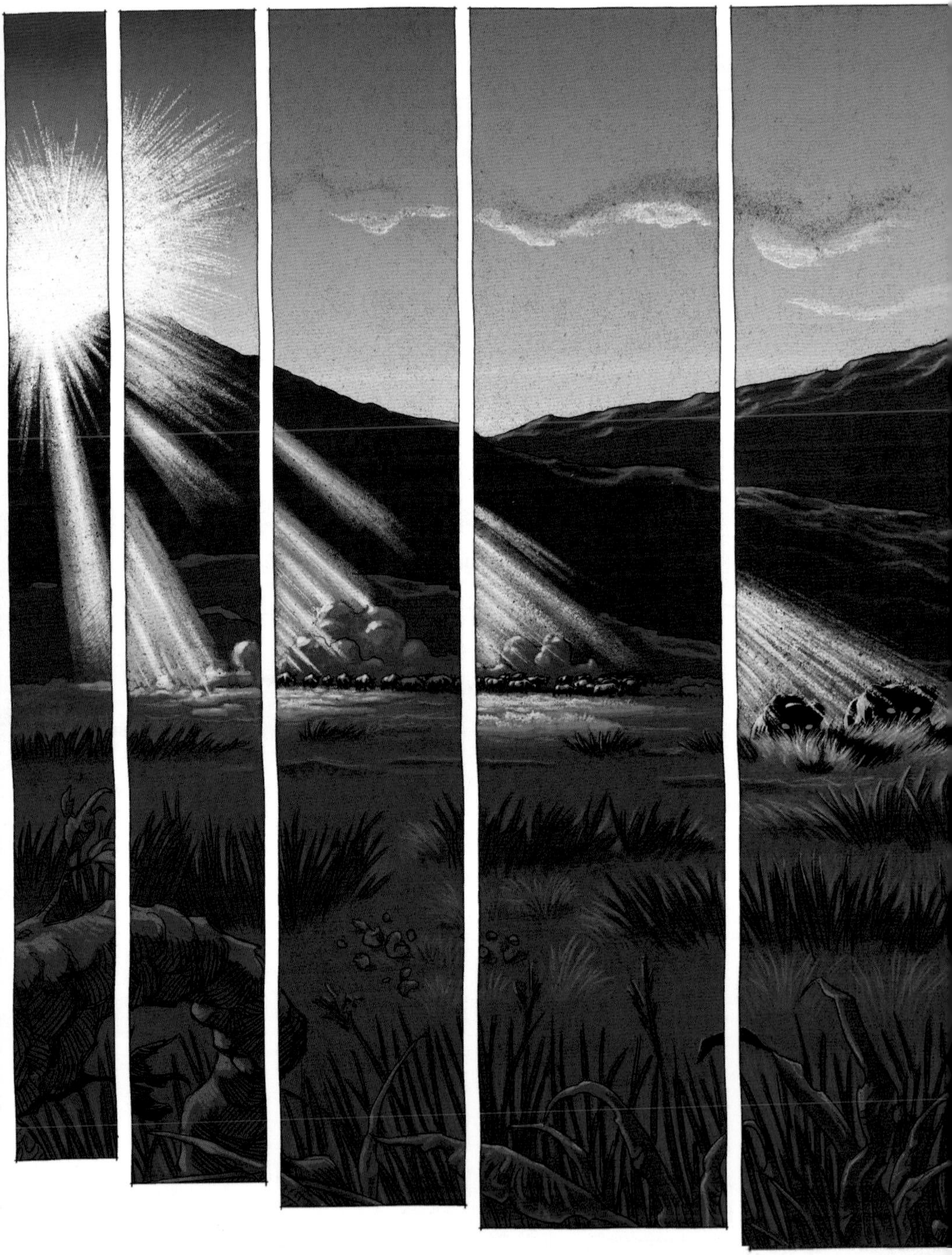

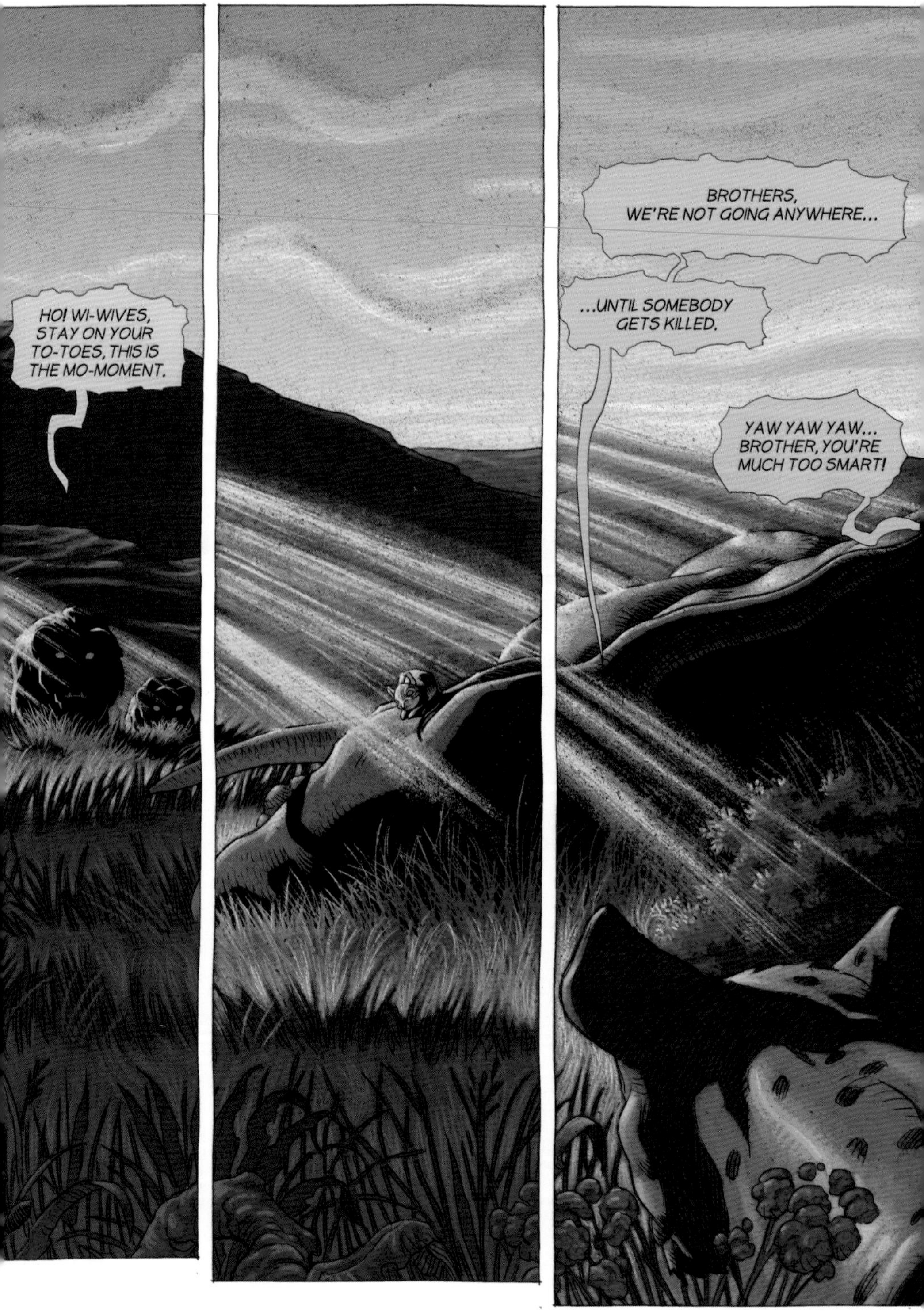
HO! WI-WIVES, STAY ON YOUR TO-TOES, THIS IS THE MO-MOMENT.
BROTHERS, WE'RE NOT GOING ANYWHERE...
...UNTIL SOMEBODY GETS KILLED.
YAW YAW YAW... BROTHER, YOU'RE MUCH TOO SMART!

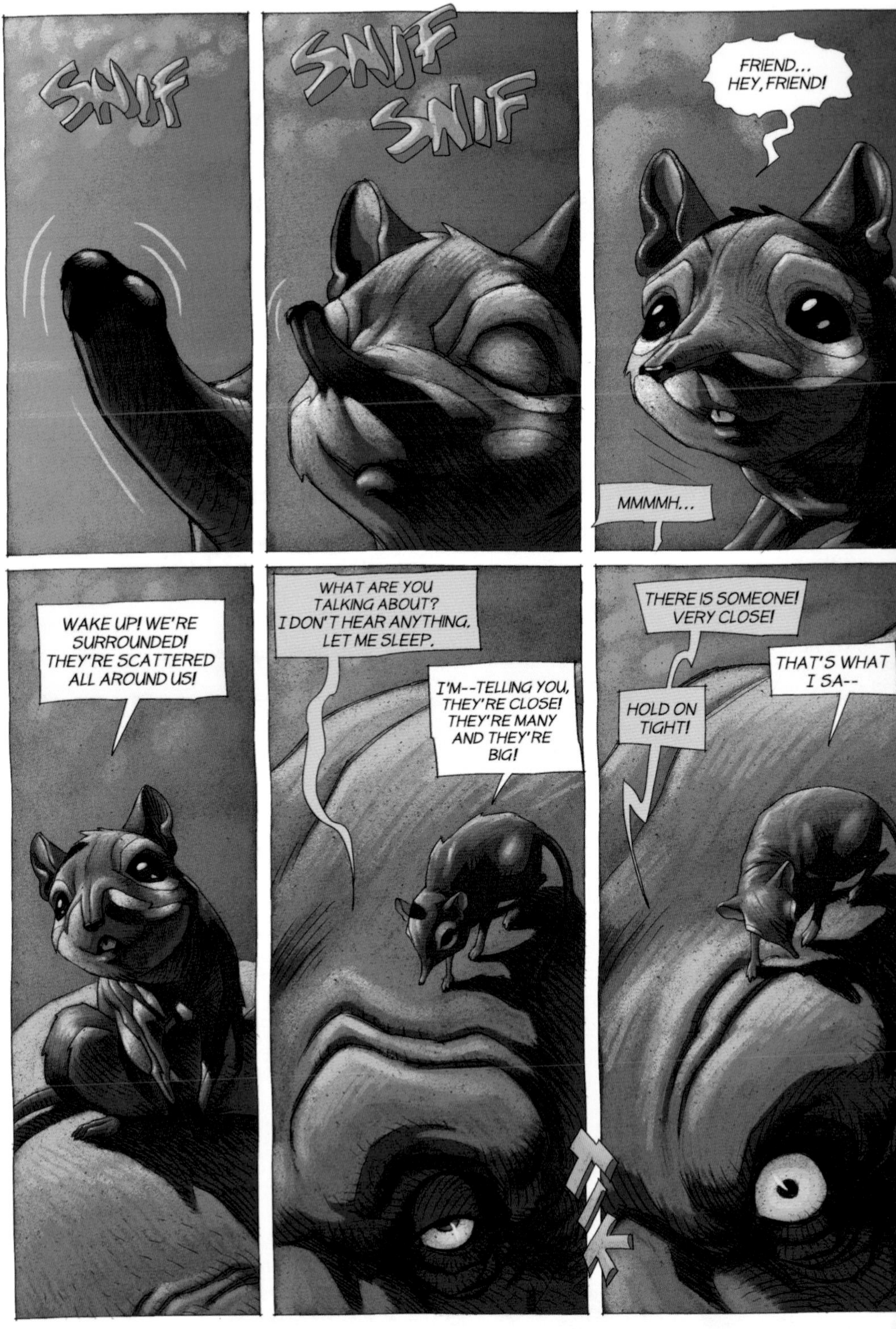
SNIF
SNIF SNIF
FRIEND... HEY, FRIEND!
MMMMH...
WAKE UP! WE'RE SURROUNDED! THEY'RE SCATTERED ALL AROUND US!
WHAT ARE YOU TALKING ABOUT? I DON'T HEAR ANYTHING. LET ME SLEEP.
I'M--TELLING YOU, THEY'RE CLOSE! THEY'RE MANY AND THEY'RE BIG!
TIK
THERE IS SOMEONE! VERY CLOSE!
HOLD ON TIGHT!
THAT'S WHAT I SA--

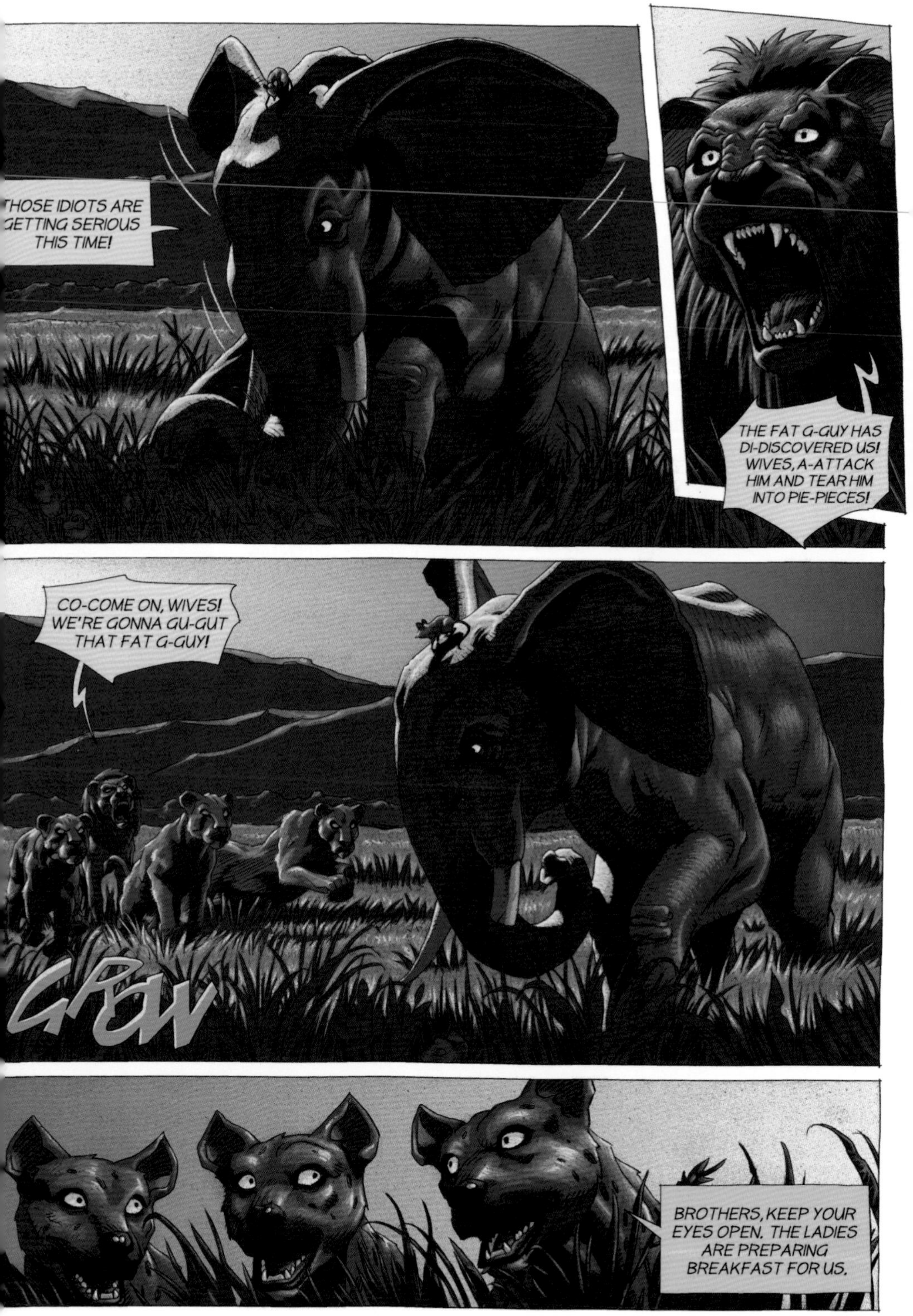
THOSE IDIOTS ARE GETTING SERIOUS THIS TIME!
THE FAT G-GUY HAS DI-DISCOVERED US! WIVES, A-ATTACK HIM AND TEAR HIM INTO PIE-PIECES!
CO-COME ON, WIVES! WE'RE GONNA GU-GUT THAT FAT G-GUY!
GROW
BROTHERS, KEEP YOUR EYES OPEN. THE LADIES ARE PREPARING BREAKFAST FOR US.

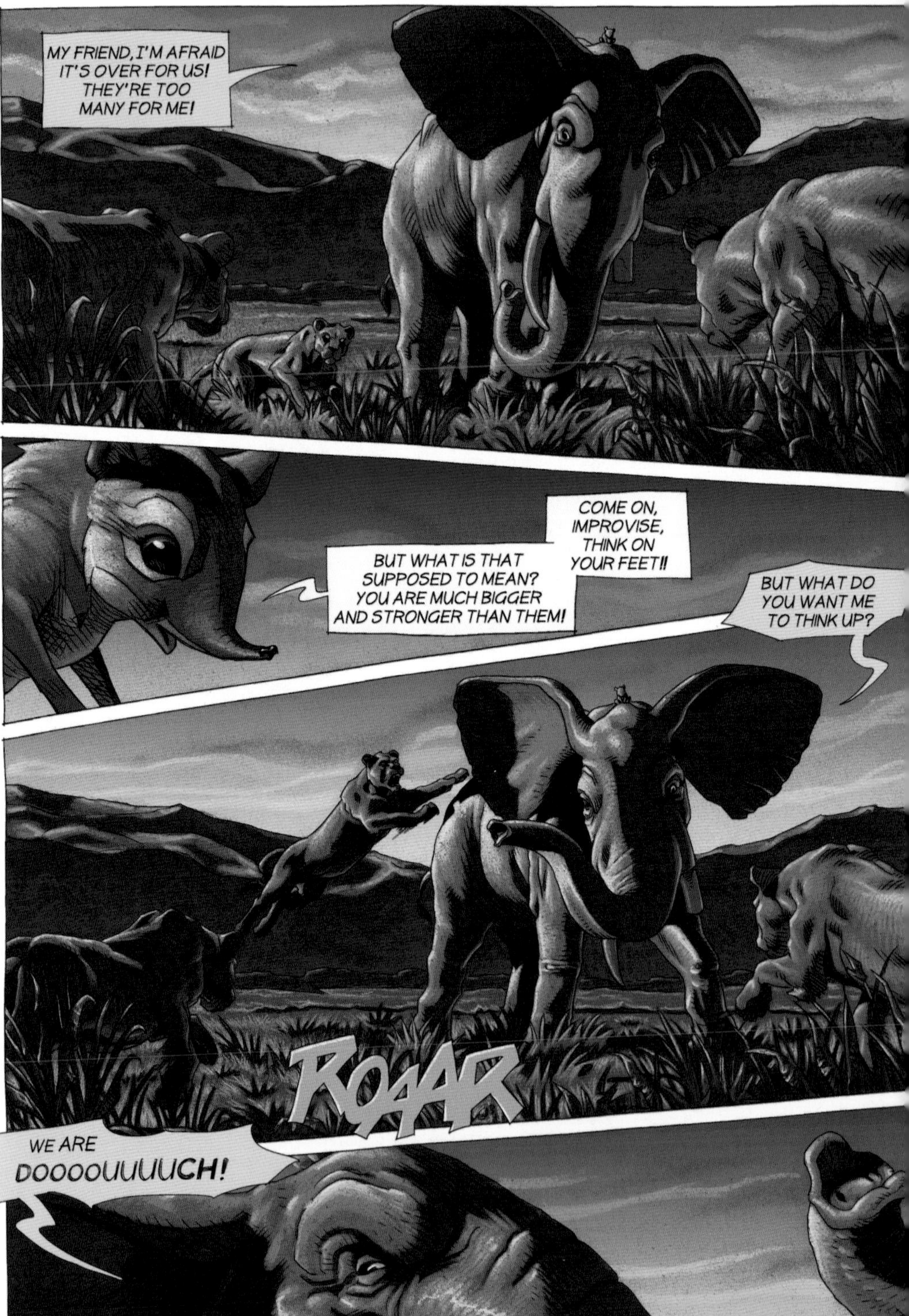
MY FRIEND, I'M AFRAID IT'S OVER FOR US! THEY'RE TOO MANY FOR ME!
COME ON, IMPROVISE, THINK ON YOUR FEET!!
BUT WHAT IS THAT SUPPOSED TO MEAN? YOU ARE MUCH BIGGER AND STRONGER THAN THEM!
BUT WHAT DO YOU WANT ME TO THINK UP?
ROAAR
WE ARE DOOOOUUUUCH!

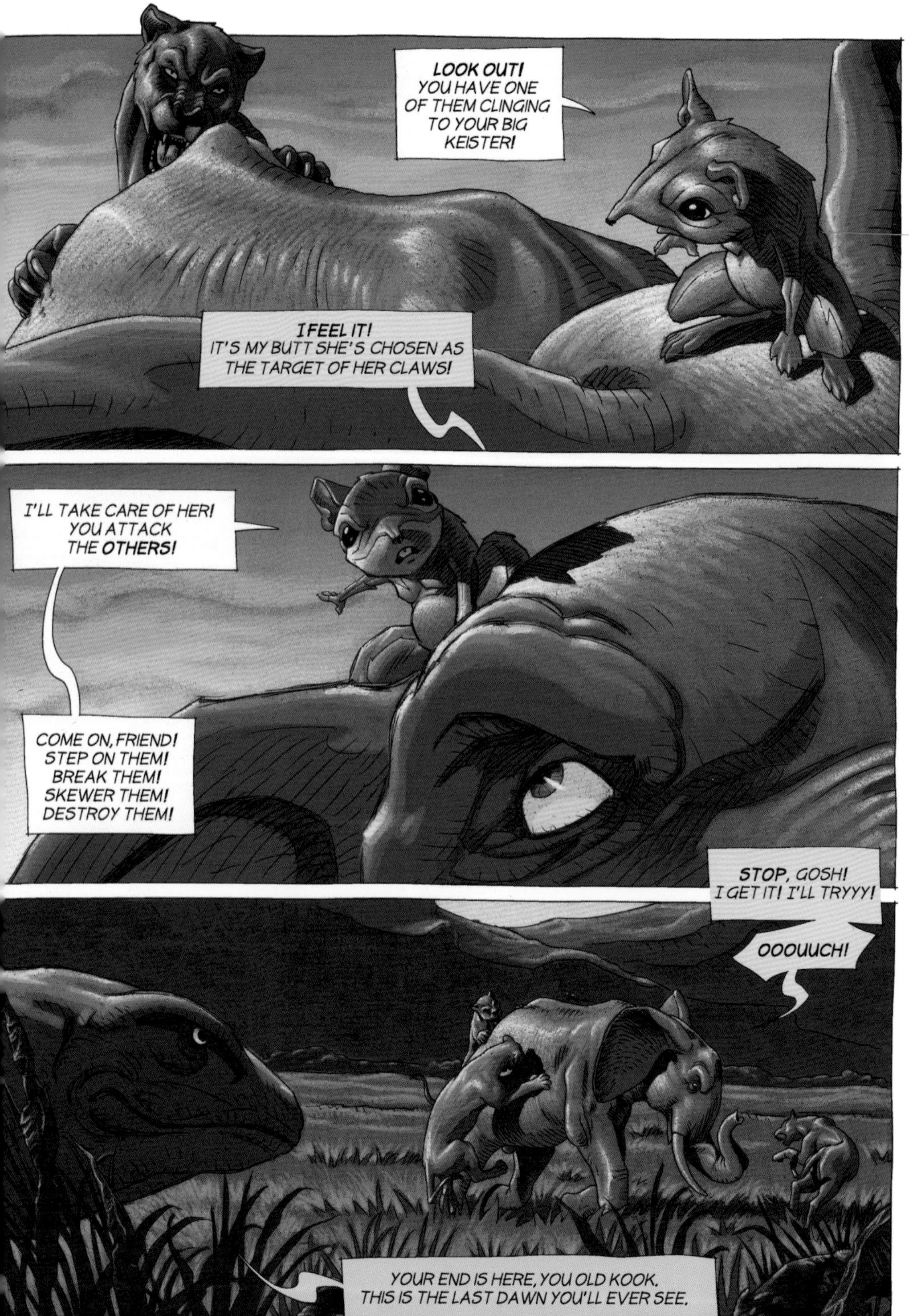
LOOK OUT! YOU HAVE ONE OF THEM CLINGING TO YOUR BIG KEISTER!
I FEEL IT! IT'S MY BUTT SHE'S CHOSEN AS THE TARGET OF HER CLAWS!
I'LL TAKE CARE OF HER! YOU ATTACK THE OTHERS!
COME ON, FRIEND! STEP ON THEM! BREAK THEM! SKEWER THEM! DESTROY THEM!
STOP, GOSH! I GET IT! I'LL TRYYY!
OOOUUCH!
YOUR END IS HERE, YOU OLD KOOK. THIS IS THE LAST DAWN YOU'LL EVER SEE.

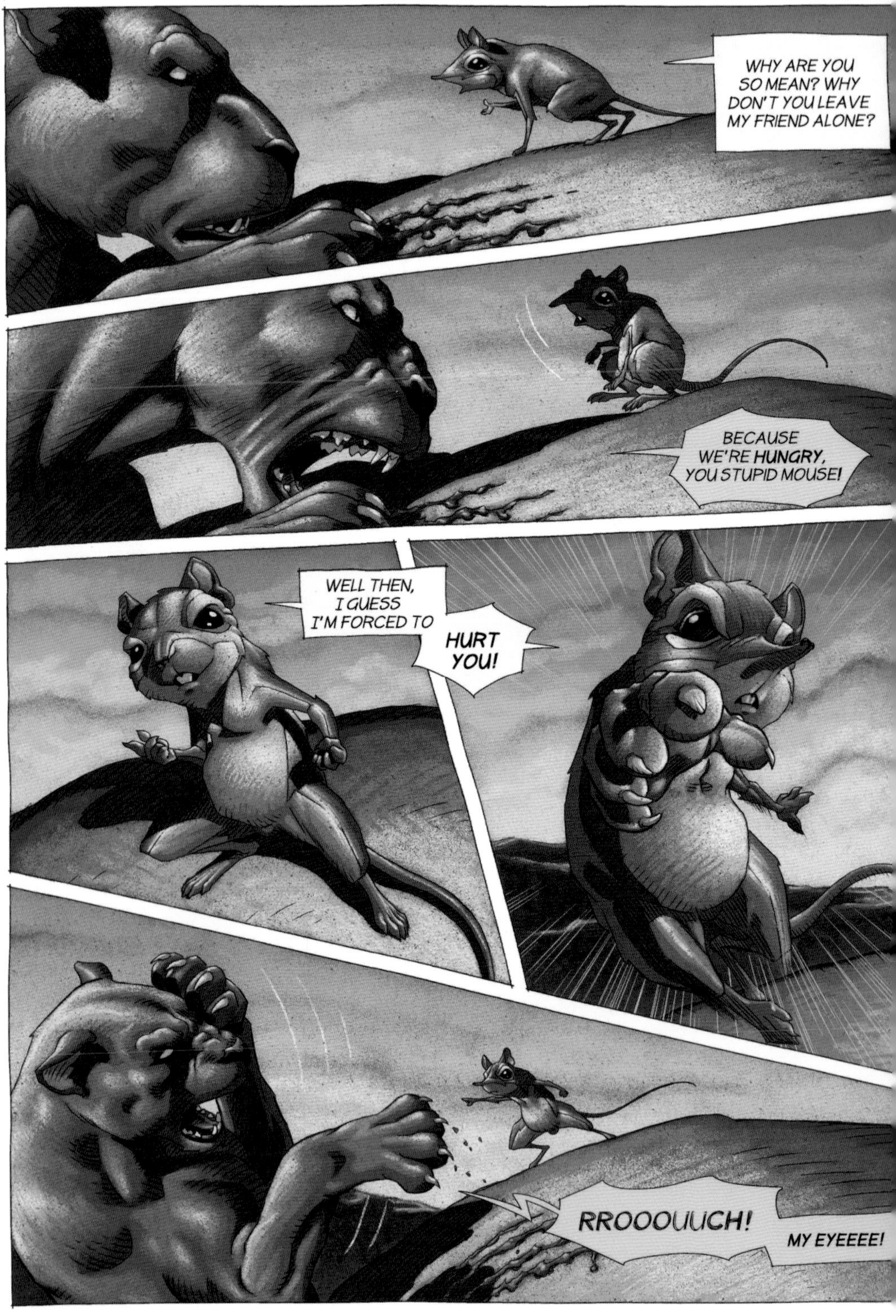
WHY ARE YOU SO MEAN? WHY DON'T YOU LEAVE MY FRIEND ALONE?
BECAUSE WE'RE **HUNGRY**, YOU STUPID MOUSE!
WELL THEN, I GUESS I'M FORCED TO
HURT YOU!
RROOOUUCH!
MY EYEEEE!

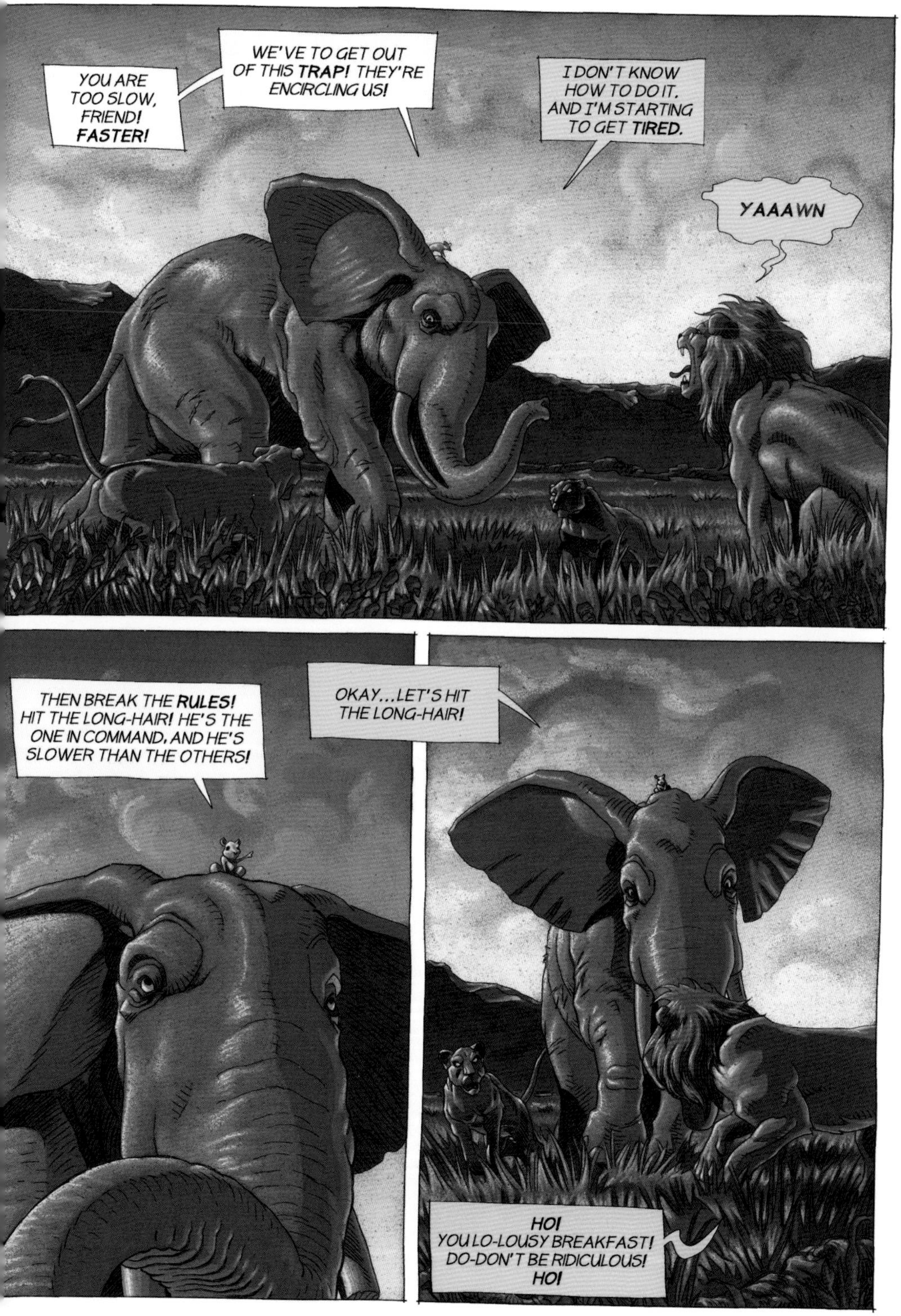
YOU ARE TOO SLOW, FRIEND! FASTER!
WE'VE TO GET OUT OF THIS TRAP! THEY'RE ENCIRCLING US!
I DON'T KNOW HOW TO DO IT. AND I'M STARTING TO GET TIRED.
YAAAWN
THEN BREAK THE RULES! HIT THE LONG-HAIR! HE'S THE ONE IN COMMAND. AND HE'S SLOWER THAN THE OTHERS!
OKAY...LET'S HIT THE LONG-HAIR!
HO! YOU LO-LOUSY BREAKFAST! DO-DON'T BE RIDICULOUS! HO!

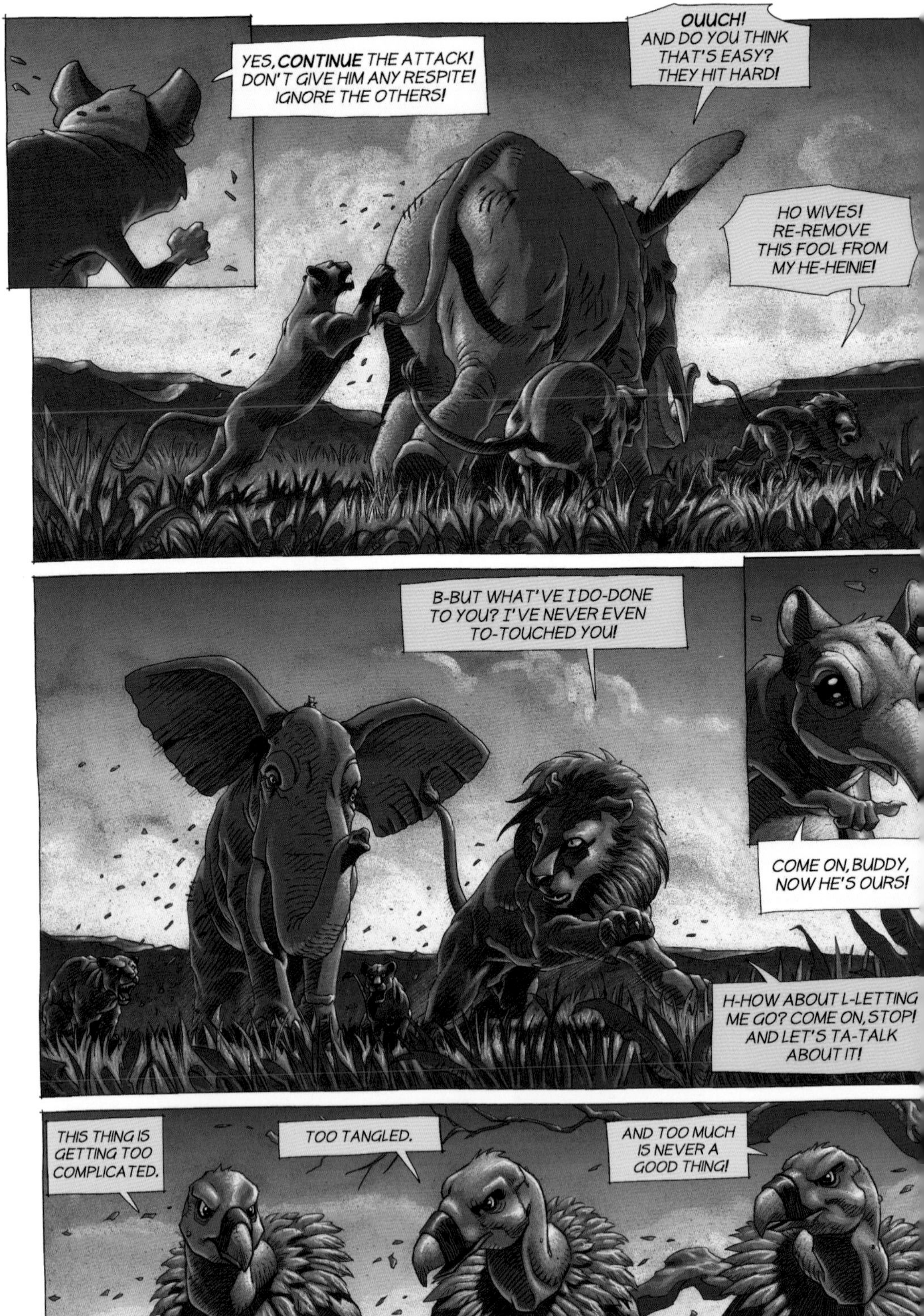
YES, **CONTINUE** THE ATTACK! DON'T GIVE HIM ANY RESPITE! IGNORE THE OTHERS!
**OUUCH!** AND DO YOU THINK THAT'S EASY? THEY HIT HARD!
HO WIVES! RE-REMOVE THIS FOOL FROM MY HE-HEINIE!
B-BUT WHAT'VE I DO-DONE TO YOU? I'VE NEVER EVEN TO-TOUCHED YOU!
COME ON, BUDDY, NOW HE'S OURS!
H-HOW ABOUT L-LETTING ME GO? COME ON, STOP! AND LET'S TA-TALK ABOUT IT!
THIS THING IS GETTING TOO COMPLICATED.
TOO TANGLED.
AND TOO MUCH IS NEVER A GOOD THING!

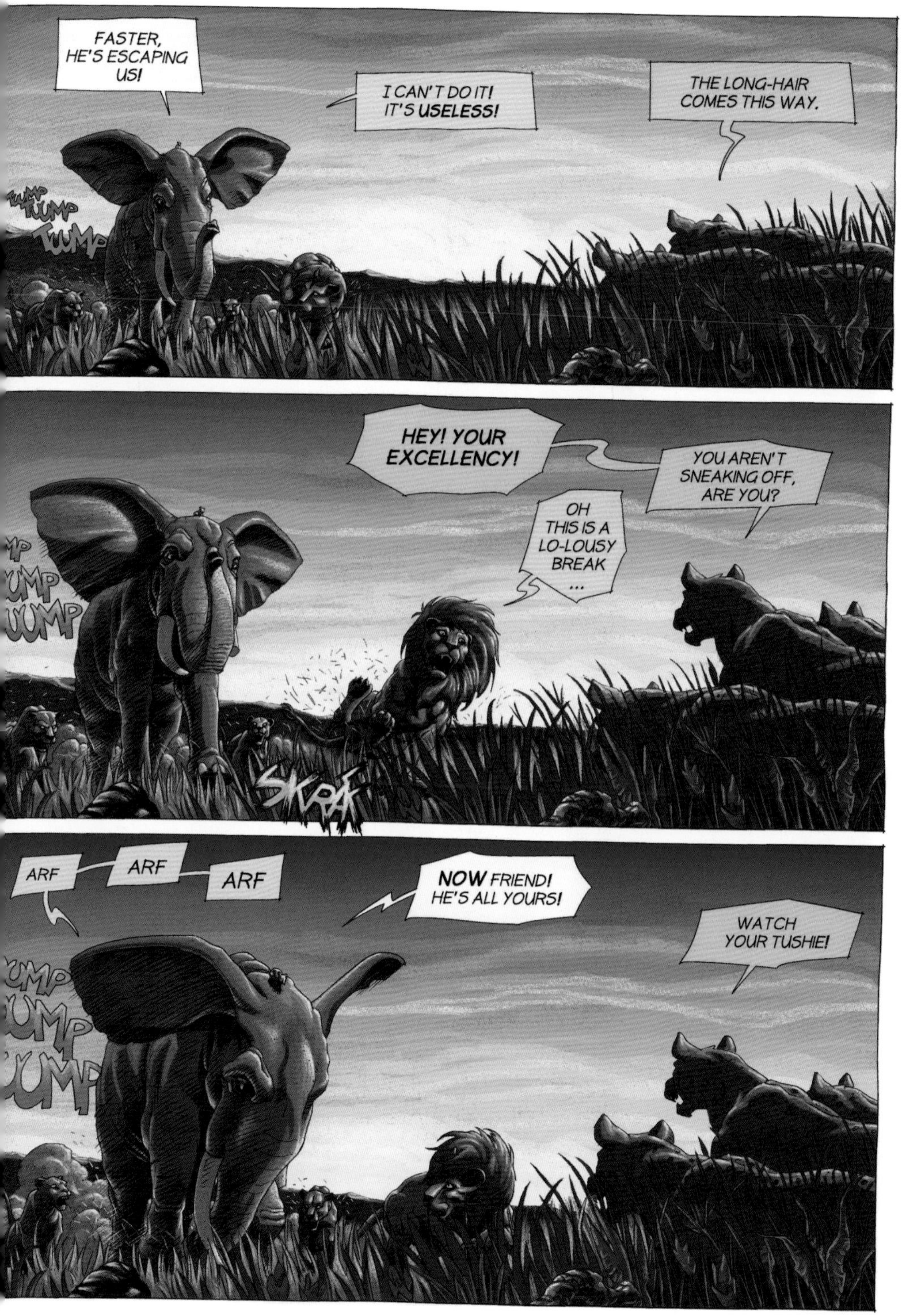
FASTER, HE'S ESCAPING US!
I CAN'T DO IT! IT'S USELESS!
THE LONG-HAIR COMES THIS WAY.
TUMP TUMP TUMP
HEY! YOUR EXCELLENCY!
YOU AREN'T SNEAKING OFF, ARE YOU?
OH THIS IS A LO-LOUSY BREAK ...
SKRAK
ARF
ARF
ARF
NOW FRIEND! HE'S ALL YOURS!
WATCH YOUR TUSHIE!

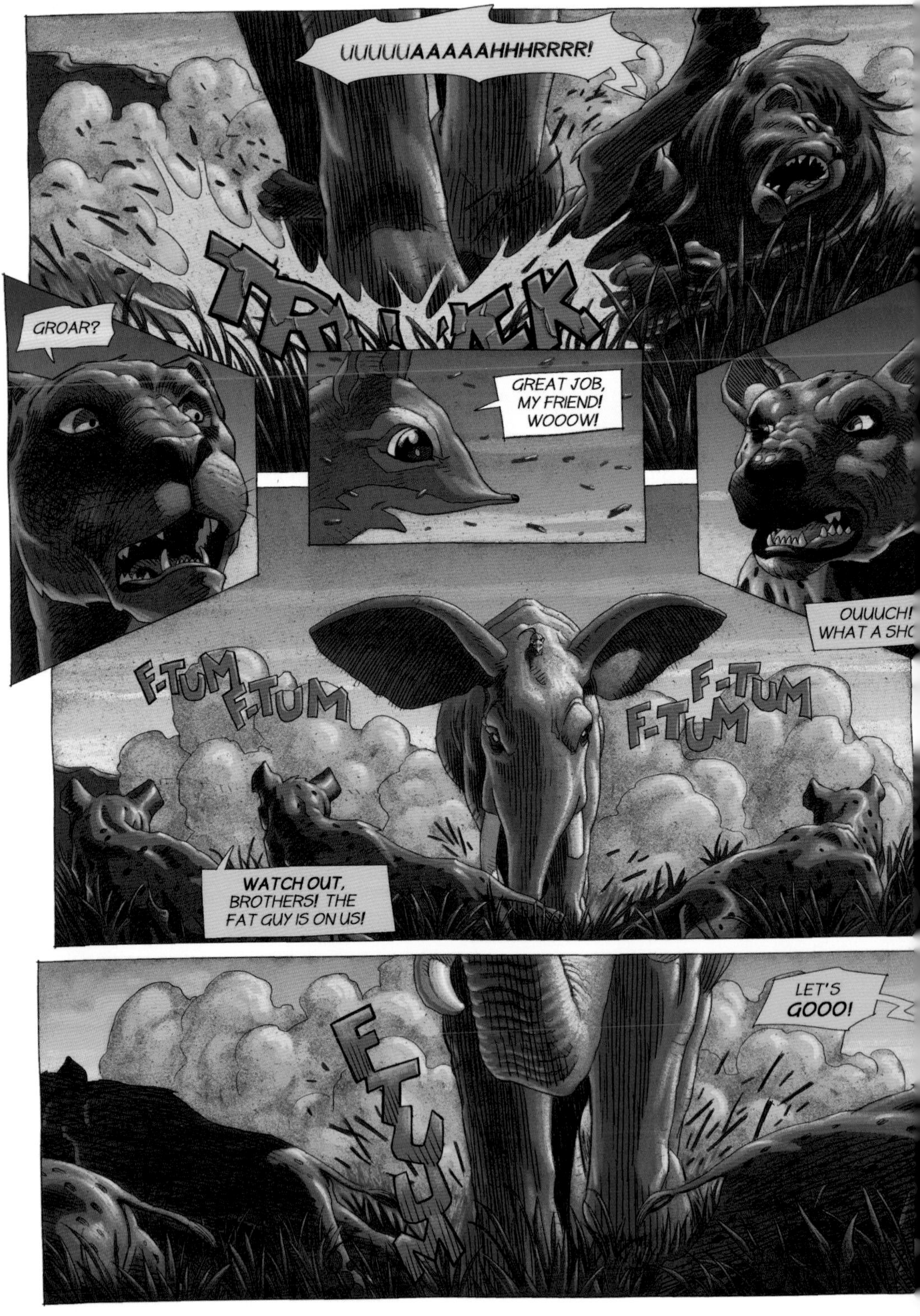
UUUUUAAAAAHHHRRRR!
TRUUNCK
GROAR?
GREAT JOB, MY FRIEND! WOOOW!
OUUUCH! WHAT A SHO
F-TUM F-TUM
F-TUM F-TUM
WATCH OUT, BROTHERS! THE FAT GUY IS ON US!
LET'S GOOO!
F-TUM

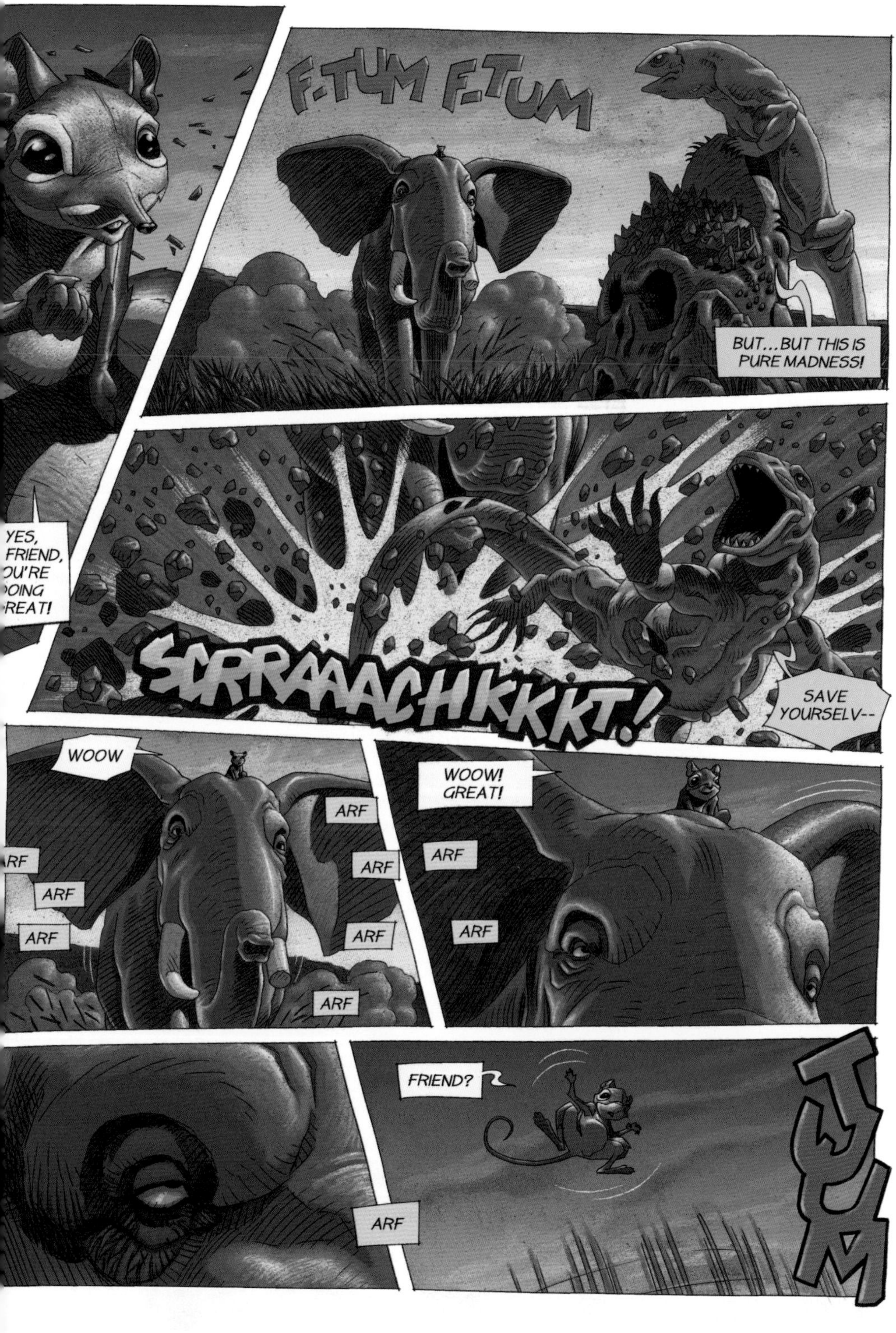
F-TUM F-TUM
BUT...BUT THIS IS PURE MADNESS!
YES, FRIEND, YOU'RE DOING GREAT!
SCRRAAACHIKKKT!
SAVE YOURSELV--
WOOW
ARF
ARF
ARF
ARF
ARF
ARF
ARF
WOOW! GREAT!
ARF
ARF
ARF
FRIEND?
TUM

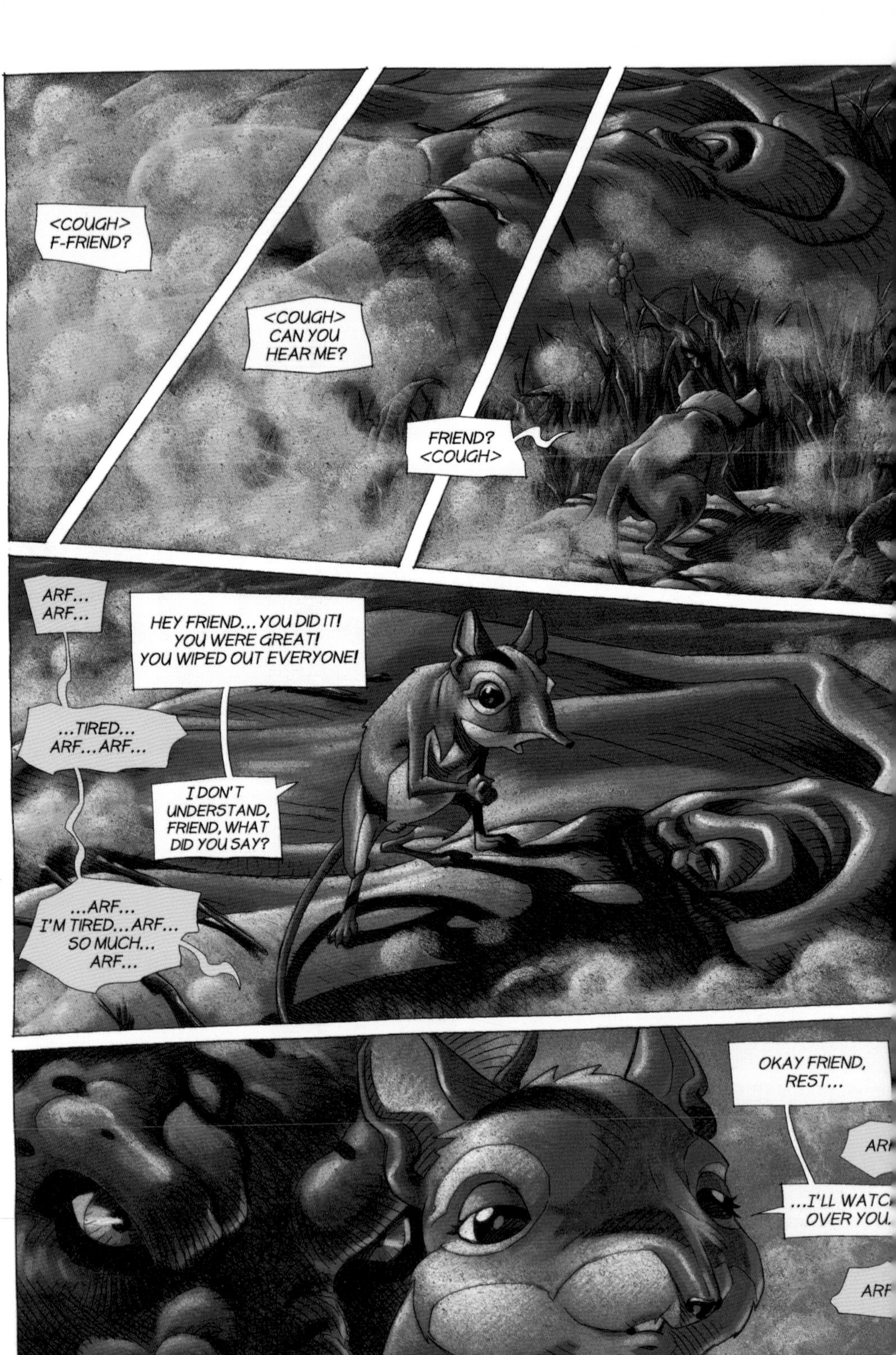
<COUGH> F-FRIEND?
<COUGH> CAN YOU HEAR ME?
FRIEND? <COUGH>
ARF... ARF...
HEY FRIEND... YOU DID IT! YOU WERE GREAT! YOU WIPED OUT EVERYONE!
...TIRED... ARF... ARF...
I DON'T UNDERSTAND, FRIEND, WHAT DID YOU SAY?
...ARF... I'M TIRED... ARF... SO MUCH... ARF...
OKAY FRIEND, REST...
...I'LL WATC OVER YOU.

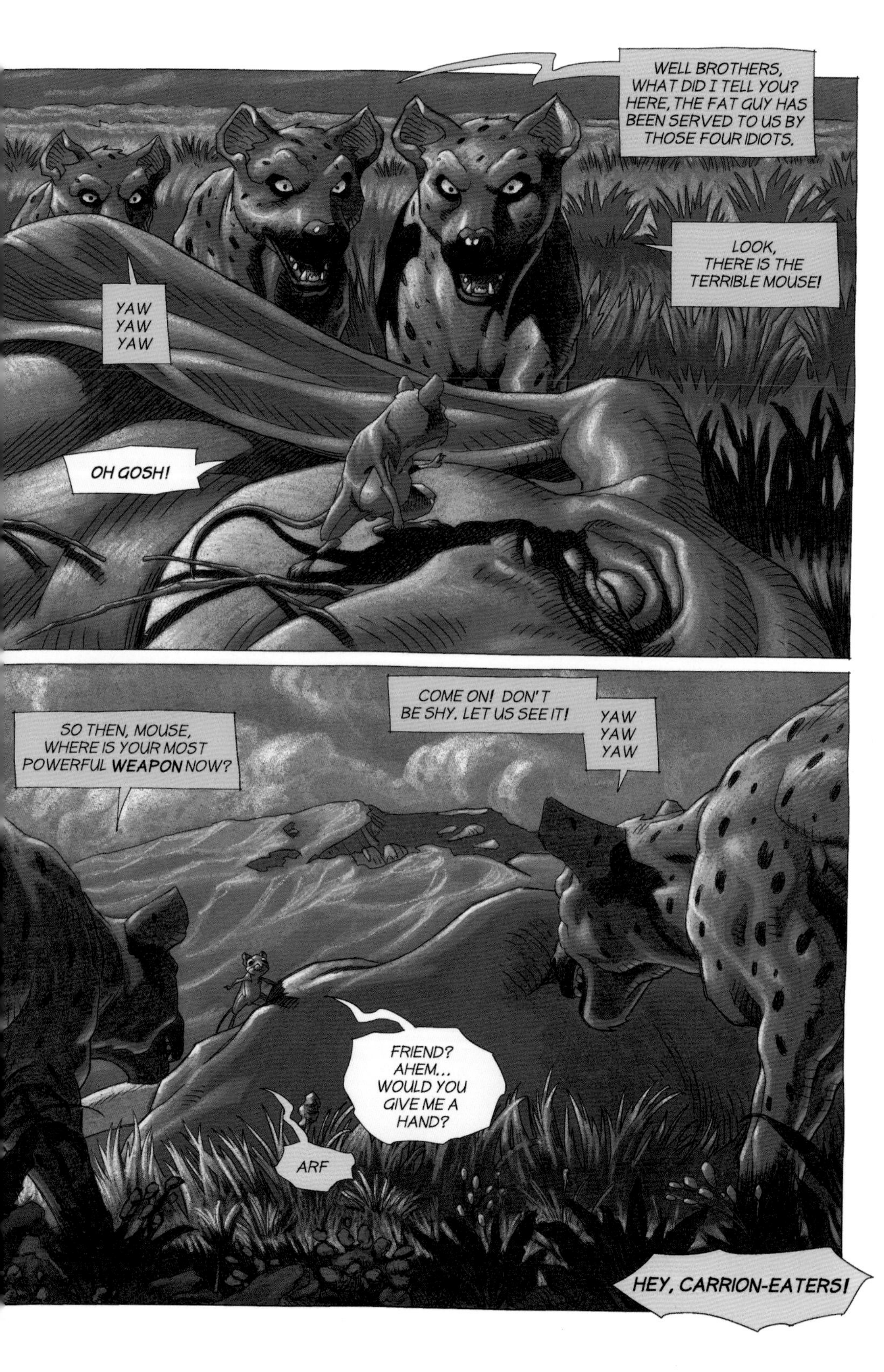

WELL BROTHERS, WHAT DID I TELL YOU? HERE, THE FAT GUY HAS BEEN SERVED TO US BY THOSE FOUR IDIOTS.
YAW YAW YAW
LOOK, THERE IS THE TERRIBLE MOUSE!
OH GOSH!
SO THEN, MOUSE, WHERE IS YOUR MOST POWERFUL WEAPON NOW?
COME ON! DON'T BE SHY. LET US SEE IT!
YAW YAW YAW
FRIEND? AHEM... WOULD YOU GIVE ME A HAND?
ARF
HEY, CARRION-EATERS!

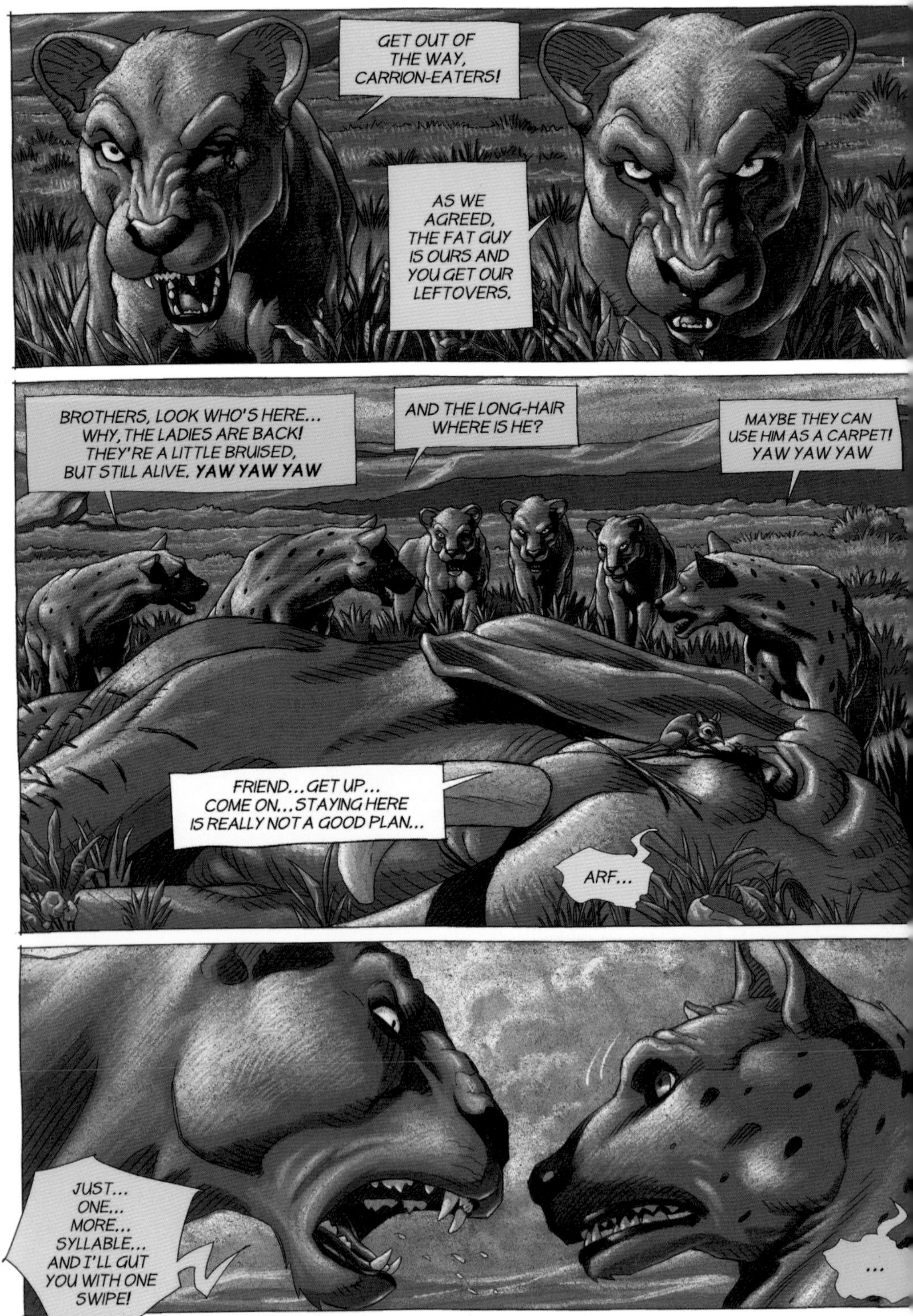
GET OUT OF THE WAY, CARRION-EATERS!
AS WE AGREED, THE FAT GUY IS OURS AND YOU GET OUR LEFTOVERS.
BROTHERS, LOOK WHO'S HERE... WHY, THE LADIES ARE BACK! THEY'RE A LITTLE BRUISED, BUT STILL ALIVE. YAW YAW YAW
AND THE LONG-HAIR WHERE IS HE?
MAYBE THEY CAN USE HIM AS A CARPET! YAW YAW YAW
FRIEND...GET UP... COME ON...STAYING HERE IS REALLY NOT A GOOD PLAN...
ARF...
JUST... ONE... MORE... SYLLABLE... AND I'LL GUT YOU WITH ONE SWIPE!
...

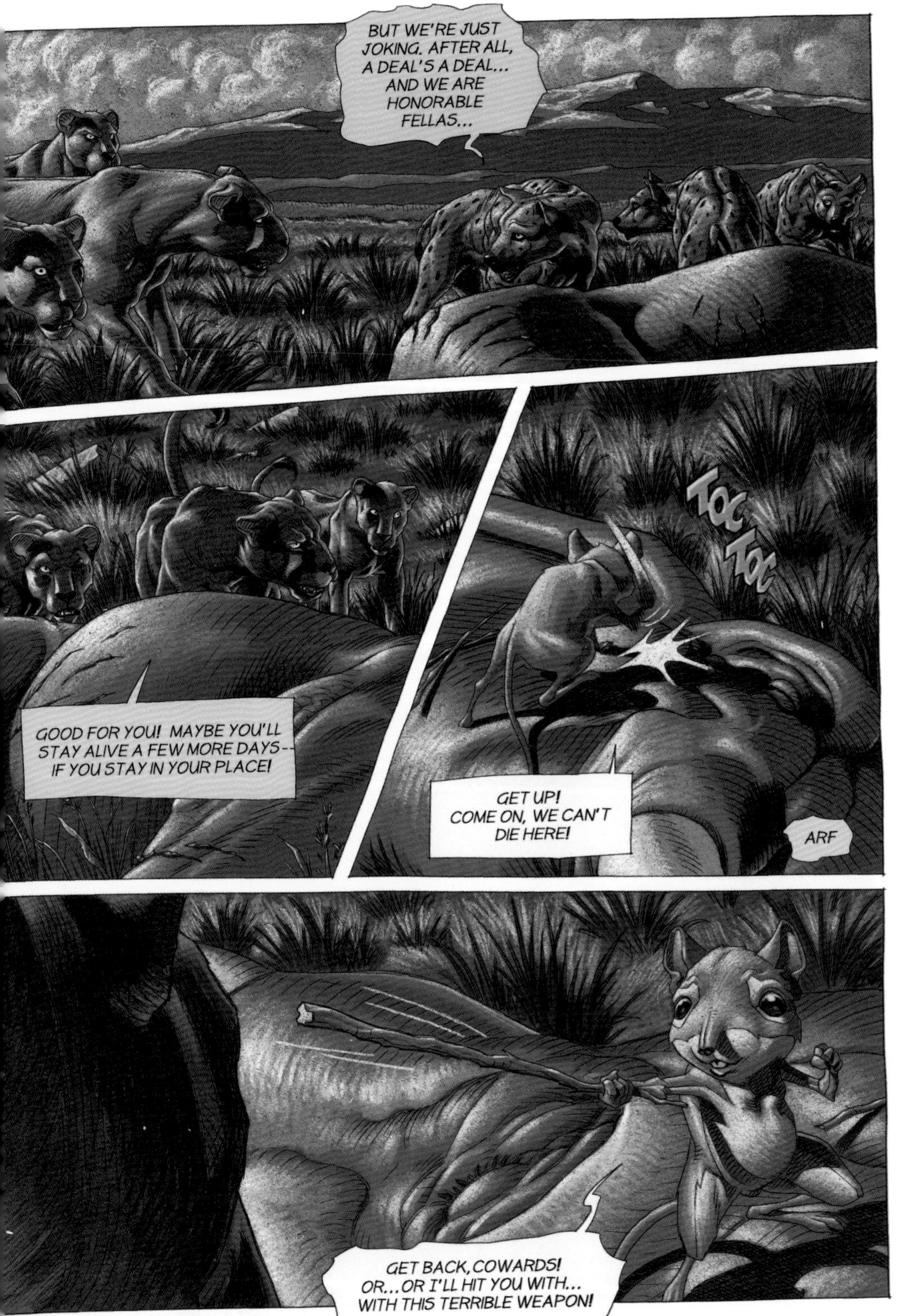
BUT WE'RE JUST JOKING. AFTER ALL, A DEAL'S A DEAL... AND WE ARE HONORABLE FELLAS...
GOOD FOR YOU! MAYBE YOU'LL STAY ALIVE A FEW MORE DAYS-- IF YOU STAY IN YOUR PLACE!
TOC TOC
GET UP! COME ON, WE CAN'T DIE HERE!
ARF
GET BACK, COWARDS! OR... OR I'LL HIT YOU WITH... WITH THIS TERRIBLE WEAPON!

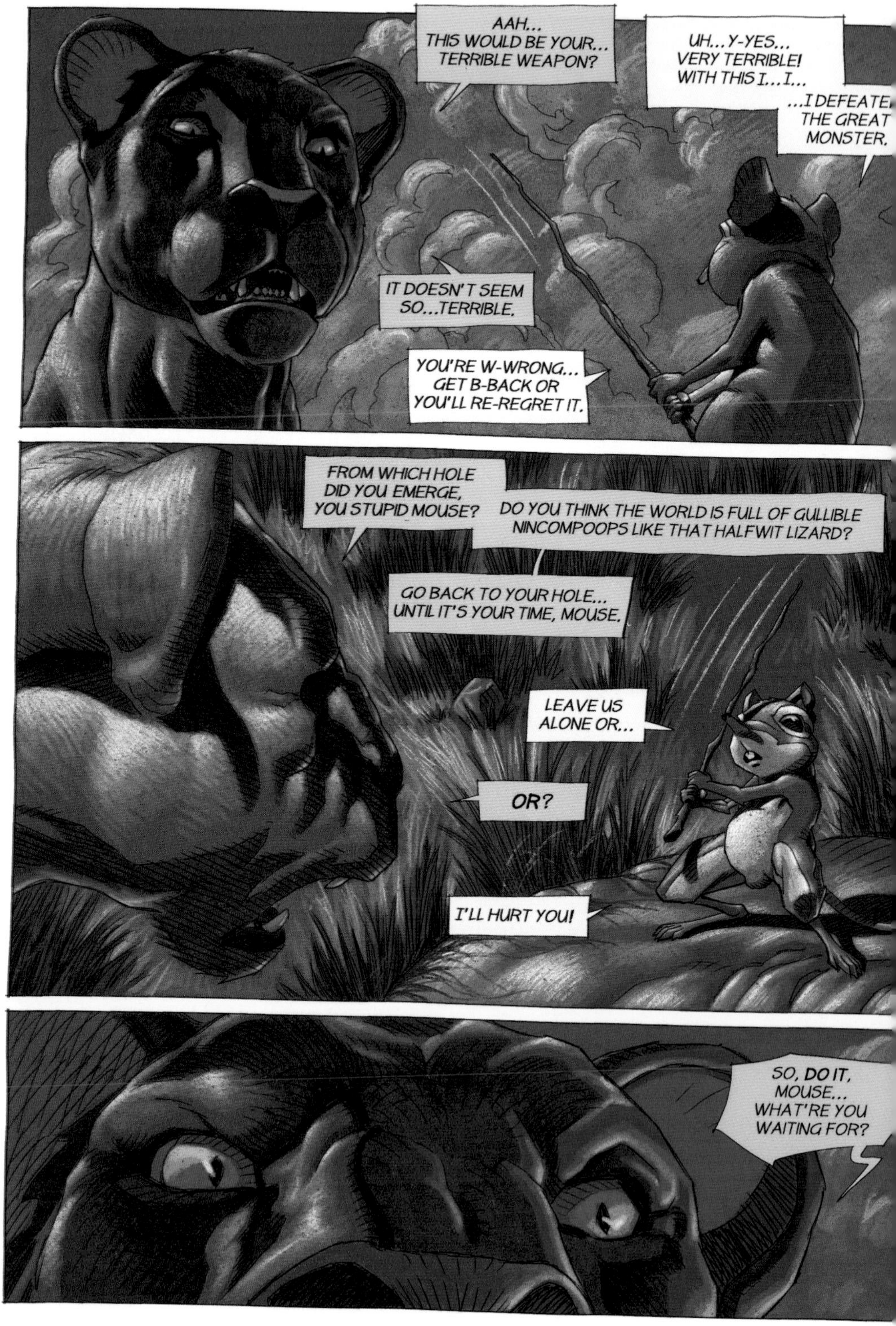
AAH... THIS WOULD BE YOUR... TERRIBLE WEAPON?
UH... Y-YES... VERY TERRIBLE! WITH THIS I... I...
...I DEFEATE THE GREAT MONSTER.
IT DOESN'T SEEM SO... TERRIBLE.
YOU'RE W-WRONG... GET B-BACK OR YOU'LL RE-REGRET IT.
FROM WHICH HOLE DID YOU EMERGE, YOU STUPID MOUSE?
DO YOU THINK THE WORLD IS FULL OF GULLIBLE NINCOMPOOPS LIKE THAT HALFWIT LIZARD?
GO BACK TO YOUR HOLE... UNTIL IT'S YOUR TIME, MOUSE.
LEAVE US ALONE OR...
OR?
I'LL HURT YOU!
SO, DO IT, MOUSE... WHAT'RE YOU WAITING FOR?

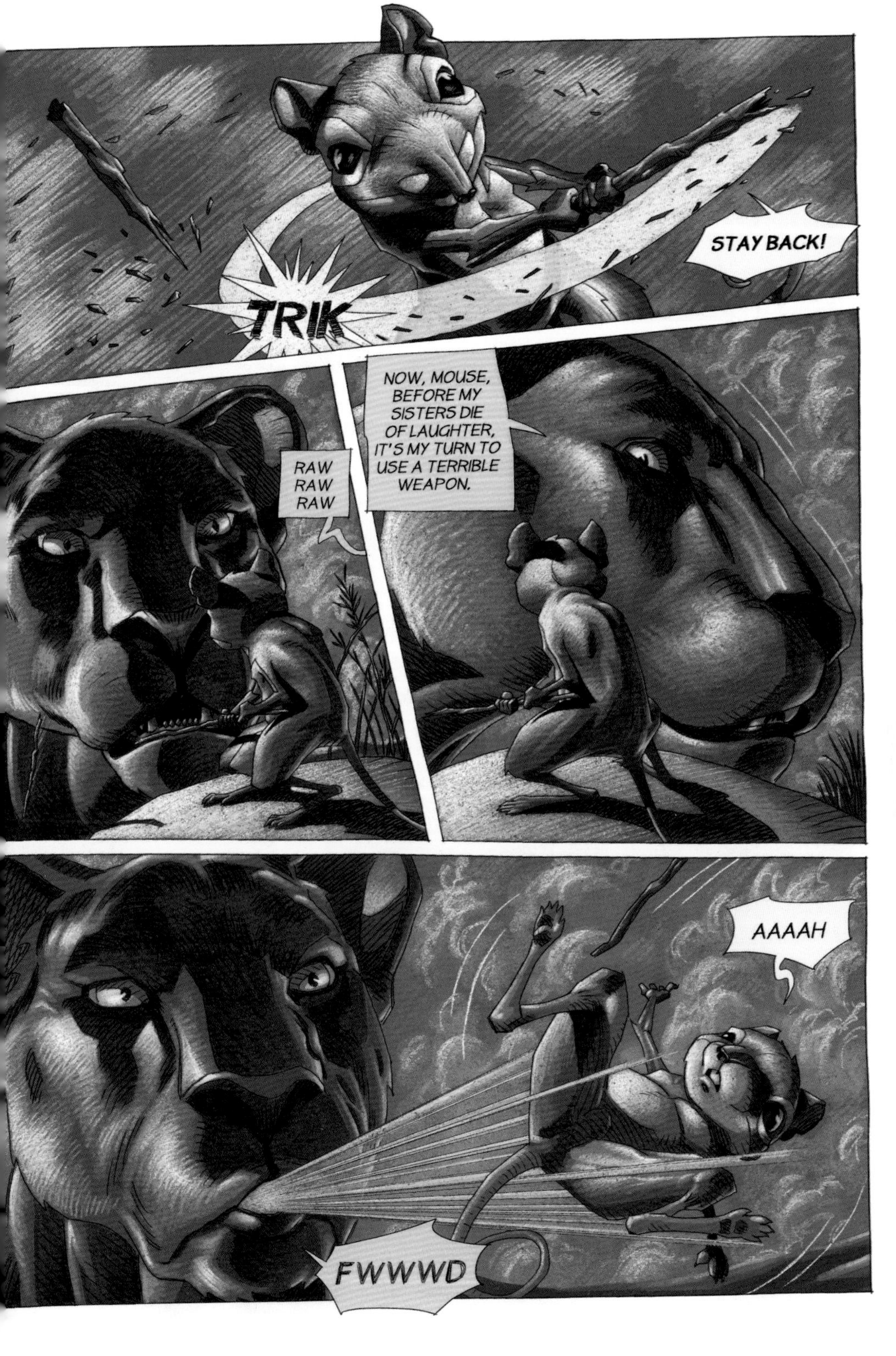
STAY BACK!
TRIK
RAW
RAW
RAW
NOW, MOUSE, BEFORE MY SISTERS DIE OF LAUGHTER, IT'S MY TURN TO USE A TERRIBLE WEAPON.
AAAAH
FWWWD

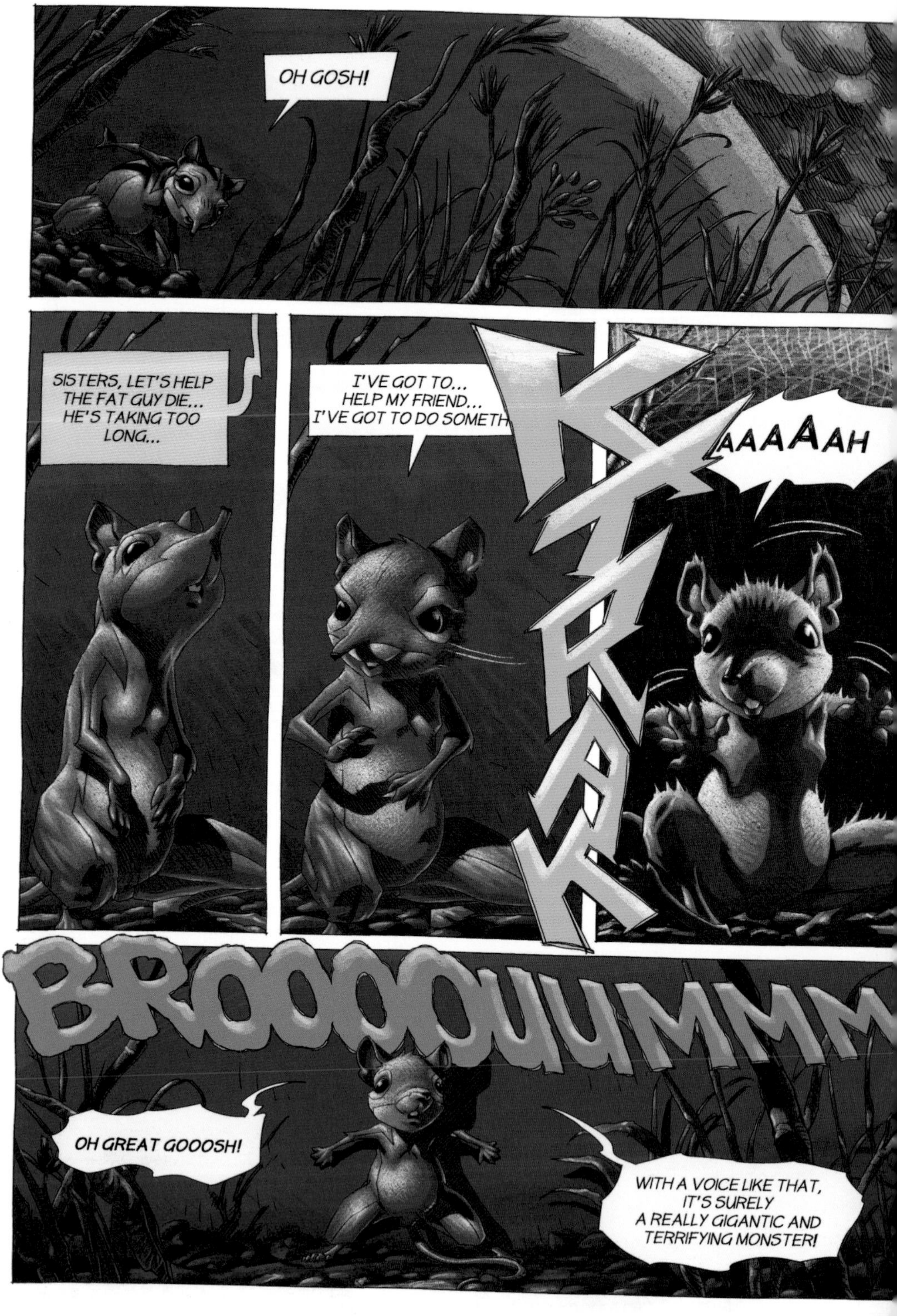

OH GOSH!
SISTERS, LET'S HELP THE FAT GUY DIE... HE'S TAKING TOO LONG...
I'VE GOT TO... HELP MY FRIEND... I'VE GOT TO DO SOMETH
KXRAK
AAAAAH
BROOOOUUMMM
OH GREAT GOOOSH!
WITH A VOICE LIKE THAT, IT'S SURELY A REALLY GIGANTIC AND TERRIFYING MONSTER!

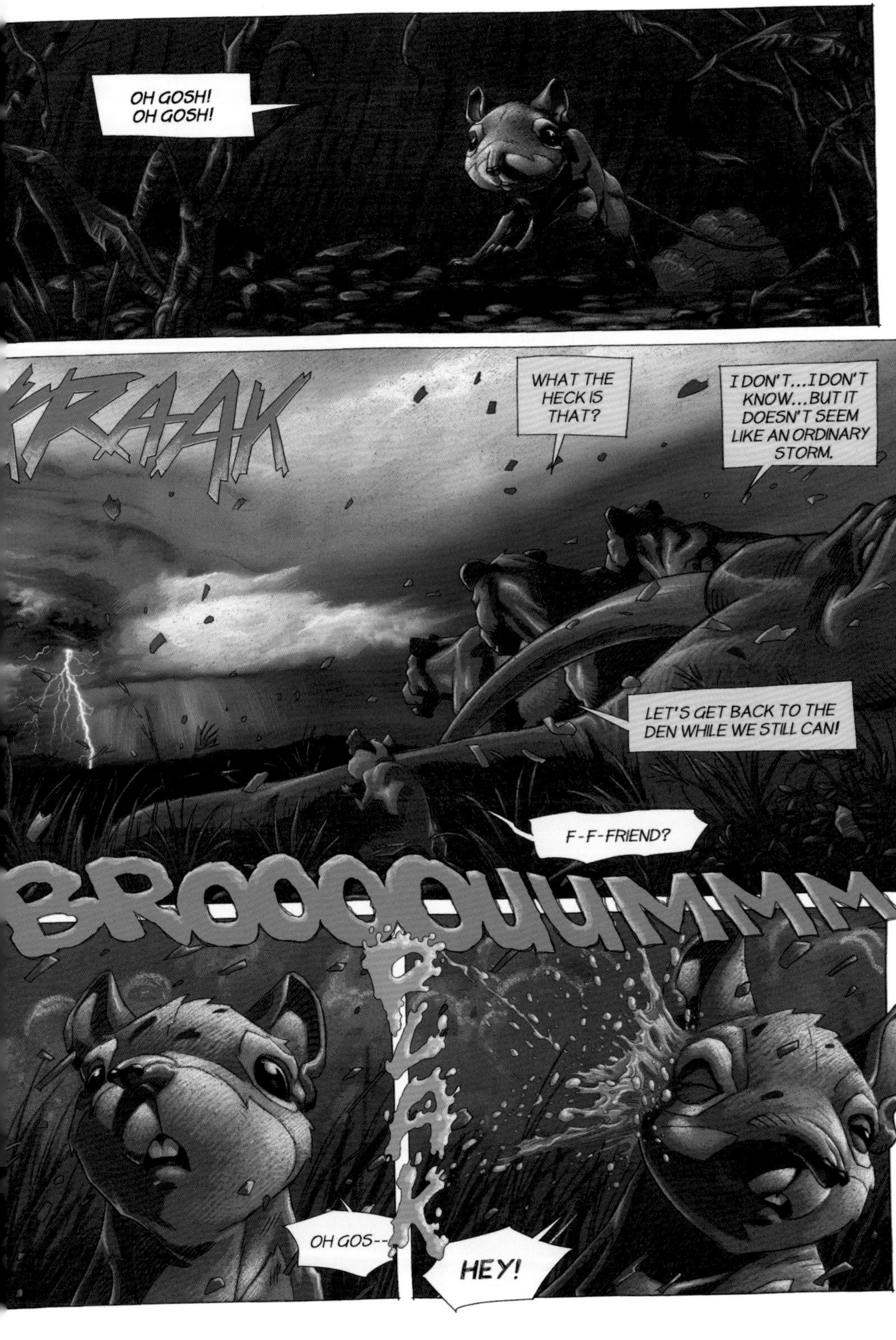
OH GOSH!
OH GOSH!
KRAAAK
WHAT THE HECK IS THAT?
I DON'T...I DON'T KNOW...BUT IT DOESN'T SEEM LIKE AN ORDINARY STORM.
LET'S GET BACK TO THE DEN WHILE WE STILL CAN!
F-F-FRIEND?
BROOOOUUMMM
OH GOS--
HEY!

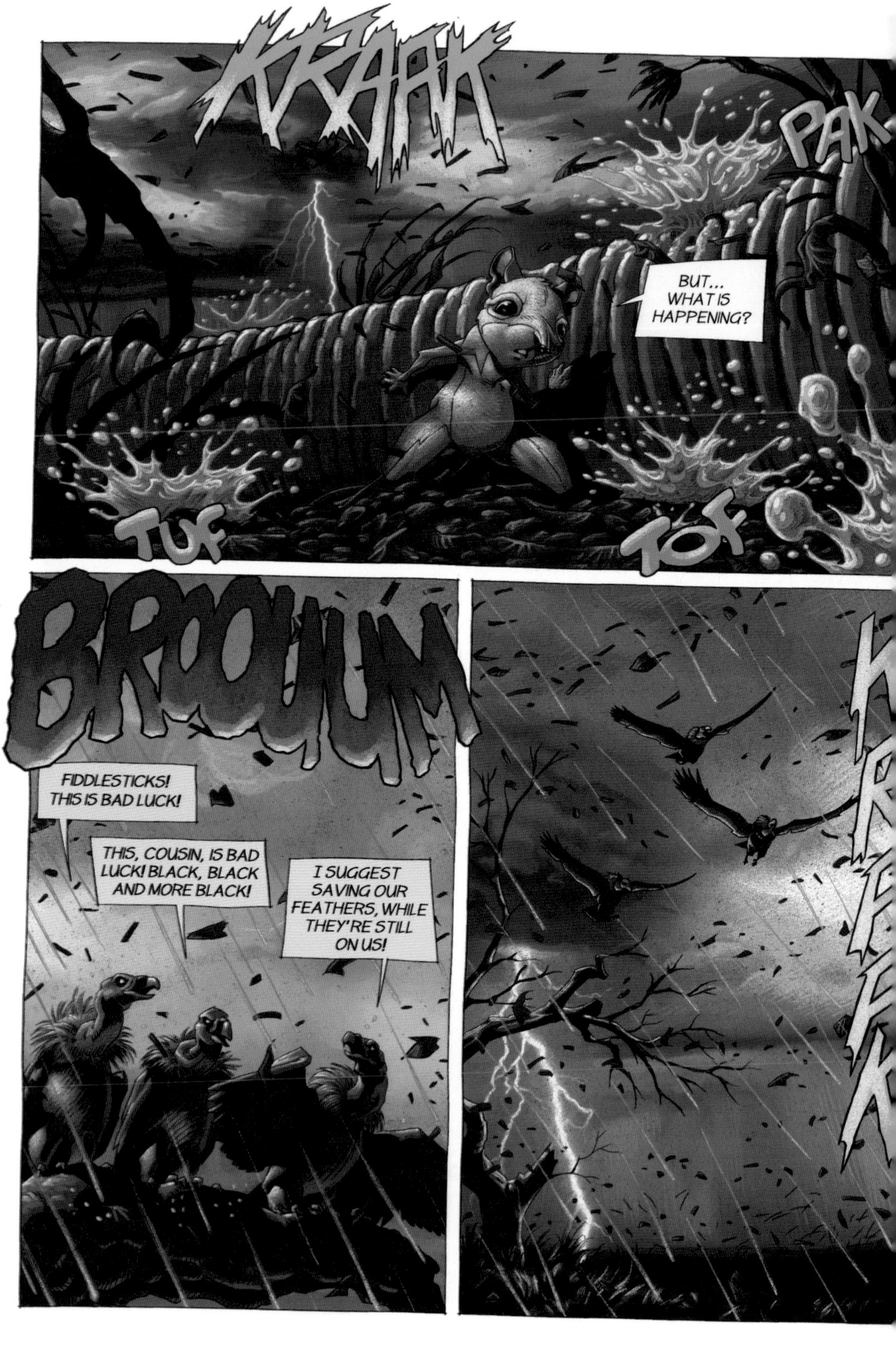
KRAAK
PAK
BUT... WHAT IS HAPPENING?
TUF
TOF
BROOUUM
FIDDLESTICKS! THIS IS BAD LUCK!
THIS, COUSIN, IS BAD LUCK! BLACK, BLACK AND MORE BLACK!
I SUGGEST SAVING OUR FEATHERS, WHILE THEY'RE STILL ON US!

BROOOOUUUMM

RAIN?
WATER...
FINALLY...

...MAYBE, I'M DEAD AND...
I'M IN THE LAND WHERE...
THE ANCESTORS REST...

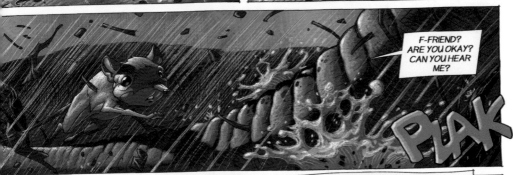

F-FRIEND?
ARE YOU OKAY?
CAN YOU HEAR
ME?

PLAK

YOU'RE NOT DEAD!
YOU'RE STILL
HERE! IN THE
SAVANNAH!

SURE IT'S POSSIBLE!
AND A GIANT MONSTER IS COMING,
DEVOURING EVERYTHING HE SEES!

DO YOU
HEAR HIS
ROAR?

THAT'S HIM,
AND HE'S
GETTING
CLOSER
AND
CLOSER!

YOU? AGAIN? IT'S
NOT POSSIBLE.

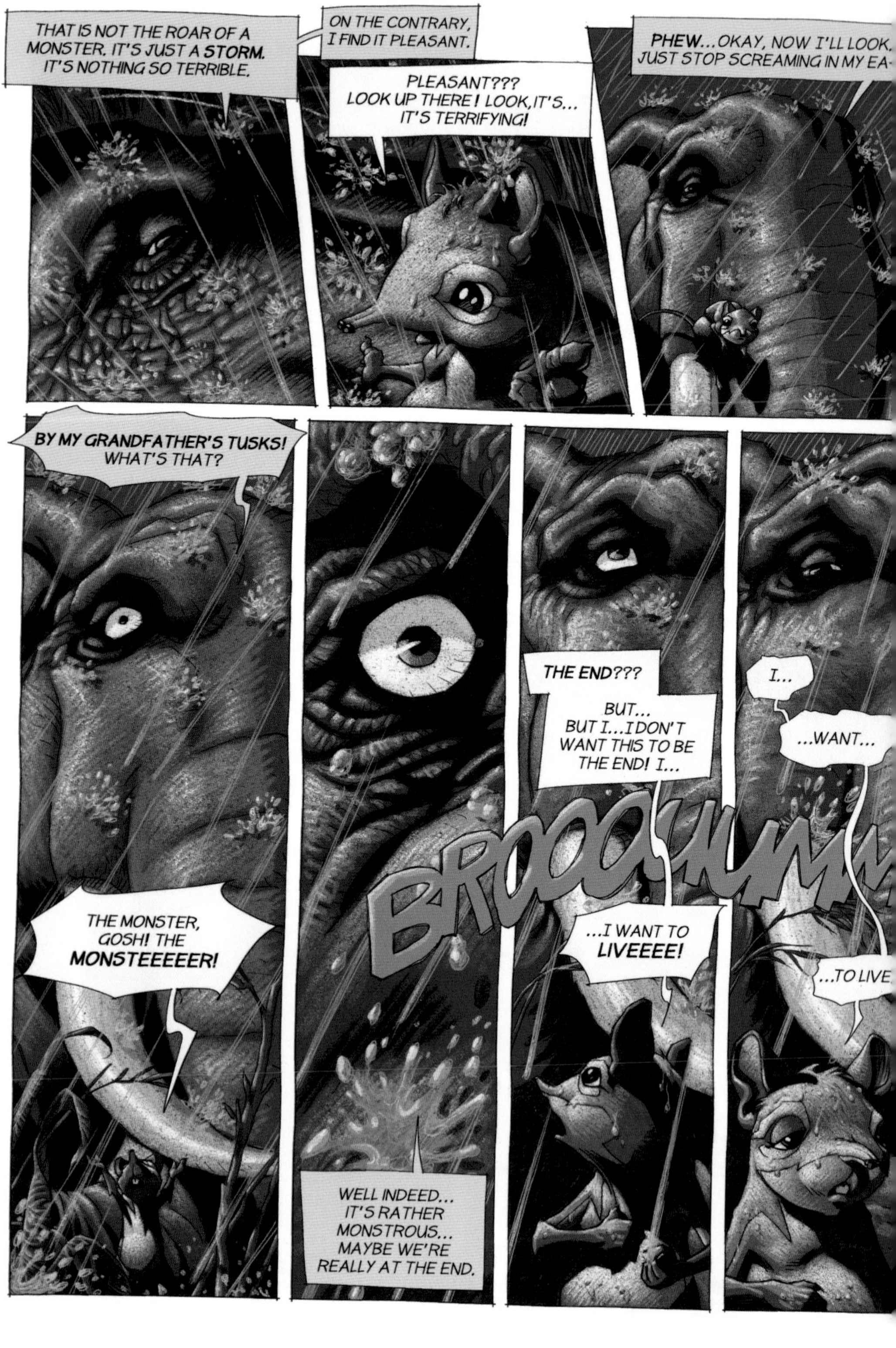
THAT IS NOT THE ROAR OF A MONSTER. IT'S JUST A STORM. IT'S NOTHING SO TERRIBLE.
ON THE CONTRARY, I FIND IT PLEASANT.
PLEASANT??? LOOK UP THERE! LOOK, IT'S... IT'S TERRIFYING!
PHEW...OKAY, NOW I'LL LOOK. JUST STOP SCREAMING IN MY EA-
BY MY GRANDFATHER'S TUSKS! WHAT'S THAT?
THE MONSTER, GOSH! THE MONSTEEEEER!
WELL INDEED... IT'S RATHER MONSTROUS... MAYBE WE'RE REALLY AT THE END.
THE END???
BUT... BUT I...I DON'T WANT THIS TO BE THE END! I...
BROOOMMM
...I WANT TO LIVEEEE!
I...
...WANT...
...TO LIVE.

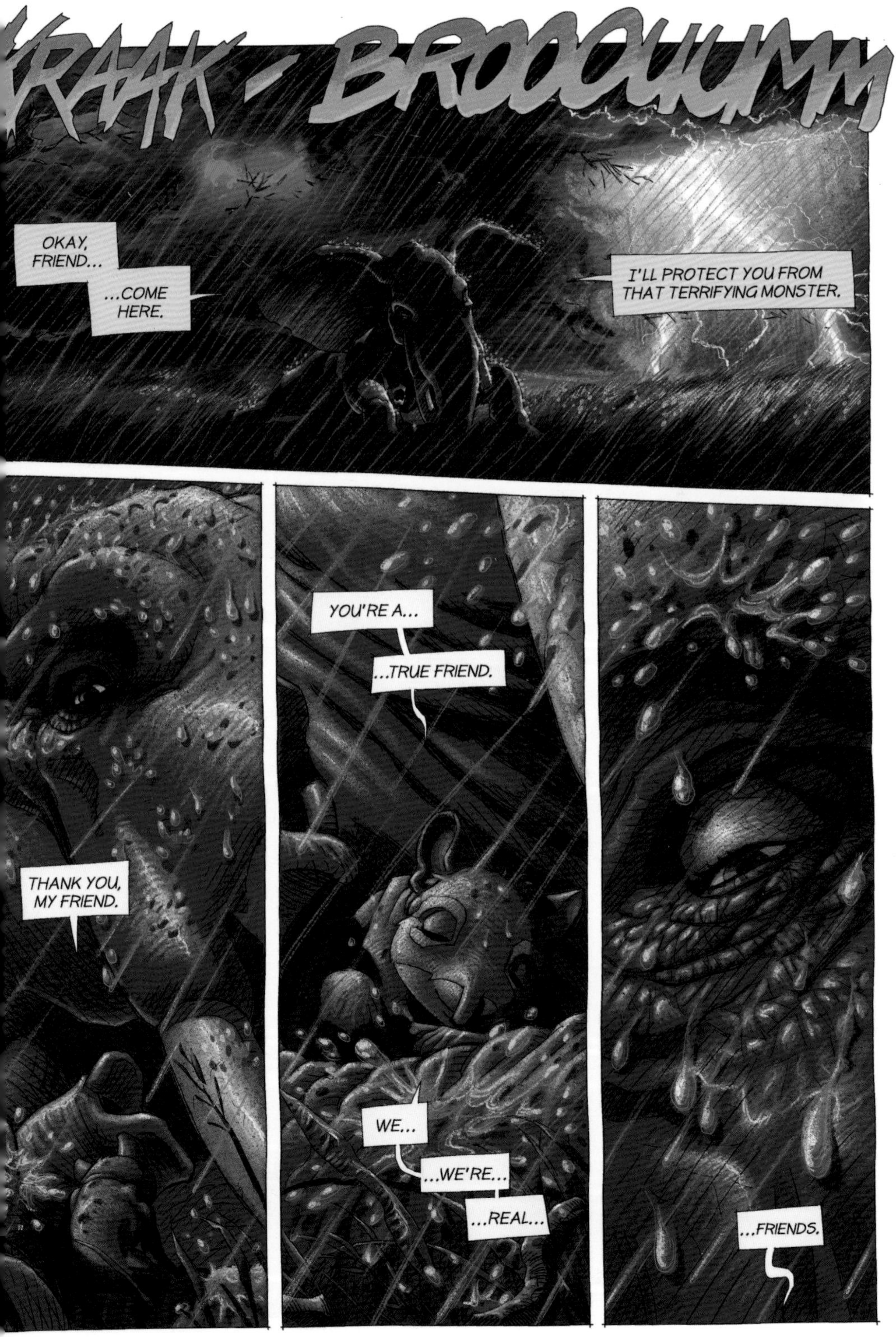
KRAAK - BROOOUUMM
OKAY, FRIEND...
...COME HERE.
I'LL PROTECT YOU FROM THAT TERRIFYING MONSTER.
THANK YOU, MY FRIEND.
YOU'RE A...
...TRUE FRIEND.
WE...
...WE'RE...
...REAL...
...FRIENDS.

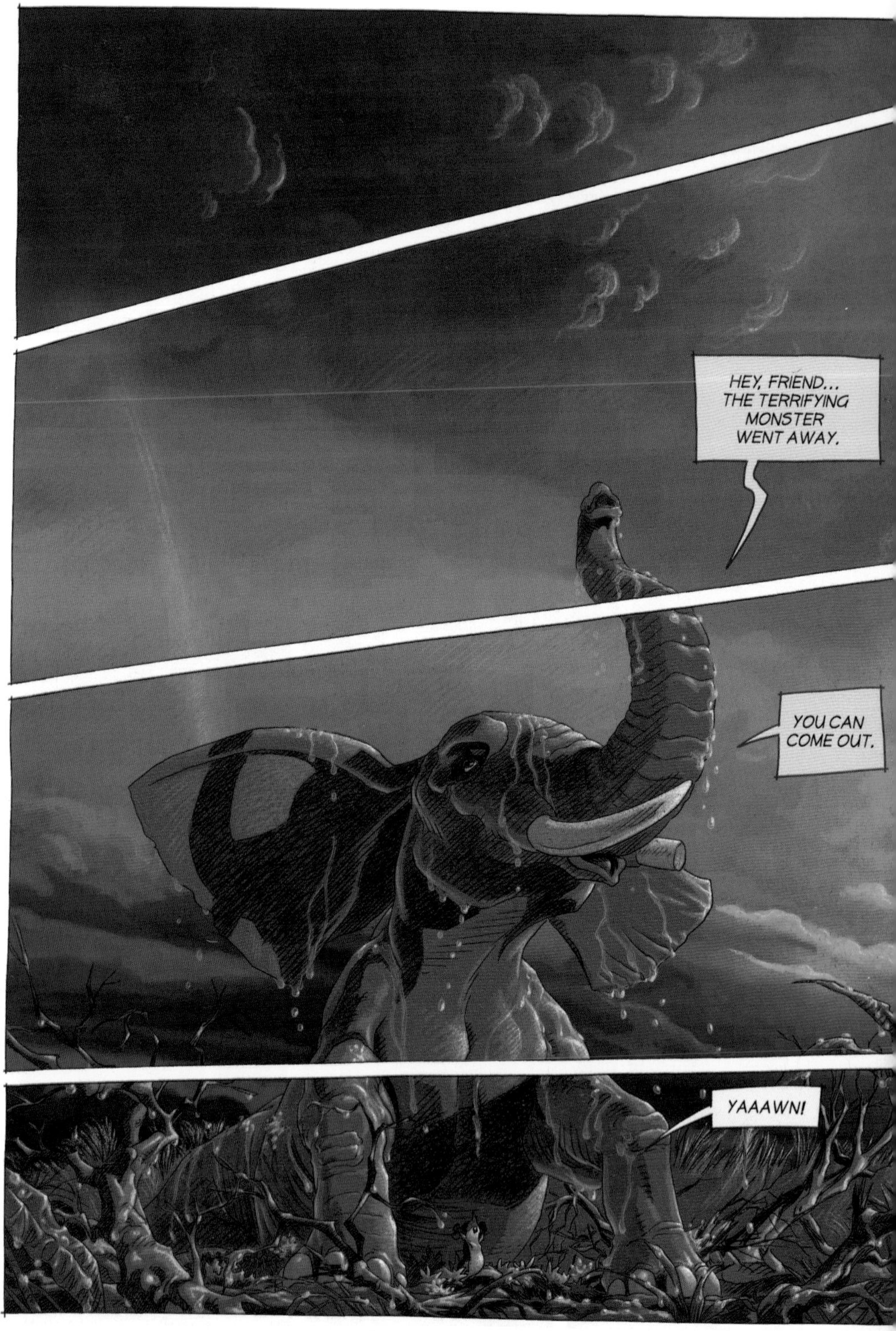
HEY, FRIEND... THE TERRIFYING MONSTER WENT AWAY.
YOU CAN COME OUT.
YAAAWN!

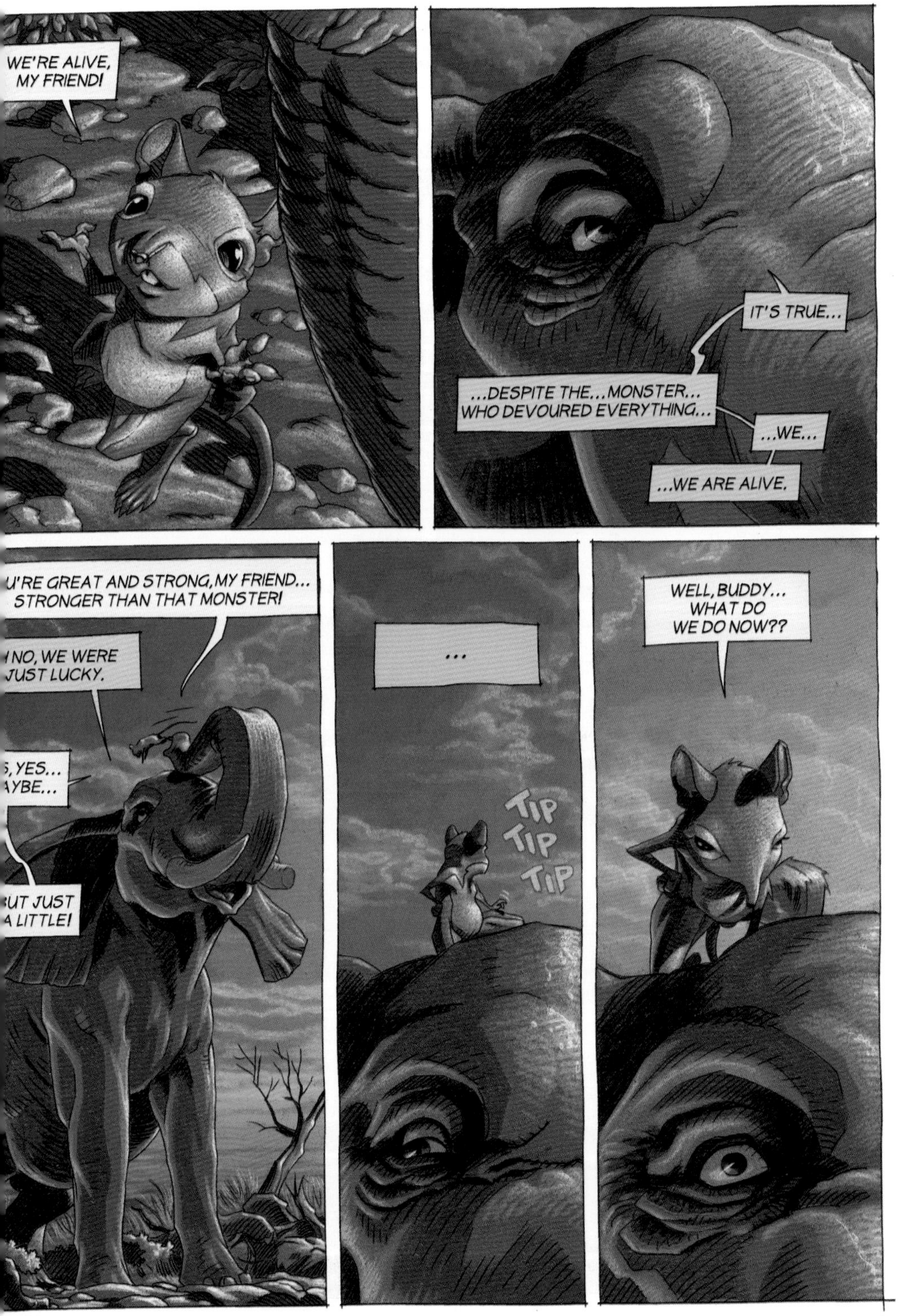

WE'RE ALIVE, MY FRIEND!
IT'S TRUE...
...DESPITE THE... MONSTER... WHO DEVOURED EVERYTHING...
...WE...
...WE ARE ALIVE.
U'RE GREAT AND STRONG, MY FRIEND... STRONGER THAN THAT MONSTER!
NO, WE WERE JUST LUCKY.
, YES... AYBE...
UT JUST A LITTLE!
...
TIP TIP TIP
WELL, BUDDY... WHAT DO WE DO NOW??

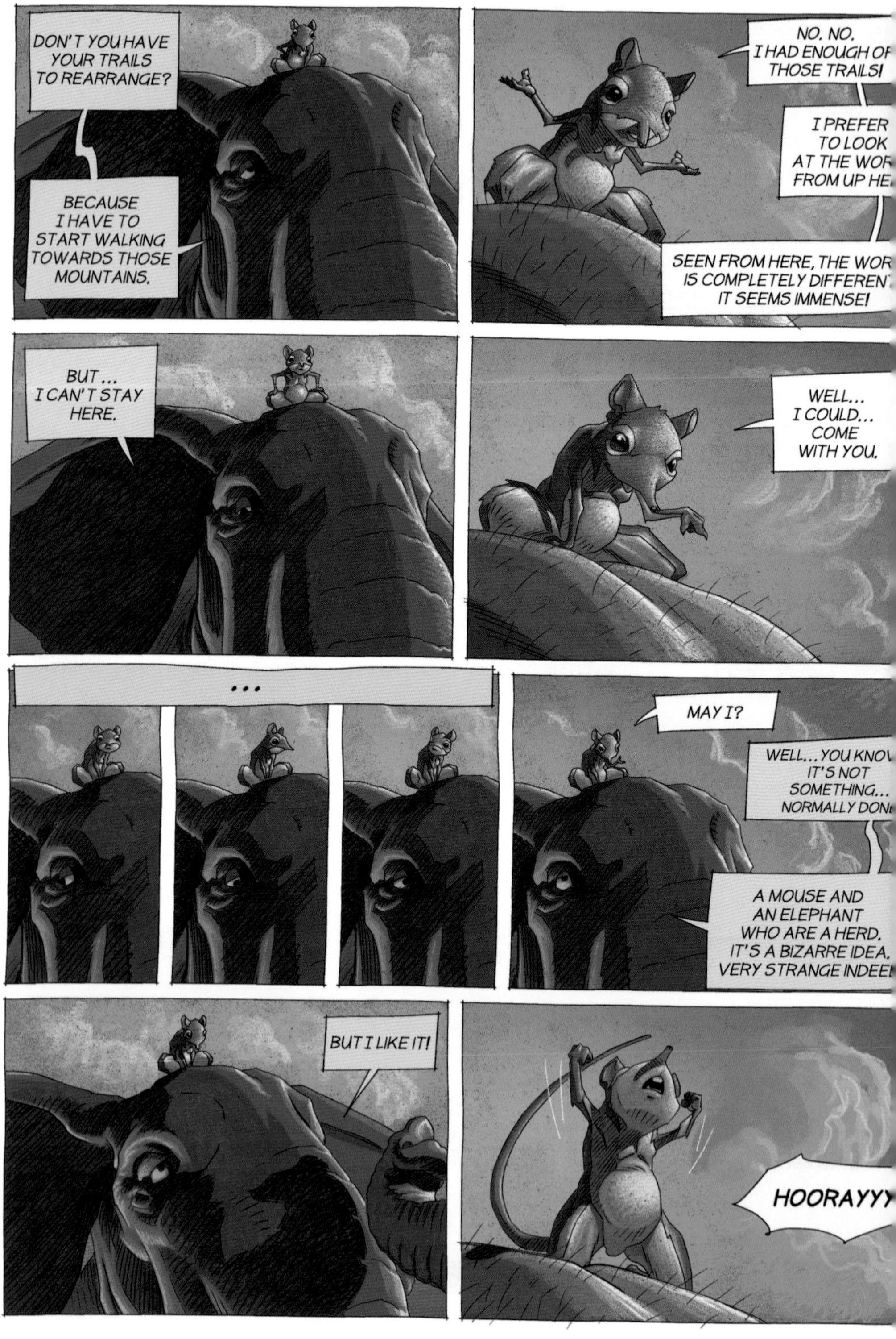
DON'T YOU HAVE YOUR TRAILS TO REARRANGE?
BECAUSE I HAVE TO START WALKING TOWARDS THOSE MOUNTAINS.
NO, NO. I HAD ENOUGH OF THOSE TRAILS!
I PREFER TO LOOK AT THE WOR FROM UP HE
SEEN FROM HERE, THE WOR IS COMPLETELY DIFFEREN IT SEEMS IMMENSE!
BUT... I CAN'T STAY HERE.
WELL... I COULD... COME WITH YOU.
...
MAY I?
WELL... YOU KNOV IT'S NOT SOMETHING... NORMALLY DON
A MOUSE AND AN ELEPHANT WHO ARE A HERD. IT'S A BIZARRE IDEA. VERY STRANGE INDEE
BUT I LIKE IT!
HOORAYY

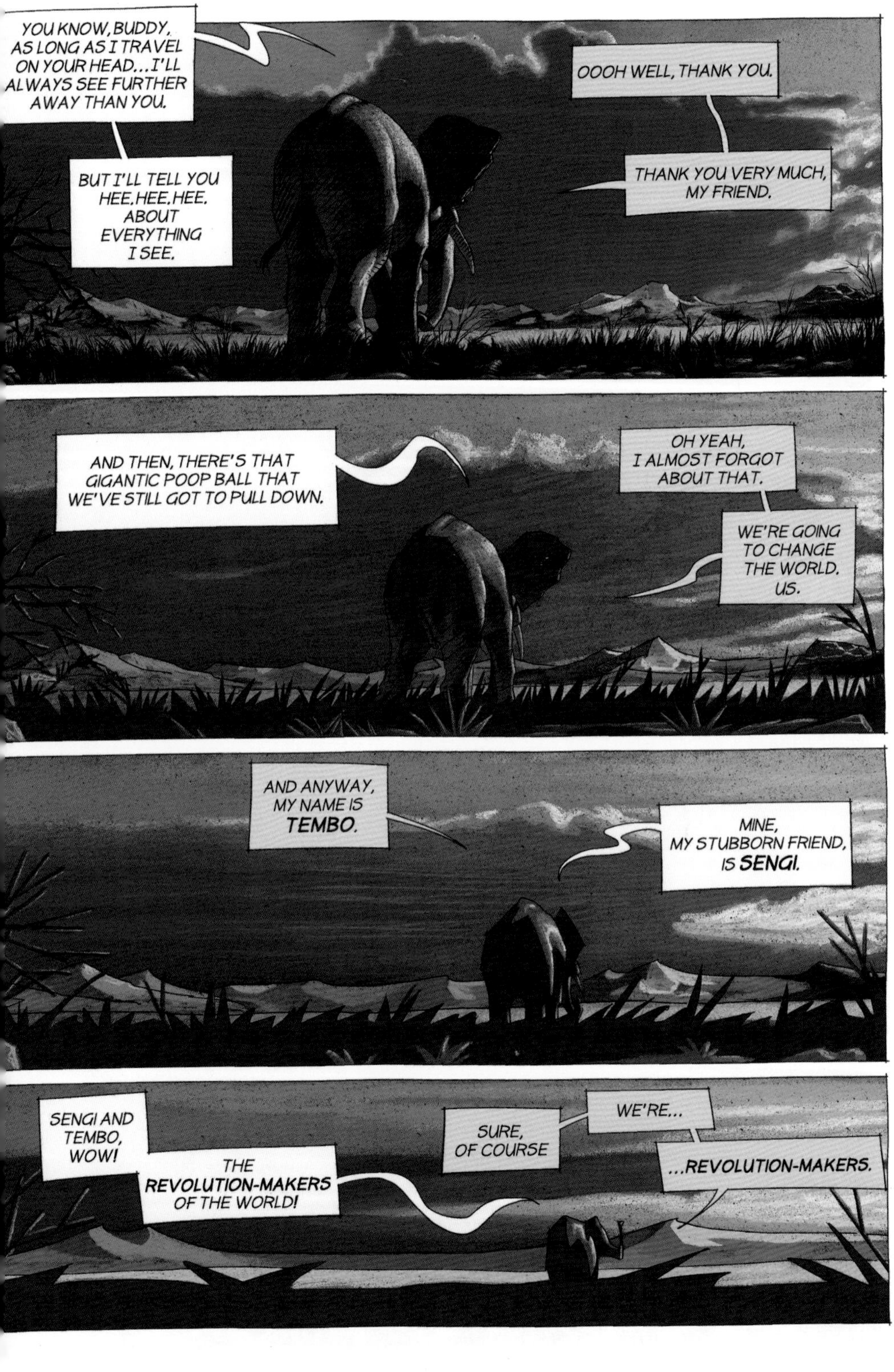
YOU KNOW, BUDDY, AS LONG AS I TRAVEL ON YOUR HEAD... I'LL ALWAYS SEE FURTHER AWAY THAN YOU.
BUT I'LL TELL YOU HEE.HEE.HEE. ABOUT EVERYTHING I SEE.
OOOH WELL, THANK YOU.
THANK YOU VERY MUCH, MY FRIEND.
AND THEN, THERE'S THAT GIGANTIC POOP BALL THAT WE'VE STILL GOT TO PULL DOWN.
OH YEAH, I ALMOST FORGOT ABOUT THAT.
WE'RE GOING TO CHANGE THE WORLD. US.
AND ANYWAY, MY NAME IS TEMBO.
MINE, MY STUBBORN FRIEND, IS SENGI.
SENGI AND TEMBO, WOW!
THE REVOLUTION-MAKERS OF THE WORLD!
SURE, OF COURSE
WE'RE...
...REVOLUTION-MAKERS.

THE NAME THEY GAVE ME AT BIRTH IS GIUSEPPE FALCO.

WAS BORN LAST CENTURY, I THINK. ALREADY IN MY FIRST YEARS OF LIFE, I
ALIZED THAT A SIMPLE LIFE AS A HUMAN BEING WOULD NOT BE ENOUGH FOR
ME, SO I STARTED READING ADVENTURE BOOKS AND COMICS. MY OWN LIFE
ISAPPEARED, BECAUSE I LIVED THE LIVES OF ALL THE CHARACTERS I READ.

Y TRAVELS AND ADVENTURES BEGAN WITH JAMES FENIMORE COOPER, I WAS
TH THE NATIVE AMERICAN TRIBES ON LAKE ONTARIO. I WAS THERE IN THOSE
ORTHERN WOODS AND IN THE CANOES THAT PLOWED THROUGH THE WATERS
OF THAT GREAT LAKE.

THEN I MET TARZAN, BY RUSS MANNING AND BURNE HOGARTH, AND FOUND
MYSELF IN THE AFRICAN JUNGLE AMONG LIANAS, MONKEYS, AND BIG CATS.

ATER, I LIVED WITH PETER PARKER AND BORROWED HIS COSTUME (STAN LEE
AND JOHN ROMITA, SR.), CLIMBING HUGE BUILDINGS AND SWINGING THROUGH
THE NEW YORK SKYLINE.

FLEW ACROSS THE GALAXY WITH STAN LEE AND JOHN BUSCEMA, SR.'S SILVER
URFER, AND I TOOK ON GALACTUS WITH LEE-JACK KIRBY'S FANTASTIC FOUR.

WITH CONAN'S SWORD I FOUGHT AGAINST WARRIORS, MONSTERS, AND
WIZARDS, ADORING THE DRAWINGS OF JOHN BUSCEMA, SR.

THEN I MET MOEBIUS, AND IT WAS LOVE AT FIRST SIGHT. I LITERALLY LOST
MYSELF IN HIS WORLD AND TIME ITSELF LOST ALL MEANING.

THESE ARE JUST SOME OF THE ADVENTURES AND LIVES I HAVE LIVED.
THESE ARE JUST SOME OF MY TEACHERS, AND IT IS FROM THEM THAT I
LEARNED TO TELL A STORY WITH BOTH WORDS AND ART.

BUT IT STILL WASN'T ENOUGH FOR ME AND MY DESIRE FOR OMNIPOTENCE.
SO I BEGAN TO CREATE MY CHARACTERS AND WORLDS, AND THEY TOOK ME,
AND STILL TAKE ME TODAY, TO PLACES THAT ARE ALWAYS DIFFERENT AND
FASCINATING. I LOVE WRITING AND DRAWING MY ADVENTURES.

SENGI AND TEMBO IS ONE OF THESE. INDEED, IN SOME SENSE, IT IS
THE FIRST STORY I'M REALLY PROUD TO PRESENT.

MY WISH FOR ALL OF YOU WHO WILL READ SENGI AND TEMBO...
HAVE A NICE TRIP AND A WONDERFUL LIFE!

# COVER GALLERY

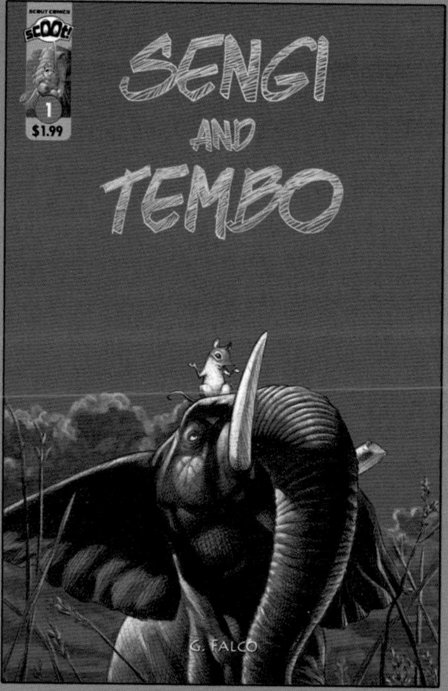
SCOUT COMICS
sCOOt!
1
$1.99
SENGI
AND
TEMBO
G. FALCO

GIUSEPPE FALCO

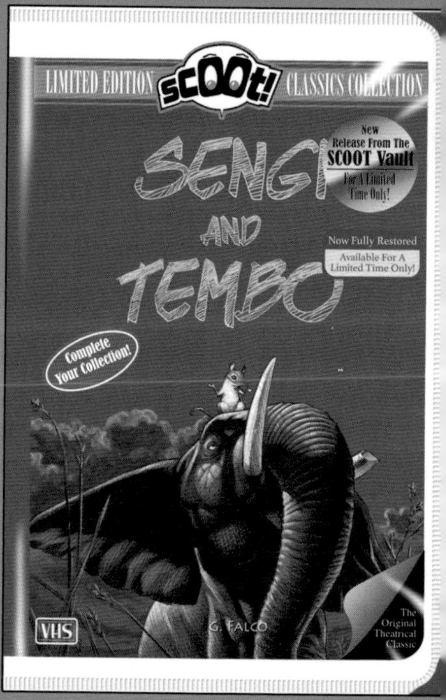
LIMITED EDITION
sCOOt!
CLASSICS COLLECTION
New Release From The SCOOT Vault For A Limited Time Only!
SENGI
AND
TEMBO
Now Fully Restored
Available For A Limited Time Only!
Complete Your Collection!
VHS
G. FALCO
The Original Theatrical Classic

GIUSEPPE FALCO

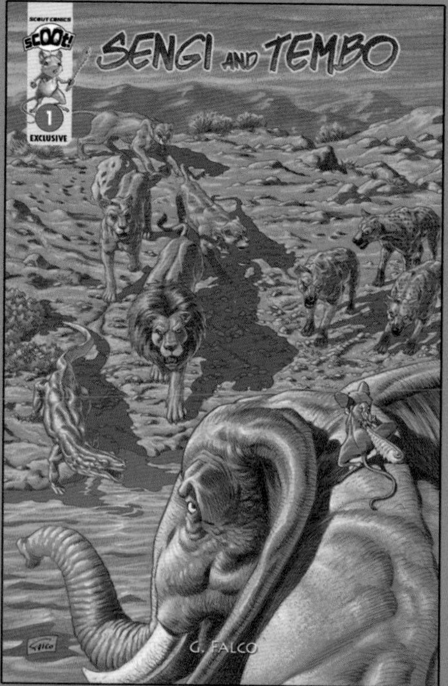
SCOUT COMICS
sCOOt!
SENGI AND TEMBO
1
EXCLUSIVE
G. FALCO

GIUSEPPE FALCO

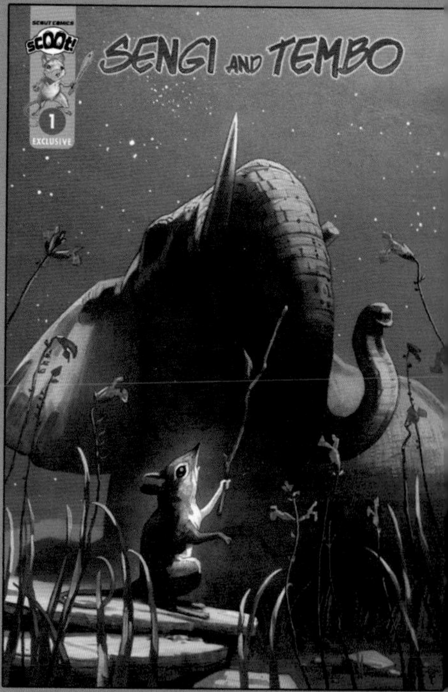
SCOUT COMICS
sCOOt!
SENGI AND TEMBO
1
EXCLUSIVE

CLARA TESSIER